A. Allan Chibi is a Canadian living in Sheffield. In his day job he is Director of the Distance Learning Association as well as an experienced professional and academic historian. When he can get a break between writing works of history and reformation theology, he likes to dabble in historical fiction, fantasy, and horror. The Stolen One is his first foray into fantasy/horror genre. His non-fiction work, including seven monographs and textbooks, have appeared in several journals and on-line sites. He lives with his wife and an overly critical parrot named Jake. Contact me on Twitter [@AndrewChibi] or LinkedIn.

This is a work of fiction. Names, characters, businesses, places, events and incidents are either the product of the author's imagination or used in a fictitious manner. Any resemblance to actual persons, living or dead, or actual events is purely coincidental.

The Saga of the Stolen One
Book One

To the Last Generation

A. Allan Chibi

The Saga of the Stolen One
Book One

To the Last Generation

VANGUARD PAPERBACK

© Copyright 2023
A. Allan Chibi

The right of A. Allan Chibi to be identified as author of this work has been asserted by them in accordance with the Copyright, Designs and Patents Act 1988.

All Rights Reserved

No reproduction, copy or transmission of this publication may be made without written permission.
No paragraph of this publication may be reproduced, copied or transmitted save with the written permission of the publisher, or in accordance with the provisions of the Copyright Act 1956 (as amended).

Any person who commits any unauthorised act in relation to this publication may be liable to criminal prosecution and civil claims for damages.

A CIP catalogue record for this title is available from the British Library.

ISBN 978 1 83794 049 3

*Vanguard Press is an imprint of
Pegasus Elliot Mackenzie Publishers Ltd.*
www.pegasuspublishers.com

First Published in 2023

**Vanguard Press
Sheraton House Castle Park
Cambridge England**

Printed & Bound in Great Britain

For my loving and patient wife, Ellen.

The following people were important in seeing this book through to the end. My wife Ellen, who was always encouraging. My readers, Jennifer MacLennan, Cathy Chibi Garant, Christi Lane-Barlow who all gave me useful feedback and criticism, and Paul Clayton-Shawley and James Burtoft for hours of amusing shenanigans.

Contents

The Last of his Bloodline 13
Long and Long Ago… 28

Part One Curses 40
1 41
2 48
3 63
4 64
5 74
6 83
7 85
8 104
9 120
10 121
11 132
12 148
13 151
14 164
15 179

Part Two Unto the last generation 183
1 184
2 205
3 208
4 221
5 224
6 225
7 244
8 284
9 288
10 290
11 295

The LORD is long suffering, and of great mercy, forgiving iniquity and transgression, and by no means clearing the guilty, visiting the iniquity of the fathers upon the children unto the third and fourth generation.

(Numbers 14:18)

The Last of his Bloodline

"What's past is prologue."
— *The Tempest (Act 2, Scene 1)*

Michael opened his eyes, glanced about, but nothing seemed familiar. It looked like the ceiling of a cheap motel room, very much of a muchness with those he had visited over the years of the Omaha — Boston route he drove. Golden white morning light was streaming in through poorly installed curtains; it was mixed with an inconsistently strobing red light of an advertising board which must have been placed near the front of the parking lot. He watched the colors chase each other across the greying white stucco above. These rooms are always too hot or too cold; this one was too hot.

Okay, he blinked and silently mumbled to himself, *so far so good, but how did I end up here?* He could not remember any specific details of the previous day.

He tried to sit up but found that he could not move.

He tried to turn his head, but he could not move that way either.

He tried, but he could not feel anything binding him, tying him down, although it seemed that there must be something. Before he could even begin to process that realization, a shrill screaming worked its way into his hazy thoughts.

Michael was so startled that the question of his immobility was instantly forgotten, only to hit him again ten-fold as he tried to get up and away from the earsplitting shrieks which were now all around him. Sweat formed on his forehead and dripped into his eyes… it felt *salty* and it stung and was hotter than the room. The comparison came randomly into his consciousness, but he tried to push the random reflection aside; he was pinned down in what was beginning to sound like a slaughterhouse or a battlefield.

A battlefield? Michael paused, having never heard a battlefield except in movies. This sounded like no movie, however.

At least the sounds were no longer getting louder or any closer, but they were all around him still. Then, under the screams, he could just make out another noise... *click-click-tap, click-click-tap*... and that one was indeed getting closer. He was inadvertently more frightened of that sound than of the noise of the screaming and dying. He grew frantic and nearly shit himself when he unexpectedly felt a hand on his leg.

He was too afraid to look down (forgetting that he could not do so).

He was too fear-stricken to scream. He did not know that any sound he made would attract no attention. He did notice that the weird *click-click-tap* sound that had scared him so had ceased, but then he heard something else under the sound of screeches and cries encircling him.

His mind was working overtime and at a frantic pace, but all he could produce to explain the new sound was the word "metal". Only slowly could he attach new words to that base sound... "metal on wood" and then "metal on... something else." Michael did not know the last sound exactly, but it was like a slap, followed by a scratch, followed by a sickening sucking resonance which suggested an awful thing to him. He also now heard the sound of squealing animals added into the cacophony.

It was almost too much to bear, then the hand, he had almost forgotten the hand, began to move up his leg, squeezing his muscles alone the way. It felt like someone was crawling up his body or pulling themselves up, testing his nerve for... *something?*

He closed his eyes again at the second thought, holding them tight, afraid of what he might see through the tears leaking from his eyes and the sweat pouring into them.

'Why?'

Why? Michael was confused by the word, by the Irish accent of a woman's voice, by the suggestion that he had done something. He was relieved too by what she had said.

'It's a mistake,' he whispered to whomever she was, whatever she was. 'You... you have the wrong room, the wrong guy.'

Thank God for that; it's settled, no harm done, go away now... please. Michael had never been religious before, but right now he could have been a Jesuit.

The hand paused; Michael allowed himself another quick sigh of relief. In a moment, however, no more than mere seconds later, the hand resumed its lateral crawl up his body. Leg to hip, hip to stomach, stomach to chest it inched upwards. All the while, Michael mentally shook his head and proclaimed the obvious error being made.

Finally, the hand reached his neck and there it paused. No squeezing, just overt menace.

Michael was afraid that he would be strangled, but after a moment the hand moved on again and came to rest over his mouth. Now pressure was applied. The hand smelled of dirt and sweat and… *beef stew*?

'You killed me, *Lawrence Pennyvale!*' The name was spat out like a curse.

No.

'You killed my husband and forced me to watch.'

No!

'You killed my son and forced me to watch.'

No, please!

'You did unspeakable things to my girl, forcing me to watch before you killed her too.'

I did not. I swear I didn't! I couldn't!

'Why?' That question again; the woman sounded desperate for an answer. 'What harm did we ever do to you English *cuntes*?'

Michael could not speak as the hand clamped harder over his mouth, but in his mind, he caught flashes of the acts the voice had described. He was like a ghost in the vision; he saw the face of this Pennyvale in the reflection of eyes and it looked nothing like his own, how could it, it wasn't him.

Why would it look like him? The whole idea was absurd.

Where the sadistic torturer in the vision was of light complexion, dirt smeared, blood splattered and sweating, Michael was of a darker skin tone. The man had brown hair, the color of a dirty potato just plucked from the earth while Michael, he would have shouted had he been able to, had hair the color of coal, a tumble of blackness.

I'm not even English!

In his mind he balked at the unfairness of this attack and the accusations of violence against him. *Could the crazy bitch not see that?* His eyes flew open, to plead his innocence or to somehow signal the mistake to her some other way. *His* eyes were blue! *Mine* are grey! *Look! Look damn you, look*! He moved his eyes as much as he could, but then he registered the owner of the hand over his mouth and forced his eyes shut again, even tighter this time. He had witnessed the impossible and did not want the vision to get into his head any more than it had.

The woman who held him down had at least a quarter of her head bashed in, and slits and gashes appeared on her neck and what he had briefly glimpsed of her shoulder through a torn peasant dress. How he wished now that he had resisted that brief terrifying glimpse, that curiosity brought on by terror. Her skin was a bleached out white. The only color about her was the brown of dried blood on the rags she still wore, raggedy, and dirty. Her one good eye was dead, cloudy with a film of... *something*; there was no mercy in there to appeal to; nothing with which to compare her victim to her previous torturer.

Around them the screams and hollering, the sucking sound, the animal cries, it all rose in volume.

It was then a strange thought forced its way into Michael's consciousness. There was an underlying rhythm to the noise... a beat. A sickly thud, a blood curdling scream, a laugh, a plea for mercy, the slash of a blade and the sound of skin invaded and skewered on repeat. Michael tried to deny the evidence of his eyes, but he could not deny the power of the hand as it gripped his mouth tighter and tighter. He would have shaken his head, but he could still not move it. Then another hand pinched his nose, a smaller hand with tiny fingers.

Oh no!

'You killed my papa. Why mister, why did you do that?'

This was a softer, younger, feminine voice. If this were the girl the corpse-like woman claimed had been attacked, he certainly did not want to see that, and Michael screwed his eyes shut as tightly as he could and then he tried to close them even more, so tight it hurt.

I am innocent, he wanted to scream.

A mistake, this is a mistake.

Suddenly, the pressure on his mouth and nose was gone. He could breathe again, and he took in great heaving gulps of air.

After a moment he tentatively opened his eyes to see a... *savior*... a soldier's head appeared over the shoulder of the (dead?) woman; a strong hand now on her shoulder, pulling her off and throwing her effortlessly across the room. He was in a vague uniform, but it too was torn, and too dirty, and too blood splattered to see if there was any real colors Michael could discern, other than that of the dried blood. The soldier followed the arch of the woman's flight, pulling a sword and swinging it up and under her.

Michael watched the arc in slow motion.

It struck off what was left of the woman's head.

Michael half expected a gush of red blood, but there was nothing but brown, dried out dust puffing out of the woman's neck. It plumed out and settled as far as his bedclothes like a fine powder. The sword then stabbed forward over Michael's chest and face, and more brown dust puffed out and choked him.

The girl was the thought in his head, Michael still could not look that way to confirm it though.

'Get up, Pennyvale!'

This was the voice of command, and it was English — not American English but something you might hear in a movie, an old movie, maybe not even then. 'You've had your fun, *ya dorre cunte* but there's still work to be done. Get on your feet, pull up your britches man, get your sword and move out!'

But try as he might, Michael still could not move, nor could he correct his savior's mistake.

'Did ya not hear me *bor*? Are ya *addled or sumptin*?'

Michael's eyes widened as the soldier's fist struck him in the ribcage, punctuating the order to move. He gasped in a great breath of dust-filled air from the new pain, which made him cough once again.

Suddenly he found that he could move after all and he sat up, only to find himself alone.

He was in that motel room bed still. Golden-white and red strobing lights playing across a stucco ceiling; a chair to one side of the bed, a side-table and cheap lamp, a television chained to a wall mount, a non-working air conditioner unit in the window.

So hot in here.

Michael suddenly woke up again with a start, realizing that the scene of normality had also been a dream of sorts.

Click-click-tap, click-click-tap. All was darkness, and the sound was getting closer, closer and louder. Michael sank into the bed and pulled the covers up to his face like a child might do, no longer seemingly constrained in his movements except by his own imagination.

§

How long he lay under the blanket was unknown to him, ten, a hundred, a thousand loud heartbeats were all he had now. Without warning and without the sound of a switch being engaged there was a bright, bright light now washing over him and through the thin fabric of his protection.

'You should know, Michael Daniel Rodriguez, that I bear you, you personally, no ill-will for the actions you've just witnessed. You are merely the last of Pennyvale's cursed bloodline.'

While Michael understood that he was now sitting up, he also realized that he was not in a bed in a motel room somewhere between Boston and Omaha at all. He was instead tied to a chair elsewhere. He heard his name through the fog of sleepiness and fright, however, and knew it came from another Irish accent. This one seemed less threatening than the corpse-woman and unseen victimized girl. His physical response to it was less frantic thereby. His task now was to try and find a way out of the mental fog into which he had been thrown and then, hopefully, make the man see reason, see that a mistake had been made by someone, somewhere.

Start at the beginning.

'I'm', his voice sounded squeaky and weak. He swallowed and started over. 'I am not... I am not this Pennyvale; there was, has, obviously been a mistake.' He had wanted to scream but he had refrained. For all the kindness there seemed to be in the new voice, his own situation was no less worrisome than before. He calmly (as calmly as he could under the circumstances) made the same appeal.

'I'm not Pennyvale.' Michael was not sure how long he had been unconscious, where he was now, and whether the corpse-woman, girl, and soldier had been a dream or not.

Was this a dream too?

'No,' came the sound of the stranger's Irish accented voice, 'this is as real as real can be and that was a vision of the past retained in your blood.'

Blood? My blood?

Michael knew the words but they made no sense to him, there was no context here for him to grab on to. When he tried to concentrate on what had really happened, on his last real memory, all he could think of, oddly enough, was a playing card. *No, not a playing card exactly,* he mentally corrected himself, *but something genuinely like a playing card.* In his mind's eye it had suddenly appeared before him, as if out of nowhere, when... *when he answered the door to his motel room.*

'I... I was in that room, the room from the nightmare, wasn't I?' Michael noted the desperation in his own voice, not unlike the corpse-woman's need for an answer or the girl's accusations.

'Yes, you were Michael.'

'But it was a mistake... is a mistake. I am not this Pennyvale, can't you see that. I'm not even English, I'm Spanish, I'm from Puerto Rico.'

'No mistake,' came a slow, considered response from somewhere nearby. 'Of course, you are not that Pennyvale. He was a man living over half a millennia ago. And yes, you are *mostly* not English, that is also true. But the cursed part of your blood is as English as can be.'

Michael was still struggling with his last real memory, so he missed the qualifying statement of his identity. None of it really made any sense to him anyway. He tried to focus on the card as an anchor; it had had a strange symbol written upon it. Try as he might he could not now remember what it had been though.

'Never mind that, Michael, you would not understand it, and it will drive you insane to think of nothing else save that.'

The voice of the other was melodic in Michael's ears, soothing in a way... reasonable. Irish, yes, but not like those from any of the New York gangs he had once ran against with the Mexicans (who accepted him as one of them despite his non-Mexican roots). That was long ago though.

Was that what this is? Some act of revenge a long time in coming?

'Revenge?' the deep, baritone voice of the other asked as if considering the word, examining it. 'Yes, of a sort it is revenge, but a longer time in coming than you can imagine young man.'

Michael risked opening his eyes again.

'I did not say that aloud...' he realized and stopped short of finishing the sentence.

The chamber, or room, or cave, wherever he was, was dark, so very dark that the point he had been trying to make would have been sucked into the void. He tried to raise a hand but found once again that he was bound tightly, although this time it was to a not-uncomfortable chair as opposed to a motel bed.

The realization shocked him. It occurred to him that he was tied up as if his comfort were a factor in the decision to keep him here, wherever here was.

'Well, we are not uncivilized my friend. We do not stoop to the level of our enemies.'

That was a strange thing to say; the whole thing was strange. The awareness of its strangeness woke Michael up just a little more. He shook his head to try to clear away the cobwebs of confusion which must have accumulated over the last few hours *or days*.

Steeling his resolve, it was time questions were answered. 'Did I? Say it aloud that is? What… what is…?' The new question went unfinished. In his confusion, in his bound state, Michael struggled to find the right words and to force them over his dry tongue. He discovered, however, that if he squinted just so he could make out the form of a tall man, sitting in the shadows of whatever chamber they were in. Presumably that was the speaker, the Irish fellow.

He wore a hat. Michael was surprised and irritated at the irrelevant detail. The man nodded, but not toward Michael.

A movement on his other side startled Michael and he involuntarily moved his head to watch which tightened his bindings ever so slightly. It was, again, a woman's hand, but this time it looked whole and healthy, a white woman, but with lightly tanned skin. One finger featured a gold ring with a big green letter F. It held out a glass of water, just before his face. The glass was raised to his lips and angled toward him.

The message was clear; the water smelled good, and so he drank. It was cool, and fresh, and tasted slightly of oranges. Another sip was offered, taken, and the glass was then removed from his range of vision.

Michael's mind could not get over the fact that the water had a fruity taste. It had been quite refreshing, what little had been given him.

'Thank you,' he said.

There was no reply and he focused fully back on the man by shifting only his eyes. The man in the shadows was not looking at him but had turned his head watching the woman walk away perhaps. Michael tried bringing his breath under control, breathe slower, calm his nerves some, lower his heartbeat. He needed to think straight. He needed to be freed. Mistakes happen, right? No harm, no foul. Who would he tell?

Someone had made a terrible mistake! He still wanted to scream it out.

Focusing his attention once more he now came to realize that there was a light source near the man, just not an immensely powerful one, providing the shadows in which he stood.

Probably not tied up somewhere in a cave then. The thought brought him small comfort.

It was puzzling. That light was clearly not meant to hurt his eyes but only to provide shadows; that light… it was illuminating enough for Michael to see the other man sitting there; enough to form an estimation of his person, but no more than that.

'Yes?' this other then said when he noticed the attention. 'What is what? Is it this place, you mean, or the symbol on the card I told you to forget about?'

Michael's confusion, and thus his heartbeat, rose again.

'Listen to me, human, and try to be at ease. My kind, well, some of us have a certain talent, if you will, a skill for reading your kind by your expressions and by the way you move your bodies when you ponder thoughts and ideas.'

'The little they do of either.' This sarcastic response came to Michael's ears from somewhere close, too close behind him, and above him too, but it was a small sound.

'Yes, thank you, Talia. That will do now. He heard you.'

'I wanted him to hear me, sire.' The voice was a little shrill and acerbic.

The man in the shadow moved his head slightly to address the woman, *women*? Did he address the one with the water maybe? Had that been her voice? Michael reasoned she must still be standing out of sight then, further into the shadows on the other side of the chair. He moved his head to look at her, remembering too late that he was bound. The bindings tightened again. Michael then moved only his eyes, straining to see. There was no one there in the scope of his vision, however; no one he could see in any case. The man in the shadows spoke again.

'Michael. You were thinking about the symbol on my card, the last thing you remember?'

'Yes,' he shifted his vision back. 'Wait... what did you say? *Human*? You said human!'

'I call it a ward, but some of my people call them goblin ciphers, even though they were not developed by goblins at all. Isn't that a strange thing?' The man in the shadows chuckled. 'The wards are meant only to confuse those who look upon them; to bamboozle, if you will.'

Bamboozle? Who uses words like that any more?

'I am so incredibly old Michael, forgive my poor modern vocabulary, and like you, English is not my first tongue either. In any case, the symbol renders the human mind into a state of stupefaction and disorder. It is just one trick my people have used for self-preservation, you understand, for centuries. It is temporary, I assure you; but were you to remember it, to think upon it too closely, you would fall into a near permanent miasma.'

Michael's confusion must have been plain.

'Ah, that means you would be in a mental fog you could not come out of. I think coma is a close approximation for the affect.' The man in the shadows fell silent watching him. Michael felt his eyes upon him. 'Let us hope you do not. You need to be aware of why.'

'*Mãe de Deus,* there is that word again, what do you want with me? I'm not rich, I...'

'I know, Michael, I know.'

The words were calming, soothing, and Michael found himself relaxing a little, falling into the voice.

'I found in your mind that you drive a large vehicular transportation machine, moving foodstuffs from Omaha to Boston, and then whatever commission you can take to transport back west. I know this already. As I said, I bear you no ill-will, personally, young man. You, personally, did nothing to harm me or mine. I acknowledge that willingly, freely. I do not find you particularly offensive, as some of your kind can be, but rather attractive in a rough-hewn way.'

'I'm not gay,' Michael said quietly but nervously, as if this was now the issue.

'They are called semi-trailer trucks, sir.' This was the other female voice, spoken at the same time as Michael's confirmation of his own sexuality, but it was still very tiny sounding. Michael somehow knew that in this case it was just perspective. This female, the water-bearer perhaps, was not Irish, and she was a fair distance away from him. He could not pinpoint where the voice came from exactly, however, just that way.

'Even I knew that, sire. I mean, come on, *large vehicular transportation machine*? How did you produce that sentence?' This was the tiny voice that was close to his ear.

There was silence from the shadow man.

'Ah, I see...' came his eventual reply, '...the "trailers" cannot move themselves, so they are considered as only half of a working whole.' He stopped speaking a moment. 'As ever, Daughter, you are a significant help to me.'

Michael noted that the man in the shadows had turned his head to address the female beyond, calling her his "daughter", but trying to look in the indicated direction himself revealed nothing but darkness there still. If the man in the shadows noted his confusion at all he made no mention of it. Instead, he picked up his address to his prisoner where he had left it off earlier.

'I have come to believe that "offensiveness", unintended or not, is bound to the pressure of your mortal existence, that which weighs so heavily upon some of your kind, Michael. Whether you realize this or not is quite another question entirely of course. But you seem carefree, which appeals to me and to my kind very much. Wealth has no bearing on my decision to take you captive or on what must come next either. Nor is it a question of whom you choose to take pleasure with.'

'Harvest,' said the small near-by voice with spooky enthusiasm.

'I have riches uncounted already,' picked up the shadow man, 'and I have no need of more. Nor do you have any particular skill I have need of, nor is this a case of extortion... blackmail you would call it, you have nothing with which to bribe me, and I do not have the freedom of action to accept a bribe in any case and still my hand. Whether you are happy or not is also beside the point, and my own happiness bears no importance. But...' the man in the shadows lifted a hand to forestall any further questions. 'Rest assured,' he continued, 'that your bodily organs are not going to be ripped from you for transfer to another, if that is a worry for you. That is a myth and practiced only in more primitive cultures than yours or mine. You have no information that I might need in my work either… well, any more than you have already provided me.' Michael struggled with his bonds.

The man audibly sighed. 'Sadly, you see, you and I are, both of us, victims of circumstances neither of us were originally party to, but which now impacts upon both of us nonetheless, and please do not struggle like that Michael, you will only do yourself an injury.' Michael stopped. 'May I be familiar with you? We are, after all, in this together.'

The man in the shadows paused as if waiting for permission to go ahead. 'I was saying, though, I have tied the ropes in such a way that if you sit still you will come to no self-injury, but the more you twist and turn like that the tighter the ropes will become until, like the victim of a python, you will no longer be able to breathe through the resultant constriction. I do not want that, and I am sure neither do you. It would be most inconvenient for us both.'

Michael sputtered, '*Inconvenient?*'

'I taught him to tie ropes that way,' said the little female voice, now with a hint of pride.

'Indeed, you did, Talia,' he regarded the source of the voice and then turned back to Michael, 'her kind are exceptionally good with things of a domestic nature.'

Michael had felt the ropes tighten about his chest now that he thought about it, so that much rang true. He decided to follow his captor's advice and sit still.

'What, what happened to my truck?'

There was silence for a fleeting time. Michael thought his captor had not heard him. 'My truck,' he said a little louder.

'Oh, I see,' said the man in the shadows. 'Only that part with an engine is your own property, while the trailer belongs to… that indoor marketplace in Boston?' The man fell silent in consideration of this. 'Hmm, a fair enough system I grant, and one not unlike that to which I am much more familiar.' Then the man paused. 'My apologies, but I am not entirely *au fait* with American idioms, despite the years of my residence here. A little remiss on my part, I admit, but I have had other matters on my mind. But rest assured, young man, that I have arranged for your… truck… to be delivered of its cargo at its destination. As far as the recipient was concerned, you personally fulfilled the contract and you were rewarded accordingly. You have lost no income or material possessions through any action of mine; the payment is already in your bank account.'

This was clearly meant to be reassuring to him, but Michael was increasingly concerned by the dichotomy between the gentle manner of the man with the melodic voice, now standing at ease in the shadows and who had somehow captured him with a squiggle on a card, with the man who now held him bound God knows where, God knows why.

'Oh, certainly your triune god knows where you are, Michael, but I daresay that he, she or it probably does not care over much about it. Have we settled then on the issue of my using your given name to address you?'

'We do not want to appear rude you know!' The tiny female voice had moved and now came from above him and to the right. Michael almost twisted his body around but recalled in time the advice about the ropes. He also heard the thrumming of the wings of a dragonfly beating nearby. He wanted to put a hand to his forehead; he wanted to rub away a new throbbing in his temple, he wanted away from here.

'Okay, okay', he stretched out the words, giving himself time to think.

The only sensible solution to his dilemma suddenly occurred to him and made him laugh. All he had really seen before was a man, a woman, and a kid. Costumes and make-up could explain the corpse-like appearance of the woman, the soldier's attire, and a little trick with accents accounted for the rest.

'Hal put you up to this, right? Is this being filmed for YouTube or something? Is this because I asked out his sister that one time and never called her back?' The man in the shadows smiled, not that Michael could see it clearly, but he felt it in the slight lifting of the mood. He smiled too, then he chuckled again, having guessed correctly, relieved.

'Does this sister of your friend give you thoughts of lust and enthusiastic sex?' The tiny voice took an interest and had moved closer to his ear.

'Ignore her, Michael, her kind have physical, erotic, dreams all the live long day.'

'Well excuse me!' She was suddenly petulant sounding.

'But to your point. Your friend…' the man paused, looking beyond Michael to the darkened recesses of… wherever this was. Michael thought he detected another light come on from there, bluish rather than the stark white of the source closer to him.

After a moment, the name of his friend, Henry Tarbuck, was announced. 'The sister's name is Marian, sir.' The man in the shadows nodded his thanks to the woman he called "Daughter".

'Your friend, this Tarbuck fellow, is not involved here, Michael, nor his sister for that matter. Although, if you wish to think of her, be my guest. I see her now in your mind, a romanticized vision of her, no doubt, but I can see why you might lust after her. Do not fret; we all see those we love or lust after as flawless. As far as they are concerned you are perfectly well and driving your vehicle still, your semi-trailer truck, onward to Philadelphia this very instant.'

'Why Philly?' The man in the shadows slowly turned his head to regard Michael once again.

'Now, now, is that really of paramount concern to you at the moment Michael, the destination of your vehicle?' He shrugged and waved it off. 'Well, if you must know, I like the name Philadelphia. Did you know that there is a Philadelphia mentioned in your Christian Bible? Yes, in the Book of the Revelation of Saint John, chapter three. That city, however, was in Lydia, in Asia Minor, although now it falls within the nation of Turkey and is called Allahshehr. Did you know that? In Greek, the name of the city meant *brotherly love*, but is now known as the *city of God*.

'Greek?' Michael was finding it hard to keep up his end of the conversation.

'Yes Greek, the language of Greece.' The shadow man's voice had taken on a critical tone. 'I cannot fathom how you could not know this? It's quite famous.' Michael sighed.

'What the hell does Greece have to do with anything? Fuck Greece!' Suddenly there was a pain in the back of his head, as if he had been hit with a small but powerful fist.

'You speak to a king, you cretin, show some respect or I will smite you!'

'Hey!' He almost tried to reach back and rub the resulting bruise but remembered the ropes and controlled the impulse. 'Okay, look, who are you and why are you holding me here?' The man in the shadows said nothing for what seemed like hours to the bound trucker, although finally he shook his head. *Smite?*

'I disapprove of your tone and your language, Michael. There is no need for vulgarity.'

'Damn right there isn't!' said the small female voice vehemently. The man in the shadows stopped talking a moment, shaking his head.

'In any case,' he said with something of a sigh, 'as for why I am holding you…' the man in the shadows stepped out of his relaxed position and came forward.

Michael did not know what to expect, but an obviously expertly tailored, dark blue suit was not on that list. The hat was a Panama design, dark blue (bluer than the suit, almost black) and silk. The man carried a walking stick, ebony, the head of which softly reflected the soft tones of the light. It had a lion's head grip. Michael checked himself; why did he notice that?

The man walked toward him and as he did so he made a *click-click-tap* sound. Expensive shoes and the walking stick hitting the floor.

The man closed the distance and bent over to look Michael squarely in the eyes.

Michael could not be sure of anything in this dim light, but the man had hair of pure white and he had large black eyes, without pupils… no whiteness, all black. Those eyes, those inhuman eyes, looked right into his soul! Michael closed his own eyes again, now afraid of his own reflection in those eyes.

Although he did not see it, the man smiled and said, '…that, Michael Daniel Rodriguez, is the most important question you have ever asked anyone or ever will.' The last thing Michael would ever know, had he risked another look, would have been long, white, sharp fangs descending from the shadow man's upper row of teeth.

Long and Long Ago…

To mortal onlookers, the four travelers would have made for an odd procession had there been any mortal onlookers to watch them pass by.

There were two men, a woman, and a donkey. The animal was pulling a small, half-laden, wooden cart. The four were travelling along the *An Seisear* path in the only true way fit for purpose, by the light of a full moon. If there had been any other travelers on the ancient trail (it is possible that someone might have stumbled upon it unknowingly) they had not made themselves known to the four, who were clearly on a mission of somber consequence. That the four were on a mission would have been obvious to even the most oblivious of drunkards.

First, the four were on the path to the *An Seisear* under the light of a full moon.

Nobody used the holy trail for anything other than pilgrimage to the blessed site. Indeed, unless your intentions were pure and true, you could not even find the path to the blessed site to start with as it was usually hidden to the eyes of mortals (unless they were very drunk, and thus their senses quite twisted). Such folk rarely found their way back home again to tell the tale. Unknown to most was that the path was protected by the *Hidden folk* and had been since before the time of the Normans, and before the time of the Norsemen before them (and certainly before the time of the ungodly English afterwards).

Second, the two men, the woman, and the donkey were all arrayed in the traditional regalia of supplicants. They were not wearing the simple garb of the common pilgrims. The three people wore special insignia — that of the king, the versifier, and the celebrant. The donkey was more than just a donkey, true, and his cargo was sacred, so he too wore regalia of a sort. In his case a forest green tabard was laid about his head (no insignia).

The path snaked its way through the forest and flatlands, now on a slight incline leading up to Holy Hill and the elevated flatland upon which sat *An Seisear*, the six standing stones of myth, legend, and song.

Third, they all looked solemn. They were going to the stones to ask the ancient gods to bear divine witness to an important act and oath, hopefully to which the gods would give their wisdom and assent.

The versifier was known as Lóegaire. He was called such in honor of the ancient herder who had once upon a time saved the famous poet, composer, and chronicler Áed Ua Crimthainn from the great fire at his abbey. It is said that as a reward to his humble savior Áed agreed to stop the persecution of those folk of the old ways who lived under his authority. This was offered on the premise that they, in turn, keep themselves to themselves, which they had been more than happy to do. The abbot's namesake could play the lute and the pipes and was said to have the voice of an angel when he sang. He had beguiled many with his songs and poems and had been a welcome guest at castles and courts from Corca Duibne to Canterbury. He made his home in Bweeng nowadays and he had been the last to join the procession.

He would speak the words of the oath to be taken.

The celebrant, not yet a woman but more than a girl (on the verge of adulthood perhaps) was known as Feidlimid. She was not exactly a princess in the strictest sense of being a daughter or sister or wife of royalty. She was, however, a druid's daughter (the second of three). She was from Magh nAla, known as "The Plain of the Stone" (for a reason now lost in the mists of time). Her village had been the site of the tragedy and of the evil acts which had taken place not so long ago. She had been away from the village when the tragedy occurred and was now one of the few living breathing remnants of the place. In daylight, it was said, Feidlimid's hair was the color of the morning sun. It had once matched her temperament too; bright, fiery even, a joy to behold it was said. She had been loved by many, respected even around Mallow (as the people of the settlement had called it). She would have married an important rival chieftain, or shaman, or a holy man even, or some other important dignitary her father needed to ally.

That was before the tragedy of course before her father was killed. She now lived with her mother's people, near Corcaigh, and could look forward to a less important marriage; one arranged by her uncle for the benefit of his immediate family.

She would function as witness to the oath to be taken.

The versifier and the celebrant walked proud on this night with the mission in their hearts. Their strides projected importance and dignity. But they also walked with an obvious air of anxiety. Neither spoke, but they kept making quick glances at each other and at the third member of this grave trinity (unfairly ignoring donkey). Though they walked beside a king — a being as regal and proud as could be imagined — they were both mightily afraid of him.

King Dubhgall was the reason they made the journey to the stones.

He would take the oath.

He would drink the blood.

He would burn the ceremonial wooden bowl which at this moment held the blood, and then he would spread the ashes on the relics while the versifier sang a song of sadness and loss written especially for the occasion by the king's own troubadours.

The donkey, nameless except for "donkey", pulled the cart which carried the relics.

To the versifier and the celebrant, they four were the only folk about on the path this night, but this was not true. Only the king was aware of the others, however. They were accompanied by dozens of others who could not be seen by mortal eyes.

These others were the court and commons of the *Hidden* kingdom and walked with them, unseen by the versifier and the celebrant, clearing the path and leading the way to *An Seisear*. They functioned as guardians for the four, secret companions, and silent protectors. They also kept the path hidden from the eyes of mortals. In their wake, lagging behind the four, confused and frightened by their own, new condition, were the ghosts of Magh nAla (which now only the *Hidden* and the king could see).

It is unknown to mortal man whether ghosts are aware of their actions or condition. Did they know why they walked this path? Were they drawn to the four or were they drawn to the sacredness of the mission? Perhaps they were drawn only to the fact that everything they had once been before the tragedy had been reduced to whatever was being carried away in the cart, so they followed along. The ghosts did not know why they were on the move, nor did they know that they would be returning again to the remains of their village after the oath was taken.

Donkey could see them. It was assumed that he was a dumb creature and he made only the usual complaints that beasts of burden have made since time immemorial.

The ghosts, lost souls that they were, would be the beneficiaries of the oath to be taken.

§

As the four marched along in silence, clearly tiring but still climbing up the path toward Holy hill, Lóegaire and Feidlimid noted that the temperature was falling and that the moon was less distinct in the sky than it had been at the start of the trek. Something, natural or supernatural, seemed to have cast a veil over the moon's reflected light. Perhaps a mist had fallen upon them… neither could say for sure. The king knew, but his attention was focused straight-forward along the path. Donkey followed along without ropes, bridle, or leads, but this did not seem unusual to the other three. It occurred to Lóegaire, however, that no one had told him to whom the creature belonged; was it the celebrant's or the king's creature? Unbeknownst to the versifier, the celebrant wondered much the same thing, he, or the king? Their occasional glances at the king revealed nothing about it.

The only sign from him that he was with them in anything more than body occurred when King Dubhgall paused a moment and appeared to consult with someone or something invisible to the others. Lóegaire and Feidlimid were forced to pause as well or else walk passed him — a violation of ancient customs. They watched as the king nodded and moved his hand as if patting someone on the shoulder — a friendly gesture of thanks. Dubhgall sighed then looked back over his shoulder at the others, the first sign of acknowledgement in hours.

'We take this pathway now,' he pointed along the ground.

The other two looked down but did not notice anything other than rockier soil. They could not see the slight indications in the soil which was meant to warn supplicants of a change in direction, a slightly steeper elevation, a harder path now to traverse from this point onwards, anything of the sort really.

The king noticed their confusion and gestured at them. 'Come forward a pace, both of you.'

His voice was soft, but the command was implicit; the voice indicated that the king meant to be obeyed without question. The two others did the king's bidding, and both gasped when they too saw the suddenly changed scenery before them.

A dark hedgerow had suddenly appeared to their right-hand side. Along one side of it the path (a clear, stone-paved path) continued forward.

Lóegaire, a seeker of knowledge, took a step back. Sure enough, the hedgerow disappeared from his sight only to reappear when he took a step forward again. He examined it carefully and saw hazel, dogwood, and spindle mixed and threaded together in an intricate almost weaved pattern. A new poem was forming in his mind already now; a song could be wrung from this phenomenon for sure.

Such is the way of artists.

'How…?' asked Feidlimid, stumbling over the question.

The king glanced at her, his eyes narrowing and saddened by the woman's plain ignorance. He turned and addressed his reply to the versifier.

'Come, bard, you must know this.'

Lóegaire nodded his head and considered the question. '*Bobne's half-league* sire.'

The king smiled and spread his hands, a gesture of appreciation. That he smiled was the first sign of good humor the king had shown toward them. He waved the bard on to supply more detail.

'Ahem, yes. It marks the path and forms a boundary of sorts. It is said to lead to the land of the *Hidden* or it serves as a gateway elsewhere.'

The young woman shook her head in confusion.

'It is the magic of the *Hidden*, holy man's daughter,' the bard explained. 'It is all around us, always, every day, but it is not…' he lost the words.

'Wise to speak out of such things?' said the king with a small chuckle. 'Attend my words Feidlimid, it is forbidden by the church of the triune god to admit such things, to speak of them, to admire such wonders unexplained in their miracle books.'

'Yes, sire,' Lóegaire picked up the explanation, 'except in Mallow of course, and less people elsewhere seem to care with each year that passes, or so it seems.'

'Fewer.'

'Sire?'

The king shrugged and smiled in a sad, melancholic kind of way, having shown evidence of a higher education than his companions and sad for the omens of a culture in decline. 'What else do the legends say of *Bobne's half-league*, bard?' Lóegaire pondered this question a moment, then he grinned as realization struck.

'Oh yes. Man is to walk only this side of the hedge. That side is dangerous for mortals to tread. To wander along that side of the hedge,' here he indicated the far side, "is to court death itself at the hands of the Hidden."

The king turned at the last few words, his eyebrow raised with a question.

'Death? Hmmm, that is a rather un-nuanced understanding, bard. The original curse spoke of "the end of one's life." That is a phrase that has many meanings as I am sure you would agree, of which death is only one interpretation.' The bard nodded but spread his arms wide.

'But how can one know sire? If they are not originally on the path, and even if they are, how can they know which side to walk?'

The king shrugged as if to blame fate.

He moved forward and shoved his hands deep into the woven branches, twigs, and brambles of the hedge. He was clearly searching through the undergrowth, unconcerned by the wicked looking thorns. It took only minutes until he found what he was feeling for though. The versifier heard the snap just before the king pulled out of the thicket a small branch of lighter-colored leaves.

There were berries on the branch withdrawn, he noted, which might have been the color of blood or the color of peat; it was impossible to say in only this muted moonlight. The king plucked the berries from the twig, and so taken, took these into his mouth, chewing and swallowing the juices and skins. He sighed contentedly and handed a small handful of the fruit to each of his companions, feeding the leaves and the remaining berries to donkey, patting the creature s head, and scratching it behind its left ear.

This pleased the beast and he brayed in thanks.

Lóegaire and Feidlimid both regarded the berries in their hands suspiciously, but only for a moment. Almost together they each took them in and began to chew. The taste was bitter, but not unappealing. Feidlimid thought, mixed with honey, a nice pie might be made of the fruit. Neither knew exactly what to expect, however, although Lóegaire suspected what would shortly happen. Each was suddenly infused with a surge of energy; fatigued legs were rejuvenated, sore backs and muscles relieved, the pains of hunger sated. Seconds later, even the fog of weariness which the pair had not realized had been gripping their minds over the course of the long march lifted, clearing their thoughts completely of fatigue and the sky free of the mists.

The versifier laughed, 'The *Pooka's Pick-me-up*? I thought it was a myth sire.'

'It is,' said the king. He smiled enigmatically at the confusion of the others and resumed his place in the forefront of the group, leading them onward along the left side of the hedge.

§

Eventually, the incline eased to a gentler slope.

The party came to the end of the hedgerow and faced a thickly grown woodland of pines, cedars, maples, and oak trees. The path continued, however, covered in needles, leaves, and whatever else nature let cumulate upon it. The king held out his hand, signaling a halt.

He turned to his companions and placed a finger against his lips.

Whether donkey understood this otherwise universal gesture cannot be said with surety, but like the two others he too kept his mouth shut (except for eating some grass on the side of the path which had been too tempting to pass up). It was clear that the king was communing with someone or something here. The other two looked around but the berries' effects had worn down somewhat already and they could no longer see any supernatural phenomena. After only moments the king bowed, nodded, and turned.

'We may proceed. The circle is not far, hidden away in the center of the woodland.'

'Is there a path, sire?' asked the bard.

The king turned and regarded the bard with a mixture of annoyance and expectation.

The bard thought a moment then he nodded. 'Of course, the *Royal League*, forgive me, sire.'

The king nodded solemnly and turned back to face the woods. He took a step forward and disappeared into nothingness. The bard and celebrant faced each other. Then they each smiled at the prospect of *Hidden* magic. Each stepped forward and found themselves on a clear woodland path not too far behind the king who was moving on and away from the entrance point.

Dubhgall had not waited; he expected them to follow as a matter of course.

The two humans took a few steps forward. Abruptly they heard donkey braying. They paused, and looking back over their shoulders, saw donkey step forward almost mowing them over. The two humans pushed on as the poles and then the cart itself became visible again too. The bard and celebrant chuckled at this wonder; the king simply walked on ahead.

§

Eventually, the four emerged again out from the woodland which had surrounded them for the last few leagues. There was no canopy now; no tall, strong trees on the sides of a pebble strewn path; the moonlight lit up a circular meadow of short grasses and flowers. In the middle, still a hundred yards away, stood the stones.

'The six,' announced the king, pointing forward as if it was not obvious, 'the royal family, frozen in time and place.'

'I thought they would be bigger,' the celebrant commented having never seen the holy site before this moment only hearing of it in tales and songs.

The king shrugged. 'They are what they are, and we are yet far away.'

The stones stood at attention on an unadorned low spur which spanned the grove and beyond, from the Boggeragh mounds to the west to the Nagles to the north-east. 'Come, there is no time for gawking.' The small troop moved again, now toward the center of the grove and the stones themselves.

'They stand west to east, sire?'

'As close to true as could be created, bard, yes. Obviously, the natural contours of the land had to be respected as well.'

'Was this grove here all along, sire?' The celebrant gave voice to a question she had been musing on for a while now. 'Or was it cleared by the ancients? Why are the stones called the royal family?'

The king did not stop moving forward but he did signal for the bard to answer the woman's questions. It was like a challenge, in fact. Lóegaire nodded to the king's back and turned to regard his companion.

'The stones are called the royal family because legend has it, they were once human. The first,' he pointed ahead, 'largest stone, the one facing the Boggeraghs in the distance, that one is the king stone. Sadly, his name is lost to legend.'

'Cairbre Cinnchait or sometimes Caitchenn,' said the king ahead of them, 'he of the cat's head.'

The bard bowed and acknowledged the king's learning, making a mental note to print the name and description for later research.

'It is said,' he then continued, 'that he and his family were turned to stone at the moment of the birth of the Christian savior.' He paused to allow the king to make amendments to the story so far, but he either could not or chose not to. Feidlimid looked between the two men.

'I know some of this story, I think. Was his wife named Queen Mani?' The bard nodded.

'That is correct, well-remembered. Not a great deal is known of her, however, save that she was the daughter of a great king far to the north of Éire. It is said she was married to the, yes, the cat's head king, as a means of peace between the North and the South. The *Ulaids* were an ambitious people, sometimes cruel but never random, trying to expand their empire of minor kingdoms into the south.'

'Yes, I remember some of that from my grandfather's fireside tales. Why was he here?'

The king picked up the tale from this point, not turning around. His voice seemed to carry back to the others clearly enough though. 'There is much speculation on that point Feidlimid. He ruled for only a brief time, no more than a ten-year perhaps, even less maybe, but what started as a promising time turned to sorrow as all his sons were blemished and put to the sword. After the birth of his final son, known as *Morann mac Máin*, nature itself turned against him and his people. The boy was born without a face, or so it is said. The stones are the three royals and three attending noble women, each of whom was with child herself. They were on their way to the sea to try and lift the curse on the boy.' The king then paused and shrugged. 'There are other versions of the story, of course, and other explanations for the stones, but none quite so,' the king moved his hand in the way people do when they are searching for the right words, '…satisfying, or omen laden, as this one.'

The bard frowned.

'Something bothers you, Lóegaire?'

The bard's eyebrows shot up in surprise. How could the king know he was unsatisfied with the legend? 'Yes, sire. The king was cursed; why is this holy place built around his legend?'

'That… is a fair question bard. I only know what my elders told me, but this is my understanding of it. The king was cursed, as you said. He had a cat's bearing about his head, and he was a tyrant as well, having killed all of fair Éire's nobles. He was himself of peasant stock, you see, king only by virtue of rebellion, so his own leadership was considered unnatural. The gods cursed him and his offspring for his arrogance and cruelty, but he did not heed the curse, instead slaughtering his children and any evidence of this taint. Mani, however, who was royal but not a native of the island, she was what we now call English, was unfairly grieved by the curse on her husband too, and the gods recognized this and recommended that she flee with her son and her ladies, to the sea, as you said. The king fled with them, however, after an uprising against his rule came to his attention. It is, generously I think, thought that the king had undergone a change of heart at the prospect of rule without Mani, but this change came too late to appease his rebellious people. It was not too late to save his soul, however.' The king paused here, as if thinking of something. 'So… here is a monument to repentance, or to love, either will do. The gods gave the royal family an immortality of sorts so that the king could thereafter hear appeals and advocate on behalf of subsequent supplicants.'

The king grew quiet. 'Petitioners much like myself,' he said under his breath.

Also under his breath, he added, 'Let us pray to the old gods and the new that this is so, many souls depend upon it for their own salvation and mine.'

§

Dubhgall was the first to approach the stones. He walked around them, inspecting the site and their positioning. 'I fear this one maiden is on the verge of falling over.' He pointed out one of the middle stones, which did seem to be leaning at an odd angle compared to the others.

This drew the bard's interest and he examined that stone as the king completed his inspection. For her part, Feidlimid did not wish to approach the stones any closer than the ritual called for. She stood back a respectful distance. The king finished his scrutiny and came to stand beside her, watching the bard work. He leaned over, 'They are merely stones, Celebrant, that is at least until someone makes the appropriate approach.' He gave her a weak smile. Feidlimid nodded at this but did not move any closer to the stones all the same.

The king took it in good turn. A great deal depended on his, their, actions, but fate must be allowed to play out as it will. If the gods did not think the appeal a good one, something or someone would intervene. 'Well, we are here now. Prepare the bowl, Celebrant. Bard?'

'Sire?'

'Come away now, we have work to do.'

The bard nodded from his position at the base of the middle stone. 'It looks like there was a shifting of the rock under that one stone,' he said, and the king nodded.

Together, bard and king approached the cart. The king led donkey toward the Kingstone and the two men placed the relics before it. When the last, a wooden toy, was placed, the king led donkey away a safe distance and unhooked him from the wagon, allowing him free movement for a time, laying out some oats for his feed which had also been brought along in the cart. He handed the bard his tome. The three of them then removed their clothing and finery, placing these neatly into the cart.

The ritual called for the king, versifier, and celebrant to be unadorned.

'Should I get naked too, sire?' came a soft voice into Dubhgall's ear. Despite himself, he smiled. He turned his head to regard the pixie sitting on his shoulder. She was so light he had not realized she had landed there.

'No Talia, this is a serious matter, you know that. This is no time for pixie jesting.'

'But naked is fun,' Talia pleaded and pouted. Dubhgall chuckled and shook his head.

'Frankly, little one, I am surprised to ever find you clothed at all.' Talia smirked.

'My parents were somewhat strict about that sort of thing for some reason.' Her face took on a sly expression, 'It is a wonder I was born really. But if the king told me…'

The king frowned. 'You know it does not work that way for our kind.' He sighed, 'Okay, Talia, you can be naked too, just do not interfere in the ritual.'

'*Woo-hoo!*' The little pixie took to the air as her dress fell to the ground. Dubhgall bent down and picked it up. He had to be gentle with it; it was woven of gossamer-like threads. He placed it neatly on top of his own garments. Lóegaire watched in confusion, unable to see the garment or the pixie.

'I have come a long way from Ragusa,' sighed the king.

'Ragusa, sire?' The bard's eyebrows betrayed his continued bewilderment, 'That republic state on the Adriatic coast?'

Dubhgall nodded to the bard, 'Yes… it matters not Lóegaire… I was merely thinking aloud. How did it come to this? You understand?' The bard smiled in agreement. 'And I think you can set the fire over by those stones there,' he pointed, changing the subject. The bard nodded and picked up the kindling and began to move the few logs they had brought with them. He turned around to find Feidlimid already had placed the bowl before the largest stone. There was a stirring in his loins as he regarded her body, but he had the awareness to think of other things and the task at hand, looking away again.

Dubhgall sighed. If anything reminded him that he was not himself, it was his non-reaction to such a fine-looking young woman as Feidlimid and a well-built man like Lóegaire. Drugal had told him that his true nature would begin to reassert itself once it had overcome the shock of the imposed changes and as the oath was closer to fulfilment.

Well, that was the theory anyway. *How did it come to this, indeed.*

Part One

Curses

1

[Mallow, Kingdom of Munster, AD1425]

In the early months of *Robarta* (which the Romans had called *spring*), in the days following *Cétamain* (which the Romans called *May Day festival*), in the village of *Magh nAla* (more widely known as Mallow), on a bright day in a backwater village in a backwater region of *An Corcaigh,* a boy was born to Rory O'Rourke (a descendent of *the* Rourke), and his wife Katherine Nic Gilly (daughter of Gil, a blacksmith of good repute from another village). It was the year that Edward Mortimer, the English king's so-called Lieutenant of Ireland, had died of the plague then raging in the Pale of Dublin. The death of the tyrant's man had been celebrated for many days across the island realm. That the boy was born shortly after the death bespoke good times to come.

Rory had already been a celebrated singer, poet, and storyteller, known far and wide as a *fili*, but one gently fallen from the greatest heights of his powers. He was the scion of the extensive line of the tribe of *Danaan* (tracing his ancestry back to the *Tuatha De Danaan* or "Peoples of Danu" and the invasion of mythic Eire), and as such, he was steeped in the centuries' old histories and lore of the rulers of Munster (then under *the* FitzGerald Earls of Desmond). The earls accounted themselves the scions of the tribe of *Tuatha*, the Danonian nobles. Already in Rory's time the story of the three tribes of the Danonian invasion, the *Tuatha*, the *De*, and the *Danaan*, had moved from history into legend. As such, their story was only half understood by the peoples of Munster, but it made for good storytelling, nonetheless. It was folklore shared widely, in song and poems told and re-told repeatedly (but often changed to suit the teller's purpose on the night).

In Rory's time it was firmly understood that the *Tuath Dé* (or "people of the divine"), were... had been... those gods and goddesses and other mythic creatures who dwelled in the *Hidden* world, sometimes called the *Otherworld*, and who visited and interfered in human affairs whenever and wherever they may (for their own sport and entertainment and sometimes, rarely, to aid a good family). As no one god, goddess, or aspect of the divinity was associated exclusively with only one particular aspect of nature or geographical region (or even name) it was difficult for lore-masters to establish the exact nature of any one of these *Tuath Dé*. Yes, *the Dagda*, *the Morrigan*, and *the Manannán* god of the sea had become well known across the entire realm but it was no longer clear how much of that storytelling was based in fact and how much merely the whimsy of previous bards.

Bards achieved and were ascribed much power on this basis.

In his youth and early adulthood, Rory followed in his father's steps and performed many crucial functions at the court of *the* Desmond, John FitzGerald, and for a brief time, in that of his son and heir Thomas (whose rule had been usurped by his uncle James in 1418).

A nephew's power usurped by an evil uncle — it is an old, familiar tale.

Rory had been loyal to John and to the young Thomas and had written (and hidden away) the chronicle of James's usurpation for future generations to read once all concerned were passed out of this life. Had an ordinary man committed such an act, committed such words to parchment, it would have been his doom. Rory's life was spared due to the fear of the *glam dicenn*. Tradition held that bardic satire, penned by a master, could disfigure, scar for life, or even kill the target of the satire, depending on the wishes and skills of the bard who wrote it.

If it were ever to be read aloud.

Tradition, imagination, and fear bound the king's hands and weakened his resolve to punish this servant of his nephew.

No one but Rory knew what the intended affect. James feared what Rory might have written because he knew the bard's skills and the lore. The two came to an understanding. Rory could stay at court and serve *the new* Desmond, or he could go into exile with Thomas to Rouen in France, or he could leave Desmond service altogether, handsomely compensated (i.e., bribed to keep his pen silent). Rory chose the third way. Golden handcuffs were crafted; but after a year, the wealth hidden with the script, Rory followed Thomas to Rouen. James hired a curse that the bard's first born would die. But no other *Danaan* would serve the evil earl. He was left without proper guidance and public advocacy. He finally turned away from his own people, and his people from him. James found succor in foreign company. He made pacts with *the* Ormond — James Butler, Earl of Ormond — and even with the English Duke of Clarence, George Plantagenet, then living in the Pale.

Thomas died in 1420 of a broken spirit (or, it was said in whispers, he died of the *French disease*), and Rory returned to Eire *via* Canterbury, London, Oxford, and finally Bristol (from which port he took ship across the sea in 1422). He brought the news and the story of Thomas's last year and of his death to *the* Desmond, who was so pleased to hear of it that Rory was given much treasure and the freedom of Munster as a reward. He could settle wherever he pleased, unmolested for life, and that old "misunderstanding" between the second and third options once given him.

Rory moved to Mallow.

There he still received the occasional message from *the* Desmond, to which he graciously sent short statements of sound advice. Rory hid much of his new treasure and he married a girl of uncommon beauty and bright red hair (one already growing big with his baby in her belly). They were blessed with a son in 1425.

§

It had been a hard birth for Katherine (she of the bright red hair); her hips were slim, *"Not birthing hips"* the midwives said. A day and a night passed; Rory had contacted all the midwives he knew to come and help and advice.

And they all were happy to oblige him.

As a wise man Rory had made it his business to know anyone of importance, anyone with even the smallest modicum of power, knowledge, or authority in the kingdom. Midwives ruled in the ridiculously small but intimate world of birthing, which the surgeons of the day considered beneath their notice. It was nature, not science. All the midwives who could get away from their current tasks did so because no one of them wished to be on the bad side of a bard of Rory's reputation.

The boy was finally pulled from Katherine's unwilling and uncooperative womb, cleaned, severed from Katherine's cord, and placed into the hands of the father. All this was done in heavy silence.

Katherine was anxious to see her son. Rory hesitated; he knew right away that the boy was not long for the world. He was well formed but sickly in aspect, purplish-blue in color, not breathing very well at all, and not crying.

All but one of the mid-wives finally left the sad little scene, each touching the bard's arm or shoulder as they passed, tacitly expressing their sorrow of what would inevitably come to pass that night or the next.

Rory signed and took the babe and laid him on Katherine's uncommonly beautiful chest. His wife, he knew, was many things but she was not uncommonly perceptive. She saw only a perfect little babe (as perhaps all new mothers do). She put herself to sleep counting and recounting his fingers and toes, measuring, saying how this feature looked like that of one relative or other: his blue eyes, his red hair, the shape of his little face.

Rory stood by with the sole remaining midwife and looked on and listened to the happy recitation and smiling, nodding along in silence at his wife's glances. When Katherine finally fell asleep Rory moved the child to a crib of his own design and construction. Then he saw the last midwife out.

'What will you do now, bard?'

'Pray, Magda. I will pray. Perhaps the *Tuath Dé* will hear me reaching back for them through time.'

The midwife shrugged as she had no better suggestion and toddled off home to see to her own children, warmly embracing each of them and then with her man too.

Rory returned to his wife's side, pulling up a fresh blanket. He then regarded the child in the crib and picked him up again. The unnamed babe's little body was still breathing, miraculously, labored though it was, and was now a very pale whitish color rather than the sickly shades of earlier. Rory moved toward the fireplace and placed the boy into the little cradle, this one the woodcarver's gift.

It was better built than his own effort, if he was any judge, because of course it was.

He sat and rocked the babe; he did not want to get too attached just in case what he expected to happen should happen. But looking down at the small struggling boy, Rory came around to him.

He sang to his son; this calmed the little body.

He eventually fell asleep with an appeal to *the* Brigit on his lips. She was goddess of poets too, and she also knew the heartache of the loss of a son. James's long forgotten curse came to pass in the night.

§

The following morning, however, it was clear that *the* Brigit had heard and answered her good servant's plea. Typical of the gods, however, the answer was not the one he had begged her for.

'All I am saying, dearest Kate, is that there is something different, something not quite the same about the boy we brought into the world last night. I am not saying I do not love him, it's just… he just looks… I do not know… different… than he did yesterday.'

Katherine, who really should not have been up and out of bed yet, scooped the child out of her husband's hands and held him close to her body as if protecting his little ears from this verbal abuse.

'Surely,' Rory said, 'you can see that his ears are a little… more pointed?'

'So? What of it? They are perfect to me.'

'So? They were smooth yesterday, not pointed at all.' The woman looked at the tiny ears, tilted her head in a little bit of confusion, but waved it off.

'It's just… embroidery.'

'Embroidery!?'

'Stop yelling!'

'I'm not…' *sigh*.

'My uncle Ogden, you never knew him Rory, had slightly pointed ears too. It did ***not*** make him a demon!' Katherine recalled that Og had been a bit of a shite though, no one would deny that, but she did not mention that popular opinion.

'I never said that!' Rory slammed his fist into his open hand. 'You always do this, Kate; you twist my words into something bad.'

'You do not love him; you do not love your own son!'

Rory groaned a heavy sigh, appealing to his loyal hounds for counselling. Sadly, they did not understand the problem any more than Katherine did; they twisted their heads from side to side and wagged their tails, grinning as dogs do when expecting a treat.

Rory frowned and returned his attention to his wife. 'Of course, I do. Sit please Kate, you will make yourself light-headed. All I am saying is that yesterday he was... well, sickly. Frankly I feared for his life and so too did all the midwives. Now, today, he is lusty. Clearly, he is healthy, if still a little pale... but obviously vital as can be and with good lungs. He will be a great singer for sure. But yesterday, his hair was red like yours, now it is black and much fuller than it was. Have you ever seen a babe with a mane? And look at his fingers. You counted his fingers yesterday; I saw you do so when I handed him over to you. You saw his fingers. Look at them now. They are twice as long as they were, at least that much!'

The woman looked at the baby's fingers and kissed them tenderly, each one. 'They look fine to me, Rory O'Rourke. Long fingers are a sign of a musician. I would think you would be pleased by that!?'

Rory closed his mouth and did not argue the point any further. The boy's eyes were open, watching him. Rory had a feeling of being judged. The boy was smiling, or so it seemed, his long fingers pulling at Katherine's robes trying to get at her breasts.

Rory shook off the thought forming in his head.

'What should we name him, Kate?' He gave up the argument.

The woman let slip her robe and sat on the side of the bed trying to get the babe to suckle. It took time; the boy only wanted to play with her breasts, but a vigorous feeding soon began. Katherine managed to pry her eyes from her son to her husband. She was so happy; tears of joy reflected the sunlight coming in through the window. Soon Rory forgot what his earlier point had been. She had that way about her.

'We should call him Tadhg.'

Rory sat next to her and put his arm around his wife's shoulder. He watched the little babe feed for a bit and thought about the suggested name. He nodded, finally, and kissed his wife on the cheek and then his son on the forehead.

'Tadhg McRory.' He rolled the name around his mind for a moment. 'Yes, I like it, and let us hope that he grows up into such a name. A great poet or philosopher he will be.'

'Or musician.'

'So be it. A welcome addition to the *Danaan* tribe.'

'And the tribe of *De*', added Katherine. 'Dah said we was of the priestly caste once.'

Rory nodded. Katherine's father was a good blacksmith, that much he knew for certain. His father by law was not the shite that was his brother Og, Katherine's uncle, had been (or so local tales had it) but still, her father did not have a priestly bone in his body. The boy opened his eyes and regarded his father; his eyes were a deep shade of violet, purple dominating the right and blue dominating the left, both giving off a hint of deviltry. Rory only now noticed the colors. He then recognized the sign; he would have spoken out, but Katherine was already drowning in those eyes, so he let go and allowed himself to go with his wife into whatever would come to pass.

Little Tadhg winked at him, or so it seemed to Rory.

§

Tadhg McRory would write poetry in the years to come, but he would never be great (or even particularly good) at it. He would think deep thoughts, but he would never be a philosopher. He had a good strong voice, and he could sing passing well, but his voice lacked range, tone, and variation so he would never make a living out of it. Had Rory consulted a sage or witch about his son's future, he would not have believed the response anyway. Who could believe that their son would be a savior and a destroyer combined?

2

[Mallow in August 1435]

Rory O'Rourke had discovered that his son of ten years was not interested in any one particular thing but had enthusiastic (though temporary) interest in everything from fauna to Latin, to woodcarving, and to reading whatever writings he could find.

It had been challenging times of late for the little green island in the Northern Atlantic. Since the death of Mortimer, the so-called "saintly" English King Henry (no more than a boy himself) had decided that the people of that other island must be held responsible for the insult to his family's honor. The king's uncle, named Bedford, who controlled events in England with more dispassion than others had in a similar position, was, sadly, mostly out of that country overseeing England's diminishing French domain. Bedford might have explained to the boy king just how unlikely it was that a selection of mutually hostile tribal leaders in a savage land had somehow allied together and decided simply to wish Mortimer dead through plague.

Not that anyone in Mallow, save Rory (maybe), really understood these political matters at any level high or low, nor could they have named the decade-dead lieutenant or the king for that matter, even were he to be standing next to them in all his youthful gold and silken finery. Rory had been kept busy in correspondence with *the* Desmond, and sometimes with *the* Butler, but mostly with trying to find things to occupy his precocious son and avoid troubling questions from his neighbors.

Precocious was not exactly the correct word to describe Tadhg, however, but it was the best Rory had to offer them. *Ripe before his time* was the expression often used. The boy was bright enough for his age, true; talented, certainly (he could play and sing, and Katherine was teaching him to dance), but he treated learning as an entertainment. He treated everything as entertainment. He took little seriously; he grew bored very quickly. His curiosity was as insatiable as his attention span was brief.

And people talked of his "oddness", his "other worldliness".

One day, while sitting at the table with his wife, Rory heard her say, softly, 'You may have been correct.'

They had been chatting over the remains of their mid-day meal. Tadhg was out of the house playing with the other village children (or so they assumed). Their son had become the leader of the village youth despite that he was neither the oldest, smartest, nor the strongest among them.

'Oh?' Rory regarded his wife and tried to remember the disagreement that had brought on this new confession, but he could not recall it.

Katherine sighed. 'Aye, a mare instinctively knows her own foal, so too does the ewe, and the nanny. So too does the stallion, the ram, and the billy. I should have trusted your instincts when time was.' Rory nodded in dawning understanding.

'Tadhg? You speak of our son. After ten years... what changed your mind, dear? And yes,' Rory held up his hand, 'I do not think that he and the son that we had that night are the same person. But... I do not care any longer; I have not cared since the second day of his life. He is my son, our son, if not our blood.'

'I know. I feel the same, but people have been talking, and finally, I have started to listen to them.' Rory stood and came around the table to hug his wife. He stroked her hair.

'It's no sad thing *flame-hair*. I... that first night... when you were asleep, I prayed to *the* Brigit for a miracle and we were granted one. I decided to leave it at that, and I think we should still. Perhaps that makes Tadhg even more precious?' He kissed the top of his wife's head. 'We dreamed of a perfect child to complete our family and we got something more special even than that.'

'I'm not questioning the goddess's gifts, husband, but all the things you've talked about over the years with regard to the *Hidden* folk and all the superstitions and all the little rituals we all do to keep the favor of them...'

Rory nodded. 'You mean to say that he will not be with us much longer if all that is true?'

He could feel Katherine's nod against his chest. 'Children leave home, do they not? Ours may be going a little sooner, but he has always been special. And well… we could try to have another, maybe a little girl this time?'

Katherine looked up and back at her husband, smiling. 'I didn't know you wanted another, husband… Tadhg is such a handful.'

'I had no plans either way dear. It just has not happened for us as yet.'

'I would like that too.'

'Well then,' Rory's hands slipped down from Katherine's shoulders to cup her breasts, gently squeezing, tweaking, which he knew she loved. He bent over and kissed his wife passionately on the lips, then took her hands and lifted her to her feet, untying the knots of her apron.

'Rory! It's the middle of the day!' She laughed as her husband led her unresisting away from the table toward their bed.

§

At about the same time as his parents were trying to determine the future size of the O'Rourke household, Tadhg was hiding in the woods from his friends. He was the absolute king of the hiding game; he was able to blend into the forest background and become invisible, somehow, even in plain sight, only provided he was near a tree or a bush. It was quite entertaining and he loved the fact that he could sneak up and eavesdrop on any and all conversations in the woods. He had also seen many of the couplings going on among the younger and between the older adults of the village too.

Tobias McKeef was particularly prolific at it, bringing different girls into the woods on a weekly basis or so it seemed. Kelly McNeil got more sheer joy out of the act than any of the other village girls. Surprisingly, to the boy's uncertain knowledge, Tobias and Kelly had never come into the woods together, even though they seemed an ideal match. Tadhg spent quite a lot of time scheming of a means of making that coupling happen; the entertainment value alone would be tremendous and well worth the effort. Sometimes he wondered why he had never seen Rory and Katherine out in the woods. He had seen and heard them in their bed often enough, and he had seen his friends' parents out here too (with or without their usual mates), knowledge he somehow kept to himself.

'Does it not seem odd to you, boy, that you do not think of them as father and mother any longer?' Tadhg spun around, almost losing his balance, but could not see who had been speaking just then. There was a laugh; it was good natured rather than mocking. 'Look closer boy.'

Tadhg tried to do so, not really knowing what the voice meant.

'Open yourself up to what is all around you.'

He tried.

'This is the *unleashing* boy; this is your time.'

Tadhg was getting annoyed at being called *boy* when suddenly his entire perspective changed, and it no longer mattered.

§

Rory always thought that maybe humans had more than the traditional five senses of taste, touch, smell, hearing and sight, and that they were also limited by the fact that they could only use these senses for the titular purpose. The *Hidden* folk, however, have the advantage of being able to use any and all of these senses, and more, interchangeably or deeper than mortals could. To hear color or to see flavor or to feel whatever is underneath feeling.

The voice again told Tadhg that he was experiencing the "unleashing".

The voice said that what this means is the time in a life when a young *fae* is suddenly hit by the uncontrolled torrent of all of their senses being mixed together and opened up to all the sensations around them, higher and lower, at the same time.

Tadhg would have asked what "torrent" meant, but his eyes were just then being bombarded with sound; his nostrils were barraged by the sights of nature; his tongue could taste the abrupt blitz of bright colors. Green, for example, was no longer merely a predominant color in nature, a simple hue with many variations. Now, suddenly, it was so much more. A thousand variations in tone, a plethora of tastes, a surfeit of textures, an overabundance of sounds both near and far, above, and below, hidden, and obvious. The chirp of the cricket was suddenly a symphony of meaningful sensations and communications. A wolf padded by a league or two in the distance, its greyness now speaking volumes to Tadhg. He could smell that

Tobias and Kelly had in fact finally found each other, somewhere far to his left, a thousand paces away. Looking in that direction he could hear them even if he could not exactly see them, surrounded as they were by the bushes and tall grass of Tobias' own favorite spot. He was saddened by the unexpected revelation that Kelly would never have a child, was incapable of it, as she smelled wrong, in a certain way he did not quite understand, but he shed a tear nonetheless for the unfulfilled life the girl had before her. No man would have her until they were each well beyond child-bearing years, and women would sympathize, but would exclude her from most of their circles. Even as he wondered how he knew this — how he could actually smell the barrenness of her womb from such a distance — his senses suddenly overloaded. Tadhg lost all consciousness and fell over.

'Well,' said the voice, 'unleashing accomplished. Perhaps tomorrow we will speak again.'

§

Tadhg did not know how to understand what had happened to him.

When he re-awakened, he was alone in the place where he had collapsed. His senses seemed to have returned to normal, all except one — he was very hungry, and he felt that very sharply indeed. It was approaching evening after all; he must have been asleep for hours. He hurried home for the evening meal hoping he had not missed it. He resolved to consult about all this with the wisest man he knew — his father. By the time he got to the table, however, he was suddenly distracted. He looked at his mother very carefully and a smile appeared on his lips, his pupils dilated with interest.

'Am I to be a brother now, Mother?'

Katherine suddenly stopped ladling out the stew she had prepared.

She glanced at Rory.

Rory looked up at his wife, shrugged his shoulders. 'Why do you ask, Tad?' The boy considered this.

'I know not the how and why of it, Father, I just know a child is forming. I can… I do not know, sense it… maybe?' Katherine laid a hand over her belly.

'Well, would you like to be a brother?'

The boy considered his father's question very seriously and nodded. 'Yes, yes, I think I would like that. It would be very entertaining. But Father, I am confused about some matters.' He spooned the stew into his mouth, no longer able to fight his hunger. 'Thank you, Mother, this food smells delicious.'

Katherine patted Tadhg's head and kissed him on the cheek. She ladled the stew into her own bowl then she placed a loaf of bread, white meat, and fruit slices on the table for whomever wanted them, finally sitting down to eat her own meal. After a few mouthfuls, Rory turned to his son again.

'What brings on this new bout of curiousness?'

Tadhg told them of his recent experience in the woods, the voice, the overloading of his senses, and how really sad he was for Kelly McNeil. He could not explain how he had come to know so much about her, by sense of smell did not seem to clarify it enough.

'Have you ever coupled with Kelly, Father?'

Rory laughed and Katherine got angry and red.

'Sooth *flame-hair*, it is just a child's question,' said Rory.

Tadhg found the way he said *child* annoying, like the way the voice said *boy*.

'No, I have not. Besides which, she is only fourteen winters' old. And most importantly, I do not wish to. I have all I want right here.' He winked at his wife, who was cooling down again.

'But you said mother was only fifteen when you took her as a bride?' Rory sighed; he had said that; he now remembered it.

'That is different, son.' Rory smiled at Katherine, who had been back to her normal coloring but was darkening again. Tadhg nodded, accepting this non-explanation as some children will from a parent. Rory's was the usual adult answer when something did not make sense to a child.

Tadhg smiled in realization, 'Oh, so is that why you and mother never couple in the woods any longer?' Katherine spit out her small beer and turned a brighter shade of red, the color of her hair. She started coughing.

'Mother, are you well?'

Katherine nodded and rose from her chair to get a rag and clean up the spill. Rory took a few moments to recover from his own suppressed need to laugh.

'That's enough talk of coupling for the day, Tad.' Rory put his hand over his son's, drawing his attention. 'Tell me more about this mysterious voice of yours instead.'

'Yes, do,' said Katherine, recovering from the shocks and happy to change the subject matter. Tadhg regarded his mother with a mixture of curiosity and wonderment. His parents talked about who was coupling with whom all the time. Why was this different? The boy then shrugged it off and turned to his father's question, describing for him a deep voice, singsong without singing, a strange accent, and he mentioned the word *unleashing*. The use of the word made Rory straighten up in his chair with an odd look on his face. Katherine, who could read her husband's face very well sometimes, noticed the change at once.

'What does it mean, Rory?'

Rory took a sip of his own mug of beer. He regarded his son very carefully.

'Are you sure that was the word, son, "unleashing"?'

'Oh yes, Father, a strange word is it not, "unleashing"?'

'It could not have been another word perhaps?'

'No, I do not think so, Father.' He paused, cocking his head, and rolling his eyes right to left as if inspecting the thatch of the roof and beams of the house. 'I do not understand. What does it mean father?'

'Yes, what *does* it mean, Rory?' Katherine repeated her question, clearly suspecting an unappealing answer, placing emphasis on the second word.

Rory leaned back in his seat, regarding his wife and son. He purposefully took his time to stuff and light up his after-meal pipe-full. He then confirmed Katherine's suspicions. 'It means that the day I have always dreaded has come at last.'

§

A little later Rory and Tadhg sat by the fire and discussed the boy's experience and what it really meant. Katherine fussed about the chamber, clearly listening too, and worrying. Rory had decided that if they were going to acknowledge the secret then he and the boy would have to have a full, unadulterated conversation. Tadhg would have all his questions answered, and he would be made to understand exactly what all this meant… if Rory's knowledge stretched that far. They spoke on and off for three days and two nights.

They paused for meals and other necessities of course, but it was important. Rory, in his wisdom, had prepared the discussion years ago just in case the need ever arose, and now it had, and he was glad he had anticipated it.

The bard spoke of many things and Tadhg's attention never strayed from his talk. He spoke of the earliest stories of the land, of the *Book of Invasions*, of Sesser and Fintan MacBochra and his sixteen, then his thirty-four, then his fifty wives, who finally drove him mad and into hiding away from them.

He spoke next of the giant Partholon, "family-slayer", who, when trying to outrun the curse placed upon him, brought his wife and children and servants to Dublin where they cleared some of the great forests for settlement.

He told of how the curse finally caught up to the Partholonians (as any and all curses will eventually do), his people, and how they were wiped out by plague and battle-losses to the dreaded *Formorians*.

Rory told next of this evil, under-worldly, demonic, sea-based, vagabond race of thieves, their battles with the next people to come to the island, those known as *Nemedians* after their leader, the great druid Nemed.

The story kept expanding in the telling as if some outside force was taking a part in it unknown to the three of them.

Rory told a wide-eyed Tadhg how the battles between the *Formorians* and the *Nemedians* were legendary. Of course, Tadhg, the son of a bard, knew the tales well enough to tell them to himself and his friends, but Rory had a way about him and brought the stories to life for his eyes. Tadhg had heard these tales in his crib, in his bed, and from listening to his father's tutoring of the children of the very wealthy of *An Corcaigh* and Munster. The *Formorians* lost their king and fortress, true, but the *Nemedians* were decimated by the last battle and subsequently spread (thinly) throughout the world. Rory used the word "diaspora", which Katherine thought too funny sounding to be a real word and chortled. Rory paused but ignored the interruption.

Whatever force had overtaken him, Rory was not to be stopped now. Continuing the story, he told his son that following the war nothing was known of the land for centuries; no one lived here; no one but Fintan MacBochra hiding in his cave still, until finally the remnants of the *Nemedians* returned one day.

They came back as the *Firbolg* though and as the *Tuatha dé Danann*.

'The Firbolger came back first,' Rory instructed in his story-teller voice, the one that Tadhg loved so well (much nicer than his angry father voice, which was frankly terrifying, the memory of which kept the boy from getting into more trouble than he did), 'and they were cultivators of land.'

'Tillers and planters?'

'No Tad... well, not exactly that. The Firbolger people both tended to carry sacks of clay around with them. They had brought the clay back with them from wherever they had been, and they would bring the clay to rocky places, and spreading it, they would transform the rocky land in such a way that crops could be sown. There were then five kings and five tribes, and they vowed not to fight among themselves but instead to divide the island between them and live in peace. The five kings created the five kingdoms we know now...' he looked at his son and he smiled a teacher's smile, 'which are?'

Tadhg paused in thought. 'Well, Father, first is Munster. Ours is the land of the arts of music and poetry and is ruled over by *the* Desmond. We are the southern-most kingdom of the island and the largest.'

'True,' Rory replied, motioning his son to continue with the recitation.

'To the east is Connacht, ruled over by *the* O'Conor. His is the land of wisdom. To the west is Leinster, the land of prosperity and once the home of Finn McCool. It is ruled by *the* FitzGerald. The English over the sea have tried to rule there from their Pale of Dublin, land stolen from *the* FitzGerald long and long ago and paid for in blood, treasure, and diplomacy. To the north is the kingdom of rocky Ulster, a hard place of hard men, hard women, and much hard fighting. It was ruled, as much as it could be ruled, by *the* great O'Neill, although his rule is much disputed by lack of kinfolk and too many rivals. It is a land of war and discord. In the center is Mide or the fifth kingdom. It is the land of the high king, once called the "Unifier". There is where the druids made their seat as well, once upon a time.'

'Good; and what happened to the Firbolger?'

'They were displaced, Father, run out by the magical arts of the *Tuatha dé Danann*.'

'Just so. I am of the *Danaan* tribe, and your mother is of the *De* tribe. We are the descendants long and long of those who stayed behind and who, over the centuries, accommodated themselves to the descendants of the *Milesians*, known as Gaels to the Latins. It is from the latter that most of the people of the island descend, not from the *Tuatha dé* as scholars like to believe. After much warfare and invading the Gaels and the *Tuatha dé* decided a pact to bring peace to the island and they also divided the land between them. The Milesians would thereafter occupy the land above, and the *Tuatha dé* would thereafter occupy the land below, that land known as the *Otherland*. They became the *Hidden* ones, sometimes known as the *fae-folk* or the *free-folk*. In their place they advanced magic. Your mother and I believe that you, Tad, are of them.'

This gave the boy pause, but then he smiled brightly as if suddenly enlightened.

Rory smiled too and when on to explain about the babe they had had all those years ago and how he had prayed to *the* Brigit and how Tadhg must have been brought to them by the goddess herself or by her servants. Tadhg, of course, had more questions and Katherine gave voice to a few of her own. Rory could not answer them all, however, but he answered several, which was quite something actually.

§

His father had filled Tadhg's now ten-year-old head with many tales over the years and especially over the last few days and nights, mixed with some history, some mythology, some with religious conviction and some with the wisdom of scholarship, but it was not up to him to sort it out and decide what to do with it.

That was up to Tadhg.

Having experienced the *unleashing*, however, it was all but impossible now to deny his true nature. It was time Rory reckoned that Tadhg return to the place where the voice had spoken to him those scant few days ago and find out what more could be uncovered.

As Tadhg later moved through the woods the next morning he would stop occasionally and try to recreate the conditions of his earlier experience.

It was a daunting task; he met with little real success but even the successes he managed were amazing to him.

He found that he was able to sharpen his senses considerably; that he could take in all the scents of all the flowers or focus his senses to the point where he could smell but one, somehow masking all the others. He found that he could limit his hearing to the buzzing of one sole bee or expand it in such a way as to locate the hive, leagues away. He held out a finger and summoned a bee to land there. He was not sure if the bee actually performed the tiny bowing of its head that it seemed to have done, but he got a sense of the joy of the little creature as he very carefully used his finger to stroke its head. He was having a great deal of fun with this experimentation, this new game, it was highly entertaining. He then sent the bee on its way back to the flowers and found himself in the presence of a man with long hair, the color of sunset but with silvery strands mixed in, and intense violet eyes, the same color as his own eyes; bluer in one and more purple in the other although in the other eye to his own.

Tadhg also sensed wisdom and age.

'So, you have returned, young *fae*. Did your bard speak truth or myth?'

The speaker had the same voice Tadhg remembered hearing before. He was sat on the side of a log, recognizable forest creatures like racoons and squirrels gamboling about his feet, chasing each other around, while small unknown creatures sat on his shoulders or fluttered about on dragonfly or moth or butterfly wings. Tadhg's eyes were drawn away from these amusing antics to the staff in the man's right hand.

It was oddly fascinating.

It was a white wood, fir, maybe spruce, worked somehow into a smooth surface with what appeared to be green leafy vines winding about it, but a moment's concentration gave proof that these were expertly embossed details rather than actual plants. The head of the staff was a silver buck with a pair of small antlers of a golden hue. When the man moved to stand, his shirt shimmered. Upon closer inspection it appeared to be made of green-hued silver leaves somehow woven into a garment. These were workings no mortal smith could have achieved.

'Who are you?' Tadhg was able to shift his attention from all these distractions back to the other's eyes.

'Can you not guess? Focus your will, focus your senses, and make what comparisons to the known are in your experience to craft.'

Tadhg did as he was bid (or tried to, new as he was to such undertakings). He drew as best he could on his senses.

The man before him looked majestic and perfectly suited to the woodland setting. His hair was not hair as such but an august mane of golden-yellow (and white) fur, which eliminated the possibility that he was human.

'Very good, youngling,' the other smiled encouragingly. 'Are the strands of my locks so vastly different from your own?'

Tadhg brought his hand to his own head and felt his own hair and was surprised to find that it was also not the fine strands of his parents' or of the village girls he had begun to experiment with. His hair too was different, not like the man before him but more the texture of a downy rabbit. This realization opened up a new field of exploration for him.

Tadhg focused his aural sense now.

The man (the creature?) before him had no heartbeat. No, that was not true; just as Tadhg made the determination a sound did appear from the other's chest, loud and clear.

'We have hearts, Tadhg, but the beat of the heart of the *fae* is much different to that of the human. It is slow by comparison. Creatures of the world all have a natural span of life, and this is measured out in beats. We are allotted a number of beats at creation, and if we lead a life uninterrupted, we should live to that measure *but no longer*. The human heart of your father, Rory, beats as unto a hummingbird's wings, whilst yours and mine beat as unto a butterfly's. What does this tell you?'

'It tells me that humans are short-lived, while we are long-lived.'

The other nodded. 'This is so. We are, all of us, creatures of the earth, the air, the seas, the plants as well, everything, influenced by the beat of the heart within. Humans are active, focused on the moment, dynamic in purpose. It gives them an urgency that we, the *fae,* do not have. But this is no dreadful thing, nor is it good. It just is what it is.'

The other shrugged, 'It is that which it is by decree of the elder gods. We are languid, able to follow our interests through to an inevitable conclusion, with patience, if we so choose, although sometimes we are dreamy, but never are we somnolent like the trees. Human movements are… aggressive as a result. So little time, but so much to do; their minds race from interest to interest, task to task, a time to sow, a time to reap, as is written in their holy books. This is what makes them the greatest source.'

'The greatest source,' repeated Tadhg, 'source of what?' The person paused a moment then spread his arms wide in indication of the world around him.

'What makes all of this, youngling? What element binds it all together, gives it purpose?' The other searched the treetops; his eyes followed the flight of a bird. The animals which had been gamboling about were now gone, although several of the smaller creatures (Tadhg had no knowledge of their names) sat on the fallen tree, watching the other, following his movements, or danced among themselves, or wrestled with each other. Some had wings and some did not; those butterfly, moth, or dragonfly wings determined alliances in the wrestling matches or so it seemed. Tadhg became aware of a soft buzzing noise and followed it with his heightened senses to these creatures. They were talking, laughing, arguing, and cursing.

'Quiet,' said the other man and the buzzing stopped.

'Now, youngling,' the other turned back to Tadhg. 'There are many names for this singular element. Human philosophers call it *quintessential*. In the language of the Roman legions this means "fifth element", to compliment earth, air, water, and fire. The human churchmen call it "God". They worship it as such, which is perfectly reasonable of them after all. The *enlightened* ones, history knows them as *wizards*, call it *aether,* or the god-essence. Of this they partake to create their wonders. We call it purity; we mold it to our own desires or can shape it into a form and gift it to the humans, or the wizards, or to the *conroicht* or even as defense against the thieves of life, the *Stolen*, the unnatural ones.'

The other spoke of concepts that Tadhg knew truly little about, although he was not completely ignorant of them. He was fascinated that sometimes the man's voice clearly came from his tongue, and entered in through Tadhg's ears, but at other times it was a mind-to-mind conversation. He was too inexperienced, however, to fully figure out which was which or how to communicate in this other way.

'These things you must necessarily learn for yourself, youngling.'

Youngling was better than *boy* or *child* at least, although it meant the same thing.

But more than this, while Tadhg heard the main points of the discussion, he also became aware that there were unspoken undercurrents as well. The man of the woods spoke one thing with his tongue but thought something else directly into Tadhg's younger mind. Or, when he spoke, he seemed to be speaking different words at the same time. Sometimes the buzzing of the smaller creatures grew too intense to be ignored, and the other would stop, listen and respond to them.

'How is it molded, sir? How is it gifted? What do the *conroicht* use it for? What…'? The man of the wood raised a hand.

'Hold, youngling, your mind races like a pixie.' Two or three of the smaller creatures stopped what they were doing and turned to stare at the other. The man smiled and regarded them with obvious fondness.

'Am I mistaken?' A moment passed, and as one, they all shrugged and resumed their play. The other turned back to Tadhg.

'All will be revealed to you in the fullness of time. This is but our second meeting after all. Your curiosity is admirable, youngling, but you are not yet ready to hold the wisdom of the ages in your heart. You are still much too much a creature of the humans.' He paused. 'This is no terrible thing; no insult is meant by me; you will need that knowledge in the years to come. But your body has been taught to grow weary, and your mind has been taught to become overtaxed in the human way. Return now to your house and eat and rest, for the day has passed while we have been at discourse.' Tadhg regarded the heavens above the trees and saw that this was true, darkness was rising.

'One more question, please, sir, just one.'

The man smiled, nodded, 'One more I grant.'

'Who are you?' It had been his first question, still unresolved. The man drew in a breath of air and slowly let this out again. In time he nodded.

'I am called Fionnbharr, but that is just one of many names I bear. I am the *Hidden* high king of this island which the conquerors called Hibernia, which the English call Ireland, and which the people of the land call Eire. I rule the *Otherland*. The *aos sí* are my, our, people and I am their king. We are the *Aes Sídhe* or *Sith*. The humans call us *The People of the Mounds* or the *Daoine Sídhe*, but that is a misunderstanding we chose not to correct. They also call us the gods and goddesses of nature, the elemental spirits. We also chose not to correct them on these points. I rule with my queen,

Uonaidh, and we are your true parents. The Bridget sought a boon from us and we acquiesced. Now, let that be enough for today. Return when you can and I, or another of my choosing perhaps, will be awaiting you.'

3

MURDER MOST FOWL! Local man Thomas Carter (43), a known chicken farmer and supplier to local stores and eateries, was allegedly pecked to death by his birds on or about Tuesday evening, July 14th, 1995. The county coroner and sheriff's office are deciding whether the birds were actually responsible or if they merely saw the true cause of death, which was said to include massive blood loss. A possible witness, a tall man with a black cane, is said to have been in the area and the sheriff would like to speak with him. Carter's wife (Nell, 44) and son Neil (13) intend to continue the farm work.

Potter County News
for July 16th, 1995
by Benjamin Corban

4

[It is mid-June 1441, in Mallow, Ireland]

By his sixteenth year it was being said quite often that Tadhg had grown into a fine-looking young man.

He had not suffered the usual growing pains of the young, however; his long black hair was always clean, and his eyes were always bright. In those eyes were reflected wonder; at times, his infectious mischievousness was balanced by a suddenly restrained seriousness of mind and action.

Tadhg was not like the other young people of the village but no one seemed to mind.

When confronted with questions over their elder boy's plans for the future, Katherine and Rory acted the proud parents in public and pretended that a fine young man was all he really was. They encouraged Tadhg to do likewise, although it was increasingly difficult for him to conform to their wishes and to the village customs and they taught Bran, their second son, to act like his older brother.

Katherine often took note of the looks that her elder son was getting from the village girls and even the women at market square or in the lodge, of late, and she suspected that Tadhg had been with three or four of them already. That was life in the village though, and she was not overly bothered by it. Her thoughts were, however, disturbed by two other recent and related insights.

It occurred to her one fine, sunny afternoon that she would never have grandchildren from Tadhg. At least, she would not through a human girl, and she might herself be long dead before he had a child with one of his own kind (a child she would love as if it were of her own blood, but still). Bran was too small to take on the burden of supplying grandchildren for at least another decade or more. Sometimes her thoughts led her in strange directions too; like did the *fae-folk* get children in the same way that humans did? She had never seen another *fae*, to her uncertain knowledge, leastwise one heavy with child. She let these thoughts slip into the open air one day and she noticed that Rory's face turned unusually mournful. He called her broody. Mary Tavish, Katherine's friend and cousin, had just had another child.

But this did not explain his mournful expression and Katherine said so.

'Just thinking,' he responded.

'About?' she prompted.

'Well, you are correct I think, *flame hair*, there had never been children born of a human and *Hidden* coupling… as far as I know.' Rory explained to his wife that millennia ago either the *Hidden* folk or the human folk had become something different to the other, or they never had really been one people in the first place (despite all the myths and legends). Whether it was impossible, well, he could not say, but to count on it happening was a fool's errand. He had not wanted to be harsh with his wife but sometimes loved ones had to be disabused of notions quickly and callously for their own well-being.

He hoped that his wife would do him the same service should the need arise.

'I am just saying that you should not long for a grandchild that will never come from Tadhg.' Of course, this made Katherine sad for a time, but she took it rather well in the end. The sadness quickly turned into something else; the other thought that kept her awake at night these days finally had an explanation.

If it was true that these couplings could not bear fruit, then Tadhg was tacitly hinting at a promise to those girls that would never come due, was he not? Marriages often began as a result of pregnancy in the small rural communities round and about. Girls gave up their virtue to boys for more than pleasure.

Rory did not seem to understand her point; not at first and not emotionally in any case.

Tadhg was indifferent to Katherine's disquiet on the point when she raised it with him.

Perhaps this was because it was more a woman's concern to both of them. Rory knew, and Katherine knew in theory, that men took a different view about love, sex, and marriage than women took. Inadvertently, however, Katherine had put another issue altogether into Rory's mind.

How many months or years of this behavior would go by before the fact that none of the girls got with child led to… questions? Questions unanswered would lead later to accusations. Was there something wrong with Tadhg? Was he accursed?

Was he different?

Belief in the truth of the gods and the *Hidden* was one thing, but no one really liked being made a fool of. If the truth of Tadhg was someday uncovered… well, at best feelings would be hurt. Rory stopped himself from guessing what else might happen. As a result of his, foolishly giving voice to this thought, Katherine became doubly concerned for her son and now feared deadly repercussions.

As mothers do sometimes do, she began to blame herself. Rory could not comfort the new disquiet away despite his best efforts.

It is known, Katherine said, and everyone agreed, that it was the way of things that the *Hidden* lived only for pleasure, entertainment, pranks, but she had long harbored the hope that her influence would show somehow on Tadhg nonetheless; that she was still, in some way, the boy's real mother. She was blind to the fact that her influence had actually been quite deep already.

Rory pointed out that Tadhg was kind and thoughtful (while everyone knew the *Hidden* were only tricksters and pranksters and amoral unless bribed), and although quite carefree in other ways he was never callous to anyone. The people of the village liked him because he was likeable; there was just enough of the rogue about him that mothers warned off their daughters (while secretly smiling and daydreaming about the rogues in their own pasts) which, of course, made him all the more attractive to their daughters.

He had a gang of devotees about him who were themselves then positively influenced (including little Bran, Rory said picking up his second son). So, when an accident happens, is it not true that, for example a broken pot, Tadhg was the first to step up and take responsibility if he was in any way involved in the breakage. But more than that, he and his cohort set out determined to set things right if they could. A broken fence was repaired; a crushed flowerpot was replaced. No one stayed mad at him, or them, for longer than mere moments. This had all been Katherine's influence *writ large*. Because of a mother's love and influence the village was a more pleasant place to live for everybody. Mothers' love and fathers' discipline kept the village alive.

For his part Rory had been teaching Tadhg the art of the bard and the poet. The boy had learned the lute, the pipes, and he had a pleasing enough singing voice. His talent was only passing though; he would never figure among the great bards (or to be completely honest, the bards of any reputation). But as if to balance out the less than perfect voice, Tadhg was naturally cheerful. When he played along with Rory on the occasional night on the green or in the lodge it was never a disaster. Indeed, Tadhg had a way of turning a missed note or sour chord into an opportunity of further entertainment for the crowd.

He was charmingly self-deprecating, which endeared him all the more.

Where another performer would be pilloried, he was forgiven.

Tadhg was laughed with, not at.

But Rory had a growing awareness that his son was unsatisfied with it; with performing, with life in the village. At sixteen summers old it was time he left home and made his own way, whether here or in the *Otherworld*. Rory hoped it would be here or hereabouts, as Bran clearly loved his brother (and Katherine was pregnant again and Rory hoped for a girl).

For the last few years, however, the other half, the greater half of Tadhg's time had been spent among his own kind. While this had Rory's and Katherine's approval (if not their understanding), they knew that eventually Tadhg would have to choose between the two worlds and he would choose the other because of course he would.

For his part Tadhg learned the *Hidden* magic from Fionnbharr and Uonaidh, was introduced to other members of the high court, explored the *Hidden* paths, learned the ways of the *fae* and that of the elementals and other extraordinary creatures usually and carefully hidden from human eyes.

The tree-folk he found slow and ponderous (not very entertaining… but wise).

The water-folk he found overly voluble and unable to concentrate long (unwise but very entertaining) and always on the move.

He enjoyed the tricks and jests of the *pookas,* but he was too serious-minded to lose himself in their incessant and meaningless play for long.

He was awestruck by the violence of the *red caps* but was too compassionate to fully take part in their bloody contests.

While *sprites* and *pixies* were great fun and usually thought only of sex and pleasure, they were too small for him to fully engage with (although there were entertaining experiments of a bodily sort tried).

Tadhg spent increased time too in the company of what few remaining druids there were about the place. These people straddled the line between the mortal and mystical worlds, similar in a way to the mortal magic workers, and Tadhg saw himself in a comparable situation. He learned much from these folks though, attending their councils and appreciating their wisdom and lore, speaking out more and more of his own thoughts and opinions.

He also found that he particularly enjoyed the company of his older cousin Drugal. Drugal, the "Silver Prince" was of the court of Armagh, the child of Uonaidh's sister Tadhg's aunt. The sisters had conspired to bring their offspring together as it was thought Drugal would be a good influence; he was principled and martial in nature (like his father), and he stood in for the ideal of a young *sidhe* noble. Drugal, for his part, needed a purpose, and mentoring his younger cousin into the *sidhe* ways seemed good for him too.

Their friendship was encouraged and it blossomed.

Still, in his mother's opinion, that is, in the queen's opinion Tadhg spent too much time ogling female dryads and wood nymphs, and she was dismayed to find that her nephew did not do enough (in her opinion) to discourage that aspect of Tadhg's nature. Little did she know that despite his advanced age Drugal too fell more under Tadhg's influence than the reverse, as hoped. It did not help the cause that the dryads, nymphs, and others encouraged the attention, such was their nature. Both sisters, both queens in their way, knew that interspecies coupling among the *fae* was common, but sometimes resulted in... accidents, aberrations even.

A half-pooka, half-dryad child was not a stain as such. No, of course not, the very idea that they would have a problem with that, imagine!? But half-*sidhe*... accidents... were inconceivable.

The word made Tadhg laugh. 'But you said...'

'I know what I said, young *sidhe*.'

His would have been the life of the beloved prince of a beloved king if it had been left to progress normally (but nothing is ever so easy as that). Also, unexplained, and unexplainable, there was sadness growing in the back of the queen's mind about her son which she could not yet put into words.

While he could, however, the prince took to it all. He was like a mop; he learned from everyone, whatever they could teach him, trivial or essential, he took it on board and wrung from it what entertainment he could.

In the human world, however, it was getting to be time for the boy to become a man; to put aside the things of childhood, to think of marriage and family and responsibilities to his people and his tribe and village. In the *fae* world there were many, many, decades of life to come before these issues became even an inkling of a notion of an idea of a concern. Still, that fact did not prevent envoys from other *Hidden* courts commenting on the prince's qualities, hinting that it was never too early to negotiate "arrangements" with the English, Welsh, Scottish or Burgundian courts.

Fionnbharr would stroke his bearded chin in thought at such fine words and considered the philosophies of suggested arrangements.

Uonaidh would hear none of it. She always seemed to know the flaws of the noble and royal daughters put forward for consideration. Common to all species was the idea that no man was good enough for a man's own daughter and no girl was an ideal match for any woman's son.

The idea of such things as "unanimous truths" (and other like conundrums) both teased and entertained Tadhg's thoughts while he was lying awake in his bed.

He did not fully grasp why Katherine disapproved of the couplings with the village girls, but for her sake he eased off, discouraged attentions, and found other diversions. She must herself have taken part in the act when she was his age; it was the normal way of life, though she and Rory did not say anything about it. For his part Rory seemed proud of his son's activities.

'Humans are irrational,' said his father the king, 'always had been, probably always would be, get used to it, son.' His other parents (in his heart Tadhg would never distinguish one set from the other) encouraged him. He had never once promised a girl marriage, although Katherine implied that he silently did so every time he took one into the woods.

'But they take me into the woods too, Mother!'

'That's not the point, Tad.' Tadhg could only conclude from these discussions, as Fionnbharr did, "That humans are indeed irrational creatures."

One day, while walking through the woods around Mallow Tadhg was idly thinking the great thoughts that all beings in the odd years between childhood and maturity think while otherwise looking out for sport or distraction. He was surprised (alarmed is a better word) to chance upon the scene of Rory and Fionnbharr in deep conversation. He instinctively knew that this was not a good thing (for himself) and he had, successfully, backed away several paces before two different hands waved him closer.

He had been caught by his fathers.

Sometimes life can be unfair even for the exceptionally privileged.

§

It had not subsequently been a lengthy conversation although it seemed interminable to Tadhg. To even call it a conversation was generous, he thought later, as that implied an exchange of ideas, a certain give and take between persons.

No, this had been more like a homily.

Not a reprimand either, exactly, but more like a long address from one father, followed up by a speech from the other.

There was no scolding; no censures (some pontification it must be said); and it all seemed very complimentary in that way people know is building up to something unwanted.

"Here is the situation", one or the other father said, and "This is the solution agreed upon", the other father would add.

Tadhg had been firmly instructed to sit, which he did.

The bard and the king took turns talking "with" him (in a one-sided kind of way), and he learned many things as a result…

That he was a clever youth.

That he was quick witted.

That he needed a wider base of experience.

That there were other places and other lessons to learn.

That he could do both his families a great favor.

Of course, he had a choice, what kind of question was that?

No, he could not take Drella the fair dryad with him, this is serious.

That the best way to learn as quickly and as thoroughly as possible about the wider human world, as well as the customs of his people elsewhere, was to be in other *fae* kingdoms.

That he was to leave the village and join with something called the *Universitas Dubliniensis.*

'Wait...' Tadhg raised a hand to stop the barrage of... learning. 'What is that?' He paused, 'This... University of Dublin?' Tadhg translated Rory's Latin. 'I thought you said that these academies were merely for the instruction of new priests of their triune God?'

'Well, yes, I did say that' said Rory, 'but you do not have to accept residence at the *Ard-Eaglais Naomh Pádraig,* son'. Here Rory explained to the king his reference to the great imposing structure in Dublin known otherwise as St Patrick's Cathedral.

'The plan we,' here Rory referred to himself and the king, 'decided upon is that you take advantage of the facilities there, the library, the city, and make connections with the other students.'

'And the Dublin *Hidden* court,' added the king, 'where your cousin Aurnia rules as high duchess.'

'Yes,' agreed Rory, 'expand all your horizons, son. The school gathers the best and brightest Eire has to offer and then some from beyond these shores as well.'

Rory placed a paternal hand on the young man's shoulder. 'From there you could move on to an English institution and then a couple European schools if you are so inclined. You have a good head for languages.'

The king put a paternal hand on the young man's other shoulder, 'And in so doing, you could learn the arts and cultures of other lands, learn the ways of our *fae* cousins in England, Burgundy, France, Castile, wherever your heart leads you, son.'

'You are as the proverbial bee, son, leaving the hive, collecting the nectar of other lands and bringing it all back with you to produce the honey of wisdom here.' Tadhg looked bemused by Rory's metaphor.

'I like that,' said the king. 'Hive, honey, bees, nicely put, sir. Indeed, I first came to the boy while he was stroking a bee.' Tadhg turned his head and looked bemused at his other father.

Recognizing that he was trapped Tadhg nodded his agreement.

'When do we think I should be leaving, Fathers?' Neither father picked up the sarcasm in the question.

'I have a friend over at St Finbar's Abbey in the city,' said Rory, referring to nearby Cork, 'and I still have some connections at the mayoral court there as well. You will be set up there as a novice. The abbey is not dedicated to any particular order, however, so you can learn the ways of all the different so-called "regulars" from them or find one you like,' Rory paused, 'that means monastic orders. You will take instruction from the scribes, archivists, and librarians there, in the sacred history and philosophy of their triune god. You will not be suspected at the university if you have some knowledge of these things, you see. You are already fluent in Latin, as much as I could teach you, so you are set in that regard. The king, your father, has agreed to set funds aside for your use and protection.' Tadhg smiled and nodded as his future was laid out before him, decades in advance. Sadly, there had been no mention of pretty, human girls, or enthusiastic fair-skinned dryads in any of the discussion or plans.

§

Weeks turned to months but all too soon it seemed the necessary contacts had been made and arrangements settled. It was time for the boy to set out on the road to manhood (or some such sentiment, Tadhg had stopped listening to whichever father's rattling on after a time). And for all his protestations (of which there had been quite a few) Tadhg actually found himself looking forward to this new phase of his life. Indeed, when the time came, rather than take the *Hidden* paths he decided to walk the human roads to the city. He reasoned that Cork was not that far away, and as he had been there with Rory on occasion, he already knew the paths well enough. He would open a *fae* pathway once he had settled (as he had been taught to do), that is, once he had found a new living space.

Katherine was teary-eyed as she waved him goodbye, holding little Bran's hand tightly as he too waved (not really understanding what was happening but wanting to go with his brother).

Queen Uonaidh confessed to the king later that she was troubled by it all.

'The boy is off on a fine adventure, my fawn,' said the king, lying next to his wife. 'A part of me wishes I were going with him. None of these opportunities existed when I was his age. Imagine these schools...'

'I don't like it, my husband, I don't like it at all. There is disaster ahead.'

The king sat up and regarded his wife. 'Disaster, you say?'

The queen turned over and looked up at the king, 'You know my prophecy is fitful, my husband. I don't know when, but I know something bad will happen to him.'

The king very seriously mulled this over. The queen was a seer of sorts, true, but her skills were problematic and sometimes unreliable. He was at times reminded that the prophecy of utter destruction for the human village she foresaw had never materialized in over two centuries, and that it was almost forgotten by all. Two hundred years of putting treasure aside, hidden from almost all and earmarked for rebuilding, gone to waste (so to speak).

'Are you sure that this is not just a mother's foreboding, my fawn? You will miss your son, as will I, it is only natural, but how long are we speaking of really, a century; two at the most? How much knowledge could these mortals have accumulated since we were naked and frolicking in the woods ourselves?'

The queen smiled at the memories of the naked frolicking (and other things) they used to do in the woods. She hugged her husband and held him tightly, which shortly led to some of those other things, which eventually led to sleep. For the rest of her life, however, the queen was convinced that someday unwelcome news would come their way.

The king should have listened.

The queen should have insisted.

5

[It is 1450]

The years since he left Mallow went by quickly, unnoticed, at least by the *Hidden*. For his part, however, Tadhg (now sometimes known as Brother Richard) was having a splendid time of it.

The myths and legends of this triune god and his followers fascinated and entertained him in equal measure, although he often uncovered borrowings from other human mythic tales through his extensive readings on the subject. The *Hidden* folk can go days or weeks without having to sleep, and Tadhg put the extra hours that his human friends did not have to particularly beneficial use indeed, deep in the depths of their libraries and in their damp and yet dusty hidden vaults of knowledge which many had forgotten but which he had found in his nightly wanderings. He added some valuable manuscripts to his own growing collection (these would have wasted away forgotten otherwise), some of which he even shared with Rory and Bran (when he could get away with it). That is, when he remembered he had a human family to share discoveries with.

This triune god of theirs, Tadhg often concluded, was clearly a reflection of the monotheism of the Jews. This was itself a blending of the polytheism of the Canaanites. Tadhg liked these big words and through them into conversation when he could. He might have pursued that learning further even though, or perhaps because, it was discouraged by all his monastic superiors. These gods of the Canaanites were utterly charming in their way though, and clearly instrumental in Greek and Roman subsequent mythmaking. Indeed, he often paused and wondered how much these god stories influenced those of his own people's folklore. *The* Dragda was known to the people of his lands as "all-father" but this was a title also applied to *Wodin* of the Germanic people, while *Dīs Pater* of the Romans was also a god of agriculture, much like *the* Dragda, and so it went on.

But Tadhg knew that the gods of his people were real beings. He came to believe that this triune god must also be real, therefore, at least as real as were the gods of all these other folklores (or perhaps they were all the same gods?) The Christians, however, had conquered so much in their brief time and in the name of their one god who is three gods that these others were disappearing fast and losing adherents as the years went by. It was the same with the followers of this Mohammad the prophet. Although they were all loath to admit it, Allah, Yahweh, and the Christian triune god were all really the same being. Tadhg might have pursued this knowledge further too, were it not also for the fact that there was so much else to learn. The more he learned, however, the more ignorant he realized he was of the mortal's world and all its charms.

He called this a "fascinating paradox", translating the ancient Latin and Greek terms into his native tongue.

The arts, the sciences, the philosophies, the myriad human languages, magic forms that for some reason the Church of Rome opposed and suppressed, all awaited the earnest scholar not afraid to pursue them.

Tadhg learned that some humans were quite magic proficient but most of whom were not associated with that Church (or any church). These few his father the king had called wizards, although they referred to themselves as "enlightened." Tadhg thought Fionnbharr had mentioned this too but coming from mortals it seemed a bit pretentious in his ear. True, the people who had "ascended" their earthly bounds and entered into mystic systems were exceedingly rare, but they were still an interesting and entertaining lot (if a little unimaginative with their art).

Really, what is the point of turning base metal into gold anyway?

Of course, they in turn had learned about the *Hidden* and some had made a study of other so-called "mystical" creatures (some even said "bizarre"). That other word bothered Tadhg though. He was instructed that it was used to mean anything which fell out of the accepted rules of nature. But he knew, of course, that his people and these other creatures were all at the very heart of nature.

It made no sense.

None of this was taught in the learning academies either, at least not officially, or not in any practical way really. There were a fair few cat baptisms (for whatever magic that was supposed to bring forth). Humans associated cats with magic.

Why?

They were irrational.

Getting back to the *enlightened*, however, it was interesting to Tadhg that the humans differentiate themselves into separate factions; they did not see that magic was just magic.

Some of the arts of the factions he had come across were medicinal in practice. Like the hermits and wild women of legend they were inclined toward the natural magic of herbs and plants. These few reminded him of the druids back home with whom he was familiar, and he was surprised (shocked, if truth be told) to learn that there were no English or French druids. There may once have been... but no more. Charmers, blessing-casters, and conjurers, there were aplenty, however. Tadhg often argued these were no different to priests. Instead of praying to God for some benefit or miracle they prayed to other beings, including, he was interested to learn, the *Hidden* folk of their own realms.

The mortals also made very precise divisions between "white" or helpful magic and "black" or baneful sorcery, which Tadhg thought of as mere hair-splitting word play. Surely, the magic in and of itself was a neutral thing subject only to the state of mind of the wizard?

Whether enchanter or sorcerer, healer, or curser, and for whatever reasons, the Church of the triune god hated them all equally. Its inquisitors would burn their books and materials and even their bodies wherever and whenever they could catch them casting spells or even just preparing to do so. After so many years Tadhg could still not fathom this discrimination (practiced not just against the *enlightened* either, he discovered).

No, these priests of the triune god also had some strange and confused ideas about the *fae*, the night creatures, and the lupines as well, as if these were not all perfectly natural creatures doing what was in them to do. The Christian clergy spoke out against all the other "mystical" beings, surprisingly, and laughably, ill-informed about it though they were.

Tadhg had been warned off enough to keep his opinions to himself, however, lest he be thought of as a troublemaker, and over the years, he more often than not did so. Jewish scholars he met were less shockingly ignorant, but they were often more superstitious, while the Islamists passionately believed only in the tales of desert djinn and little else. He shook his head, waved it away, and silently marveled that so many of his seniors in the Church (whatever church really) still, nonetheless, consulted with wise men, witches, fortune-tellers, and astrologists (in defiance of their official canons) on such a regular basis.

It made no sense.

"Humans are irrational creatures." His father's words rang in his ears.

One thing these clerics of the triune god did well, however, was illuminating manuscripts. They created beautiful inks, drawings in gold and silver leaf, and they could bind books and manuscripts in such a way that despite varying sizes they would fit aesthetically well together in vast libraries. The scripts, the colors, the gold and silver embellishments, it was sometimes literally breath-takingly beautiful art.

Tadhg found the archivist's profession and the conservationist's trade relaxing and stimulating work. He took to it like a calling, and as time went by, he was entrusted with increasingly important tasks, from mixing the inks to preparing the vellum sheets. He learned the best ways to bind, the best skins for the best results, how to fix rips and tears to the point where no one could see the repairs at all. When he was not being indulged as a prodigy (which amused him immensely), he was also the leader of great cohorts in whichever city he currently inhabited.

Tadhg was the child of a generous father after all and was able to move seamlessly from the noble to the gentle to the common worlds through mere illusion and speech. He had come to understand quickly that the *Hidden* have no real firm understanding of wealth (in the human sense of the word). His people valued natural beauty above material possessions which they really had little desire for otherwise. Tadhg shared the *fae-folk* philosophy, but he also came to understand the human viewpoint as well. A piece of gold was in and of itself a scintillating work of art certainly, but it could also buy anything from companionship to peace and quiet. It gave Brother Richard a status in the world of monasteries and churches, but it also gave Sir Richard Rorison (Tadhg's noble personification) status in their secular societies. With a little simple will-working, a change of hair color, a little height, a little weight, better looking clothing Tadhg easily passed effortlessly from one to the other strata and back again.

§

[It is 1455]

As time passed and Brother Richard advanced from post to post in the monastic system of the Church of the Triune God, he came into contact with more and even greater wonders.

Tadhg knew that one day he would return to his home in Ireland's otherworld reflection, and he wanted not to forget his grand adventures of this human world. So, of late, along with the letters to his human family, which had grown in his absence by another brother and a sister, he sent Rory and Bran diverse selections of manuscripts (including a couple Tadhg had penned himself along the way), strange musical instruments, little statues, and other miscellaneous items (including gifts and trinkets for his mother and siblings too). He sent works of art and other precious trifles to the king and queen. Amazingly wrought pieces of clothing and jewelry were bundled up with coins from many realms with pictures and portraits etched into them, gifts from other *Hidden* courts, of course, and weapons from many armies, carefully managed and handled.

His mother, Queen Uonaidh, was charmed by silks of many colors.

His mother Katherine was intrigued by carved ivory and the idea of elephants, imagining them to be much larger than they actually were. Return letters from his human family noted such things as illnesses and deaths, new births in the village, marriages, crop reports, and Tadhg took it all in. If Munster was any example, then Ireland as a whole was doing well for itself.

§

[It is 1459]

Time passed quickly; Tadhg sometimes forgot that he was not a mortal human being (even though he looked like one and had learned to act the part almost but not quite flawlessly).

Ideas and events entered and left his awareness; some things made an impression on him based on whatever he was currently interested in or how entertaining they were, but not much further than that and he would always return to books.

The great war between England and France gave way to other battles across Christendom, and then with the armies of Islam. He sometimes took an interest in these events whenever he was assigned by monastic superiors to archive diplomatic materials or to function as a witness to negotiations. In England one half of a noble family made war on the other half for the right to set themselves up as targets of greed, jealousy, and assassination. This conflict, somehow, spilled over into Ireland, which still sometimes caught his especial regard. He would write home (*via* the *Hidden* paths or through monastic networks) for assurances that all was well in his little village. Mostly it was.

He was surprised to learn that Bran, now seventeen and a man by village standards, had gotten a girl with child and was now married. Rory had bought them a parcel of land and the men of Mallow had built them a house on it, leaving enough room for this Margaret girl to have a little garden, plant some vegetables, and keep a cow while Bran plied his trade as a smith. Of all things... a smith. Bran had inherited none of Rory's artistic ability. The news of all this brought Tadhg boundless joy (temporarily) as well as a little sadness (also temporarily) as he would not have the opportunity to meet this girl for many years to come, if ever.

Tadhg told the recipients of his letters, Rory, Katherine, Bran, that he would have liked to have met Jean d'Arc but had been in Aragon at the time and missed her celebrity. He was disturbed by the founding of the Inquisition there, later in the century, he wrote, but by then he was in Bavaria cataloguing some destitute noble's book collection for an estate sale. As the cataloguer he was able to keep some of the better volumes out of the public eye and added to his own massive collection *on the sligh* (as they say). This he carted around from place to place or had stored here and there under specific conservational conditions.

Sometimes as Brother Richard, sometimes as Sir or Baron Richard Rorison (depending on his mood and need for social status in a new surrounding) Tadhg also studied the arts of illumination under Simon Marmion and had discussed musical composition with the famous (some said infamous) Flemish musician William Dufay. He had laughed along with others at the anecdotes Nicholas da Conti had brought back with him from darkest Cathay (some of which were true, or so he said). When Gutenberg demonstrated his new press apparatus, Tadhg had been in the gathering and had been impressed. He had been less impressed with a drink call Scotch whisky (after the country of its concoction thinking that the Irish could do it better). In Venice he opened one of these new-fangled bank accounts and heard a concerto written for harpsichord.

At some point in all this travel he was sad to discover that his mother Katherine had died and that he had been missed at her life celebration service. Five years later, Rory followed his wife into the mortal version of the afterlife. His human family had been reduced to Bran and people he mostly could not identify by sight or scent.

Tadhg had been saddened by the loss of his human parents of course (when the news finally came to him *via* the *Hidden* paths and the monastic networks), and he made arrangements that his three human siblings be watched over and cared for by his father the king (and he provided the details of the bank accounts in his letters to the king his father and to the abbot of St Fins to be passed on). Tadhg fancied that he would become the secret hidden patron of their descendants (a *fae-folk* practice he had never shown much prior interest in, but which now sounded highly entertaining).

Although he was not as proficient as the queen, his mother, in the seer's arts, he did know that Ireland was in for some bad decades ahead. He told his human brothers and his one brother-in-law that they should become as accommodating to the English as possible without compromising their essential Irish-ness as much as could be done. This would put them at odds with their fellows in the short term but which would pay massive dividends (that was a banking term) in the long term. Advantages they might use on behalf of those self-same people. He wrote many letters, but he did not return to his human homeland. About twenty years after leaving Mallow, he had been assigned (as a high-ranking churchman in his own right) to be part of a negotiating team for peace and trade between the Kingdom of Hungary and the expansion minded Ottoman Turks. He had not been to the tiny Republic of Ragusa before, so he remained with the mission rather than returning to Ireland. Besides, it was said that Richard the Lionheart had lived in Ragusa for a time, and this interested Tadhg.

§

[It is 1461]

The Hungarian company to which Brother Richard had been attached as head secretary arrived in Dubrovnik in the frigid winter month of November. A chill wind was blowing in-land off the Adriatic Sea and up the Dalmatia coast, and it had dogged the carts and coaches all along the journey from their starting point in Buda. Tadhg had not been put off by the icy rains so much as his comrades, creature of the elements that he was, nor did he consider the inclement weather the ill-omen that some of his company thought it to be. Hungarians, Transylvanians, and Wallachians were overly superstitious folk (not to mention irrational).

Tadhg would smile whenever that word came to mind.

This is how he had come to understand the profusion of incense sticks burned against the influence of *lidércs* (especially the devilish sort). Tadhg had spoken with a few of the native *Hidden* folk of Central Europe (unfairly but amusingly called *incubi* and *succubi*) and he had found them quite entertaining and quite misunderstood by the mortals, not to mention very accommodating.

But that was a common lament of all the *fae*.

In any case, negotiations would take place in the Rector's Palace in the center of the city. This "palace" turned out to be a squat, rectangular building, whitewashed to look more like a merchant's guildhall than a political manor. But as the Republic was ruled by a merchant-based aristocracy this was not an unexpected discovery and so Tadhg merely shrugged his shoulders.

The King of Hungary hoped to pacify the Ottoman Sultan for a season or two further, but negotiations were dull, time-consuming, and mostly, sadly, unamusing. The king's party would only parley in Latin. The sultan's party made the grand gesture of parleying (only) in Greek rather than Arabic. Master secretary was ensconced with the small contingent of translators, which hoarded and bottlenecked information and which practice also gave them a great deal of influence. Brother Richard was one of those few summoned to both public sub-committees, and *in camera ad hoc* gatherings. His translations were held up as both honest and un-biased with a dash of uncommon accuracy.

His reports were all of these things too because, as neither a Christian (in truth) nor a Muslim, as neither a Turk nor a Slav he had no poker in the fire. He was not averse to customary bribes from either side; was a guest at many a sumptuous feast;, and as he always had been, he was fine company for all. Whenever he could, however, Tadhg let slip the clerical persona and explored the city in the guise of a Venetian nobleman named Paulo de Costa.

It was in that guise, one particularly cold evening, when he met her.

§

Their eyes met at the exact moment when, back in the Irish *Otherlands*, Queen Uonaidh came down with a debilitating pain in her head (cause unknown) which was rare for the *fae,* but not as rare among the seers.

6

Reports have come to our attention that a local Watertown woman, Janice Haymaker (34, nee Pierce), has been "murdered" in the early hours of the morning after she and her husband, Robert Haymaker (40) stopped at a 24-hour self-service station on their way home from her sister's home in nearby Medford. They pulled into Makie's Gas, which is next to Ferguson's Grocery, at or about 1.15 am, just as the store was being robbed, allegedly, by the **Lords of Watertown** gang (of local ill-repute). Details seem confused at this time, but according to witnesses, and despite the alarm going off, the **Lords** took the time to load two cash registers and several bottles of whiskey into a pickup truck and a car and were taken by surprise by two police officers responding to the alarm. Gun fire was exchanged, at which time Robert was knocked unconscious and Janice was killed on the scene. The **Lords** escaped arrest with a hostage described as a tallish man, expensive blue suit, Panama hat, and exquisite walking stick (possibly with gold and silver aspects). A bizarre twist to the story has appeared, however, in that eyewitnesses placed the **Lords** several miles away from the scene at the time of the crime. If any of our readers have any further information about these events, please notify the editor.

The Boston-Gazette, and Country Journal
for September 17th, 1984
by Margaret Jonson

7

[It is January 13th, 1463 — the woman's name is Mikaela]

Tadhg could not help but take notice of the woman. She slyly entered the Greek-focused *taverna* in which he was currently sat. He was drinking with a newfound group of Italian merchant cronies, to which a couple friendly Turks had attached themselves (clearly in defiance of what Tadhg understood of their religious conventions). She strangely had no colors.

Her aura was grey and featureless.

An attractive, pale-skinned, red-haired woman was revealed when her black satin hood was pulled back from her face. It rested gathered on her slender shoulders. *Interesting,* thought Tadhg, *that her eyelids should remain hooded even as her face was revealed.*

She could not be far into her third decade, *If that,* Tadhg reckoned, tilting his head this way and that to get the best view he could of her.

In the midst of all these olive-skinned, dark-haired Dalmatians, swarthy Slavs, and darker-skinned Turks, she was almost ivory white in complexion. Her skin had a sheen that was not perspiration; it was porcelain-like in texture. Initially Tadhg thought her face might be a mask the way the light reflected off of it, but it was not so. As she looked around the drinking room her right eyebrow suddenly arched in haughtiness, but Tadhg did not take the gesture as a sign of conceit or arrogance. *No,* he thought, *it was more… a calculating reveal.* As he observed, her pupils dilated and contracted as she passed her attention over the crowd. Tadhg could also sense a great sadness about her; he unintentionally sat up straighter in his chair while watching her. Her hips rolled suggestively as she moved closer to the bar; she moved with a confidence, a swagger even, which should have been beyond a girl her age.

Also, as she entered the tavern and moved inward and about, Tadhg notice that the noise level dropped an octave or two as conversations halted to silence. He made note of her fine, tightly bound hair, bound in black ribbons, which he would have said were onyx changing to sometimes anthracite as different shades captured the firelight in her movements. Her eyes were also black, but with more of a liquid impression... a rich ink.

Tadhg was absorbed by her.

He smiled as he noticed her nose wrinkle at the smell of the place; she sneered, and he found that amusing.

As the noise levels rose back again, and his attention was drawn back by the table-talk around him, only then did he discern barely audible curses and blessings circulating nearby among the native Dalmatians. He heard the words "creature", "she-devil", and "succubus" aimed in the woman's direction, among other profanities in the many different dialects spoken here (some of which he did not yet know and had to assume were oaths by the tone of the speakers).

He was having a gay time nonetheless and laughed and dismissed such irrationalities. She was too pretty to be a prostitute; she had too fine a garment to be common (a word which did not really mean what the English meant the word to convey, but nonetheless).

Then, remembering who and what he was, he looked at her again the other way.

She was human, that much was clear, but there was something odd about her. She was breathing (a slow and steady rhythm), and blinking her eyes, although both actions were oddly perfunctory. That colorlessness which surrounded her though, that was the most curious thing. Tadhg concentrated further and found that there was a very dark element underneath it all... not a color so much as an absence of light and a negation of color. He ignored his companions and concentrated his other senses (which had been used to block out the worst of the odors).

She used a fragrant scent, but this was meant less to attract and more as... a subterfuge; used to mask her more natural scent which Tadhg identified as decay. *No*, he shook his head, *that's not quite it, "torpor" perhaps, motionlessness*.

Tadhg blinked away his *fae*-senses to look her way again without mystical enhancements.

This time he found, to his surprise (and some inexplicable joy), that she was staring at him now, with, it must be said, a charmingly confused expression. Whether her countenance was the result of non-human powers of perception or simple bemusement at the way she had found a man looking at her, he decided at once to find out more.

He rose from his chair and made his excuses to his new friends.

He brought his fine silver cup with him to where she was standing against the crude bar, sipping what smelled to him like some heated spiced wine. He stood nearby, jutting his chin forward with confidence and indicated her near empty cup.

'May I buy you another, my lady?' He said this in the Venetian dialect.

She turned, smiled shyly, surreptitiously looking him up and down. 'You may, if that is your wish, my lord.'

He was surprised that she conversed in the same dialect, but hers with a Slavic accent. The only conclusion was that the woman had the benefit of an education, a rare quality. Tadhg got the bar-keeper's attention easily enough and indicated two more mug fillings of the exotic smelling wine.

'Are you Transylvanian?' Tadhg said turning back to face the woman.

She shook her head, 'Wallachian, my lord, it is a common mistake.' She paused, 'But you, I think, are not Venetian, despite your fine attire and educated tongue.'

Tadhg's eyebrows shot upward in surprise. 'You have a good eye for detail, my lady… may I know your name?'

'Ah, you seek a boon of me so soon, my lord. For the price of a mug of wine am I expected to reveal such details and sell a part of my soul to you?' Tadhg smiled and mused on this.

'Well, it is good wine.'

'True.' She paused in consideration in turn, sipping from her re-filled cup. She then placed this down on the bar, decision made.

'Mikaela, my lord; I am Mikaela Florinescu.' She looked into Tadhg's eyes and studied them, looking out for evidence of schemes, swindles, or dishonesty. 'I have now given you a measure of power over me; a gentleman would make some recompense.' Tadhg thought this curious phrase over and assumed it was some Slavic tradition or proverb.

'Visconti Paulo de Costa at your service, my lady.' He bowed, keeping up the dialect.

She raised her cup again, turning to face the wall beyond the bar, 'If that is your wish, my lord, Venetian then. I think perhaps that your skin reveals a more northernly origin... England perhaps? But no, if you say Venetian then so be it, I will accept it for now.' She turned and raised her eyes to regard his directly again, raising her mug toward him, 'A toast, then, Paul of the coast.'

Tadhg matched the action with a smile and a nod, 'A toast, child of Florin.'

Their cups came together and made a clinking sound.

§

In far off Ireland, Queen Uonaidh, Tadhg's mother, passed out suddenly from the pain in her head.

§

Tadhg was charmed that night by Mikaela (to say the least) and she in turn seemed to enjoy his company, wondering at the small deception he maintained which she tried to wedge into the conversation from time to time.

It turned out that they were both there (well, she and Brother Richard, that is to say) for the same reasons; she was tangentially attached to the Ottoman negotiations. Although Mikaela was not a direct participant she did stand for, unofficially, the interests of her political master, the great Voivode of Wallachia, the infamous Vlad III. Tadhg knew the name from his work with diplomatic papers, of course, but little else beyond the common gossip.

Vlad III, sometimes called *"Impaler"* for his treatment of captive enemies, was from the Romanian House of Basarab or, more accurately, from the branch of that dynasty called the *Drăculești*. It was interesting information to Tadhg because, as he pointed out to Mikaela, this Wallachian family of her master was very much like the Plantagenet family of England, where he had gained some education. Where the Yorkists battled the Lancastrians for power, he opined, these *Drăculești* battled their cousins of the *Dănesti* branch. Tadhg asked a great many questions about this and Mikaela even answered some of them, switching roles with him as questioner and respondent throughout the evening. After some time, as they spoke on, Tadhg indicated the large fireplace. 'Two chairs have just been vacated my lady, would you care to move closer to the fire and continue this talk in more comfort?' She turned and considered the move but rejected it.

'It is late, my lord, or perhaps now quite early, and I should return to my rooms. I have duties in the morning.' Tadhg nodded but frowned.

'Then I insist on walking you back to your chambers.' She raised an eyebrow at this.

'You insist?'

'I do. It must be done, and I must do it.'

She smiled shyly, nodded absently, and raised the hood of her cape to cover herself again. 'Well, my lord, if it must be done then who am I to blow against the winds of fate ' She was about to turn, but stopped. 'Where is your cape, my lord?' He shook his head.

'The wind and chill breeze do not bother me so much.'

She shook her head and rocked back and forth on her heels; most would not have noticed, but Tadhg had. This meant that she was deep in consideration of a point.

'A true Venetian,' she finally said, 'would have over dressed for such weather, layers upon layer. But you, my lord, seem to embrace it.' She smiled triumphantly. 'That confirms my suspicions. Not English, but definitely not from these southern realms. You are surely of a kingdom in the north. Well,' she concluded and turned away, 'have your mystery, come, and walk with me if you insist.'

The two of them left the tavern together.

Some patrons, those witnesses left behind, breathed a collective sigh of relief when the door closed again. Some of them also shook their heads at the sorry fate of that nice young Venetian noble who had been so free with his purse these past few weeks. It was unlikely another like him would appear here any time soon.

§

Outside the taverna the winds of the Adriatic had picked up as the evening hours had turned into early morning. Tadhg breathed in the sea air deeply and took the arm of the now covered woman. He was pleased that she led him in the direction of the palace; her rooms must not be too far from his own monastic cell (and near to the well-appointed suite he rented as a cover for his aristocratic persona).

'Seriously now, my lord, how is it that you are not cold?'

'It's merely my nature, my lady, nothing more than that. I find the breeze refreshing after the stuffiness of the taverna.'

'Visconti... my lord... Paulo of the coast, if you wish to maintain this ruse,' she shook her head and raised a finger in an accusatory fashion, 'as you are not being entirely honest with me. You have not said... well, you have made a lie of omission, I think.' Tadhg enjoyed the huskiness of her speech.

'My lady, child of Florin, the same might be said of you.'

She dismissed this with a wave of her gloved hand. 'I can see that your visage is something of an illusion, my lord. May I say it is a quite brilliant disguise? I can see no make-up or lines at all.'

Tadhg gave her a little bow.

'And I,' he said in replay, 'can see that your aura reveals something dark lurking beneath the beautiful surface, my lady. While your voice is angelic and alluring, your words have no color and no music.' They walked on, arm in arm, climbing the streets toward the top of the hill upon which sat the squat palace and other governmental buildings taken over for diplomatic lodgings.

Finally, the woman sighed and stopped short at a crossroad, a market square by the looks of it. There were no others on the street and the surrounding windows were all closed and latched against the weather. There was only the light of the moon and stars to illuminate the scene.

'I am not sure what these words mean, my lord, "no color and no music", perhaps I am... do you see a monster my lord?' She grew quiet again. 'You are charming and kind, sir, perhaps it would be best... please do not pursue me further, Paulo.'

She turned away; she wished to hide tears now flowing down her cheeks. Tadhg, touched by the warning, reached around her, placing his hands firmly on her shoulders. He turned her back round to face him again and she gave only a token resistance. He wondered briefly, cynically, if this was a calculated move on her part but then realized he did not care if it was.

'Are you a monster, Mikaela? I do not know. But you should know that I am not human,' he admitted, 'but you knew this already did you not, or at least guessed it might be so? I think you are too charitable to make too close an inquiry. Do you fear what you might find in me?' She shook her head. She took his hand and held the back of it up to her cheek.

'Your blood is warm, my lord, mine is cold. Can you not feel that?'

'I spoke true when I claimed to be a creature of the elements, my lady, hot or cold, warm or cool, is all much the same to me.'

She let his hand drop from her cheek but did not let go of it. In fact, she turned slightly, paused as if deciding, then pulled him in a direction which would lead them out beyond the city walls rather than higher into the government buildings. They passed the walls moments later and moved into the wild places surrounding the city.

'I know a place where we will not be observed or heard, my lord. Will you come?'

'Gladly, my lady,' Tadhg said with an edge of curiosity. In the back of his mind, where it could be easily dismissed, was the thought that this was unwise. Then again, unwise decisions had often led him into the grandest of adventures.

§

Mikaela led Tadhg through gates in the wall of the city which had been left mysteriously open, down an isolated path, and finally into a grove hidden from the walls and towers of the city by large rocks and thick bushes, isolated from the winds off the sea as well. Not a cave, as such, but certainly sheltered from what rain might fall. Tadhg noted that there were other dark places nearby so there were caves hereabouts if hiding was required.

'We will be undisturbed here, Visconti.'

'So,' he said, looking the area over, 'you are not part of an embassy then?'

'Oh no, that much is true.'

'How do you know of this place then?'

'I do not spend all of my time indoors, nor do I have a need for much sleep. But truthfully, I only scouted this place two nights ago. I have always liked to have a place secret from the people of the city wherever I am. There are times... of... need for such an escape,' she had searched for the word but was less than happy with her choice, 'and less chance of intrusion here.' Tadhg nodded.

'I see. I sometimes have much the same...' he stopped talking.

In that moment he started to feel an unfamiliar, yet also remarkably familiar, tingling in his mind. He fell silent; he looked around for a source, knowing the *Hidden* cannot hide from the *Hidden*; but this was amateurish, the working of a child perhaps. He saw nothing, however, in the rocks and bushes and trees surrounding the grove and was ready to dismiss the feeling until he took note of Mikaela staring at him with great concentrated effort. Her eyes had expanded and taken on a reddish hue much like the gleam of a cat's-eye reflecting the light of a lamp or a fire.

He smiled and spoke with good humor, 'Is that you trying to force your way into my mind, my lady?' She huffed and frowned, and the tingling sensation stopped.

'That usually works.'

Tadhg's smile pulled on the already upward set of his lips, 'I did warn you that I was not human, my lady.' She nodded but still frowned, confused, and flustered by the failure of something which came easier to her before.

'*Mikaela.*'

The woman started, yipped, and turned as if about to be attacked from another direction. Seeing nothing, she quickly scanned the surrounding trees, as Tadhg had just done moments earlier. Finally, she turned back toward Tadhg, only to be confronted by amused eyes and a boyish grin across the small, rocky clearing which separated them. In the time it took her to swing about, however, she had physically changed. She turned away again quickly, but Tadhg saw the change and the smile fled his lips (although perhaps not entirely).

In the few seconds she had turned away from him searching the origin of the voice calling her out, the skin of her face had grown a little tighter about her bones, her hair a shade darker (Tadhg could see in the dark almost as well as in the light) and a little more brittle; two bright, white fangs extended from her upper row of teeth, and her fingernails had grown out into deadly talons, which she had raised as protection against whatever threat she had feared coming out of the trees with attack in mind. The change had been almost instantaneous.

Altogether she was still an impressive, beautiful creature, and Tadhg could do naught else but smile again his delight at finding one such as her here and now.

'A *dearg-due*,' he said quietly, 'or are you *leanan sidhe*?'

As her talons withdrew back into her fingers and her fangs receded back into her upper set of teeth Tadhg in turn dropped the illusion of the Venetian nobleman. He grew a little taller, a little thinner, his face elongated as his chin formed a pointed end with a tuft of hair growing there. The hair on his head now tumbled over his shoulders and down his back, now also a fairer shade, yellow, almost white, the tips of his ears pointing upward and back through the canopy of his hair. His eyes were no longer brown but their natural violet (bluer in one, more purple in the other) and had again taken on their more natural almond shape, no longer the roundness of the western world's human eye. His aura was golden, bright to those who could perceive it.

'I stand revealed.'

Mikaela shaded her eyes from the effect and impact of the reflected moonlight as if it were a physical manifestation, and Tadhg concentrated to mute the glow that surrounded his true form. 'That's... that's you, my lord, talking in my head?'

Tadhg nodded.

'Are you an incubus?' He shook his head, smiling, but held up an index finger.

'Are you a succubus?' he responded, and she shook her head as well.

'What are you then?' they both asked the other simultaneously. Tadhg laughed aloud at this coincidence; the woman smiled shyly and turned her face downwards.

'After you, my lady,' Tadhg bowed and indicated she should begin.

'Do you swear not to reveal what I say?' He nodded. 'And you, ever the gentleman, will be explaining yourself, your true self, to me as well?' He nodded again. She seemed satisfied with this arrangement.

'I do not know these words you said, "deargdue" and "hannanshee" mean nothing to me. I am called *bamiiup* or *vrykolakas* or sometimes called *vukodlak* in my native dialect, but we Slavs have so many dialects, my lord.' Tadhg mulled these words over.

'I admit my ignorance of your native tongue, my lady.'

'I have heard it said that the Latin translation is *hair of the wolf*. And yes, my hair does take on a fur-like quality (Tadhg clapped his hands together softly) when I am in the other form, as you saw, but it is not coarse like a wolf's might be, softer, as a fox's would be, despite appearances.'

'Ah, so you are called a *werewulf*?' She nodded that this was incorrect.

'That is what we are, what I am called, but that is not what I am. We are... I am... the natural child of a *strigoii*... a cursed person and an uncursed person. I am *strigoii* by birth, but *moroaică*.'

'*Moroaică*?' Tadhg swirled the unfamiliar word about in his mind. 'Is that the feminine noun?'

She smiled, 'No, my lord. In our tradition the *strigoii* is both the common description and the word for the evil curse — the curse and the cursed. We are all *strigoii* in the eyes of the church until we are seen to be *moroaică*. That is, "not malevolent"; I guess that would be the proper Latin phrase to use. We are still considered dangerous and to be avoided as unholy, to be killed if necessary but not as a matter of course.'

'I am dangerous to know, my lord, but I mean no harm. I must... feed on blood. No other food or drink keeps me better sustained.'

'And... so beautiful.'

The woman raised her hand and moved back over her ear a stray strand of hair the wind had teased out of the binding pins. Tadhg could see her blush, but her surrounding colors were unchanged in his *fae*-sight.

'Perhaps, I am not so old, my lord, less than three decades.'

'Then I am not so much older than you, my lady, in human terms. To my people, the true Irish, you were so close with guessing English, we are called the *Hidden*, the *fae-folk* or the *Tuatha dé*, and sometimes we are called *Otherworlders*. I am, however, considered quite young by the standards of my people and I am away from court to become educated in the ways of the mortals.' Her unrelenting stare revealed that Mikaela was interested in this talk. She narrowed her eyes in thoughtfulness, mulling the words over repeatedly.

'*Tündér*,' she finally said.

'Is that not a Magyar term?'

She shrugged, 'It is the closest term we have in Wallachia to what you say. You are a *spinner*.' Tadhg was taken back and amused by this term.

'I assure you my lady that I do not spin. Well, not often. I am no dervish.' She laughed, and Tadhg found immense joy in the sound of her laughter. It was genuine.

'No, my lord, not a man who dances… a *spinner* is a weaver but said as if that were an insult, so to speak… a spider, you see? The *tündér* are known to weave fine fabrics, but these are… not as they seem… illusions, used to fool fools and innocents.'

Tadhg laughed in turn. 'I think we have come to an ethnic misunderstanding. Spiders are very much maligned in my view and are often quite beautiful, not to mention particularly useful.'

'Yes, that is so.'

Tadhg walked forward, approaching Mikaela. Her smile turned to a more anxious expression though and this was reflected in her upturned eyes.

'So, would it be so bad now if one such as I were to pursue one such as you?'

He put his hands on her shoulders and looked her firmly in the eyes. He could so easily lose himself in those deep, black liquid pools.

Mikaela looked up. She suddenly took a step forward and embraced Tadhg, moving passed his hands and into his arms. She laid her head against his chest. She listened to the strangely slow beating of his heart. It was not in the mortal place, and clearly not beating at a mortal pace. Tadhg's hand took her chin and raised her face to his.

'Is that a… no?'

When she did not deny him, he lowered his head to kiss her lips. They were cold; they were soft and full, but cold. After a second, she started to kiss him back. Sometime later, when they broke away from each other, without letting go, he said, 'I'll take that as a no then.'

She smiled. Hand in hand they left the grove.

§

At about the same time as this, in far off Ireland, Queen Uonaidh suddenly roused herself from a restless sleep, screamed, and passed out again just as quickly. The king was concerned for his wife, but not so much alarmed at this behavior. She did come from a weird family, even by *fae* standards, and she was known to show such odd behavior from time to time. She would recover her senses in a couple of years' time, he considered, or she would not. By that point it would too late to heed the warning signs the king and court should have recognized all along.

§

The negotiations, so called because men spoke at each other, stretched out interminably into months and years.

As one of the *Hidden,* Tadhg could see the colors of the words passing back and forth between the king's and the sultan's agents as he watched from the surrounding gallery. He could see them, taste them, feel them squirming their way towards the other side. While they often sounded diplomatic, to mortal ears, even friendly at times, the lies were revealed to Tadhg's senses. There were bad intentions on both sides; dishonest oaths; underhanded plotting; implied violence.

The fraudulent promises were black, off-key, and even smelled bad.

'Of course,' Mikaela would say when they could be together at the end of a long day, 'one did not have to be *fae* to realize that there were falsehoods aplenty being spoken.'

Tadhg knew well enough that the real art of diplomacy was in arriving at a point which both sides could momentarily acknowledge as not entirely unfavorable to themselves which, at the same time, seemed to give them some advantage over the opponent. At that point they would agree to move on to the next subject on the agenda, which could be anything from a trade discrepancy to a perceived insult already months out of date and long forgotten. The scribes and translators took their notes and later changed the words so that either side almost got the same idea, but not quite. The Ottomans always had the choice of backing out and moving their larger army further into Christian territory, while the Slavs had the choice of calling in favors from the Muscovites, Germanics, Poles, and French.

Delay actually suited both sides.

Mortals came and went as the months passed.

In the early mornings, when the sun was not as yet too high in the sky, Tadhg might catch glimpses of Mikaela. He enjoyed these very much.

Perhaps she would be slipping out of a hallway, or carrying some dispatches away to her own overlords, or talking to someone, wheedling, convincing, or using her skills or beauty or both on lesser minds. He never acknowledged her or revealed himself; she and Brother Richard had never officially met and there was no reason they should do. He took these glimpses with him to his rest at the end of the day as he read in his cell on those nights when they could not be together for whatever reason might arise.

If the woman thought there was anything familiar about the monk there was no sign of it whenever they did happen to pass close by. Sometimes, in the evenings, when he could slip away from the monastery and the other scribes and scholars Visconti Paulo would appear and drink with his rogues' gallery of cronies, facing down the gawps from the natives of the city who had seen him leave (or heard about it) with the blood-headed woman so many months ago.

Nothing had happened to him, he swore, while hinting at some or other exotic delight. Sometimes they would cross themselves when they thought he was not looking.

Sometimes the red-headed woman herself appeared at the taverna and they would sit together and speak of many things right there in the public eye! Some of the others would cross themselves when they thought neither was looking their way. Tadhg never considered what Mikaela did when he was not around, and since the owners of the residence where the Visconti had rooms never bothered him with messages from her, he assumed she afforded him the same respect of privacy. The time they were apart was theirs to do with as they pleased; there was no contract or agreement between them on that point as yet, and they had never discussed one.

Sometimes Tadhg met Mikaela in her secret grove for more intimate assignations and over the months that passed he had grown to appreciate her practices and approaches to life (if not to fully understand them). Like most of his kind Tadhg had very few inhibitions; Mikaela, he discovered, like most of her kind had much more old-fashioned (one might say conformist, even reactionary) views.

Where she was reserved, he was spontaneous.

Tadhg grew to love Mikaela's surprising modesty and her peculiar impulses. He often pondered the fact that, even when there was no chance of interruption or discovery, she was unwilling to completely disrobe in the open air under the light of the moon and stars or in the daylight (which sapped her energies quickly she said). She was *not*, however, averse to his doing so and Tadhg loved surprising her.

Like his own kind, he loved being fully exposed to the elements.

Of course, he knew what modesty was, he was just never a devotee.

Back in Mallow, once a woman was paired off with the father of her child, very rarely was she ever caught naked with another man, and her man was rarely caught naked with another woman. Nature had brought man and woman together and the people were content to leave well enough alone. It worked well enough, mostly; generations, in fact, had lived that way. Very rarely did cases come before the chief of the village for judgements and rarely did he need to punish an immoral man or sinful woman. Tadhg could not even bring any to mind; he often meant to remind himself to remember to write home to Bran and ask him or send a message to the king his father… but he never found the time those days.

Modesty was a strange concept to the *fae,* but Tadhg understood the self-reproach that the religion of the triune god put upon its followers, of which Mikaela was one (surprisingly). The priests said that the god wanted them to be fruitful and multiply, which was fine, entertaining even, but also to do this only in societal approved ways, which was confusing for him. The ways of rural Ireland, it seems, were not the approved ways but that did not seem to stop trysts in the woods outside of wedlock.

So, under the moon and the stars and sometimes the sun, the woman was modest. Perhaps she thought her god was watching them. Oddly enough, when she could sneak Tadhg into her private rooms in the house hired by her superiors, Mikaela was much less inhibited. There she was almost licentious, wanton in her secret apparel, unconstrained in her pursuit of the pleasures of the flesh. In the grove she was a quiet lover; there, in a house with other people almost certainly within earshot, she was loud and unbothered by what others might think or hear. At first Tadhg found this behavior confusing and he had tried to untangle the reasoning behind it. He could find nothing in the triune god's holy books that suggested He could not see-through walls. Later, Tadhg just accepted it as her personal eccentricity and enjoyed of her what he could, when he could.

Neither was aware that something unbelievably bad was brewing in Mikaela's heart. It was not her fault, just the nature of the beast she was.

§

[It is April 23ʳᵈ, 1468, in the Republic of Ragusa]

Time passed quickly; Tadhg had not written home to his human family in five years.

Negotiators came and went but Tadhg and Mikaela remained much the same. Something was coming their way though. While Tadhg had not been gifted with his mother's foresight (unreliable as *that* was) to any significant extent he was mildly aware of some vague threat in the unforeseeable future. Whenever he mentioned this to Mikaela, she waved it away. No believer in prophecy she.

'Of course,' she would say. 'Dangerous things come and go all the time, which is life my love.' Tadhg had no convincing reply to this truth but the feeling remained.

When he awoke some mornings of late, however, he had begun to experience mild headaches.

He reasoned this new phenomenon away as the result of a frustrating day ahead, or the lasting mental effects of the frustrating day earlier. One side or the other in the meetings would try to alter the previously agreed upon points, or events, or word and this would delay the talks further and further. The entertainment was wearing thin. And while this was true it was not particularly prophetic on his part given the setting and the nature of the work, but so be it. Headaches due to the stresses placed upon the body, mind, and spirit could affect even the *fae*. Tadhg was growing increasingly and frustratingly bored with the whole ordeal though and he was denying his nature not to simply move on; lately he even pined for simpler times as back in Marrow.

He could read the signs and omens well enough (when he chose to look out for them or remembered to do so), but he was not a natural *oneiromancer* like his mother's people.

This particular morning, late in April, he awoke with seriously distressing aches, almost stinging sensations in his head and around his body, making it hard to move. He put this down to too much of the local hard alcohol and too little food to balance the forces in his stomach (which had never been a concern in the past). He decided that he would use his own wooden spoon from this point on rather than the crude iron implements of the native Dalmatians; perhaps that is what his *fae* nature was objecting to.

That was not the problem.

The day's labors had not been particularly arduous, but his persistent aches and pains made them seem unending, tedious and dull. Tadhg kept his wits and his good humor about himself (he rarely ever snapped at anyone), but it was an unfamiliar and exhausting strain on his being. Moreover, he had planned to see Mikaela that afternoon (they had been apart for at least a fortnight) but instead he took to an early bed in his sparse monastic cell.

The pains were growing worse. He never associated the pains to separation from the woman.

His was a fitful, nightmare-filled sleep.

His mind was beset by images of a dark woman calling out to him; pleading for him to come to her. She was sometimes demanding: "Come now", sometimes demure: "If it please you to come". She was almost shy in her way then suddenly a shrew, then sorry, then prideful, then embarrassed. In his unconscious state Tadhg knew that the dark woman was the *strigoii*, and he knew what she was trying to do without her even knowing it.

She wanted to lure him away and to herself. *Strigoii* generally do not make long lasting emotional connections.

He was not immune to her power; but he was able to resist it. A mortal man would not have been able to do so.

Feelings of loneliness came to him; lustful thoughts, shameless thoughts came to him; seclusion was hinted (which meant to meet her in the grove); unabashed, immodest images were planted in his mind of Mikaela dancing naked or wriggling suggestively. Scenes were played out of their earlier couplings, over and over and over again. While these were all quite entertaining, Tadhg was still able to resist them.

He did not want to resist, which was odd, he did not know why he should but he did so, nonetheless. As he had never really faced a life-threatening situation Tadhg did not know that this was his *fae* nature working to protect him.

Next to come were angry images and painful sensations including threats of violence, hints of bodily harm, and mental tortures. Tadhg could discern the lie of these even in his sleep though. His Mikaela was not a vicious creature; she was one used to getting her own way, however, and his resistance disturbed her mightily. Underneath it all was a desperation he did not recognize for what it was. Mikaela's essential being was taking over; she was starting to lose that part of her called *humanity*.

Over the next few hours Tadhg was treated to more unusual imagery, frightening scenes played out, but he was at pains to interpret it at first.

Suddenly, whilst in a dreaming state, he could see the ground passing far below. It was as if he were some manner of night bird searching for prey in the trees and rocky outcroppings near the walls of the city. He saw peasants on the out bound roads crossing themselves upon hearing a loud screech, and then walking faster toward their homes in the surrounding hills and villages, some practically running. Suddenly his perspective changed to ground level; bushes became as tall as trees and trees as tall as giants. He seemed to be scurrying among the leaves and twigs. Even saplings looked massive from this new perspective; what few mortal he met were monstrous and loud as thunder when they laughed.

Mostly, whatever this was, it was ignored.

Then, in his mind's eye, he squeezed under a strangely familiar door. Tadhg had the feeling of crawling along known walls; of pausing when a mortal man, who seemed recognizable to him, walked by; and then of hiding in a shadow here or under a chair there. Under it all was a suspicion of great confusion. Wherever he was in the dream, it was not where he was expecting to be. Suddenly he imagined he came to another familiar door, paused with hesitation, and then squeezing under that one too.

The perspective of his dreaming mind changed once again then. The unconscious Tadhg found himself looking down at himself, still confused by what he saw — a monk asleep on his cot. He was clearly uncomfortably lying there; a slight sweat had broken out on his forehead. An arm reached out tentatively from beyond his mind's eye's perspective, and a hand, a woman's hand, Mikaela's hand was placed, gently, against his sleeping cheek.

'I see you under this disguise, Tadhg.'

It was a tender moment to witness.

The hand moved up to his sleeping but uneasy brow, brushing his hair away and feeling for a temperature. The hand withdrew from his sight, and he followed the movement through the head and eyes across the room. It came to rest on a wash bowl, a jug, and a cloth. The water in the jug was found to be cool to the touch, and was poured into the bowl which, with the cloth, was brought back over to the cot.

A hand reappeared in his mind's eye, dripping some of the water. There was a sensation of the cloth, damp, and cool, being patted against his brow. Tadhg saw that this offered some relief to his sleeping likeness; thanks were mumbled.

The hand moved the single blanket lower and was laid out on the sleeper's chest. This felt good to Tadhg and was met with more mumbled thanks. The hand fussed his hair and soothed his brow a little further. These were the machinations of a nursemaid or a caring wife.

The machinations of the *strigoii* followed soon enough, however, when these simple gestures turned into something less wholesome and innocent.

The heart wants what it wants, when it wants it, is an old saying, and sometimes the mind does not offer useful restraint when needs be.

In his mind's eye, through which he continued to observe the actions even as his body lay unconscious and prone before him, the hands of the *strigoii* grew restless; caresses turned to kneading; nails like talons emerged out of the fingertips and the gentle machinations grew rougher still. The thankful mumblings of the sleeping body turned to pleas for gentleness.

Suddenly the cover was thrown from the bed.

Hands and mouth, hot with the breath of demanding lusts became busy rousing the sleeping member of the body in the bed. A momentary blackness, deeper than the shadows of the cell in which he slept told Tadhg that Mikaela had thrown off her clothes as well. Her breathing became the panting of an animal, pawing at her own breasts and testing the wetness of her own unique femininity. Then Tadhg felt the pressure of Mikaela climbing on top of him; her hands easing him inside of her; the gyrations of her hips on him, hands pushing into his chest, talons scratching. Through his own vision he saw his body responding to her even though his mind was displaced by it all.

But tonight, she demanded more!

The vision was so intense that Tadhg felt the release even though separated from his own body. But it was at that point the vision went dark.

He was conscious again only long enough to see Mikaela's wild expression, to hear the howling, and to see the fangs descending toward his throat. Almost in slow motion he saw her wolfen incisors, long and white, descend; he felt the momentary pain of her bite, never before experienced. He felt her take in his ichor. He could not protest, too weak from the fever, but he saw her open a vein in her arm and press this to his lips. There was nothing he could do about it; he took in her blood.

That simple reckless, ignorant act cursed both of them.

Tadhg was instantly tainted; his *fae* pureness corrupted.

For Mikaela it was a more lenient curse. Neither had known that the ichor of the *fae* was poisonous to what would become known as the *vampyre*.

§

In far off Ireland a tear ran down the cheek of the sleeping Queen Uonaidh, unseen, and thus unheralded. Her heart broke, and with it, her spirit faded away.

8

[It is 24 April 1468 — The day after]

The tale that Tadhg had been told in the morning following the previous night's visit of Mikaela was startling and confusing to hear.

Some of the monks, visitors like Tadhg and the foreign-born residents, did not know how to explain the monstrous din that had been heard throughout the building. Without warning the shrill sound had roused all the brothers from their slumbers, then from their beds, then from their cells and herded them into the communal areas where great consternation and confusion reigned for a time (but there was safety in numbers). No one knew what that sound was, whether it was of great joy or great suffering, whether it had been a warning or a seduction. No one knew where that sound had come from as it seemed to have been at all places at once within the monastery.

An elder of the community and native to the region sat calmly aside and said it was the cry of the *strzyga* and that it meant death for someone. A search was then instigated (after the brothers were calmed down again).

And at least everyone was present at the gathering.

'Where's Brother Richard?' Someone noticed the absence of the foreign-born archivist-conservator. Men started talking all at once; Richard was immensely popular with many of the brethren and his advice had been sought out by the abbot on numerous occasions. His absence was troubling; his was the first cell searched.

The abbot and prior both produced pass keys at the door and went inside. Tadhg was found asleep in his bed, mumbling denials, and shaking his head vigorously. His thin body had been stirring in the night; that much was obvious to everyone who could see in. That Brother Archivist was found naked was not raised as an issue in and of itself; many of the monks slept without added covering. But the fact that his blanket had been thrown across the cell and had been ripped at some point in the night did arouse conjecture.

It was cool in the cells at night; no one would purposefully sleep without a cover unless he had a fever and certainly no one would tear into a cover like a wild animal.

Brother Prior checked Tadhg over and he nodded, yes, a fever.

Brother Physician was summoned from the infirmary, and after a quick examination of the body, a cool compress was applied to Tadhg's forehead. In this naked state, however, some of the monks mumbled that Brother Richard did not look *quite right*, but no one of them could say exactly what was wrong, having had such a limited view before Brother Physician arrived, covered the sleeping monk, and closed the cell door.

As the three principal monks stood in the cell, as Brother Physician tended the sleeping brother, the abbot and prior made a concerning discovery; a selection of female garments had been strewn about the cell, all torn, some jewelry as well. There was no evidence of a female to wear them, however, or of one having worn them, and they were of a size too small for Richard.

'Did *strzyga* leave clothing behind, Abbot?' asked the prior. The abbot shrugged.

Brother Prior, an enterprising man rather than a contemplative man, opened the door to the cell and regarded the other brothers' concerned and confused expressions. He asked the pertinent questions, but there were no reports of a sighting of any females in the building in the last week. Yes, the cell's door had been locked shut as was that of the great entrance itself — still bolted in fact. Only the member in the cell, the abbot and the prior had keys, and all of these were found where they should be. Brother Richard's key was hanging from a little hook on the back of his door undisturbed.

The feminine clothes became a mystery and would be a talking point for years to come.

Where had they come from .. was the only pertinent question at the moment.

The prior could find no box to hold them in Richard's cell, and no one standing without had ever seen them before. As no answer was ever forthcoming, it was dismissed as a sign of nothing other than an eccentricity on Richard's part.

"Too small for his frame", was heard mumbled.

Well, it was said, these items reminded him of something then or they were connected to the reason behind his original decision to become a monk in the first place. That the garments were covered in some dried mud was also commented upon, but to no sure conclusions could be drawn from the limited evidence. Moreover, some of the mud had the consistency of dried blood.

No one was satisfied by the conclusion but what more could be said at the time?

Ever practical, the prior had the clothes were hauled away to be washed and mended.

In his delirium, Brother Richard said nothing about any of this or of the blood, if blood it was, as it was clearly not his own. What few windows there were in the entire building were all checked, and none found to have been disturbed or opened. All of them were shut, and locked, as they should be from the inside.

Other than the muddy garments, Richard's cell was clean enough; spare clothes neatly hung up; books neatly stacked on a table with an ink well (capped), a quill (freshly cut), and parchments partially covered in research notes and translations. Brother Abbot looked over the notes but nothing was related to females, or males for that matter other than negotiators; it seems Brother Archivist was teaching himself some Slavic tongue. The abbot shrugged; this was useful for a diplomatic translator but did not explain anything.

He shook his head; there was a mystery here and he did not like mysteries, as they took attention off the necessary work.

Tadhg came to his senses sometime during the abbot's inspection of his cell, but Brother Physician advised that raising questions now would be pointless as the fever would still have a scrambling effect on the brother's memories.

By sext, curiosity about the noises had been replaced by rumors of a curse on Brother Richard, and whether this was sure to spread to the rest of them or no. When he was awake and his fever down, the abbot and Brother Physician asked Tadhg about all of these oddities — the scream, the clothes, the locked cell door — but his answers were less than helpful. Brother Richard looked terrified and backed away from the abbot as far as the headboard would allow him to do. His eyes bulged in terror at the abbot and at the doctor, sometimes the cow-eyes of disbelief, sometimes the bug-eyes of fear or horror.

'Your words have no color; they taste wrong!' he yelled at them, in a language neither understood.

The abbot thought about this, then turned to regard the head of the infirmary, raising his eyebrows in interest and question. Brother Physician shrugged in return.

'He said much the same to me earlier, my lord abbot. I have no idea what it means, but I think it's Gaelic.'

The abbot nodded and regarded the patient again, while Brother Physician tried to help Tadhg back into a more comfortable position on the bed. The doctor also tried to get Tadhg to take a sip from a draught he had brewed from a cocktail of herbs and other medicinal plants, and finally succeeded after taking a small sip himself.

'I don't understand what this means, Brother Richard,' said the abbot in Latin, and in as soothing a voice as he could manage while the patient drank some of the offered potion. Brother O'Neil, a gardener, and an Irishmen, who had come to the monastery ten years' earlier and was known to have spoken with Brother Richard many times, was consulted. He translated the statement for the abbot and doctor.

'Should my words have color, as you say?' The abbot asked Tadhg in Latin. Tadhg lowered his head, slightly calmer, less frightened, but with a mind still obviously muddled.

'I don't know,' he replied, now also in Latin, '...yes, I think they should. You have no aura either. What kind of creature are you?'

The abbot pondered this. 'I am a man as God made me. Should I be something else?'

'The triune god, you mean?'

The abbot's eyebrows raised in unison, 'Well, yes, of course!' The way Tadhg stared at the superior was beginning to make him a little nervous.

'Do you know your own name, brother?' asked the doctor, refreshing the cold cloth and replacing it again on Tadhg's forehead. Tadhg turned to look at the other monk.

'Prince Dubhgall?'

The two others shared a look. It was not impossible, of course, that a monk could, in an earlier life before vows, to have been something as exulted as a prince. He might have been a third or fourth son, his family displaced and unseated, any number of explanations could explain why a prince was in a monastery, but Brother Richard had never made such a claim before. 'No. My name is Tadhg?'

'Tiger?' The two others regarded each other again for a moment. 'But' said the doctor, 'this is the name of a beast from southern Asia brother, not a man like yourself.'

'Rory?' The abbot smiled.

He turned to the doctor, 'Well, at least that is a man's name.'

Tadhg lay in bed as the others let their questions remain unspoken. Left in this relative peace, he looked around the infirmary (as if for the first time). His forehead was puckered with an anxiety the potion had not settled; his eyelids were closed into slits, but whether with anger or distrust the superiors could not say. There was a troubled awe in his expression.

The abbot stood and moved away from them summoning the physician to a more private meeting. 'What do you think, Brother Physician?'

The doctor looked back but spoke away from the patient. 'He has clearly been addled by the fever or whatever happened to him last night; it should pass I think, like a nightmare.' The abbot raised a hand to his chin at this and stroked his longish greying beard.

'Perhaps…' his lips were set in a firm line.

The doctor turned and read the new expression as fear. 'You have another explanation, my Lord Abbot?'

'I don't know, Brother Physician, I don't know. I think I will send a message to Bishop Venier just as a matter of caution.'

'I can't hear what you're saying over there! Why can I not hear you?' Both monks turned at the sound of Brother Richard yelling at them.

The abbot paused and leaned in a little, 'He grows agitated, Brother Physician, perhaps… restraints and a sedative of some kind?'

'What did you say? What did he say?'

The doctor agreed this might be a wise precaution. He left the abbot alone with the patient. The abbot approached the bed again to keep Tadhg calm. It was a skill he had carefully cultivated over the years and had served him well. Brother Physician's mission now was to find something which could be used as restrains, as well as a couple of strong novices to give aid, should the situation need something more than a soothing manner. He also gathered the necessary ingredients for something that would put the patient to sleep.

It would take four times the normal dosage to finally have the desired effect.

§

Later, the abbot sent a missive off to the bishop as well as a copy to the general of his order.

The general tone of the missive was one of concern. It noted that one of the persons of the visiting community, and a member of the diplomatic embassy, had somehow fell victim to a strange sort of possession. Not demonic possession as such, he assured the bishop, at least as far he could figure out, but an unknown influence nonetheless, at least unfamiliar in his experience. This Brother Richard, an Irishman, had remained mostly *compos mentis*, but he had a sudden obsession with matters sensual, insisting sound had taste and textures had sound, other such nonsense. The abbot described the bewildering case as best he could, having never encountered the like before, and dispatched the letter hoping that these men of greater experience and authority might know more than he.

As the hours turned into days, and the days into weeks, the letter went unanswered (as often happened).

Brother Richard, however, grew noticeably quiet and observant until he was strong enough to leave his confinement. He was not the same man he had been before the incident, that much was clear; he was no longer calm and carefree, no longer interested in the life of the monastery, or interested in his translation duties at the never-ending negotiations.

The other monks found him suddenly listless in company; he was lethargic in his religious duties, and apathetic toward anything inside or outside the monastery except the library, where he was found most hours doing secretive readings.

A month following the events of the scream another brother was found still in his cell long after the prime prayers had passed.

He had not slept in, however.

He had been murdered in the night. The corpse was still in bed, bedclothes undisturbed. There were two puncture marks in his neck; the blood had been drained not very efficiently from his body.

Had the cell door been open? Why had no alarm been raised? These and other questions failed to be answered, but an elder said that the *strzyga* must have returned to feast. They had been invaded. They were all doomed.

The others did not know what to think about that opinion.

The following morning, Brother Richard was discovered gone. He had requested no permission to go; he had left no prior notice of his intentions or note explaining himself. He simply left, never to return. He was never to be heard from again as far as anyone in the monastery was aware.

§

Mikaela was still very fresh in his mind.

The last month or so had given Tadhg a great deal to think about, but the monastic library (such as it was) revealed only the vaguest of answers to his many, many, questions. When the other monk was killed Tadhg decided that the time had come to put distance between himself and further temptation. That inexplicably mighty hunger had been sated, but it had not been satisfying and Tadhg feared escalation.

What few possessions he had kept in his cell were moved into the caves at the secret grove where he and Mikaela had spent so much time together. What had been stored in the noble quarter suite was also surreptitiously retrieved and moved to the caves. Mikaela's essence was strong here and Tadhg did not feel so alone.

But it wasn't long before all that she was began to fade away.

If he did not act fast Tadhg would lose all clear memories of the woman and he reasoned that his memories of her were key to his survival now… somehow.

He decided to remedy the situation by sneaking into the house of her former overlords and remove all her possessions from there. Her favorite dresses and jewels, he took. A silver brush she had used on her long red locks, he pocketed despite the fact that no hairs were in evidence (only strings of ash remaining). The silver pins she had used to hold up her hair, to fasten her cloak, he also took these. Her collection of a few finely bound manuscripts that she had proudly displayed on a shelf, carefully arranged, were also removed and taken to the caves of the grove. He also found a journal in her handwriting skillfully hidden under a loose stone in the hearth of her chamber. He hugged this to his chest.

Overnight, all evidence of her existence outside the grove was as disappeared as was the evidence of his own mortal existence.

§

One day, Tadgh came to the sudden realization that he could not remember the exact color of Mikaela's hair.

Before her death Mikaela had been showing Tadhg examples of the native Wallachia tongue in written form; it was a dialect of old Slavonic. He had taken a very leisurely approach to it then as both teacher and student assumed they had all the time in the world to teach each other new things and build memories together.

Cruel fate had disabused him of that belief.

And as the days and weeks passed, Tadhg grew desperate to find answers to his many questions and the only source he genuinely had was the woman's journal. Although his memory was usually potent, he found himself in heated debates about her exact wording in conversations he had only listened to with a mind preoccupied by many other thoughts.

Curse the frivolous nature of the *fae*!

He had to remember what she had said, he had to recall the words, the meanings, and allusions, and insinuations; he had to re-learn a great deal of it from unsure recollections in order to adjust to his new life. From such humble beginnings the words he remembered were reworked, the symbols redrawn, and every time he remembered something it was written down. New words were added to his knowledge base and each and every one was cherished as a means of hanging on to Mikaela.

But it was a slow, laborious and painful process. Words only slowly turned into sentences and sentences into concepts. These, however, were more difficult to turn into practical knowledge. In the solitude and quiet of the grove, which he now rarely left, he managed to slowly dig out useful intelligence. In the meantime, when he was not studying, he spent the hours in meditation. How much of the *fae* remained within?

It was difficult to tell; he could feel it was inside him still... but hiding from the creature he had become. When Tadhg was not re-reading the journal and when he was not reviewing his luminous notes, he tried to coax out the *fae* and merge it with the *strigoii*. It was a struggle: the native *fae* resisted the invader and the invader derided the worth of the native.

§

Even as Tadhg debated with himself the exact shade of the woman's eyes, or the way she combed her hair, he recalled clearly that Mikaela had had very sharp senses. She could see and hear as well as Tadhg could, but in her eyes a leaf was simply green without particular sounds or textures. Tadhg found that while he could still easily discern the green of a single leaf on a tree from a great distance, even at night, the other *fae* sensations were, if not entirely gone, now greatly dependent upon hard concentration of his will. When he listened to the voices of the creatures of the mountains and the woods, he could no longer discern the precise meanings of their sounds as such, although he could achieve a limited sense of what they meant — a kind of fellow-feeling — by paying closer attention to the tenure of their sounds, but again only with great concentration. He could not manipulate the elements as he once could, but he found that he could enter negotiations for cooperation. His impurity and tangled natures confused everything natural. It was now his place to prove his intensions whereas before his needs and desired had been met without question.

It was frustrating and he sometimes slashed out in violence which, of course, put back his progress.

As Mikaela's form grew less sharp in his mind and as her scent was being unwittingly aired out of her gowns, Tadhg sometimes lost himself to the rage of frustration. If there was one saving grace, however, it came when he realized that darkness and shadows were his to command almost at will. He had never before known just how resilient a lack of light could be; shadow became almost physical in his hands. He could track both humans and animals as easily as before, relying on one or two senses at a time rather than all of them at once, and he could get into the minds of humans without too much mental exertion. Mikaela had been able to do that.

He less often searched for his fellow *fae*. If there were any hereabouts, he could not find them, nor find any signs of their passing. After a time, it mattered less and less.

Tadhg found that he did not much care for the taste of mortal blood but at least it was better than that of the rats, cats, dogs, and boars. After the accident in the monastery... *how long ago was that?...* he had become much more careful not to inflict mortal wounds; he fed only when he was at the beginning of a hunger cycle. He made note in his own journal of the intensity of hunger pains compared to the days or weeks since he last fed. He swore he would never let it get desperate and he fought against an inner demon trying to control his mind and actions to simple feed whenever whim dictated.

It had not been a theme he and Mikaela had even discussed, nor had she ever mentioned it, nor did she write about it in his journal beyond hints and misgivings. As for the hints, well, these words he might still somehow be misunderstanding. Without a separate guide he was blind; he resolved to consult a larger library when he could find one.

That would mean leaving the grove for extended periods, which he was loathe to do.

The particular magic of the *fae* had been denied him in this form, that much was clear, but he also saw deep within himself that the spark of the *fae* was still there also stirring with rage. He determined that he would have to find a means to bring it back out again or at least tap into that heightened fury. Until such time, however, he struggled and strained to create a magic of his own... neither *strzyga* nor *fae*, a magic unique to himself.

He just needed to be left alone to do it.

§

He could no longer pick out the tenor of the woman's voice in his memories of her. Her words were still there, but the voice given them was now his own.

Over time (he was vaguely aware of its passage) Tadhg developed a means of calling out to the creatures of the region; he developed a sympathetic understanding with his caves, with the grove, and with the surrounding hills. He was a part of them and they were a part of him. He knew when someone was nearby, for example, and he knew when wolves entered what he now thought of as his territory. Sometimes the predator creatures came and paid him homage, bringing fresh kills, and leaving these in the paths where he was sure to find them.

We will kill for you, this meant, *do not kill us*, was the offered bargain.

He developed a skill at reading of the signs of the coming weather. He found he had a sense of danger which, he reasoned, must have been inherited from Mikaela, although his new condition may merely have heightened his once fragile prophetic skills. He found that he could... imitate... the magic of the *fae*, after a fashion, which would have to do for now.

It was a small, unsatisfying victory.

Tadhg would meditate many an evening and whole day away trying to recall the lessons he had once had at the knees of nameless and now faceless druids, hermits, wild women, and bards (particularly from Rory, of course). He remembered the making of wards, and placed many about, corralling wanderers into traps using his own spilled blood to power the lures. Rumors spread in the city of the dangers inherent in wandering the mountains alone nowadays, and over the months which passed fewer and fewer people were ensnared. This meant that Tadhg either move on — there was forested terrain about and a whole island off the coast in fact, no more than an hour's swim away — or prepare to make forays into the city once again in times of need. He wanted to remain in the grove with the memories of Mikaela, weak and fading as they were, so his decision was more or less forced upon him — venture back into the walled city.

§

Tadhg could no longer remember if the woman favored this jewel or that one, this gown or that one, these shoes or those, and he packed all of it away and buried it, only to dig it up the next day struggling with feelings of profound sorrow. One day he simply stopped opening the crate.

In the city he found that the diplomatic embassy he had once been connected to had moved on to other things weeks and weeks ago. He learned this while sitting at the back, in the shadows, of the Greek taverna where he had first met Mikaela. His intention in coming here, at first, had been to scout; to learn who was still in the city. Did he know anyone? He made enquiries as to whether anyone recalled a certain light-hearted and generous Venetian nobleman. The few conversations he had started since then resulted in little added wisdom. The Visconti was remembered with sadness when he was remembered at all.

"But friend, that was years ago! I was but a boy then."

The native Dalmatians gave the new patron, this Hungarian scholar, plenty of space; somehow, they knew his presence in their little Republic was an ill-omen of something to come. Tadhg had once been warned away from Mikaela; he remembered and wondered if anyone warned the people who sat and drank at his table now away from this stranger named Stephan Hunyandi, who claimed kinship with the famous Bans of Severin?

Perhaps they did.

This Stephan was said to have an undeniable charm, however, even if he was moody and given to emotional rants, as Magyars are said to be. Both aspects attracted some followers, however, much to his surprise. His clothes were once again of the finest cuts the city had to offer. This told people he was a man of wealth and culture, which attracted still others to his table. Tadhg could, of course, also converse in many languages, which made his table the center of attention on many a night… for visitors and diplomats, merchants, and clergymen, alike… but rarely for the natives.

None could say where he lived.

None could say with certainty from which direction he approached the taverna.

The women (and men) he left the taverna with could not relay much detail about his personal life when they next came to drink. Some recalled deep philosophical discussions into the early morning hours while others blushed and whispered of this Magyar's odd sexual habits and stamina, of wild orgies, of soft and tender caresses in the night. Other travelers at other tables dismissed this as crazy talk and spoke instead of tangible new terrors in the woods and mountains surrounding the city. This new threat was called *crna magla* by the Croats and *mávri omíchli* by the Greeks. This new dread was to the Slavs called *čierna hmla* and to the Turks, whose sultan held Ragusa as suzerain these days, the words used were *kara sis*. They all spoke of the same thing.

The black fog.

This physical manifestation of evil was said to hover around the city of a night, but always outside the walls. This malevolence was said to be black, always there at night, and always containing within it the sounds of children laughing and animals baying, or so it was thought, warning sounds trying to lure the unwary out on missions of investigation, rescue, or simple mercy. It was said by some that this talk was all nonsense, but natives said, there was something big waiting in the wicked fog for the imprudent, that much was certain and true.

It was known!

Figures, they said, both large or small, no one is sure, dart out in front of the carts of merchants, frightening the horses, and unnerving the drivers into making terrible mistakes. Oddly, however, no cargo was ever stolen as far as anyone knew, but the drivers seemed listless and weakened when they were eventually found after they began to be missed. It was said that the fog was brought on by the sounds of pipe music, a form of music not native to the region, but sweet to hear, nonetheless.

Tadhg sat and took in all this rumor, but he wondered who was playing the music?

It is not himself, and he had never heard it.

Maybe what is imagined by the victims was mere added flavor for the tales they were telling. But why is the music described so reminiscent of that from his homeland?

It is a mystery he determined to solve, but never entirely solved.

§

Mikaela was more a memory of a memory of a real woman; an emotion here, a color there; the chance finding of a bloom brought her fragrance to mind, but little more than that. When he could bring himself to prise open the crate, what came out were faded and threadbare rags. Soon even the rags were unrecognizable as once having been anything else.

Tadhg had also come to the conclusion that his unconscious mind did, sometimes, take control of his body and act without his mental knowledge. He found a set of pipes hidden away in the trees; pipes clearly constructed in the fashion of Rory's patient instruction of decades passed.

One evening Tadhg was studying her journal again, carefully; the pages were fragile, torn in places, over scribed by layers of notes in his own hand. The goal of reading had been to understand this newly realized aspect of his nature… this unconscious activity. Perhaps it was another by-product of his mixed humors? He turned the pages by the light of the moon and the stars, and he searched for hidden meanings in her words and in his marginal and interlinear observations.

He was suddenly surprised and angered to find a man standing in his grove, not twenty feet away from him.

§

The man, who was armored in artistically filigreed silver, seemed familiar, somehow, but Tadhg could not at once place him and merely stared.

The stranger then bowed, formally, at ease with the situation if not aware of the danger he had placed himself in.

'Sire,' he said in a language Tadhg has not heard in years. 'Dubhgall?'

Tadhg stared at the man for a long moment still, not having really heard the address, and only realized suddenly that this man was not a man at all. The man, whatever it is, turned his head to the side, confused by his odd reception.

'Do you not recognize me, your own cousin!?'

Something sparked in Tadhg's mind then; a name, drudged up from long and long ago. 'Drugal?'

The man-like creature, dressed not only in silver armor, but silver fabric under the plates, from head to toe, clapped his hands, laughed, and approached closer. Tadhg rose to his feet, alarm plain in his features, and a clear warning in his countenance. A wolf howled in the distance in answer to the otherwise silent distress call.

Drugal stopped suddenly, confused again.

Tadhg could hear the other's heart suddenly galloping (for a *fae*) in his chest. Something told this stranger that this was all wrong. Tadhg can smell his confusion, the unexpected fear on the other. Tadhg could also now smell something new, something old and familiar still — ichor; the blood of the *fae*. He breathed in deeply. It smelled good, rich, and tangy. His fangs and talons extend, and he took a step closer to the interloper.

'What… what is this!? What has become of you, Cousin?' Drugal steps back, draws his silver weapon as Tadhg takes another step forward. 'Have I been tricked, lured to my fate by Abarta?'

'Abarta?' The name brought Tadhg to a halting stop. *Is that what I am now?* He pulls himself together, talons and fangs withdrawn and he took a step back.

'Drugal? What in all the hells are you doing here?'

Tadhg can plainly see that Drugal is frightened. He knows, from memory, that Drugal has rarely ever been frightened in his centuries of life and certainly did not expect to be terrified here and now by his younger cousin.

For his part, Drugal can plainly see that Dubhgall is not the Dubhgall of his memories and recollections. The Dubhgall he came to find no longer exists, his mission a failure… or, it occurs to him… maybe…not? As Tadhg watches, evaluates, listens, Drugal takes in a deep breath, sheathes his sword, lets the air out of his lungs slowly. He is stalling, lowering his racing heartbeat but unsure now of his actions and of himself, which has never been the case before. He starts again, 'We,' he says hesitantly, 'that is, the court… you see, Dubhgall…'

'What are you stammering about… Cousin?' Tadhg sounds a note of warning, spitting out the last word as if it is some kind of poison, and waving away the matter, impatient. 'You bite at your lip; I have never known you to be insecure. What do you want here? Speak or leave, it is your choice, but I will give you this choice only once for the sake of our common blood and old times.'

Tadhg's eyes narrow in expectation of a response, considering whether or not if Drugal runs will he give chase? The ichor of the *fae* is a taste he has not experienced yet. But then he stops this line of thinking, *is that not what killed Mikaela?*

'Mikaela?' asks Drugal, daring to make a personal observation despite the danger. 'Who…'

'Never mind that, Cousin, my question goes unanswered.'

'Yes, about that. I have been looking for you long and long, Dubhgall.'

'Call me Tadhg.' He spreads his hands, 'Okay, you've found me all right, deliver your message and be gone.'

'Dubhgall… umm, Tadhg, if you like, you must return with me.'

'I must!?' Tadhg sneers. 'I will be the judge of what I *must* do, Cousin.'

'Of course, of course, it's just that the court needs you. Munster, I mean, the *Hidden Court* in Cork.'

'The court needs me. Why?'

'Why!? You are its king.' Tadhg laughs.

'My father is its king.'

'No more.' Drugal grows noticeably quiet and very still letting the implications sink in.

'What of my mother, the queen?'

'She died decades ago, even before the king. How did you not know this, Cousin?'

Tadhg sobers quickly, shaking his head. It is a good, but a troubling question. *How did I not know that?*

He is neither angry nor surprised at it though, recalling old dreams and a banshee scream he once heard, or thought he had heard, one night long and long ago. He sits back down at his makeshift desk and quietly closes the book on Mikaela's last few observations. He then waves Drugal over, indicating a rock shaped like a seat opposite him, still distant in manner but less unfriendly than earlier.

'There is wine in the cave behind you, Cousin, and food too if that is your wish. Take whatever you need, then sit and tell the tale you have come to tell.'

9

A robbery: Last night occurred an armed robbery of a small, family-owned restaurant north of Sussex which had tragic results. Coffee and wine were stolen after hours from Hannah's Café of Sussex, New Brunswick, where a caretaker (Kenneth Hope, 60) was tortured and killed on the scene. He is reported to have had the blood drained out of his body, although Doctor Sanderson, the coroner of this country, will neither confirm nor deny this rumor. There are, to date, no witnesses to the crimes come forward. Regular readers will recall that Hope and his wife Denise (56) tragically lost their son Michael (who would have been 25) when the Sussex Post Office was robbed three years passed. Services will be held as St Peter's Church of the Redeemer on the 28th.

The Kings County Record
for December 23rd, 1956
by Thomas Shaffaer

10

[It is June 1498 in Mikaela's Grove]

Drugal sits down after re-emerging from the indicated cave. He has brought out a couple bottles of a fine red wine and some tasty cheeses. He pours two glasses and hands one across the makeshift table. Drugal has begun a troubling tale of slaughter and death, but before he can speak on Tadhg stops him.

'What year is it now?'

Drugal is nonplussed a moment, pauses in confusion, and thought, 'Well, by the Christian's reckoning, Cousin, it is now 1498. June or July,' he waves this away, 'whatever the mortals call the divisions.'

'And this massacre of which you speak, this happened... what, six years passed?' Drugal nods. 'And you have been searching for me all that time?' Drugal nods again and chuckles, holding up a hand in response to Tadhg's raised eyebrow.

'We did not know that you were still alive, Cousin, as you stopped sending missives to the mortals and the court. Our best diviners could not find you. I had begun to fear that you were no more even as I searched on knowing in my heart you were. The monks in Cork knew only that you had left them some fifty years earlier for the learning academy in Dublin. The scholars there were aware only of records that you had left them for advanced training in England. In England it took me several months to untangle your trail from those of two dozen other brothers, Richard.'

Tadhg smiles despite the seriousness of this recitation. 'Could you not have selected a less common name?' Drugal sighs and then also smiles.

'The *Hidden* courts,' he says pressing on, 'were not much more accommodating to me. Oh, you left strong memories and impressions behind all right, Cousin, but you told them little of your actual future plans or travels.' Tadhg smiles again, accepting the truth of this statement.

Yes, this sounded very much like me… the old me. He frowns.

'I had few actual plans then.'

'Yes, well, speaking of which our cousin, Queen Habundia, sends her regards from Normandy. She misses your company very much, or so the other Norman *sidhe* say under their breath. How often did you visit her bed chamber?' Tadhg answers with a shrug.

'I vaguely recall her at all, Drugal. Our cousin, you say?'

'Yes.' Drugal regards Tadhg with a quizzical expression. 'How could you not remember *her*? So dark of hair and so fair of skin, her eyes, the green of the sea those eyes, and stormy seas at that. The mortals there call her the queen of the witches, utter nonsense of course, but she does nothing to disabuse them of this notion.' Drugal laughs quietly, a jeer of disrespect in his tone.

'These Normans… her people would tell me little or nothing without first demanding boons of me. It is a bad sign cousin, a bad sign. The Munster court has fallen so far that it is of little concern elsewhere. When these boons were performed, the *lutins* pointed me in the direction of Bavaria while the *lutines* pointed north to the lands of the Swedes. That misinformation alone cost me many months of fruitless journeying.'

Tadhg considers this, 'But Fée Esterelle knew my plans were to the south, such as they were.'

'Perhaps, but she was not taking visitors when I was nearby.'

'I see,' Tadhg recalls, 'yes, she has always been flighty.'

'True, and her subjects are equally so.'

'It is said a court resembles the ruler.' Drugal regards Tadhg while sipping his wine, saying nothing for the moment. 'What of the white ladies of Lorraine?'

Tadhg fidgets under Drugal's inspection, 'They… they also knew my agenda.'

'I was not in Lorraine, Cousin. I did, however, spend time in the presence of Melusine.'

'I hope it was not a Saturday?' Tadhg smiles at the unintended humor of the question; he knows the story well enough.

'Of course not, we all know *Pressyne's curse*, but it was too late in any case. King Raymond could not abide knowing what she got up to on a

Saturday and brought the curse down upon her… and himself.' Tadhg nods and shrugs; a small laugh at the whims of fate.

'Was this at Château de Lusignan?'

Drugal affirms that it was.

'And what of Melior and Palatyne? I've enjoyed their company many a time.'

'According to their sister, Melior stays in Armenia with her sparrowhawk and Palatyne awaits rescue still from her prison in Aragon.' Tadhg considers this.

'Funny, I had thought once upon a time to travel into Aragon and visit her, perhaps claim some of that vast treasure as a reward. I guess I just assumed by now she would be free again.'

'Our French cousins are less than… stable, let us say.'

'Aye, that's a good description.' Tadhg sips at his wine. 'After France?'

'After France I moved into the empire. I travelled along the Rhone, for a time, seeking out the wisdom of the terrible Drac.'

'Is he still abducting maidens from the banks?'

'Yes, more or less.'

'I'm glad some things never change. Speaking of which, I presume he told you nothing?'

'Of course not, the old bastard, and he made me help him in the abduction of three virgins for it.'

'How odd… what does he need virgins for? They can't nurse his children for him.'

'It was a cruel jest, nothing more. He released them unharmed at once and escaped me into his watery kingdom before I could mete out some punishment. His laughter haunts me all these months later.'

'You were played upon, Cousin.'

'Don't I know it?! I was left alone facing the wrath of three virgins and their village.'

'You were always quick, Cousin, I'm sure you outpaced them easily.'

'True, but I also had to find three human men to marry a nereid, a limnad, and a mermaid, all because they wanted mortal souls. Why would they want mortal souls?'

Tadhg shrugs, 'To eat? I've never understood the *undine* races, Cousin, mad the lot of them.'

'Aye... mad. But that was nothing,' Drugal smiles, 'compared to the white-furred dwarfs of the Swiss Confederation.'

Tadhg pauses in thought. 'The... *barbegazi*? They of the massive feet?'

'The very same.'

Drugal slaps the table, forgetting that it is just a flat rock. He cradles his hand, 'I spent a winter aiding them in finding and rescuing mortals caught in the snows of the mountains, and a summer with them digging out new caves and tunnels. I was not allowed to leave before the next snow fall. They, at least, were helpful and pointed me in the direction of the Carpathians. Finally, there, a Wallachian noble diplomat recalled you, in your monk's garb, and told me of how you must have grown sick and disappeared. From these clues it was into the Balkans for me, and finally here to Ragusa.'

'So, here we are.'

'Aye, here we are.' There is a long pause in the conversation then.

Finally, Tadhg asked the important question. 'What happened in Mallow, Cousin?' Drugal hesitated now, delaying his reply by pouring another glass.

'That... that is a less easily answered question cousin, and a far less entertaining tale. It would seem to involve a red and a white rose and civil conflicts in England.'

'Yes, I am aware of the conflict, but I thought it resolved by the last Lancastrian... this Welshman named Twudor?'

'Aye, seemingly so, but seven years ago the mayor of Cork, a man named Atwater I believe... remember that I am not from that region... took under his wing a young Frenchman pretending to be a son of the dead English king named Edward, fourth of the name, I was told.'

'Pretending?' Drugal spread his hands in a helpless gesture of ignorance.

'So, it is said, Cousin, so it is said. In any case, this Atwater gave aid to this boy and the cause of the white rose remnants and meant to induce others to rebel against *the* Welsh king of England.'

'Let me guess. *The* Twudor ordered a reprisal against the supporters of this pretended son of York?'

'Those I have spoken to say that nay.'

'Oh?'

'*The* Twudor was indirectly the intended beneficiary of this bloody deed, of course, but not the instigator of it. That was said to be a certain Sir Thomas Herbert of Basingstoke, wherever that may be, England, I guess. He is the one who sought to attract the attention and favor of *the* Twudor *via* an attack against this Atwater. The mayoral court at Cork was to be taught a lesson as well in meddling in the affairs of others, and it was assumed that the capture of this boy, this Warspeck I believe is… was… his name, would be a boon in this Herbert's cap. The sad thing is cousin that the boy had long since left Cork before Herbert's small army was formed and closed in. With no way to storm the city, and no real cause so to do, they picked at random a smaller target to loot and make example of.'

'Mallow?'

Drugal nods. 'Late in the day, the sun already below the tree line and darkness rising, when things were all settled after the working day, Herbert's band charged into Mallow's tiny market square and so began the wanton destruction of every household, every man, woman and child. I have been told such tales of it, Cousin, such tales as to sicken the spirit and pain the heart to hear. Women and children herded into houses and burnt alive; the men slaughtered in the commons. Each and every building was set aflame. It was said the fire and smoke was visible from Cork. Perhaps Atwater got the message.' Drugal paused and took a steadying sip. 'Well, I have heard the word apocalypse whispered from the men of other towns who assembled to help Mallow, but they arrived too late to do so. It was cruelty on a massive scale.'

'Where were the *fae* of the *Hidden* court? The noble *sidhe* did not join the fight? The wrathful *redcaps* and mischievous *pookas* did not involve themselves? This is hard to hear, my father the king was sworn to protect Mallow by the ancient gods themselves and agreements inherited from his father and his before.'

'He… the king… your father, my uncle, was… not the *sidhe* you would remember, Cousin. The sudden and unexplained death of the queen had… broken him. The *Hidden* were elsewhere that day, scattered about Munster, avoiding his misery and his sad court. He led a charge, of course he did, but with so few *sidhe* to lead the other ranks they were beaten back, their magic not enough to counter the weapons and maniacal, drunken, energy of the soldiers. Still, they killed half the human enemy before they could fight no more. More than forty enemy soldiers rushed in, less than twenty crawled out. But Tadhg,' Drugal looked down, regarding the dirt, 'those few obliterated Mallow from the face of the earth in less time than it took to prepare an evening meal.'

Tadhg listened, sipped at his wine, but found it had turned sour.

He put the glass down again in disgust and steepled his fingers before him, laying his elbows on the flat slab of rock he used for a table. Try as he might, however, he could not bring Mallow to mind.

Had it been erased from my memory as well?

'So, the king and some others were killed in the defense of the settlement.' It was not a question as such, more a simple restatement of the facts as heard.

Drugal did not respond as there seemed no need to do so, but he carefully watched his cousin's face.

'This was a sad tale you relay to me, Cousin, a sad tale indeed. But be of cheer! You have succeeded in your quest; you have found me and relayed these ill-tidings. You are relieved of the *geas* taken up. Spend the night if you will, I would welcome the company for a change. We shall drink to old times; speak of old friends and conquests.' Drugal's mouth hung open, his eyes wide in surprise. Tadhg's smile fled before it. 'Is there more?'

'I did not make this journey only to relay a sad tale, Cousin, I have come to bring you back.'

'Why?' Drugal stood suddenly and threw down his goblet at this innocent question.

'Why!? You are the king; you are the *Hidden* king of Munster! You are the *High Hidden* King of Ireland, in point of fact!' Tadhg shook his head, waving away any significance to these words.

'I have much more important work here, Cousin, and I want nothing more to do with that life any longer.' Tadhg shrugged. 'You be the high king now, Cousin. I give you the crown and staff of my own free will. Fetch another *sidhe* here; I will swear before a witness if that is your desire.' Drugal laughed bitterly.

'You know as well as I that cannot be done. Yes, you and I share some blood, but you are of *the blood,* not I! Your father, the late king, was only my uncle by his union with the late queen. The longer you delay a return, the worse off mortal Ireland will become as a result.'

'Bah! *The* blood!? What the hell are you talking about, Drugal?'

Drugal sat back and regarded his cousin as astonishment spread across his features. Tadhg saw this; it was not the reaction Tadhg was expecting to see, and it gave him pause. 'Wait, what exactly do you mean, Cousin? Clearly there is more here than I understand. Speak on and I promise to hear you out.' Drugal sighed and returned to his makeshift seat.

'The late king, your father, my uncle, intended to have such a discussion with you in later times, perhaps after your eventual return, but there must be a *Hidden* high king for the land to prosper, Cousin, there must be, to keep the connection between the mundane and the divine, if you will. The high *Hidden* king of the land provides order, and fertility, and the blessings of the gods for the entire realm.'

Tadhg takes on a dismissive aspect. 'Yes, yes, I've read *Le* Morte d'Arthur too, Drugal. I was less than impressed with all that literary mystical symbolism.'

'You think that is all fiction then?' The question is met with a mere shrug. 'Listen, Cousin, for all the time we have known each other have I ever misled you before?' Tadhg raises an eyebrow, smiling wickedly. Drugal shrugs, 'Okay, point taken. Let me rephrase; have I lied to you about anything important?'

Tadhg waves a hand, conceding this truth.

'Then listen now. Without a king of the blood there can be no definition of the land, right order falls into abeyance. The king of the blood supplies the energy that is translated to the people, all the people, as right feeling and community. You are the center of us, Cousin, whether human, Hidden and whatever lies between. Why do you think when called upon by the Bridget to give their son to the mortals your parents did so? And did so gladly?'

'She was sorry for Rory and Katherine, loyal followers, true to the old ways. It meant little to my parents, ten, twenty years apart from a child. That is nothing to us.' Drugal nods enthusiastically and points a finger in demonstration.

'Yes, true, but why you in particular, Cousin? Why not the child of any other sidhe of the Munster court? Would not any have done?'

Tadhg shakes his head. 'Well, I've never considered it beyond that point, Cousin.'

'It is because you, as high king, need to understand both worlds. Your father my uncle the king that was, in his time, had also been raised partially by humans of that village. Did he tell you that?'

'No. But… now some other things begin to make more sense.'

'He would have told you, given time. The king, the high king, must be a conduit; the joint kingdom cannot flourish unless that is the case. The kingdom, Ireland, will be lost if you do not return.'

'I always wondered why Mallow was the center of the kingdom and seat of the Munster court.' Tadhg regarded his cousin, his words beginning to filter through. 'You offer me only a kingdom of dust if what you say is true.'

'No!' Tadhg has never seen Drugal this animated before. 'No, just a kingdom momentarily covered in dust, obscured by darkness. It awaits its true king to cleanse the dust away. Already the Desmond and the FitzGerald have grown weak and unable to resist the foreign rule of the Twudor, and the Church of the Triune God exports priests and bishops all the more so for this weakness. We have become as nothing more than territory for others to walk on and exploit. The chiefs are falling into a kind of madness cousin, fighting each other for the scraps from the tables of the Twudor and this pope of Rome. We are becoming civilized, modernized, but ruled from afar. Soon, without Munster, the other realms will follow suit.'

Tadhg huffs cynically, 'And so, I am to shepherd the land.'

'You must be more than that, Cousin, so much more! You must be the warrior too. It will be a challenge, of course, as you must now also reclaim that which you have lost in your person. Be not the victim any longer Dubhgall, sire, return and assert your will upon the land. You must, I suspect, become a destroyer for a time; you will need to cure the ill and cut out the disease…'

'I am less than I was, Cousin, and more.'

'Oh, yes, I see that, I am not blind. You cannot save the land as you are, however, certainly not entirely. Dubhgall, my cousin, seems to be but a shadow of your aspect now. A small part of the Tadhg you have become. You are less than *fae*, as you say, but you are more so too,' he pauses, searching his cousin's eyes. 'It seems your passions have been replaced by instincts, and only the one primal drive now stirs you entirely to action. If I understand your condition correctly, I am not fully aware of it. You seem more akin to the tick-like *nosferatu* of England than the *fae* of our home. I am not blind to it, and neither will be our people. Your aura has become dull, no longer vivid like you once were, so vivid… once. You have become the motherless child, sire, but you must once again become the magician, the knower, the king.'

'A fine speech…'

'Please,' he raised a hand to forestall whatever Tadhg planned to say, 'but you know it to be true, I see it in your aspect. You no longer accept these truths as true even though you know they are still there within you, lurking, hiding from what you now are. Your world has been shattered by imputed change, Cousin; what was once within you does not now function, except in an iniquitous fashion. You have become profane, true, but the sacred is still within you. It remains to be drawn out. You have been stolen, Cousin, but you can bring yourself home.'

Tadhg held up his hand now forestalling Drugal's words. 'Even if I grant all that you have said, and I do not, but for the sake of argument. You are forgetting that my father's was a summery court, Cousin. What would mine be? Autumnal at best; such a court has never been tried in Ireland. It would be wintery, almost certainly. How will summery fae make that transition?'

'It will be hard but so be it! The high court and lesser courts will adjust to it, they will have to. And wintery is better than dead; wintery is necessary for springtide to come again and bring us back to summery. Perhaps the change is necessary; perhaps the gods decreed this; perhaps… well, it need not be forever, Cousin.'

Tadhg's eyebrows shot up, 'Not forever? If you have something in mind, Cousin, tell me now.'

'We'll walk the pilgrim's path to the royal stones. We will make an appeal to the gods… for guidance, and and, well, I do not know what else. But Cousin, are you happy this way?'

Tadhg laid an elbow on the stone surface and rested his chin on his fist. Drugal watched him searching the grove with his eyes, seeing shadows and specters of times past, and clearly thinking of happier days.

'I have made this wild, rocky land my own. My... heart is here now, Cousin, perhaps it always will be.'

'This... Mikaela?'

Tadhg nods, his expression sad.

'Tell me of this creature, sire, she must have been something amazing.' For the first time since he came here, Drugal notes a happier expression on the king's face.

§

The tale takes what remains of the night and some of the following day. The cousins grow tired, though, one from the telling and the other from the hearing of it.

'I fear that I will lose her completely if I leave, Cousin... already she fades in my remembrance.'

'Hmmm,' Drugal now matches the posture earlier held by Tadhg.

'A thought?'

'You met this... s*trigoii*...'

'*Moroaică*.'

'Yes, the *moroaică*, when you were still pure.'

'A strange way to put it Drugal, but yes, I was unchanged then.'

'Well then, don't you see, if we can somehow lessen this taint about you, she will return to your purer memories. You can have her with you as long as you want.'

'You promise much, Cousin.'

'Much is at stake, Cousin.'

'I can no longer travel the *Hidden* pathways. I have tried to pry them open; they refuse my call. And my court, it would accept me? Like this?'

'They cry out for you, Cousin. I can go back and prepare them for your coming... explain to them...'

Tadhg is silent a moment. 'I would welcome your company on the trek, Cousin, it will be long in the undertaking, and I need... re-tutoring... in the use of the *Hidden* magic. I have been able only to simulate what once came naturally to me.'

'Of course, I will make the trek at your side. I am as bound to you as you are to the court and realm.'

'Besides which, you will not leave me alone until I agreed to return.'

'There is that.'

Both Tadhg and Drugal chuckle at this observation. Still sniggering a moment later, Tadhg's smile turns sardonic.

'I will return with you, Cousin, provided you can meet one request.'

Drugal's expression turned from one of joy to suspicion. 'Which is?'

'I must build my strength, but food no longer gives me nourishment. I need blood. I will need your aid in this matter.'

Drugal's mouth opens and closes as he starts to reply, then reconsiders his words. Tadhg lifts a hand to forestall further attempts.

'I promise that no one need be killed. My requirements are modest, I think, and you will be there to watch in any case. Find the ill or old and dying ones; find the young who would gain a boon from me in return; negotiate what you will to gain volunteers along the way. Agree to this, and I will return with you. And prepare them back home.'

11

[It is October 22nd, 1499]

It has taken Tadhg several weeks, months in fact, to get back to Mallow and the mental and physical effort has been much more taxing than he had expected; more so than Drugal had promised him. But as difficult as the effort had been, the final revelation was far worse. Drugal's words had not sufficiently prepared him for what he now saw, and he had not prepared himself for the mental impact it would have (or was supposed to have had in any case).

Tadhg had no emotional reaction to it at all (except annoyance over the wasted time) and already he was planning his journey back to Ragusa. He stood before the burnt-out husk of what had once been, long and long ago, his home of sixteen summers and fifteen winters. As he looked about him now, he longed for the little grove which he had come to think of as his home (certainly more than this place), and from which he had been lured away by false promises.

He felt another emotion, the stirrings of anger.

He tried to conjure images in his mind; images that would have meant something to the old Tadhg, but which meant nothing to him now. As he looked around this place his cousin had brought him to, he tried to recall the colors, and smells, and sounds of the village… but these would not come to him. The mortals who raised him through childhood were decades' dead, so too were his adopted siblings and their children, whom he did not know even the names of.

Tadhg did recognize an emotion connecting to these last thoughts, however. He was gladdened by the fact that Rory and Katherine had been spared this atrocity.

Their true children, Bran, a girl named Tara, another boy named Sean might be alive still, somewhere, had they moved on elsewhere when time was. He searched his memories, trying to recall any correspondence about them, from them, but was unable to bring any to mind... save for the notion that one of them had been a smith. Of course, the monastery nearer the city would have declared Brother Richard dead or missing long ago. Perhaps his adopted siblings had been informed and had given up hope of a return, reunion, introductions. He fought down the will of the demonic invader within, which seemed to say *seek them and drink them dry*. To his surprise he found that it was less of a struggle to subdue the other aspect of himself than once it had been.

'You are learning, Cousin. That is a good sign.'

A bright silvery light blinked to Tadhg's right side. He was used to it now though; the comings and goings of his self-appointed royal bodyguardsman and confidante.

While an annoying presence at first, what with his near omnipresent optimism, Drugal had done what he had promised, more or less, and seen him back safely to what remained of Mallow. Drugal had met his obligations on the trek as best he could; he got blood where he could, mortal blood, and tutored his king in whatever *Hidden* crafts Tadhg had forgotten (which was quite considerable). When the magic would not come, Drugal helped him forge new paths of his own devise using the power of the ichor within.

Tadhg nodded a greeting to his cousin without turning to regard his eternal smile. Drugal joined him and put a friendly hand on his shoulder, the other hand fanning about the remains of the village.

'Not a sight I would wish on my worst enemy, Cousin, but you had to be made to see it for yourself.'

'And now I have.'

Tadhg regarded his cousin a moment, who seemed to have missed the sarcasm. He then ducked out from under the physical contact. He walked forward, deeper into... whatever this place now was.

It is so small, he thought to himself. *Was it always so?*

Mallow had once been his entire universe, but in fact, it had never been larger than a few hundred souls, some small gardens, a smithy, a few small farms, a central market, and not much else besides. Speaking of which, he squatted down before some broken device and brushed the dirt aside. He found a grinding wheel broken into three pieces.

He stood again and looked through the doorway into the dilapidated building and recalled how the blacksmith of his day, O'Casey was his name, another later, used to work. It had been a place of heated sensual impressions and hot passions.

Was it Bran the smith?

He entered to find that a few rusted tools lay in the accumulated dust and rotted vegetation that had fallen in through the no longer extent roof. The forge had been broken up, and the bellows taken or long rotted away, whichever was the case it did not matter now. Why someone would go to the effort of breaking down a forge Tadhg could not imagine.

'Probably just for the sake of viciousness.' Drugal stood in the doorway.

'Opportunism.' Tadhg turned and regarded his cousin. 'I thought I was much improved in shielding my thoughts from being read?'

'What read?' Drugal smiled and raised his arms and shoulders in an expression of innocence. 'You were frowning at the remains of the forge. I did not need to try to understand your intent to know what you were thinking, Cousin.' Tadhg nodded and let the issue drop.

'More trouble to destroy than it is to re-build. Perhaps some other villages' youths come here to explore, or to take materials for their own needs.'

It was Drugal's turn to shrug and shake his head. 'No one comes here any more, Cousin.' Tadhg turned and regarded the other with a raised eyebrow.

Drugal took this as a call for explanation.

'The mortals think it a haunted place. Their church forbids approach, and for us, the purity is gone out from it. Only the ghosts stay, and they speak to no one.' Tadhg picked up what looked like the head of a hammer. The metal caused his bared hand some pain, but he grimaced and endured it, conquered it. He threw down the defeated hammerhead finally and stood up again, wiping the dust from his hands. A final look around said he was done with the place. He turned toward the doorway and faced his cousin once more.

'And you wish me to do what here exactly, Cousin? I am not the *sidhe* I was, that much is obvious. I am more *unseelie* than any other can be so wintery that spring and summer may never come in my presence. Even if I were able and willing, how do you think I could fix...' Tadhg spreads his hands wide, 'all this? I have no magic wands, no amulets of power. I am not sure that I even care to believe in those things any longer. You are the "Silver Prince of Armagh" and I say again, is there naught you can do?'

Drugal shook his head. 'I can perform your duty, Cousin, but I cannot fulfil your responsibilities. My powers are limited to the purely physical in this case cousin, I told you this, yours is *the blood* not mine. The connection of the land hereabouts to the *Otherland* is in abeyance as well; the web is getting thinner every decade that passes without the king to forge the bridge anew, the weave unweaves, the hedgerow withers, the path obscures. The English move in and overturn all the traditions of the people as well; soon the sons of Eire will be just other Englishmen, lesser Englishmen in fact, impotent, but as coldhearted... well, as you. Mallow was once a major source of purity for us; but there are fewer and fewer sources these days, further between them. The pathways are closing down hereabouts. When the last is gone, the true Irish, the people called the *Tuatha de Danann* will be no more. A land without its king has no true energy; the people cannot live in a right community; there is no fellow-feeling about them any more. You, sire, Cousin, are the heart, the center of both the mortal and the *Otherfolk* alike.'

Tadhg smiled a cruel expression.

'Those are fine words, Drugal, they are as fine now as they were back in Ragusa, as they were on the road back, as they were each time you repeated them, but this,' he waved his hand about, 'all this means naught to me.' Tadhg continued to wave his hand around, first indicating the empty forge and then the empty village, 'Did I not say so then; I cannot use the old paths of power. I am obviously not as I once was. I... regret... that your time and mine were both wasted on this, this... a fool's errand if ever one there was.'

'Was it, Tadhg? I wonder... I am not so sure fool's errand it was.' Drugal looked down and about the destroyed smithy. 'Certainly, I can't argue that as you are now our quest may have been pointless, but you could be yourself once again Tadhg or should I say, Dubhgall O'Fionnbharr.'

'What is this you say?' Tadhg frowned, angered now. 'You know as well as I that this curse cannot be lifted. Yet you call me a name I have abandoned, one stolen from me.'

Drugal acquiesced but waved the point aside.

'A name is a name, Cousin. As for the curse, no, not in this land, not as it is, never again, but in the *other*...' he raised his eyebrow with a twinkle in his eye, 'the wisest among your people, of this and many courts, have examined the issue long and long and they believe that it is not... let us say, as impossible as you think.'

Tadhg grinned at this reply. It was not an expression of pleasure, however. This was a predator's expression, one who had discovered a weakness in his prey. Maybe it was also that of the wise man dealing with the fool and knowing thereby he cannot win the argument for trying.

'You hold out false hope to me, Cousin, and call it good. You offer a golden crown that will turn to grime should I ever grasp it. It is a kingdom of dust you offer and a crown of rotted twigs.' Tadhg pushed passed Drugal and left what remained of the smithy to search the rest of the village (*for the sake of curiosity* he told himself), leaving Drugal to his sweet fantasies of renaissance.

Outside again, no buildings exist now in the places where he knew them once to have been; no gardens gave signs of the life they once nurtured. Tadhg searched a few of the other burnt-out husks, but found nothing more than a half-charred toy, a wooden horse, a clay pot, and a chair mysteriously left unharmed by the surrounding fires and not stolen in the meantime. In another he found some coins left untaken by whichever thieving invaders had passed them by. He too left them where they lay, even though silver and copper did not burn the flesh of the *fae* (or the *vampyre* or whatever he now was), but because he had no need of them. Let the next poor wandering fool find them and take away some small profit or curse.

Tadhg finally settled on the rock wall of what he remembered was... had once been... the old well in the center of the village's "marketplace". He noted that the hole had been filled with stones and other debris, almost completely. He glanced inside but chose not to guess on what else might have been tossed down there when time was.

Wherever Drugal had gone in the last hour Tadhg did not know, but he too finally returned via the *Hidden* paths and came to rest on the old well, seated beside his cousin once again.

'Why do you think, Cousin, that when called upon to do so your parents gave their only son, their only child, to be raised by mortals? Gladly, I might add.'

'What new tact is this, Cousin? Did we not have this conversation back in my grove?'

'Please, humor me once again.'

Tadhg paused, searched Drugal's eyes, and then relented some.

'Surely it was to serve *the* Brigit.' Tadhg glanced at Drugal. 'Besides which, to be ten, fifteen years without their son is no time at all for such as us... as you.'

'True, but that is only half the story, Cousin. Why did you take on the robes of a monk?'

'It was not originally my idea, Cousin, my fathers... but... to yes, to better understand the mortals, of course, these mortals, and to learn what there was to learn of this world and their triune god. It was easiest to move about in such a guise. The brown, or grey, or white robes are known throughout the world, and they provided me with both authority and anonymity.'

'The question remains unanswered.'

Tadhg turned his head and regarded Drugal again, pausing for thought.

'To slake my precociousness was said by Rory, as it was unbounded and could not be slaked here or, so the king thought, perhaps to start my journey into wisdom. My... journey,' Tadhg waved the issue away. 'I do not know what you want me to say here, now, Drugal. It was what it was, long and long ago.' Tadhg pushed off the well, stood, and moved a few paces away. The moon was temporarily clouded over, and he thankfully could not see the remnants of the buildings. They seemed to have been closing in on him.

Drugal was undaunted. 'As we speak, Cousin, Eire gets smaller...'

Eire gets smaller. Tadhg sighed angrily and waved this old argument away again.

'No, listen to me, Tadhg. It cannot flourish without you in your proper place. Things cannot be right without them in their proper places. You can, though, cleanse it simply by being what you were born to be. Accept your responsibilities.'

Tadhg looked to the heavens in annoyance, a silent appeal to the gods (if they were still there at all).

'Look at what has happened since you left,' Drugal rehearsed the old arguments once again. '*The* Desmond has grown weak, as has *the*

Fitzgerald. They are not kings and chiefs of the people any more, but they take on English titles and are advised by English lawyers and Roman priests. Some of the priests are Irishmen! They, our humans, can no longer resist the invaders from the Pale, or the Scots to the north, or the churchmen of Rome… everywhere they come. Bishops sit in fine churches and priests crouch in every corner of the land…'

'There were priests and bishops aplenty when I lived here, Cousin, some were good men.'

'Fine, some were, I do not argue that. Many are still, they have good intentions I grant you. But these are still foreign ideas, foreign goals. Our lands grow small, our people grow small, our ancestors, the *Nemedians*, the *firbolgers*, all of them, all of them are reduced to nothing but figures of fun and fables for children. Finn and *the* Brigit are minor saints now, did you know, long forgotten, all of our heroes of old are no longer heard in bard-song. Bards have been reduced to drafting poems of the triune god of the Christians and the adventures of the Christ-man or not at all. Eire has become little more than territory cousin, parcels of land and lines of a map to be traded away like so much head of cattle. While the English gain, what remains of the old has fallen into a kind of madness, fighting each other for scraps and shrinking freeholds. The gods knew! The wise women in their forest huts knew! The sages in their caves knew that this time was coming! Your mother the queen, my aunt by blood, she knew even if her power was weak. *The* Brigit and your parents agreed that you could become a bridge, once again closing the gap between what Eire was and what it could again someday become. That is *your* purpose; I cannot do that for you… no one can.'

Tadhg's eyes glared a harsh red and he spun around, his fangs had descended, his face had grown taut, his fingers had turned into claws. 'There is the flaw in your argument, Cousin. Look at me! See me for what I am! If they,' he waved a talon at the sky and the forest, 'knew my absence would bring this about, why-ever did they let me walk away? Why was I given no hint this would come? It is circular; *pro hoc ergo propter hoc* as the logicians say.' After a moment, his anger calmed. His fangs withdrew. His claws reformed into hands with fingers.

'It means *after this, therefore, because of this,* Cousin. It is a logical fallacy you present me with; you correlate, and you discover causality here where none exists. How… how…' Tadhg was gearing up to make one final devastating point before stalking off into what remained of the night when he suddenly stopped, becoming aware of a scent, an exceedingly small but both unfamiliar and familiar. He turned toward it, toward the dark woods, eyes wide to capture what light there was on offer.

'What is it, Cousin?'

Drugal was concerned by this action. He had seen Tadhg's sense of danger on the road and was instantly at attention. He made to stand while withdrawing his glowing sword, but Tadhg signaled him to remain where he was. Having pin-pointed the direction of the scent, his eyes bright and severe, he beheld a strange sight, and he heard a long forgotten but familiar buzzing sound getting louder.

Finally, a lone pixie came walking across the ground toward him, her dragonfly wings ratty, bent, and worn. She was carrying a clay thimble; it was the contents of the thimble that Tadhg had sensed and immediately identified — *fae-ichor*! That which had killed... her.

The little creature approached slowly, the thimble clearly a burden to her but it was never shaken and no ichor was spilled though she was clearly afraid.

Tadhg glanced back at Drugal, suspecting a trick of some kind, a new false inducement. He suspected Drugal had set this up as some emotive demonstration, but he saw his sword and that he was as confused at the deed as was Tadhg himself.

Tadhg turned back and crouched before the quivering little creature. The pixie fell to her knees and held the thimble up toward her prince in a clear attitude of submission.

'What is the meaning of this?' It was spoken not as a challenge, although Tadhg had long ago abandoned softening his voice or catering to the disposition of others.

'It is a humble offering, sire,' a small buzzing answer came to his attention.

It had been long and long since Tadhg had heard such a voice, such a manner of speaking, and he had to concentrate his mind to make words out of the buzzing sounds.

The pixie continued unbidden.

'I heard of the mission of the great Prince Drugal to find and bring our king back to us. I heard that he, that is, you, had been stolen by the dead ones. I heard that the dead ones drink nothing but blood. I have collected and preserved the ichor that runs in my veins since then, to make this presentation to welcome you home, sire.'

Tadhg glanced at Drugal again, just catching him in the act of wiping a stray tear.

To be fair it had been a great while since Tadhg had been so touched by any act and this little pixie gave him a moment of peace from himself.

He turned back and smiled upon the little thing, not the grin of the predator now but the smile of the homeward bound at journey's end. He bowed and accepted the offering, gently taking it from the pixie. He raised the thimble to his lips.

Its scent alone was intoxicating.

Ordinarily, and as he had learned through a single harsh lesson, the stolen of whatever sub-species, could not drink the fluid which was the lifeblood of the *fae*. The creature... her... Mikaela had infected him in ignorance and in her madness. As a result, she died in agony, leaving Tadhg no choice but to kill and hide to preserve himself. Still, it had been... forever, since he fed on anything but the dull blood of the drunkards and vagabonds Drugal had lured in, no *fae* had volunteered their ichor in exchange for future favors along the way.

This was offered freely, gladly, it seemed.

He drank the offered draft.

It was pure ambrosia.

It was as manna in the desert would be to the dying man.

Tadgh half expected death. He got life. It was as if he had been watching the world go by and was suddenly once again an active participant.

It was the *unleashing* all over again.

It took a minute, perhaps longer, before Tadhg remembered more than just the circumstances of his existence, and while he was not yet himself, he was one small step closer now than he had been in decades. He knew himself once again (or had an understanding now to go on).

The stolen ones go mad because the mortal mind is not capable of processing the implosion of sensual, physical, and spiritual energies contained in even the smallest thimble full of the ichor of the *Hidden*. And while his heart did not start beating again any faster, nor did his lungs pull in air any more regularly, Tadhg sensed that these organs were still within him just waiting to be reawakened to the world as once they had been.

He was not a dead thing; he was a dormant creature.

Perhaps Drugal had not been on such a fool's quest?

Tadhg lowered the thimble back to the pixie. He held out his palm for her to climb on to, which she did, readily understanding the gesture. She hung on to a finger for stability as he stood up again. In the background he now noticed many others gathered just outside the limits of the village, waiting in the trees, and cowering behind the bushes. He waved these forward too, but his attention was focused on the pixie.

'What are you called, you brave, noble little creature?'

The pixie giggled and covered her mouth with her hands. Collecting herself again she gave him a curtsey and almost fell off his palm. 'Talia. I am Talia sire.'

Tadhg nodded, glancing at the others who were all also clearly carrying vessels of one sort or another. The rich scent of enticing ichor held out a promise now of some positive thing… redemption, salvation even? Perhaps more ichor was gathered here in one place than even a *nosferatu* could drink in a fortnight, maybe a month even.

There were *phookas* in their real forms, lithe *bogies*, stocky *boggarts*, and dwarf-like *bugbears*, squat of shape but muscled, mischief makers all, now appearing solemn as judges, all looking to him for… what?

Direction?

Leadership?

Acknowledgement?

Goblins came, and a hairy, smelly, but smiling *hobgoblin*. They all stood around and mixed in with the smaller *fae*. He nodded to them, even recalled a few names and faces here and there, and they all bowed or curtsied back as was their wont.

Tadhg waved them forward again and there was a great cheer.

Those closest came and made their submissions, paying their respects with their own life's blood. Next to come were happily naked *brownies*, of all sizes and shapes, using the tools of their trade to bring their offerings, in pails, and in buckets, or in jars and pewter mugs. Some of them were familiar, but most were unknown to him. The *bogles*, cousins to the *boggarts*, brought the skulls of their victims with them, mortals who were murderers and worse in life, having collected their vital liquids in their trophies. The trickster *bogans*, who had supplied so much laughter in his earlier life, now stepped forward giving aid to their own idiot cousins, the *dobies*, who were eager but also hindered by almost no self-awareness (and they offered finger and toenail clippings and locks of gnarled, greasy hair).

Tadhg almost laughed, but he held back and thanked them for it, winking now at the *bogans*, who offered little more than distain for their cousins, but acknowledged the sentiment, nonetheless.

From the malevolent *bogeys* to the benevolent *ùruisgs* (who were as delightful as the *bogeys* were ugly), they came forward in their dozens, in their dozens of dozens. Next to approach were the larger *fae*, those less able to hide themselves in the human world and those consequently seen less often (unless one knew where to go to find them). Again, some were familiar, and some were obscure in his memories. The surly *clurichaun* and their *leprechaun* brothers came, as did massive *trolls* or fat *ogres*, handsome warrior *sidhe*, and beautiful siren-like *siths*, charming *fauns* and prancing *satyrs*, the spirits of the trees called *dryads*, and the dreaded *banshees*, the screamers in the night. Tadhg recognized ambassadors for the other courts of the land. They all came and gave of themselves to help restore their king, to humble themselves before Tadhg, whom they now called the *dark majesty* or *the stolen one*.

'Did you arrange this, Cousin?' he said in an aside to Drugal, who was just then waving at a young *sith* in green diaphanous attire (that left little to the imagination and thus creating all the more effect for it). He then heard the address and shook his head.

'I wish I could say that I had, Cousin, but this is not my doing.'

Tadhg looked down into his open hand. 'Did you have something to do with this... Talia?'

The pixie smiled awkwardly, her fidgeting hands hidden behind her back, her right foot cumbersomely wrapped around her left ankle. She finally nodded and quickly looked off to the side. 'I may have told someone something about what I was going to do, sire.'

'And the rest of you followed suit?'

There were nods of agreement.

'Cousin,' said Drugal with a nervous quality to his voice, 'I think others would be acknowledged as well.' Tadhg regarded his cousin, curious as to the nervousness. Drugal was now pointing toward the remnants of the houses opposite the gathering of the *Hidden*.

At first, he saw nothing when he glanced there, but that was only because he was unpracticed in the art of seeing spirits and ghosts. He felt their presences in his reawakening senses, however, and then saw shapes slowly forming nearby and apart from the ranks of the *fae*. Specters, ghosts, and phantoms dressed still in the ragged clothes they had died in, said nothing, but Tadhg somehow understood them, nonetheless. In some way he did not fully understand they acknowledged him as their king as well; they too looked to him to correct what had been done to them years earlier… to take responsibility, to bring justice, to avenge.

If Tadhg wore a beard, he would have been stroking it in deep thought.

Careful not to spill the pixie still in his hand, he bowed in acknowledgement of the submissions and offerings, now including the spirits in his movements. If it meant anything to them, he could not know. Two *trolls* then came forward with a great chest carried between them.

'What is this now?'

'This belongs to king… you king,' said one in a stentorian voice as powerful as thunder.

'There are many chests, King,' said the other with an equally booming, but in his case, more sing-song speech.

'But this one most important,' said the first.

'Aye,' said the other in agreement, 'most important is this one. We keep and watch over chests long and long.'

Together they put down the chest, backed off, bowed inelegantly, and stood aside.

Tadhg acknowledged their words but was taken aback some. *Had their blood not been tribute enough?*

You misunderstand, Cousin. It was the voice of Drugal touching his mind. *He said, "this belongs to you." Whatever it is, it is already yours and not tribute.*

Tadhg nodded and glanced at Talia, who seemed to understand. With some effort she flapped her wings and flew a lazy, looping circuit from his hand to his shoulder, taking hold of a strand of hair for support, finally lowering herself into a sitting position on his shoulder.

'Take hold of the other side, Cousin,' Tadhg said to Drugal, 'that lid looks quite heavy.'

It was a chest constructed of a heavy rowen, with iron constraints attached to it.

'Be careful.'

Drugal nodded and took hold of his end as Tadhg did the other. Together, neither as strong as a troll, they lifted the lid off. Tadhg did not know exactly what he expected to find, but it was not what he actually did find within.

It was a shirt of green-hued silver leaves laid atop gold and silver coins and objects both for display and for use. A circlet of gold with a silver wolf's head at the center sat beside the shirt, but clean and bright. Tadhg remembered the first time he saw that shirt, the first time his father wore that crown in his presence, showing off his son to his court. He noted his mother's jewels and other adornments laid-out on velvet cushions. He might have broken down with emotion had it not been for his *strigoii* curse (although a bloody tear did well up in his left eye).

From amidst the hushed gathering a new voice could be heard, 'Make way, move aside you lumps!'

A *red cap* emerged from the surrounding wood, pushing through the assembled ranks unburdened by protocol and politeness, making way for what followed. A *dullahan*; there could be no mistake about what he was. He was given a wide berth, of course, for everyone knows and respects the *death-callers*. Tadhg could feel Talia stand and move behind his neck, putting his body between her own and this new arrival. If the various species of blood drinkers knew of the *dullahan* they would no longer think of themselves as such fearsome creatures.

True to his breed, the *dullahan* carried his own head in his hand; it was bulbous, bare of hair, a hideous grin, with void-like tiny eyes darting this way and that taking in the scene. The head of the *dullahan* had an aura; this one of phosphorescent green of the swamp will-o-the-wisp. Had there been mortals in the company they would have died or been just blinded… if lucky. Tadhg remained where he was stood, greeting the newcomer.

'Crom Dubh,' he said, reaching back into his memory. 'Also known as *far dorocha,* and the favored of High King *Tighermas*. I remember you somewhat, sir. You were the messenger of my father's court as well.'

He spoke the words; he had named the creature. He had been afraid of the fiend all those years ago. The body of the *dullahan* bowed before him.

It was thought by humans that the *dullahan* could not speak but this was something of an untruth. They could, but they were limited in how much they could say by the whim of whatever god created them. It was always the truth, however, whatever they said. They relayed messages from *Hidden* court to *Hidden* court across the world, and sometimes they appeared to cursed mortals as the last thing they would ever know. Whatever this creature had to say now it was clearly meant for the prince returned.

'Speak your message, *far dorocha*.'

The *dullahan* raised its head above its shoulders, turning it to face the crowds, the *Hidden* and the ghosts alike. Words came from the mouth, but it was as if they were struggling to get out, only then to leak out too loud, too soft, indistinct, and all too clearly intermingled with other less sensible noises.

'Dubhgall, son of Fionnbharr, if you face *the* Crom then I am faded into the next life. Your mother preceded me as have many of my court. Drugal the Silver will be sent to fetch you back. Hear his words and consider them, for he is wise, and he is capable. By now, the *trolls* have brought the chest.' Tadhg glanced at the sudden movement of one of the *trolls* proudly elbowing the other in the ribs. 'Our treasury is now yours; you are the king. Bezel tells us that the future of our people is dim, black, but not yet of the void. Whether you can save us… them… is unknown, but my son, my beautiful son, if any one of us can, you will save us all. To aid you Bezel has another item, yours by right. Use it well.' The *dullahan* turned his head to take in all the company then lowered it back to his side.

'If you need me, sire, you know how to summon me.' He then turned sharply and stalked off only to disappear into the night again. Talia, who had been peeking out from under Tadhg's long hair, now re-emerged into full view.

The *red cap* stepped forward after the departure of the other.

He shivered, 'Never liked those things; gives me the shivers they do.' He shook one more time, as if shaking off the remnants of a nasty fall into a mire.

'So, you are the king now, sorry about your father and all, he treated us well he did. Okay, you are a dark one, that is true and no mistake, not like silver breeches over there. Personally, I like that. Maybe we can now do what needs to be done!'

Tadhg eyed up the vicious little creature, Drugal taking offense in his peripheral vision. 'You have something that belongs to me, Bezel?'

'Aye.' He reached into his leathery jacket and pulled out a stick. It was a fine-looking stick, cedar, or some other white wood. Try as he might, however, Tadhg could not place it among his father's possessions. 'Oh aye,' said Bezel, 'it looks like not much now. But here, take it, and all will be revealed, as they say.'

'Who says that, *red cap*?'

Bezel turned his attention to Drugal, his expression one of contempt. 'They do, *sidhe*.'

Tadhg made a chopping motion with his hand to cut this frippery. He took hold of the stick.

Everything went quiet.

The air seemed to hold still in the moment.

No insects or birds were heard.

It started as a small, localized buzz around Tadhg and the stick. At first Tadhg thought it was Talia, but there were no words within the buzzing noise. A small breeze caught his hair and shunted it around, exposing Talia where she still hid, now from the *red cap*. The breeze became a gust, and then a less than gentle zephyr, lightning flashed overhead and caught the stick in Tadhg's hand. Talia flew off into the night, frightened.

He now remembered the item.

The weather grew fiercer around him; the stick shook and shone and slowly expanded. He had been holding little more than a twig, but he blinked in the small typhoon and saw a baton, which then grew into a staff, taking on the very elements themselves. Rain fell all of a sudden and it was absorbed into the device; lightning struck it; earth swirled around him and that too was absorbed. The staff widened and lengthened, making room for more of the elemental materials. Next came fire; a small stream from the sky, like a falling star hitting the staff. Tadhg smiled in the midst of the event; unhurt, lifted even by the happening, a joy he had not experienced in long and long.

Talia watched on from behind a decayed pail as Tadhg was lifted into the air before the gathered creatures and turned; the coins from the chest were pulled into the maelstrom, molded by whatever ancient magic this was and formed into a golden ram's head with massive and curled silver horns.

It should have stopped with the head, but the storm continued unabated.

Now, the shadows themselves were sucked in; the staff, with Tadhg and the court knew to be white, forever to have been white, slowly turned black as jet, black as ebony, as if to reflect the dark soul of the new owner.

Suddenly the violent weather died out and Tadhg was lowered to the ground once more.

The king's staff stood revealed, back in the hands of a king it was an awesome, horrifying device. Where his father had held a white staff of justice the son held a black staff of vengeance. The moonlight reflected in Tadhg's black, pitiless eyes; his hair as white as a cloud, but his features were pure *sidhe* again, noble, elegant, and terrible to behold if angered. Where once the *Hidden* High Court of Corcaigh had been a summer place, warm and luxurious, it would now be a winter place, stark, harsh, hard, and awaiting whatever re-birth was to come. In the words of the old world this was the end of the *seelie* and the start of the *unseelie* times.

The *red cap*, holding his blood soaked cap in his hand, waved it, and proclaimed: 'Behold the king,' bending his knee before Tadhg. The king acknowledged the act of fealty and nodded his thanks as the others did the same.

12

WHO KILLED KAREN LONGBOTTOM? New information has finally become known after twenty years, thanks to our own intrepid reporter Patrick Williams. To recap the now infamous tale.

On March 14th, 1947, the blood drained, ravaged body of Karen Longbottom (24) was discovered in a vacant lot right here in Wilmington, Delaware, reminding the reading public and police of the earlier and now much more famous incident of Los Angeles known as the Black Dahlia murder [of Elizabeth Short] on or about January 15th of that same year. No novels or films for our Karen though, but like the Short case, professional and amateur sleuths here in Delaware have continued to pore over the details looking for clues and hoping to bring the killer or killers finally to justice.

Is there more of a relationship between the two killings than the police know or are willing to admit?

Longbottom, like Short, is said to have bounced around homes most of her life, both women having lost their mothers in childbirth and their fathers to untimely deaths while the girls were young. Karen lived variously in Delaware, New Jersey, and New York states, until age 24, she was living in Wilmington (a mere 4 months) before her premature death. According to the official police reports, Longbottom's body was found about 9.30 AM near the new construction zone, but unlike the Short murder,

Longbottom's body was not torn and bisected or tortured, although, as in that other case, her body had also been drained of blood. Short had been missing a week before her discovery; Longbottom had been reported missing only three days earlier. The police could not find where she had spent those missing days.

That is, until now!

The personal journal of local entrepreneur Anthony 'Tony' Fustier, which came into our reporter's possession through an anonymous source, supplied an answer (of sorts, to some of the questions). It seems that the younger Tony witnessed three men hustling a covered body into an otherwise empty warehouse on the outskirts of town three days before the discovery of the body. He writes that he did not report the event for fear that the man with the cane would find him after chasing him and threatening to kill his family should he speak out about what he'd seen. Tony wrote the details in his journal but never revealed the information to another living soul to the end of his days. He noted that it had been dark, no light but the moon illuminated the scene of two large men dressed in official uniforms of some sort (police?) and a thin man in a dark suit and a Panama hat. He noticed the scene only because of the glinting of moonlight off the grip of the man's stick. Records of the town council show that the warehouse had been rented out to an Irish charity concern known as the D.o.F., but investigations led to dead ends. If any of our readers know of this organization, please call Patrick, now in the editorial office. Next week we begin a new feature called "The Longbottom case", which will serialize Patrick's new and on-going, investigation.

The News Journal
for March 20th, 1962
(Editorial)

13

[It is 23 October 1499]

The celebrations of the previous night had been subdued but happy nonetheless, and the morning brought new purpose to the court for the first time in many years.

Tadhg stood by the old village well watching a small troop of goblins, who must have arrived at some point earlier in the morning, re-excavating it. The work was as nothing to them, of course, earthen creatures that they were. They clawed through the rocks as if the stones and boulders were barely there, debris flying out of the hole in all directions save one, none hit the king. Other *fae* passing by sometimes got a face full, but no one complained too bitterly; most laughed it off. Tadhg would turn his head away to sneer or smirk at those who took offence, but otherwise said nothing beyond a hearty good morning. The goblins' antics amused him, but he had now to appear above taking sides between the summery and the wintery *fae*.

Eventually Drugal found and joined him at the side of the well, the little pixie Talia with him. Tadhg returned their greetings.

They stood in silence watching the dirt and small pebbles fly around them.

Drugal broke the silence. 'Why?' nodding toward the hole.

'I intend Mallow be reborn. It is my responsibility, or so I have been informed.'

Drugal regarded his cousin a moment searching his face for sarcasm. 'Is that why the others are collecting debris?'

'Not debris, Cousin, remnants of the destroyed lives of the villagers.'

'Ah.' He paused a moment. 'The difference being...?'

'The difference being that debris is waste, abandoned, unwanted and un-regarded, while remnants are reminders of something once alive and real.'

Drugal accepted this explanation. 'All right, fair point, but may I ask to what end?'

'A dream, call it a vision perhaps, I do not know. I think it is expected of me to safeguard these remnants for some later purpose.'

'I see.' No *fae* would gainsay what might have been prophetic vision. 'And the brownies there, sweeping out the old huts?'

'The same end.'

'I was told by our fellow *sidhe* that you've ordered them to scour the kingdom for druids, sages and wise women?'

Tadhg affirmed this was the case. Just then the attentions of the three were drawn to a near-by structure. A great crackling sound was heard; the roof, what was left of it, was seen to be shifting.

'*Trolls?*'

Tadhg nodded again. 'I asked them to go about and try to re-set fallen beams as best they could.'

'Why sire?' Any human ears would have heard the sound of a buzzing insect, but Tadhg was getting quickly re-accustomed to the languages and dialects of his people. He took in a breath.

'Talia... Mallow, insignificant it may be as a human settlement is important to the court of Munster as our greatest place of power... once greatest. It needs to be cleansed and re-stocked with villagers, re-vitalized with life, and dreams, you might say.' Drugal's attention snapped to his cousin again.

'You expect humans to come back here?'

'Yes, I do, Cousin, it is imperative they do, but of course, only the right kind, those who still worship in the old ways or who have the capacity and temperament to do so.'

'Mallow was destroyed, Cousin; the old pacts may no longer apply.'

'True, perhaps that is so, I do not know with certainty. Yes, the people who were here at the time are dead, long dead, but others lived here and went elsewhere for whatever reasons, maybe some can be lured back.' Tadhg shrugged. 'I will go to St Fin's myself later in the day and examine the old charters. I know where they are stored. It is my thinking that the spirit of the wording stands still even as the letter elapsed. The population was killed, true, but Mallow is still here, it physically exists.'

Drugal made a show of looking about, 'all evidence to the contrary.'

'*I* lived here,' continued Tadhg with a tone that suggested Drugal take some caution, '... once, and there are records affirming that in the city so this can be shown to be my home... Brother Richard's home. The pacts, however, were made between the Church of the Triune God and Mallow itself, no one particular person or persons there. If new residents can be attracted here it will be all the better for them and for us. I have asked Bezel and Crom Dubh to spread the word out to the outposts, dependencies, and protectorates of the kingdom, to the druids, the bards, the old men and women who may remember a different circumstance. Our kind elsewhere will surely know who supports the old ways and how many can be spared to come here and settle anew. The young...' he paused. 'Hopefully we can bring in new families and new blood.'

'Spared?' Drugal smiled knowingly at the pixie on his shoulder and assumed Tadhg's point.

'It is a wise approach. The humans bring us the spark of power, but we cannot simply order the wider members of the court to hand their people over to us. We would strengthen the center, true, but weaken the limbs. But a small portion of power from many weakens them only in insignificant ways, temporarily, while combining to strengthen the heart. So, of ten people of the old ways living in secret near Blarney, perhaps one would come here to live free and help re-build.' He turns his attentions back to Tadhg, 'but why those two?'

Tadhg shrugged the question off. 'The barons, counts, knights and ladies will know the message is truly from their king if a death speaker appears; it is a plea of mercy for Mallow and a sign of serious intent from me. I spent much of the last hours of yesterday speaking with Bezel and Crom Dubh and I found them wise, both of them. Winter falls upon us, Cousin, tough times call for hard measures, and hard folk to do the work.'

'I can be hard, sire.'

'I know, Talia. You are sufficient to the work. If anyone tells you otherwise send them to me.'

'My people can help, let us help. Give us a task too.' Tadhg regarded the small creature and found himself more impressed than he was with her the previous day. He gave the request serious attention.

'It seems to me, Talia, that while Mallow can be rebuilt new villagers will be starting with little in the way of needful items. Tell the pixie folk to pass the word near and far, tell the surly *clobhair-ceann*, the jolly *leprechauns* and the *boggart* pranksters to collect the neglected and forgotten pots and pans and spoons and discarded cups. Bring chairs, stools, and mats; bring tables from out of old workshops from carpenters now passed on. Knock on the doors of all the *seòmar bhrùnaidhs* across the kingdom and enlist their aid in this work.' Tadhg looked at Talia, wide-eyed now, mouth open but speechless. 'That is your task, Talia; your people are best suited to it.'

'Yes, sire,' she jumped into the air, spinning, and giggling merrily before flying off toward the north and into the woods only to return instantly heading in the opposite direction. Drugal looked on doubtfully at all this, and for his lack of attention got a small clump of dirt on his no-longer shining breastplate.

'Ah... filthy goblins!' He turned in a huff and sauntered off.

'I wonder if perhaps this court has been *seelie* too long?' Tadhg's utterance was met with squeals, laughter, and other joyous sounds from within the well.

§

'I know where the chieftain hid the true treasures of the village, Drugal.' Tadhg answers his cousin's question.

They were sat in council later in the evening of the first day. The new high court — the proud *sidhe*, the prudent *pooka* had representation; selected others who had become indispensable to the king sat here as well, Talia, Bezel, Crom Dubh.

'It is hardly dreams of Croesus, but it is a start. Perhaps you could make inquiry with the Queen of Armagh, your mother, my aunt, if donations could be sent?' Drugal nodded in approval of the request. It is an appeal because Drugal may be a *sidhe* and a prince in his own right, but he represented another, semi-autonomous, realm. Tadhg does not yet feel able to simply command the dukes and duchesses; soft persuasions are the order of the day.

'And I also know where my father, Rory I mean, stored the treasures I sent home from abroad as well as his own collected riches. There is magic in the written sagas of a master bard. Of course, these are not entirely mine to exploit as Rory had two natural sons and a daughter, who are my siblings by law of adoption if not blood and who are owed shares of it. I am the *Hidden* patron of the O'Rourke clan, and any future cadet branches; I shall act the part.' This announcement was met with general sounds of approval. All *sidhe* and some of the other *fae-folk* as well took on the wardship of human families. 'Perhaps soon we will all have humans to care for once again, to annoy or aid as the case may be, and arrest the decay of our collective might.'

§

[It is mid-November 1499]

Since Tadhg could not call upon the *Hidden* pathways for the time being, and since he insisted on taking on the task personally, he had to ride, and when the land got too dangerous, he had to walk and climb. He was heading toward a place of power known as *Cnoc Bui* or sometimes just Yellow Hill, the highest peak in the county. It took more time to get to the foot of the Boggeragh mountains, however, than it had to get to the nearby village of Balligagree, which was itself half a day's ride south-west from Mallow. It was the last settlement facing *Cnoc Bui*. Despite the presence of houses dedicated to the triune god of the Christ man, the village featured many megalithic stones, sacred monuments, and other markers of a distant past left undisturbed, all of which had to be visited and to which homage paid.

Tadhg was heading toward a point just below what once would have been the snow line, long and long ago. There was a cave, well concealed, where chieftains of ancient Mallow had stored the treasures of the village since time immemorial. Tadhg knew where it was because, age twelve, he had followed the chief of his Mallow just to see what there was to see.

It had been great fun and highly entertaining.

What amounted to treasure in the eyes of a child, even a *fae-child*, however, was often disappointing to the adult seeing it again, but Tadhg had prepared for that eventuality and was genuinely surprised to find not an unimpressive collection of trinkets, coins, weathered weapons, dried out scrolls (badly prepared for the environment in which they were stored) and other miscellaneous relics the meaning of which had passed out of the village's collective memory. The old archivist within him rose to the surface and tutted at the sight. It brought back to mind all his years in the monastic system learning the methods of parchment and artefact recovery and restoration.

It also surprised him that this one-time passion was still in his heart.

Am I responsible for that as well? He smirked.

'Drugal!'

Moments later the tell-tale signs of a pathway being opened began to appear, lighting up the far corners, nooks, and crannies of the cave, harkening a new arrival.

Drugal stepped into view.

He kept the gateway open; *trolls* carrying crates and chests stepped through followed by a few other volunteers. Tadhg directed their efforts, keeping the *trolls* to the heavy work, *pixies* collecting stray coins, and a *sidhe* woman who he had come to favor managing the precious, delicate scrolls with the application of magic. She had brought many to-purpose fashioned holders at Tadhg's direction. It would not be a long operation this, gathering all the necessary treasures, but Tadhg had further work to do so once satisfied with the effort, left Drugal in charge and slipped away toward his more personal mission. The cave was tagged now by the *fae-folk*; they could never lose knowledge of it. The trolls could seal the cave if Mallow ever assembled a treasure worth hiding away again.

§

Rory had been a canny man.

The family treasure, much of which Rory had assembled over the years of his travels (augmented by that bought and sent back home in Tadhg's), had been stored not in the Boggeraghs but in the Shehys far to the east. The lands were known everywhere for their peat bogs, coarse grasslands, and grand conifers. It is good growing land, sheep grazing land, and good hunting grounds as well (but mostly only for hare). Like old Yellow Hill, the foothills and valleys here also had the signs of long mortal habitation, monuments to ages gone by, ringforts, and *fulachta fia* or ancient cooking and brewing pits indicative of one-time settlement. Rory had written historic sagas of the land and life of the Shehy folk, including mention of stone constructed sweat houses built to capture the steam and heat of the stone boiled waters, which were said to have kept the warriors mighty and the pregnant women safely delivered of babes.

Tadhg had yet to see evidence of this innovation as he passed one site after another on his way to Gaugane Barra, the little island where Saint Finbarr had built his hermitage long and long ago.

The closer he got, however, the more pilgrims he met.

Oh, they were pleasant enough folk and assumed him to be one of them, a fellow traveler as it were, and he was invited to share meals and drink with one group or another at the end of the day's journey. As Tadhg preferred to travel in the evening and early morning, taking refuge from the day in the afternoon, he was usually gone from whichever group he had spent the evening with by the time they were up and moving. He had left little tokens of appreciation for the company and conversation, payments for the food and drink, and as tacit apology for stealing their blood as they slept or for taking his pleasure with some of them (those men and women who came to him in secret).

The pilgrims on the island clustered around the hermitage itself exploring what remained of the stone structures and bothering the resident Eremites only a little. Tadhg stood aside from all that, however, merely watching the comings and goings for a spell. This was not the first time he had been here, although never before without Rory leading him onward. Tadhg tried to bring to mind memories of those treks from Mallow, but memories rely on emotion, and Tadhg had suppressed his own for so long that it was still difficult to call them back to mind.

The ghost of his father was not walking beside him, as happened in so many fairy tales written for children.

Tadhg grew tired of the charade in time, shrugged, and moved on, following a well-known but highly personal path which used the hermitage itself only as a starting point. He did not have to think about it. Another hill, another cave, this one protected by *fae-magic* cast by Tadhg himself on one visit after he had learned of his heritage and been taught a few trickeries by his people. It was the same trick he had used in Ragusa, only reversed in effect. Rather than draw the wary in toward a trap, the symbols carved into rock faces here repelled the curious away. Rory had had an amulet of amber and silver so that he would be protected against the effect of the magic. Tadhg wondered briefly where that amulet now was? As the eldest it should have come to him; somehow, he knew it was in the possession of Bran's eldest son (whose name Tadhg could not recall… if he ever knew it at all).

It just then occurred to him that Bran or his son may already have come and removed the family treasure for safe keeping closer to their own home.

The thought did not really bother him much; he was interested, genuinely interested only in Rory's sagas, which had emotional value and upon which he had partially pinned the struggle against that which Mikaela had gifted him in her madness. Although he did not need assurances that he was on the right path, he knew he was the prickly sensations attacking the foreign aspects of his nature was a sure sign. Tadhg ignored them as best he was able. Hours later he came to a familiar rocky outcropping, a familiar oak tree (much bigger than he recalled, but somehow not as grand), he came upon the *fiadh* he knew was there.

The *fiadh* Rory had built with his own hands, before marriage, before children, before Mallow became his home. It only occurred to Tadhg then that he did not know where Rory had been born either. He had never asked; Rory had never volunteered the information.

Did that make me a bad son?

Tadhg paused and considered this question as he rested on the stone walls of the steam and cooking pit taking a drink from a skin (it did not hold water).

Had the bard shared that only with his *real* children?

Tadhg instantly regretted that word. In all the ways that mattered Rory had been his father. 'Sorry, Father,' he spoke aloud, 'that thought was uncalled for and unworthy of you.'

Having made amends, Tadhg regarded the ground carefully, mustering as much *Hidden* magic as was in him to use. The ground of the *fiadh* was layered in dust and dirt. Tadhg could see no tell-tale signs of disturbance (except small animal tracks). He put the skin away, stood, and moved to the back wall of the pit, feeling around the stones there for the loose ones, moving this one or that in a pattern which preventing the whole thing collapsing.

Where had you learned to build this way, Father?

The more important question was perhaps: *Did you share the knowledge in your saga?*

Tadhg thought of this and many questions he would have asked Rory when time was, too late now, but it was enough to pass the time away.

Hours passed.

A passing wolf paused nearby; he watched Tadhg labor without offering to help before finally moving off when another howl split the night. There were the sounds of insects singing to each other, the occasional bird call, and Tadhg was put in mind of his grove back in Ragusa.

Will I return there someday?

It was a question he could not answer in the present.

These and similar thoughts went through his mind as he worked, piles of stones gathering high on either side of him, working a growing hole in the wall and in the ground level of the pit. Although he could have squeeze through some time ago, Tadhg realized that he was enjoying himself and his commune with the spirit of his father too much to stop.

He could see by the lightening sky, however, that dawn was upon him. Early morning was the best time to go inside the cave, because the hole faced the sun directly at this time for at least a couple of hours.

He sat back and waited for the sun to break between the trees. Rory had cut a few down when time was to make the wait shorter although that contingency had long been usurped by nature.

Finally, Tadhg deemed the time right and slipped into the hole, dropping down about the height of a normal man to the sandy floor of a cave.

There, sitting against the wall of the cave as if expecting him, was Rory.

Well, the white bones, tattered robes and leather shoes of Rory.

It occurred to Tadhg just then that he had never been informed where the body of his father had been laid to rest long and long ago, assuming him to have been cremated in the traditional Marrow fashion and spread over the forest he so loved. This came as a surprise indeed.

Rory still, after a fashion, wore the amulet too. It had fallen through his ribs, some of which had crumbled already, and rested tangled against what remained of his spine, amidst beaded necklaces, a silver necklace, and a leather strap (which Tadhg could not recall ever having seen, but which had the look of child's work).

Tadhg bent down near the body. Another might have shed a tear, but he could not yet bring one on this time, although he was aware of an internal struggle between the aspects of his nature — *strigoii, fae-folk*, and human too. Rory had come here to die.

How did he re-build the wall from the inside?

Tadhg looked from his father's resting place back to the wall of the cave with this question in mind. Admittedly, he was stuck for an answer. It was then he noticed the clay pot leaning against the big bone of his father's right leg, and he knew what it was, a scroll-holder. He reached down and picked it up. The pot was solid enough still, no breaks, and the lid held tight. It was one of many that should be here.

Tadhg opened it, carefully, and looked inside. Sure enough, there was parchment within, a few sheets by the looks of it. Evaluating the pages, he found that they were not yet too brittle, the pot had kept them in fairly supple condition...

My son,

I hope you remember the old cipher we developed. It was play then, but serious now, should these old bones somehow be found.

If you are reading this, then I was correct. I knew you would come here, someday; I knew it. I also knew that something dark was coming toward Mallow. How did I know? Your true mother the queen, Uonaidh, convinced me of it. Therefore, perhaps she was correct as well, finally.

After the death of my dear Katherine, I was given the honor of frequent meetings with your other father and mother, your other parents, and in an aside one day Uonaidh recalled an old vision of her own which had not yet come to pass after long and long. It foretold the destruction of Mallow, perhaps, it was unclear precisely as visions often are, but much death, bloodshed, and great confusion was to reign in the aftermath of this disaster to come. She and the king had come to dismiss such thoughts as mistaken, saying that your mother's gift was flawed and imperfect. Much was seen, little came to pass, or so it was told to me. Although she did not say so, I believe that she still believed in it, her vision that is, and I came to believe in it too for reasons I do not know why. Call it artistic intuition if you will, I make I have thought of you often son; no one of us held it against you that you did not return home. I did not expect you would. None of this is your fault, everything has a purpose. Always remember that everything has a purpose; the gods are sometimes queer but never without end. Many dreamed of undertaking a journey not unlike yours, and some did, the friends of your youth. I do not know where many of these wanderers went, some few came home with marvelous tales, but others did not. Perhaps one or two found you? I will list them below; their tales are recorded in the parchments bound with the red ribbon. Perhaps you can find them and theirs' after whatever is to happen comes to pass.

You cannot have failed to notice that amulet you crafted for me still hanging from these old bones, now bleached white and cleaned by little creatures, or laying in the dust from my bones once laying here. I did not pass it on to Bran or Sean, obviously, because you needed to find this note; it had to be you; they would not have understood; this is your legacy.

They do not know.

We never discussed it in their presence. Bran was too young to have anything but hazy memories of you. Many of the trinkets and toys you sent had been left with your siblings for whom they were meant, taken when they left home, or discarded where and when they may. Don't be angry with them for that; humans are irrational creatures; children even more so.

The documents from this "bank?" you wrote of, in Venice, where you had deposited coin for your siblings... those are with the canons at St Fin's, safeguarded. You will know how to retrieve them and pass them on when the time comes. I thought it best your brothers and sister does not know of this other largess; in case they should fritter it away. Bran may not have; Sean is not overburdened with wisdom and Clara dreams only of tending a home with a man and children within. Time will tell if this was a wise thing to do or no. See that these parchments get to their rightful holders' son.

As you have now seen, the least valuable of my, our, treasures have been left in plain sight, including one or two of the more valuable items should some grave robbers find them. It should prevent them from looking too much closer. The more valuable, coin from many a land, gold and silver from my time and from your travels sent home, are all in the rabbit hole. My saga and the manuscripts and bound books you sent are in the fox hole, wrapped as you wrote against age and clime. I hope I did it correctly. Forgive me, I could not bear to look, fearing I would be lost in time and unable to do what must be done.

I grow tired; the pain in my arm cannot long be ignored. I think my time has finally come. Forms take place before my eyes, Katherine, with a babe in arms, my forebears, some old friends come to escort me. You were always loved Tadhg, always. Find the time to say what must be said, to do what must be done. Ask forgiveness when needed, forgive when asked. Trust in your own judgement and that of our gods. I do not know enough of this triune god, but his son seems like a good fellow. Take my best ring for yourself, my second best to Bran and my third to Sean. Give your mother's ring to Clara, or her daughter if time has passed as far as that. Be fair with what remains.

Rory

P.S. Your father the king sent some goblins to shadow, and protect, and finally to bury me here. Already they are placing the last few stones. In case you were wondering.

Tadhg laughed at the final notation as he rolled the scrolls back up and placed them carefully back into their pot. He stored the pot in his own carrying bag. He wondered if he should now bury the bones of his father as he lifted the amulet out of his ribs, removed the necklaces, rings and bracelets symbolic of his office, rank, and profession. It would not matter to the bones either way, and the cave made a good sepulcher.

'Drugal!' His cousin had been waiting for the call and appeared out of the opened pathway.

'Oh!' was the first thing he said, 'is that…' Tadhg nodded. 'Typical bard!' he commented, 'dramatic even after the end comes. I presume there was a note?' Tadhg nodded again.

'Have a troll bring in a couple large crates. That should be enough for my purpose here. I will pack them myself.' Drugal did not ask why, he knew, and simply did his cousin's bidding.

Tadhg searched the holes that Rory wrote of, which were actually hidden sections of the cave system, finding all was as it should be, and he started moving materials and packing them securely, some of which he recognized, some of which were new to him. The O'Rourke treasure was not a king's ransom, but it had noteworthy value and Tadhg was careful with it. As he worked, in his mind he labelled what should go to Bran's family, what to Sean's and what to Clara's, or their heirs at least, separating these into particular crates, and what few trinkets and mementoes he would keep himself, packing these into his pack. He held on to an ivory elephant for a moment recalling the circumstance of its acquisition, likewise a silver cup, and a golden French coin, and a clay Magyar idol, these, and a few others, held long forgotten but now remembered recollections of his earlier life.

Once everything was packed up, Tadhg supervised the removal of the crates giving clear instructions what was to be done with them until his return to Mallow, a journey he would undertake on foot. Just as Drugal made ready to leave, Tadhg bid him stay a moment longer.

'Cousin?'

'I was thinking matters over, Cousin, and I think a trek to *An Seisure* is necessary, at least for me. Ask a druid to stay near Mallow and await my return. I would like to know the best time to go and seek out the gods' wisdom.' Drugal bowed and spread his hands silently saying that he would do so; a trek to *An Seisure* was a serious matter indeed.

14

[It is December 1ˢᵗ, 1499]

The time was right, the time was now; everything was in place.

Tadhg and Drugal had consulted on the details of the ritual ceremony with the druids back in Mallow over and over again, and the king now got about the work of setting everything else in place. He would kneel before the bowl, on the opposite side of which were placed the relics, all before the Kingstone. The versifier and celebrant would stand behind and to either side of him. Forming an arch behind them would be the spirits of Mallow and in a semi-circle around all of them would be the king's *Hidden* court. Drugal, as a true kin of the king, would officiate.

Tadhg made a hand gesture to begin.

His left hand was set straight out with the thumb pointed down while his right hand was set out in a similar way, though with the thumb pointed up. He brought his two hands together forming a kind of rectangle, through which he peered at the assembled creatures. As he pulled his hands apart, expanding the rectangular viewing window, he tacitly called upon the darkness to lift itself away, and the ghosts and *Hidden folk* were suddenly visible to the two mortals. It was necessary that the assembly hide nothing from the gods or from each other. Whether the spirits of Mallow were any more aware of their participation than the donkey was unknown.

When all was quiet; when the two mortals had signaled their readiness and moved into position, Tadhg turned around and knelt before the Kingstone. He bowed his head and made a silent prayer that everything would go as planned.

Drugal then stepped forward as if out of the Kingstone itself.

The light effect that the king had cast reflected off the *fae* prince's silver armor in all directions. It must have looked as if a god had manifested before them. Tadhg heard a muffled "Zounds" from somewhere behind him, recognizing Talia's voice.

He smiled despite himself and the seriousness of the situation.

The Silver Prince made his way carefully through the relic field, finally approaching the bowl (now uncovered). Tadhg could smell the blood collected within. It had been mystically purified and preserved, which gave it an appealing quality. It was the blood of the two humans mixed with the king's own tainted ichor, the uncorrupted ichor of some of the *Hidden* (voluntary), and particles scraped off some of the relics and burnt-out buildings of Mallow. Drugal opened his hands and the bowl moved (as if by its own efforts) to rest in his grasp. Tadhg was impressed with his cousin's fine control of elemental forces.

'Who comes before An Seisear?' Drugal's voice had taken on a tone and timbre that was suspiciously stentorian. Perhaps the gods were paying attention.

'I do,' said Tadhg.

'And who are you?'

'I am the Hidden King of Éire and of the aos *sí*, the children of Érui. I am the Prince of Munster and Duke of Corcaigh, son of the High King Fionnbharr and High Queen Uonaidh. I am also Tadhg McRory, son of Rory O'Rourke of the blood of *the* Rourke and his wife Katherine Nic Gilly of ancient Magh nAla now called Mallow. I am the *Stolen One*; I am the one of the *Otherland* who cannot return to the *Otherland*.' Drugal nodded and turned to the bard.

'And who are you?'

'I am called Lóegaire of Bweeng, known as the Bard of Corca Duibne. I am the versifier called for in the ancient tomes, and I will speak the words of the oath to be sworn by the king.' Drugal nodded in acceptance and turned to the woman.

'And who are you?'

'I...' she stumbled over the words, but quickly righted herself, 'am Feidlimid of ancient Magh nAla, now called Mallow, the druid's daughter. I am the celebrant called for in the ancient tomes, and I will witness the king's oath-taking.' Drugal nodded in acceptance.

'And these others?' As one, the spirits of Mallow wailed piteously.

'They are the wronged,' said the king after the wailing had died down.

'And those beyond?'

'We are the aos *sí* and Hidden Court of Munster,' the host replied as one. Dubhgall could not be sure, but he thought he also heard a muffled giggle.

'They are my congregation,' said the king. 'I belong to them and they to me, but we are isolated one from the other.'

'And why have you come here this night, Hidden King?' Lóegaire stepped forward a pace as Tadhg bowed his head in supplication.

'He comes in search of knowledge, exalted one. He would avenge the people of ancient Magh nAla, now called Mallow, for the crime committed against them, against all decency and justice. He would learn who is to blame for this crime. He would know who to punish and how this must be done. He would also beg a boon of the gods. Let the curse upon him be lifted; let this great wrong be righted once again and let the king return to his people in the *Otherland* of Éire.' Drugal nodded as the bard took a step back into his earlier position. He turned his gaze upon the king once again.

'You seek no vengeance against the creature that cursed you?'

Tadhg shook his head. 'No. She was cursed already and did not know that which she did, and I loved her.'

'And what say you to this request, Celebrant?'

'I say it is worthy.'

'I believe so as well,' intoned Drugal, 'but it is not our decision, maiden.' He turned and faced the Kingstone, offering up the bowl of blood.

All heads were bowed.

All was silent.

The seconds seemed like minutes; the minutes seemed like hours. The silence was becoming heavy, unbearable for the three main supplicants. Then, without warning, thunder rumbled in the distance. And then again, moved ever closer to the assembly. All of a sudden, a deafening boom reverberated around the party, shaking the ground just as a bolt of lightning struck the stone in unnatural sequence. When the sky grew quiet again Drugal turned to face the assembly, but it was no longer the noble being they all now knew. He was something more. His eyes were black as the void; his hair was standing straight out around his head; his voice, when he spoke, was no longer his but someone's, something's, other than his own.

'We four have heard your plea, Stolen One, and we answer you thusly...'

Drugal's aspect took on the suggestion of tempest and fire; his silver locks turned to the bright oranges, yellows and reds of an inferno.

'I, the Mórrigan, The Crow, The Doom-sayer, She of Fate, bless this request. In exchange for my blessing, however, death must be meted out by the king himself. The blood of the wicked must be wiped out, to the last generation. Do this, and vengeance and justice will both be served.'

The voice faded and Drugal's aspect changed again, now to a suggestion of moonlight in a glade, shadows played around him, and the scent of medicinal herbs was plain.

'I, the Brigid, The Healer, The Poet, and the Patron of Smiths, bless this request. In exchange for my blessing, however, the king must take the blood of the wicked into himself so that it can be mixed with the offering and the taint erased for all time. Do this, and the soul of the king will be healed.'

The voice faded and Drugal's aspect changed again. There was a suggestion of forests and flowers blooming about, petals now falling from the sky.

'I, Eriu, The Land Personified, and Guardian of the sidhe, bless this request. In exchange for my blessing, however, the wicked must be made to know why they are punished so, no matter how far the acorn from the oak. Do this, and the land will have its hidden king again and it will recover from the scars it has gained and has yet to gain.'

The voice faded away and the petals faded from view. Drugal's aspect changed yet again, this time to a suggestion of happiness and humor, laughter in the background.

'I, Ogma, He of the Golden Chains, The Eloquent One, and He of Persuasion and Prophecy also gives blessing to this request. In exchange for my blessing, however, the king must keep a record of his acts for posterity. These acts must be witnessed by the Hidden; these acts must be aided and abetted by the mortals, the people of the celebrant and the versifier. Do this so that none can say thee nae; none can say we were not involved. Do this, and the king shall know the wisdom of the ancients and of the gods, and peace shall be brought to the land as fraction and fiction yet to come will be healed and forgotten.'

That voice did not fade; indeed, all four divine respondents spoke in a voice of powers ancient and formidable. Drugal spoke with the voice of all the gods.

'Drink of the blessed blood, oh King, and seal your fate and seal that also of these here assembled. Tied now to your own fate are those of the living and the dead.'

The bowl was lowered to his waiting lips and the king drank deep and to the dregs.

Drugal held up the now empty bowl for all to see and witness; it would shortly be burned in the sacred flame.

'It is done. The oath is taken. Let it be known to one and all of the Hidden the actions taken this day. Let the wicked suffer to the last generation of their blood. Let the healing commence. Let the witness be appointed, and let the humans know their parts. We have spoken and will say no more until the end.'

Drugal shivered and dropped the bowl, almost falling over.

Tadhg reacted fast, reaching up and steading him again.

'What happened, Cousin? Did it work?'

'For a moment you were the voice of the *gods,* Cousin.'

'Did they give their blessing?' The king nodded.

'And more than that, Drugal, much more, but let us finish here.' Drugal nodded, picking up the dropped bowl.

'Bard,' he said, 'fetch your pipes and play us a somber tune. Celebrant, take the bowl as instructed and place it on the fire.' Most of the Hidden broke ranks. Some moved to watch the bowl burn, which would slowly char to ashes while others gamboled about in their ranks and spoke of days to come and the meaning of the various blessings. Tadhg would remain where he was for the time being, before the Kingstone and the relics, considering his divinely appointed tasks.

§

After the ceremony, when the somber tunes were finished, when the relics had been blessed with the ashes of the bowl, when all was packed back into the cart, silence had descended upon the pilgrims. The spirits of the victims had faded away a while ago and returned to their haunts. Even the *Hidden* host had wondered into the secret passages and returned to the woods around Mallow. Now, only seven remained. Six sat around the fire; one was off searching out more of the succulent grasses.

Tadhg, Lóegaire and Feidlimid had donned simple shifts and sandals, neither ceremonial dress nor nudity needed any further, besides which the night air was too chilly for the mortals to stay unclothed. Even Drugal had removed his more usual bright armor for more casual attire. Talia, sat now on the king's shoulder, was dressed again and wrapped in a little shawl for added protection from the elements. Bezel, in his rags and red cap, sat scowling and poking the fire. The *fae* remained visible to the mortal pair as they were all bound together now, much to the red-cap's distaste. He did not like being nice to mortals, or to *sidhe* (he was none too pleased with the gods for that matter), but he stoically accepted his fate.

Lóegaire had secreted some wine and stronger spirits in the cart, and these were now passed around, Talia drinking from her thimble. 'What does it mean, sire, *to the last of their generations*?' Despite her diminutive size Talia's voice could be heard clearly by all, and the humans could understand it, divinely bonded as they now were to the king.

'*To the last generation*', Tadhg corrected. 'It means every one of their direct blood lines, children and grand-children and such.' Feidlimid nodded sadly.

'Children are innocent,' she said.

Tadhg regarded the girl, or woman, a long moment and wondered if she had children of her own. 'I agree with you in principle, Celebrant, but the reasoning behind the task is not unfounded in logic. The wickedness of the despoilers is now a taint in their souls and in their blood. This will be passed on and down to descendants, if left unchecked much evil could spring up again.' The woman regarded the king with some confusion, but his words had attracted the interest of the others around the fire too. Tadhg noticed this, 'Here, let me explain.'

'You see, my father was a king, so I am a king by right of birth. There is a mystical connection there in the blood of my fathers and between my being therefore, and that of the people and the land over which he was king.' He winked at Drugal, who smiled and nodded. 'Now, a weak king creates a weak land.'

'Ah, 'tis true,' said Bezel.

'Our land, Ireland, has been without me since I was stolen from it. The mystical connection has been almost broken. As I am cured, that is to say as the curse upon me is lifted, so too will that curse cast upon the land by the despoilers. The land will become strong and pure once again. Just as you are the child of a druid, Celebrant, so your blood is touched by the wild places, just as his had been. Your children and their children will always have that mark. Perhaps an affinity for animals or the ability to bring forth life from exhausted soil will give truth to the connection.'

'Still,' Lóegaire looked up from the fire, now burning low but strong. 'Killing children… seems wrong. It is wrong.'

'I agree with you both,' Tadhg nodded, 'so this is my promise. No child will be killed by my hand. We will watch them, note their movements, and the passage of time, but no one will be killed until they have at least made an approach to their third decade.' Bezel shook his head.

'This is no time for sentimentality, sire.'

'I find myself in agreement with the *red cap*, Cousin. That is all very noble sounding,' said Drugal, sipping at the wine. Bezel quickly regarded the hated *sidhe* and snorted in his direction, just as quickly looked away again. 'But that also means that the taint of the wicked has a chance to infect another generation. No offense is meant to my two new friends here, but mortals breed quickly, and they do not often wait till their third decade to do so! It could be you are extending the time before which the penitent act can be completed.'

'We have time yet, Cousin.'

'Why can we not just kill them all now and be done with it?' Bezel growled out the question. Mystical connections be damned, he was no friend of mortals.

'Aye, *we* do.' Drugal said, ignoring the interruption. He indicated himself and the king as he spoke, but then indicated the man and woman sat with them, 'their kind does not. As long as the wicked blood is still present on this good green earth you cannot be lifted of your curse and Ireland cannot be cleansed of its troubles. You heard the words; this land will suffer great misfortunes until the *Hidden* king is back in his proper place.'

'Then we must work as quickly and efficiently as possible.'

Drugal heard the words and intent of the conclusion, but he was clearly left without any further understanding of the king's meaning. 'I agree,' Tadhg continued, 'that delaying justice upon children is an added burden upon us all, there are other ways that we can act to alleviate the delay, however. I will need volunteers to take the case to other *Hidden* courts. This should be simple diplomacy; the gods said that all the *Hidden* are now bound in this quest. There should be no question of aid granted. Once we find the names of the soldiers of that fateful day, we can track them down and keep watch upon them and their heirs. Who better than the *Hidden* to undertake such a mission, Drugal? The *sidhe* can appeal to the kings and queens and nobles and our *red caps* and *trolls* can appeal to their kin in those foreign lands. And how far afield could these soldiers have gone in less than a decade?' Drugal nodded.

'True.'

'You might be surprised sire just how far a man can go in his small time.' Everyone turned to the bard.

'The bard speaks true,' growled Bezel, showing Lóegaire a modicum of respect. 'You know that I have had much interaction with mortals, particularly the scum of the race, and they are surprising in many ways. Lord Silver Breeches is right too.' He thumbed in Drugal's direction, 'They breed like rabbits, and they live… fast lives. Blink and a mortal child is old, blink again and they have a brood of twenty or more running about them. And these men, they were soldiers, right? They dip their wicks everywhere they can. Probably, they's got little bastards here, there, and yonder too. Do all of them count?'

Tadhg slowly nodded his head. 'They must do, blood is blood.'

Bezel pointed at Feidlimid, 'I reckon the bitches know how many bastards they have, but these men will not know and why would they? Nothing to them really are they now?' Feidlimid's expression grew angry, but Tadhg placed a restraining hand on her arm.

'Don't take offense, Celebrant, his are a rough people, but wise in their way and our abrasive cousin here is quite right beside it. You mortals do have strange ways.' He thought about the issue a moment.

'Bezel, you *are* wise in your way, and I am glad I thought to include you in my company and at my table. I might not have thought of the by-blows of human lusts. I think perhaps the situation is not so dire as you fear, however. The creature that I have become, although a war within me rages still, affords me an advantage yet. Although I have rarely considered it, the act of supping on blood floods the mind with the memories of the blood. I think if I could concentrate enough upon it, events forgotten by the man may well be revealed to me in the blood. The man may forget an action, a face, a name, a place, but the blood remembers to the end of its days.'

Bezel was listening to this with close attention. 'You mean to say,' he wondered aloud, 'that a man can fuck a girl in Dublin one day and forget her the next, but his blood will supply a name years later?' Tadhg shrugged.

'Perhaps not so cut and dried as all that. He must first have known a name. A face, certainly, would be imprinted, a place too and the time in his life I should think. If such is the case, careful investigation, a few calculations, should reveal the rest. Age the face, the time, the place, and search the town. We'll ask questions in taverns, if a child resulted, we'll uncover the details soon enough.'

'I have a question, sire.'

'Talia?' All eyes turned to the little pixie.

'Well,' she wrung her hands, 'what if all that is the case, but we are too late, and the child is already dead?'

'Ah, yes.' The campfire crackled in the silence of the stalled discussion.

'What does that mean?' The king regarded the red cap across the flames.

'It means that the blood may have dried up.' Drugal took a sip of his wine. Bezel shrugged and poked the fire back into a little more life.

The bard spoke. 'The gods do not set impossible tasks. They burden us with perhaps a little more than we can carry to force us to get stronger, however.'

'Yes,' said the king, slowly, considering the case and question raised. 'We need not overthink it, lest we be digging up leeches once used by barber-surgeons on the field of combat. Besides, the situation may not arise. But,' the king held up his hand to forestall Bezel's objections, 'if it does, we will consider our actions then.'

'And what of us, sire?' Tadhg regarded the bard again. 'The word of the gods mentioned us too,' he indicated Feidlimid and himself.

'Yes, and I have considered it, Lóegaire. You and your people must be, are, involved now. There is no way that is not the case.' He fell silent in thought.

'I believe that it would be best if your kind did none of the actual killings; that will be my burden alone, my responsibility, my oath to fulfil. But there will be much that will need to be overseen elsewise, as we have been discussing. Aid the *Hidden* in the tracking down of the tainted souls; protect my people from yours should they be somehow uncovered. Keep a record of these things, of all the findings, as *the* Ogma demanded. I would see no other harm come to wives and husbands of the tainted ones, perhaps your kind can arrange… compensations, gifts of treasure, sent anonymously after the fact?'

'But you too will have to work in the shadows. Your kind will be aided in turn by the *Hidden*. A journal must be kept, so says the will of the gods. I will write it, but I cannot carry it around wherever I go. How many books this will tally out to is beyond my guess. A library full which must be kept hidden and secure somewhere. Your descendants, Lóegaire, and those of you Feidlimid, and those alive now who escaped the fall of Mallow, will fulfil these other, no less important roles. The sons of Lóegaire and the daughters of Feidlimid will be creatures of destiny and never forgotten or abandoned to cruel fate by us. They will be, as the two of you have now been, gifted with the ability to see the *Hidden* in their truest forms, and the *Hidden* will know your descendants for who and what they are, blessed of the gods and the king. The gods demanded witnesses, so yours will fulfil that role too.'

He paused, 'Be fruitful, we will aid your legacies. Your descendants will be of the best families, noble in both spirit and character, the children of wealth and privilege in fact from now until the end of days. Neither of you are currently married…'

Lóegaire shook his head and so did Feidlimid. 'But I was,' said the bard. 'I have two sons and a daughter already. Are they too included in this divine charge?' The king paused, shrugged.

'I do not believe that they *must be*, as preceding the ritual, but I see no reason that they *cannot be* if that is your decision, Versifier. From this point on, however, the children of your bodies, and the children of theirs, will be so blessed. That is all that is certain.'

'I am my uncle's ward, sire,' said Feidlimid. 'Under the law I have no choice but to marry where he directs.'

'True, but the *Hidden* have ways and means of… influencing the acts of mortals. We can find you a better, more suitable and superior mate than one your uncle might ever secure, and he will be happier for it. We will also scout out the best specimens for your prosperity. Your descendants will be the best of your race; kings, queens, and champions to be.' The two human members of this little society were pleased by this promise and clearly happy with the decision.

'Yes, well, that's fine, Cousin,' said Drugal, 'but the gods said that you must be witnessed as well by one of *us*. Is that the role I am to assume do you think?' Tadhg smiled across the fire at his most noble cousin, but shook his head no.

'For a time, Drugal, I will by necessity be away from my people... again. But they cannot be left without a ruler. You must act for me in that regard and Bezel will aid you. I can trust no one more than you to do it and he to advise. You must be my eyes and ears among the *Hidden*, you must speak, but when you speak, they must hear *my* voice. You will be my regent. When an ambassador to another court, an envoy to a new land, is needed, you will judge the worthiness of those volunteers and find the right candidate. You will administer and manage my personal treasure; use it as you see fit; arrange for whatever payments will need to be made out of it, any number of things, you are more familiar with such tasks than I. In time you will tutor me once again, just as you have been. Then, when the time is upon us, you must step aside for me to resume my destined role. For a time, Cousin, your demesne in Armagh will be wed to mine in Munster. You will be the most powerful *Hidden* monarch in the world, though I wish no harm on the queen your mother my aunt. Can you undertake that mission in the knowledge that you will have to give it up, the greater part at least, one day?'

'Can I do something too, sire?'

Tadhg smiled and turned his head to regard the pixie.

'Would I leave you out, Talia? You are most loyal, my first proclaimer in fact. You, if you wish it, will be my companion and chief witness in the years to come, however many these may be. My immediate protector and my guardian in the height of the day should I rest, the keeper of my notes too. You are my amanuensis now. There will be a thousand tasks for you, if you wish to do them?' The pixie nodded, more solemn than she had ever been, eyes big and bright.

'I can do that; I will be a good soldier sire, I really will. Ah... man... usus, Talia, I will be the best one of those ever!' Tadhg winked across the fire at Drugal, who shrugged his shoulders at the wisdom of this particular decree, but accepted it, nonetheless.

'I have no doubt, Talia, no doubt at all. Anyway,' he turned to address the rest of the small company. 'I would suggest that you all sleep now; Drugal, Talia, Bezel, if you wish to remain with us, fine, but you have leave to return *via* the hidden roads if you wish it. In the morning, for a time I may wish to rest in the cart and the two of you,' he addressed the mortals, 'will be alone for the walk back. Donkey knows the way, worry not for him.'

Lóegaire and Feidlimid glanced at each other and as one proclaimed, 'Resting in the cart?'

Tadhg sighed. Drugal and Talia took on worried expressions. The king regarded the two humans a moment longer. 'You deserve to know the truth; we are tied together now.' He fell silent and gathered his thoughts. Talia looked concerned and placed her tiny hand against his cheek as a signal of support.

'You could not have failed to hear the gods call me the *Stolen One* and speak of lifting the curse upon me.' The king looked from one to the other mortal. They both nodded. 'The word *stolen* is rarely used among our kind... no, let me begin again. Do either of you know what the *abhartach* is? Bard, you must know that word.' Feidlimid glanced at the bard as well.

'Aye,' he drew out the word, 'it comes down to us from long and long ago, from ancient Slaghtaverty. There was this dwarf, or small man, who was said to have been a magician, and with his power, he was corrupted into a dreadful tyrannical ruler who perpetrated great and terrible cruelties upon his people. He was vanquished by *the* Fionn Mac Cumhail, chieftain of a neighboring tribe who finally heard the wailing of the victims of his neighbor. The *abhartach* was killed and laid to rest, buried in a standing position as is the custom. However, the curse of it had not been removed. He was back the next night, appearing in his old haunts, crueler toward his people, and more vigorous in his tortures upon those who he charged with betrayal. He now drank their blood. *The* Fionn came and slew him a second time and buried him again, but as before, he escaped the grave and now spread terror across the whole of the land. *The* Fionn sought the wisest of the druids, and according to his advice did slay the dwarf a third time, buried him in his grave, but this time head downwards. This confused his magic and he never again appeared. The grave is still there to this day.'

'I know this story,' said Bezel, 'but the druid calls the dwarf *neamhmairbh* or, the walking dead. He must be killed with a sword of yew, the grave surrounded with thorns, a large stone covering.'

The bard nods, 'Yes, I have heard these changes as well. But sire, you are hardly a creature of mindless destruction or dead.'

Tadhg smiled and accepted the statement.

'There are many legends from many lands of such and similar creatures, bard. I have met some of them and know of others. I am one of them, of a sort. I am *strigoii* but *moroaică*.' He sighed, remembering the first time he heard these words spoken. Perhaps not so terrible a curse as the *abhartach* or the bloated *nosferatu* of the English but cursed nonetheless.' The gathering fell silent until Tadhg raised his eyes from the fire.

'But call me by my name, Lóegaire, you as well Feidlimid. As I've said we are bound together by the ritual and the gods' blessings and decrees. Alas, my friends, I am one of those cursed beings. You may doubt, but when we first met, and when we travelled the mystic road, you were frightened of me. It's true; I could see it in your eyes. It is my imposed nature. *Strigoii* are not the walking dead; nor are we wild creatures of mindless destruction, as you said, at least, not in the first years of our condition. When a creature such as I, of whatever kind, infects a mortal they do so out of loneliness more often than they do out of maliciousness. Such was my case. I loved her and she loved me. But she... your kind... was not meant for an expanded life, much less immortality. Your minds cannot bare it because you were meant to live no more than three score and ten, perhaps a few years more or less. You know from your own experiences that old mortals often have the minds of children. This is why such creatures when uncovered and confronted appear mad and wild.'

'The mortal body can live on, shored by the curse of unnatural immortality. But the mortal mind degenerates beyond reasoning skills, beyond sure memories, or even any of the kinder virtues. All that finally remains are the basic instincts of survival, finding food, shelter, and reproduction. Our two species, by which I mean the *fae* and the mortal, are incompatible. We cannot successfully produce offspring together. This fact somehow stayed the hand of the dreaded curse within me. The *fae* can be infected by the curse,' the king moved his hands, now claws, in demonstration of the fact, 'but this brings on an internal war between our true nature and the imposed nature. My noble cousin found me at the point where I had almost forgot myself, and he aided me in the struggle to return. My true nature is asserting itself, finally, this is true, but I can never be rid of the curse within without divine succor. While I can think like the *fae* do, my body cannot withstand the light of day for long without growing very,

very tired; my senses are subdued then in ways you could not understand, yet also sharpened to the point where a natural predator like a wolf would be envious. I can keep the creature at bay within, employ the benefits without giving in to the weaknesses, but it is a constant battle. Even now, I can hear the blood circulating through your veins, your heightened heartbeats, Bezel's and Drugal's slower beats, and the shortened breaths of the prey confronted by the marauder.' Tadhg raised his hand, the hand of a *fae* again, with palm out to forestall further anxiety.

'I am in control of these faculties provided I do not go long and long without nourishment, and I will add with considerable pride, that my people have generously supplied me with nourishment aplenty. I mean no offense by this, but the blood of your people is weak compared to the ichor of the *fae*, it could barely sustain me. This is perhaps the case because I am not a human man, was not, so that only the blood of my own people is truly satisfying to my condition.' He fell silent and his companions said nothing, merely watching the leaping flames of the fire.

'In any case,' he finally continued, 'as you must trust me, I must trust you in turn. I cannot walk for long and long in the light outside of this magic glade, but I also cannot in this condition employ the hidden routes of the *fae*. I am not pure. So, I must trust you to return me to Mallow where my people will guard me and the ghosts surround me. The two of you and your descendants are my people now as well until the end of days. This I swear.'

Lóegaire was the first to speak. 'Then so be it. You will be safely returned, whether the rivers overrun their banks or run dry in the meantime. You have my word.'

'And mine,' added Feidlimid. 'Although, I am no combatant, ah... Tadhg.'

The king nodded his thanks. 'I am touched by your trust. And worry not, Feidlimid, you have but to call for help and the *Hidden* will always respond. You are the sister of their king, and you, Lóegaire, you are his brother by ties closer now than blood. You are all such to me now, Drugal, Bezel, and Talia.'

'Well,' said Drugal, 'that is settled then. I must return to Mallow and begin preparations for... well everything to come, it seems. Talia, do you wish to come with me?' Talia looked from the prince to the king and back again.

'I will remain here. I am the king's am... amun... nuisance.' This caused a good deal of laughter and chuckling. When a smiling Tadhg took pity on her and explained the difference, Talia turned red and crawled under his tunic to hide.

'She'll be fine with me, Cousin. Godspeed, and farewell 'til we meet again.'

'And you, Cousin, and to you as well my new friends… Bezel?' The two mortals returned the salutation. Bezel thought about it.

'I'll stay with the king. I have my axe. No harm will come to any of them.' Drugal nodded, turned and walked off, vanishing from sight.

15

THE CURIOUS CASE OF CHARLES LA RUSHE Ten years ago, Charles La Rushe wrote down a cryptic message then he seemingly disappeared into the night, never to be heard from again. Could this final note be the key to understanding his MURDER?

East Sussex has given us a few bizarre true crime scenarios over the decades of the twentieth century — the classified ads cannibals, the rolling stoning, and the Combe Haven hangings, to name a few. But rarely, however, has the shire given us something quite so strange and unsettling as the MAGTZA-fall, or the MAGTZA case.

While it may sound like a word one might question on a SCRABBLE board (if one had a particularly demonic opponent) it is, in fact, the cryptic first clue to a puzzling death that remains unsolved to this day.

The year is 1954.

Kitty Kallen is riding the top of the charts with "Little things mean a Lot", and Charles La Rushe is an unemployed motor engineer on the Strade. He can't hold down a job; he has problems with the bottle, and a precarious financial situation. But these are lesser worries for La Rushe who lives under the large shadow of CLINICAL PARANOIA. He had the creeping belief that he was being targeted by a mysterious and sinister presence, but no one would listen to him. This included his wife Cynthia, who told the Observer that every now and then for weeks before his disappearance La Rushe would mention his fears of 'him' or 'them' coming for him. There was no more detailed description of the shadowy figures, except for a black cane. Whoever 'he' is, whoever 'they' are, La Rushe was desperate for someone to believe that they intended him great harm.

On the evening of November 18, La Rushe was at home, in his bedroom, sitting cosy in his chair. The radio is tuned into a classic station, and he is reading a book. Cynthia is in the parlour. Without any warning she hears her husband shout, "That's it! Now it all makes sense! I'm no killer!" As she runs into the room her husband is scribbling down the word 'MAGTZA' or perhaps 'MA6TZA' — investigators are split over whether the 'G' is in fact a number '6' or no. According to Cynthia, seconds later her husband calmed down, crossed out the mysterious message, and abruptly left their house.

It's late, but La Rushe has decided he needs a drink. He has climbed into his 1952 Ford Consul and heads for the nearby town of Silverhill. Witnesses place him in his favourite pub, the King Henry, near St Matthew's, where he ordered a pint of bitter. Before his could drink it, however, La Rushe collapsed to the floor, injuring his nose. Witnesses are surprised by the tumble. Everyone says that he was perfectly sober at that time.

This episode happens at 11 PM, but for La Rushe, the night is far from over.

After regaining consciousness, he left the bar, drink untouched, and for the next two and a half hours his whereabouts are unknown.

At approximately 2.30 AM La Rushe is next sighted in his childhood hometown of St Leonards-on-Sea. There, he sought out a woman from his youth.

Kelly Mason tells us that she was quite put off by the early morning visit and did not invite La Rushe inside her home. Instead, she braves a lengthy and rambling monologue where he warns her of an upcoming "horrible and tragic event." Mason said she heard La Rushe out, then told him to go home to his wife who is no doubt worried for him. Instead of taking her advice, however, La Rushe vanished for another two hours. Then, at 4 AM, two truck drivers spotted a wrecked Ford Consul off the Old London Road.

Inside they found La Rushe, naked, bloodied and slumped over in the passenger seat, dead. The truckers both note that as they pulled up on the scene they saw a group of men, one with a walking stick, leaving it, or so it seemed, but the men ignored calls to stop. La Rushe had been completely drained of blood, but this detail is complicated by the further baffling discovery made by the police investigators that he had not been killed at the scene of the car wreck at which he had been found, but instead had been moved into the car wreck from wherever he had been killed.

MYSTERY?

PARANOIA?

COVER-UP?

Much had been made over the intervening years of La Rushe's death, his seeming premonition of a tragedy, what exactly was meant by the word MAGTZA, and the odd chain of events that led to his being found naked in his car dead from injuries sustained in a separate incident elsewhere. A prevalent theory was that he had been run over or transported by a vehicle bearing a license plate MAGTZA or MA6TZA (which has never panned out) and that his bizarre behaviour in the earlier part of the evening is evidence of some sort of psychic episode. Had he not turned up dead, cause unknown (besides unexplainable blood loss), the obvious reason for his actions — writing down a seemingly random string of letters (and number), the public collapse, the visit to the old acquaintance, the rambling stories — is paranoia attributable to loss of sanity.

Amidst all the speculation, however, is the fact that La Rushe's death was officially ruled a crime by East Sussex police, currently unsolved, a *cold case* to quote our American cousins. Individuals from around the world continue to speculate on the truth of MAGTZA or MA6TZA.

The Hastings & St. Leonards Observer
for November 18th, 1964
by Lawrence Tacklebury

Part Two

Unto the last generation

1

[It is October 13th, 1510]

Sir Thomas Herbert of Farnborough was having a day (a year, frankly) to forget.

He did not care so much about the linen business or the woolen trade he was heavily invested in. He had no good relations with the Staple in Winchester anyway, and he had only ineffective agents at the docks in Southampton and Portsmouth. He had made no firm friendships with the Hansa agents or in the Hampshire political sphere, so he was never put forward as a candidate for anything, and thus he did not sit in the Commons like some of his more successful peers. Sir Thomas's interest was and had always been building up his own reputation at the Tudor court as a soldier and commander of military men, but that was getting harder to do every year without a real war.

His entire life had been built around over-coming his illegitimate birth and the social and legal disadvantages that had accrued to him as a latter-born son. Then Henry VII, for whom he had done some good service in the past, died, leaving an untried boy on the throne. Henry VIII did not know him, or care about the bastard of a cadet branch of a minor noble family from Wales.

At least that is what he read between the lines of the communications from Bishop Foxe (who finally considered it time to reply after only three pleading and servile letters!)

Why am I Foxe's client again?

Nothing was available at court for him.

Well, I can accept that, he told himself repeatedly. I am no politician or diplomat and never had much use for them. I am a man of action!

Nor was there need for his skills in the bishop's service at Winchester (he was told).

Well, fine, I am certainly not a priest. I have much higher morals than that! He would jest to his reflection in the mirror or alone before a meagre fire.

There was no position for him at Cambridge University (or so he was informed). The bishop was the chancellor and could have found something which could be performed by a deputy, *surely!?* Sir Thomas could readily admit that he was no scholar; he had clerks for correspondence and an estate manager, such as his private holdings were.

There was no position for him at the Lord Privy Seal's office (he was told) which the bishop controlled. Sir Thomas was neither a lawyer nor a financier of any type; he did not expect there would have been a position open to him in that office.

He never really had trusted either profession, truth be told.

Sir Thomas could serve very capably in a war though; he had proven that repeatedly to the Tudor monarch's father. It was in the old Tudor's service that Sir Thomas had met Richard Foxe. The skilled churchman had risen as the Tudor had risen, but now Foxe was opposed to war.

It made no sense to Sir Thomas.

So too opposed was the Lord Chancellor and Archbishop of Canterbury William Warham. Between the two of them all patronage was allotted and what little remained was not afforded to soldiers.

Too many bishops! Not enough worldly men of action!

Sir Thomas and his ilk cared about this world, not the next. He angrily crumpled the pages of the latest disappointing news in his closed fist. 'Some mischievous *titivil* confounds me at every turn!' He slammed the desk with the palm of his hand.

'My lord?' asked a guard who entered the room at the sound.

Thomas regarded the man suspiciously; he was new to the Herbert household and did not yet know his place or his boundaries. Thomas raised his hand, his shaking hand, to yell some vulgar epithet at the man about his birth but then he remembered his own lowly origin.

Sir Thomas Herbert was many things, but a hypocrite he was not.

He swallowed his pride, breathed out the curses which had just been on the tip of his tongue, left unspoken, and drew his hand back down to lay it gently on the table. It settled just beside the crumpled pages of the bishop's latest and long overdue letter of regretful news. He shook his head at the sight and calmly dismissed the man, wondering how much longer he could afford guards and liveried servants.

He turned his attention back to the letter, the very disappointing but very courtly letter, into which he had placed so much importance (and not a little money — a "donation" to whatever cause the bishop chose to patronize this month — *himself, most likely*).

He placed his thumb and index finger on either side of the bridge of his nose and tried to rub away the mental stress. He had seen others do this, but it never affected any change in his own state.

The guard was still standing in the doorway.

'I wasn't speaking to anyone specific, William, thank you for your vigilance though, you can go.' Sir Thomas had gathered his nerves again and spoke kindly, but the guard hesitated. 'What is it?' Thomas said with anxiety.

'My lord, there's a man in the parlor. He claims to be an agent of the Duke of Burgundy.'

Thomas's head snapped to, he looked upon the guard, now smiling, he breathed in this wonderful news. *Maybe things are finally looking up?*

There was a buzzing sound. The idiot guard had let some insect in, *damn him.*

Never stopping to wonder at this sudden visitation, at this time in the evening no less, he stood up a little too fast and gave himself a worse throbbing in his head, which made the buzzing louder. He sat back down, hard, which was none too kind for his aching backside.

The lord of the manor swatted at whatever it was making the noise. 'Why didn't you tell me sooner, man? How long have you kept the envoy waiting?' The guard, growing used to Sir Thomas' behavior, took the accusation in stride.

'I came directly from him after seeing him into the parlor, my lord.' He reached over and deposited another paper before the head of the house.

'What is this?'

'His paper of introduction I believe, my lord. I could not find master secretary.' Thomas glanced at it.

'It's written in… foreign.' *Where is my secretary?*

'French, I believe, my lord. I do not really have the education…'

'No, I expect not.' *What an impression my household must be giving.*

Thomas picked up the page and scanned the writing (pretending to read what was written there although his French was poor at best). It looked like the secretarial chicken scratching the bishop would call an "Italianate hand". Thomas was loath to admit his own lack of learning to anyone, however, especially a common guard like William.

'I'll see to him… um, William. Go back to the gate now.'

'And what should be done with his entourage, my lord?'

Thomas sighed, 'Entourage. of course… how many are we speaking of?'

William paused, 'A good dozen at least.' Thomas considered what he assumed to be the guard's witless counting skills and reckoned a dozen could mean anything between ten and twenty-five.

'Put them in the dining hall for now and alert the kitchen. Feed them whatever we have in stocks.'

William the guard saluted and turned sharply about to carry out his instructions.

At least there is a loyal man, thought Thomas to himself. He picked up the letter again, stuffed it in a pocket, and went to his private bed chamber to put on proper dress.

§

Half an hour later Sir Thomas, in his best silk and leathers, entered the parlor.

He was ready to apologize profusely for keeping the envoy, engaged as he unfortunately had been deep into local business matters, matters which only he could deal with. Before he could say anything, however, he was at once struck by the appearance and attire of a tall, if pale, youngish man perusing the titles of his ridiculously small library (or "the bookshelf" as it was sarcastically called).

Thomas at once felt dull and underdressed in comparison.

His eye travelled up and down the stranger, taking in his dark blue doublet, his pink sleeves, the quality of his silks, his loose long black hair (worn in the French style), the magnificent hat set at a jaunty angle on his head, its turned-up brim, the sword at his side (which was worth more than Thomas' entire dining room). Sir Thomas especially liked the fancy black walking stick the man carried, silently admiring the intricate gold and silver dragon-headed grip. The other man, noticing the entrance, turned and performed a flamboyant bow.

'Ai-je le plaisir de m'adresser à Sir Tomas Herbert?'

Thomas recognized his own name of course and nodded. He did not like the way it was pronounced with too much emphasis on the second syllable, and he thought he had heard a girlish giggle in accompaniment.

The man clapped, 'Bien, bien. Bonjour, Monsieur Tomass, comment allez-vous?'

That giggle, there it was again, and the buzzing sound, how many insects had that fool William brought in with him?

As for the envoy, his words sounded like a friendly greeting, evidenced by the fact that the man took off his hat, came over and took Thomas into an embrace, kissing him on each cheek. Thomas (not a diplomat, never liked the breed) assumed this was some French custom, but he did not know what it meant or how to respond to it or even if he should. He thought he might have heard the question before though. If only his wife were here, she had spoken French. *Damn her to hell, and where is my secretary?* Sir Thomas resisted the urge to yell out for Henry. The envoy raised an eyebrow at him, clearly in expectation of some response though.

Tadhg, fully acting the part of the flamboyant Burgundian and enjoying it immensely, threw himself further into the role and took the time to eye up this English so-called "nobleman". He adopted an expression with subtly suggested that Sir Thomas was being found wanting, at best.

And that damned giggling, where is it coming from? Sir Thomas noted the envoy waving his hand about, so he must hear it as well.

With any number of questions streaming across his mind, insects invading his home and girlish laughter in the air, Thomas fought desperately through the growing mental miasma to produce 'Umm, parlez... English... Anglo... plait vous?'

Tadhg pretended to look confused, glanced at Talia who was holding her hands over her mouth really tight. He then pretended as if he was teasing out the meaning of Thomas's badly broken French.

'Ah,' he clapped, 'do I speak your language? Yes, yes, I do, Sir Tomass.' The accent Tadhg had adopted for this was thick, but the words were clear enough. Thomas sighed, smiled, and welcomed his guest properly (in English, *dammit to hell*).

'May I offer you some wine... umm, my good sir?'

'Ah, yes,' Tadhg placed his palm against his forehead, 'where are my manners? I am Etienne-Michel Faillon, Vicomte de Forcalquier, at your service sir.'

'Vecont?' Thomas repeated the word, badly, again to himself. He could not recall precisely where such a title would fit by comparison into the English aristocratic pecking order. He assumed (correctly) that it was much higher than his own lowly bastard position, but whether his was a position that was represented in Burgundy (*which was in the Low Countries or France maybe?*) at all he did not know. He blinked a couple times, which bore witness to the slow working of his mind.

He never thought to question the man's name and claim to the title he presented; never thought to question why he was here. He gave the man back his (un-read) introduction papers. He did his best to make an impressive bow of his own, and only failed a little bit. He then invited his guest to seat himself and rang for a servant, forgetting that his dining hall was also filled with guests and that he had a limited supply of servants these days. A couple uncomfortable minutes passed before a man finally answered the bell; wine was ordered.

'I apologize, my lord, but I am having severe difficulties in finding appropriate servants at this time.' Tadhg waved this away.

'Think nothing of it, Sir Tomas, soon it will not even matter and be only a bad memory for you, eh?' Thomas was obviously confused by this response and the ominous undertones it held. At least the giggling had stopped.

'If I would be not too rude, my lord, what is the nature of this visit? I am hard pressed to think what I could do for the Duke of Burgundy. Unless, unless he needs commanders for an army?' Thomas's eyes took on a bright sheen at the new prospect, only for this to be at once dashed by the response. Tadhg frowned and shook his head, but upon seeing the disappointment of the man opposite, he smiled.

He reeled his victim in.

'But be of good cheer, Sir Tomass. I am not here as the envoy to his eminence the Duke Charles II, the queen's uncle, which is just the fact of my *employ*, as you English say. *Non*. I am here, unofficial, as you say, on behalf of the duke's cousin, Wilhelm IV of Bavaria. This was clear from the letter of introduction, was it not?' Thomas raised his hands in a gesture of assurance.

'Of course, my lord, I was momentarily confused by the esteem with which I hold all these great persons you speak of.' He nodded, happy with that bit of off the cuff rhetoric there.

Hmm, maybe I could have been a diplomat.

Tadhg nodded, 'I understand, of course.' He paused, assessing Thomas in some obvious but suspect fashion. 'But monsieur, you knew this day would come, non?'

Again, Thomas was caught off guard.

'You were not expecting me, or someone very much like me?'

Thomas shook his head, clearly confused.

'But you know why I am here, non?' Thomas sighed.

'I can only apologize, my lord. I received no prior notice of your visit.'

Tadhg stared at Thomas for a moment, pretending to assess the situation again and projecting confusion on to his own face. Of course, there had been no prior letters, but Sir Thomas did not know that.

Tadhg frowned in his turn. 'I am then the messenger of sad news, it seems, Sir Tomass. I am sorry to inform you that your father has passed away. Your brother has taken his rightful place on the throne, of course, and he would now have his brother come home and serve him as Regent of Landshut.' Tadhg smiled and raised his arms in celebration. 'So, this is not such sad news after all, eh?' He paused, waiting for some response, but none seemed forthcoming.

'Why, you are being called home, mon ami! Does this not excite you?' He smiled as if this was wonderful news, but the smile soon faded as if to suggest that he had clearly not been expecting further confusion from Sir Thomas.

Tadhg looked the man in the eyes. 'You did not know this, did you? You do not know who you really are, do you? This news has taken you unaware.'

Sir Thomas sat staring blankly into space, ignoring the buzzing around his head. In his wildest dreams he could not have imagined being told… well, anything like what he was being told, that is a certainty. For most people this might have been a cause to question; Sir Thomas played right into the Burgundian envoy's hands.

'I fear all this was kept from me, my lord.'

Tadhg looked confused a moment. 'Your mother, that is, your true mother, never told you of her brief tryst with Duke Albert? Your "adopted" father, in truth a hired guardian, never mentioned the funds set aside for your use when you came of age?' He paused in feigned thought. 'There was speculation that you must have died in a war or some such thing, but Wilhelm has all the letters.'

'Letters?'

'The letters you wrote as a boy, learning the Bavarian tongue?'

Again, Sir Thomas's pride blinded him. 'I wrote no such letters, my lord. I do not know what language is spoken in Bavaria. Frankly sir, I could not point to Bavaria on a map.'

'Could it be that your uncle took the money, the thousands and thousands of golden thalers sent, and tricked the duke with false letters in reply?'

Tadhg threw himself back into his chair pretending offense and anger, but keeping Thomas's responses at the center of his attention. Thomas, for his part, was unsure if this question had been directed at him or not. He was impressed by the play of emotion across the envoy's face though, from incredulity to anger, confusion to acceptance.

'No matter,' Tadhg dismissed it all with a wave of his hand, 'I will instruct you on the way myself. Although this was not my instruction, I am having some latitude.' He stood up and began pacing in the small space of the parlor.

'But this raises a serious question, Sir Thomas.'

Just one? thought Thomas to himself.

'What is that, my lord?'

'The funds your uncle embezzled, well, we do not know that for certain, do we? Let us be charitable, eh? These lost funds were meant to pay for your journey and for the establishment of a household commiserate with your position, my lord regent. It is unthinkable that you should come to your brother with less than a hundred liveried equestrians, servants, not to mention a wardrobe suited to your position, not this...' he indicated Thomas's attire, '... not that these... English clothes... are not suited to who you are pretending to be.' Tadhg clapped, 'Ah, of course, you choose to live here, with no servants, as a ruse, non?' Thomas was unsure whether to be insulted or grateful. His "brothers" had told him he was lucky to get as much of an inheritance as he had done, bastards having no legal standing in law.

'One cannot be too careful, my lord.'

Tadhg smiled as Thomas slowly sounded out the carefully ambiguous response and turned to regard him, nodding agreement enthusiastically.

'Absolutement! Your brother will be awfully glad of your wisdom.'

'My brother... this William you mean?'

'Well, Wilhelm, the W is pronounced as a vee, in German.'

German. 'I am not a Herbert then, illegitimate or otherwise?'

'You are not an 'erbert, non.' Tadhg was on the verge of spitting out the word, but he paused instead, as if a new thought had occurred to him. 'En réalité si...' he stopped, pretending to remember where he was, 'I am certain that there is nothing preventing your remaining in this... situation, if that is your wish. I am not commissioned to force you to come to Landshut, only to find you, present the invitation, and help you with any... legalities, as you English, umm, the English say. I have connections at court which can be used to hasten matters. It is entirely your own choice, of course.'

'Matters?' Tadhg nodded, Herbert falling right along.

'Mais oui, you, that is Tomass 'erbert must be... how you say, erased? Is that the correct word in English? Removed,' he made a motion with his hand, 'from the official record, you understand? Here at least Tomass 'erbert ends. Once we get you to Calais, Tomas Wittelsbach appears.'

Tadhg looked around in an exaggerated way until he located a leather case.

'Ah,' he stood and retrieved the case, opening the flap and withdrawing a selection of papers. He returned to the table with these, placing them before his host. Thomas glanced down and saw they were written in what he presumed was French.

He never thought to question why Germans would use French in their legal documents, but then it was all foreign to him anyway.

'These are?' He glanced at the envoy.

'The necessary legalities,' Tadhg pointed to the papers. 'You will sign over your properties, deeds, leases, and whatever possessions you can absolutely do without to one of my people, who in turn will assume your position until such time as it can all be sold off and Tomass 'erbert made to look like he... suicided? Committed suicide, yes? Took his own life. The money raised will be used as compensation for the necessary travel and new wardrobe you will need, as well as immediate, if temporary employ, of armed escorts once you are safe on the continent.' Thomas regarded the documents.

Where is my secretary?

'Once you have endorsed the papers, I will take them to my retained lawyer at Lincoln's Inn in London to be recorded while my entourage helps you to crate up your possessions here. That way nothing is lost, and no outsiders need be involved. You can dismiss your servants as you will and pay off your debts however you wish. Another choice is to sign the papers and disappear, or we can start the rumor that Sir Tomass 'erbert has been killed in a tragic accident.' Thomas's mind was swimming in these details, and he was finding it hard to think clearly.

'I...' he pushed the documents away. 'I will have to consult with my secretary, wherever he has got to, and act on his advice.'

'I understand. It is a large step and not an easy one to take. Some men would be put off by the prospect of rule and sudden grandeur. But I cannot tarry here long, Lord Regent, I am expected to return to the duke and inform him of your travel plans at once. I can afford you the evening to think about it. Will that suffice?'

'It seems it must.'

'Excellente!'

Tadhg stood and clapped his hands in a celebratory fashion. 'I shall have my servants bring in my baggage. You will direct them to your guest chambers, oui?'

Thomas nodded absentmindedly, not hearing what Tadhg had actually said. By the time his senses returned to him the envoy was no longer in the parlor but had gone to the entrance and opened it to signal the carriages. Men scrambled to take down crates and chests, bags and boxes, and move them into the house, awaiting Thomas's direction. The guests' chamber had not been prepared for any visit in the time Thomas owned this manor, so he had no choice but to direct the servants to the master chambers.

He would think of something later.

The envoy returned to the house, and with him now was master secretary, chatting amiably with the envoy and clearly enjoying himself.

'Garrison, where have you been all day? We have guests, we must accommodate them!' Tadhg waved these concerns away.

'Lord Regent, you did not say that Henri Garrison was employed here. I know this man; we have corresponded much over the years. We met,' he paused and then snapped his fingers. 'Where was it, we first met Henri?'

'At the archbishop's palace at Lambeth I believe, Faillon.'

'Oui, oui, this is correct. I have missed your quick wits.'

The secretary turned to Thomas smiling, 'Imagine my surprise, Sir Thomas, to find Vicomte de Forcalquier in the courtyard!' Thomas closed his mouth, shook his head as if nothing made sense any more. He sighed.

'See to the comfort of the vicomte and his entourage, Henry, I must address matters in the kitchen. When you have time look over the papers on the desk there,' pointing to the documents, 'and tell no one about it. I take it,' he turned to the envoy, 'you have no objections to Henry knowing the details?'

'Non, not at all.' Tadhg clapped Garrison on the back, friendly as could be, making Thomas jealous and not a little angry.

My secretary had connections to the great and the good all along and said nothing?

§

Somehow, by some miracle, the vicomte's entourage, servants, and gear had all been housed, fed, watered, and entertained for the few hours remaining of the evening/morning when hospitality was needed. Cook was to go into town before first light and when the markets opened, he was to buy whatever wasn't chained down and could be eaten. In the still of the early morning, however, when his secretary was finally finished making merry with the envoy and his entourage, the two of them got down to the business of examining the agreement left on the desk.

'What do you think, Henry, can this be real?' Thomas put his hand down on the pile of documents. Henry, stifling a yawn, nodded.

'It's simple and straight-forward, Sir Thomas, and therein lays the strength of its legality. The fact of the matter is that, provided you are of sound mind, and I see no evidence to suggest otherwise, the properties and possessions listed or implied are legally yours to do with as you please.

Your brother... well, none of the Herberts for that matter, need to be consulted here on any point.' Thomas nodded.

'Yes, that was my understanding as well.' Garrison smiled and indulged Thomas' ego by simply agreeing to this claim. Thomas sat back in his chair, pondering the issue.

'Can it be true?'

'Sir?'

'I admit that as a bastard son I often dreamed of something like this. My real father would come, make himself known. He would take me away and I would be heir to a castle and vast estates. I had such a dream not long ago in fact. Then, seemingly unexpectedly a Burgundian dignitary shows up, on behalf of a Bavarian duke no less, weaving a tale and claiming that he has been searching for me for years, now, finally, prepared to offer me everything I ever dreamt of. Master secretary sighed and nodded in response. 'And all I have to do is give up a life I was never happy in.'

'It seems impossible, my lord, certainly improbable, and yet, here is the man. I guess you would have to ask yourself what is the alternative explanation for all this? Is there one?'

'To make me look foolish ..'

'By what means? Hiring a Burgundian aristocrat to play out a role? I mean, no offense, sir, but it would have cost more to set up this ruse than could possibly be gained here.'

Thomas nodded, 'If he is who he says he is, if the claims are genuine, if, if, if.'

'Well, I know Faillon to be who he claims to be. So, there is that much truth.'

Thomas regarded the secretary through lowered eyes.

'Otherwise, I can find nothing untoward in the documents.' Garrison got to his feet, picked up the empty pitcher and the used mugs. He turned to leave but paused at the doorway.

'Sir Thomas, we've known each other a good while now have we not? You've had a long day, and you've certainly had a surprising, nay, a shocking one. Get ye to bed. Perhaps by the morning's light all this will become much clearer. Now, my lord, if there is nothing else?'

'There is one last thing, Henry. Would you be prepared to move to Landshut with me?'

'Yes, yes I would.' There was no hesitation.

'Good night, Henry.' The secretary bowed his head and left the room.

Thomas sat a moment longer. 'Tomas Wittelsbach, Regent of Landshut,' he whispered aloud. Liking the sound of it he too then made his way to a bed (sadly, not his own bed).

§

'What are they saying, sire?'

Sitting in the lord of the manor's adequate chair, by a fireplace where the ambers were still reddish orange, the so-called vicomte sat with his fingers steepled before him in concentration on the manipulation of air currents. In this way the conversation between Sir Thomas and his secretary had been made as clear to him as if he had been in the same room sitting at the desk as well. Tadhg smiled.

'He cannot believe his fortune, Talia.'

The pixie shrugged, flew over and settled on to a pillow on the bed and instantly drifted off to sleep. Tadhg regarded her a moment. He too would have slept, but his work for the night was not yet finished, just one more thing to do.

§

Thomas had strange dreams that morning.

It all stemmed from the documents on the table in the parlor. In his first dream he signed the documents. His life was a blur thereafter, but large fanciful castles, significant meetings with important imperial figures (who all spoke English after all), introductions to eligible daughters, honorariums, his name in published books of poetry, science, and theology, acknowledgements came his way as the true Renaissance prince he was. Where he walked, the people stooped and bowed. He wanted for nothing. He lived a long and happy life. He had a young wife, and mistresses. He had many sons to pass on his name and daughters he allowed to take advantage of his love. He had a brother who genuinely wanted his company as well as his advice on matters of state and diplomacy. It was a very satisfying life indeed.

The second dream was frankly terrifying.

He rejected the documents as too suspicious to be true, and his luck did not change. The bishop's patronage dried up completely and no other patron would take him into their faction of supporters. Neither his so-called family, nor his peers, returned his begging letters any longer. His fortune gone, his debts mounting, he could do naught but throw himself on the mercy of the crown.

Sadly, he found no mercy in the young King Henry.

The mind-scene shifted to a rat-infested, rubbish strewn back alley. A body was found there by someone. He cannot see the face in the dream, but he knows it is himself somehow. In the dream no one claims to know the dead man, the body is finally thrown into a peasant grave and covered in a sprinkling of lime but otherwise left exposed to the elements. Over the weeks more bodies are thrown on top of him until, finally, he is crushed under the weight of so many dead bodies. This happens in the dream, but Thomas can feel the weight on his own chest in a bed in Farnborough.

§

Tadhg, as Faillon, remained awake and active long enough to take breakfast with Sir Thomas. It was not much of a burden, and Tadhg was having fun, like the old days.

Their discussion was inconsequential, truth be told; the dream had scared the man into signing the documents as quickly as he had laid eyes on them. Tadhg took the papers in hand; he excused himself, explaining that he has correspondence to consider in light of Sir Thomas's agreement. Sir Thomas is instructed to make sure he is undisturbed for the next several hours. Returning to the master suite Tadhg not long resisted the pull of the curse gifted him long and long ago. He could take a draught from one of his many flasks, but instead he secured Sir Thomas's bed curtains, creating an oasis of darkness around himself. His people, sons and daughters, will manage matters from here.

§

[It is January 3rd, 1511]

Thomas, sea-sick from the short voyage between Dover and Calais, stepped out on to the docks, his head still accustomed to the roiling motion of the ship. It took him several minutes to re-accustomed to solid land beneath his feet once again. His travelling companion, the viscount's servant, took his arm and held him up until he could move again of his own accord.

'Thank you, umm, Lóegaireson.'

The other man, normally quite taciturn, merely bowed his head in acknowledgement of the words spoken, no more, no less. This habit had been quite annoying to Thomas at first, but the ride to Dover (*why not Southampton?*) and the voyage itself had given him time to think about the hectic last few weeks since the viscount's surprise visitation. He had questions now that he realized he should have asked weeks earlier.

Who was his real mother and why had the baron (the man he had always claimed to be his natural father) never spoke of these other matters?

Why had it taken so long to retrieve him (he was well passed his age of majority)?

Why had he not employed a lawyer of his own?

What had happened to Henry? His secretary had said he would come along.

These and many other questions had disturbed his days and nights on the road, and the quiet and reserved Lóegaireson had been little or no help with any of them.

Thomas shrugged. He was to meet with the viscount again shortly; all would be cleared up then. For some reason, however, despite his own caution and suspicious nature he had trusted the envoy from the moment he'd met him.

Sir Thomas never once questioned that.

'This way, my Lord Regent.' The urgency in the voice surprised Thomas.

Lóegaireson had tapped Thomas on the shoulder and indicated a direction. He picked up what little luggage the nobleman still had, including his purse, and started walking away with it.

Thomas had no choice but to follow.

The man, who Thomas had lectured often in the last few days for his slow pace had suddenly developed a swift and long stride, which had caught his charge completely off-guard. Thomas ran to catch up but could only manage to keep the man in sight, never quite closing the gap developing between them.

Thomas began to perspire.

Going in and out of dark alleyways was giving him a headache now. The torches, wherever they were placed, he found were hurting his eyes. From time-to-time Thomas actually lost sight of Lóegaireson, but always a call would set him off again.

'This way, my Lord Regent.' The voice seemed to come from behind him now, drawing him in another direction, deeper into the maze that was the streets of Calais.

It never occurred to him that the voice had changed.

Sir Thomas emerged into another torch-lit alley, but this one had no exit. It was a dead end. He stood facing a tall, grimy stone wall, his hands on his hips and breathing heavily.

'Ah, Sir Tomass, at last you appear.'

Thomas spun around, having heard no one approach from behind him.

To his surprise it was the Burgundian envoy. But the flamboyant, vivaciously garbed man who had visited him in Farnborough was gone. Now was a man in black silks and leathers (although the sword and cane were much the same) as was the ostentatious hat.

'Faillon!'

Tadhg bowed in the French fashion.

'At your service.'

'What the blue blazes is going on here? Where's Lóegaireson and my possessions? Why this merry chase through these godforsaken streets?' Tadhg made a show of taking in a deep breath. He smiled.

'What is the most obvious answer to those questions, Sir Thomas?'

'Lord Regent!' he corrected. Then he stopped short of any further angry retorts. 'Why has your accent changed? You're not Irish.'

'Technically no, I come from an older bloodline than that. My question stands, however.'

'I... I don't know... question? What? To, to confound me I would guess?'

A screaming soldier came rushing out of the dark alley, a naked sword raised high in the air as if to strike him down. Before Thomas could shout a warning, however, the man moved passed the envoy and came directly at him. But Thomas was an experienced soldier and dodged the blow to his neck. Instinct made Thomas reach for his side arm, which he now realized he did not have. The soldier took another swipe at him before running back out of the alley the way he had come.

'What, what is this? What was that?'

'What was what, Sir Thomas?'

'How did you not…' A woman screamed from somewhere outside the alley. Then another woman, a different voice, this one cut off mid-cry. Then a child's voice was added to the cacophony, squealing like a whipped pup. A woman came running into the light near Thomas, a peasant woman by the looks of her, old, tattered clothes, barely on, no shoes. A soldier followed shortly thereafter, laughing, a wicked gleam in the eye.

'Come back, you whore, I'm not nearly done with you yet!' Thomas was shocked to realize that the soldier's uniform looked familiar to him. It was an old livery, true, a Hampshire regiment. He made no move to help the woman, now on her knees begging for mercy. The soldier did not even pause but slashed her throat.

'For the Tudor!' the soldier yelled out his victory and turned to run back into the fray beyond the alley, which Thomas could now hear clearly.

'But but this, that, that cannot be,' Thomas whispered. 'I, I know, I knew that man.' He thought a moment, desperately trying to sort out conflicting ideas. 'William, William le Penne, yes, that's right. But he died, years ago.'

He looked down, but the woman's body was gone.

Noise from the entrance forced him to look there again. Many soldiers came marching into the alley, all with the old livery. They were all carrying bloody trophies; little boxes, goblets, a hat, whatever had value. They marched passed Thomas, passed him and into the stone wall, passing right through it in fact. The final soldier, on a black horse, Thomas was shocked to see had the prominent Herbert badge on his shield. His sword was not very bloodied, and his visor was drawn down over his face.

Thomas would have known that horse anywhere though.

'Midnight,' he mouthed.

At the sound of the name the horse stopped before him, neighed, shook his head up and down and regarded him in the eye. The rider looked down too, moving his hand to raise the visor.

'Please don't,' begged Thomas, who now fell to his knees, his hands clenched together in a supplicant's posture. The ghost, shade, spirit, whatever it was, did not pause, however, and lifted his visor. Thomas screamed out when he saw what he knew he would see — his own face. His younger self, arrogant, smug, gleaming from the victory he had imposed on...

'Mallow?' asked Tadhg.

'Was that the name of the place? I don't think I ever knew it.'

The rider shook his head sadly, spurred his horse on, riding into the wall and disappearing from sight, to catch up with his troop.

The night grew quiet again, except for Thomas's quiet sobs and heavy breathing. Tadhg could hear the thumping of the aristocrat's black and poisoned heart. His inner demon, he had heard the term *vampyre* bandied about, urged him to take the man, bite his neck and take in that hot, hot red nectar, but Tadhg resisted the urge for the moment. It was not yet time. Instead, he walked up to the kneeling man and put a friendly hand on his shoulder.

Thomas looked up and saw the envoy through his tears.

'Why, Faillon, why?'

Tadhg smiled, gently. 'Not Faillon, Sir Thomas, Tadhg Rorysson. But to answer your question, it was all to fulfil an oath.'

'An oath? An oath?' Thomas started to laugh, repeating the words, having lost his senses in all the turmoil his mind had just undergone. Tadhg reached down and took the man's chin in his hand, turning his face back up so that he could look into his eyes.

'Calm yourself, Thomas.'

It was said quietly but with authority and Thomas found himself unable to resist the command.

He stopped sniveling.

His tears dried.

He was suddenly able to think clearly again.

Tadhg studied him a moment, then squatted down before Thomas with his hand still on the man's chin, a firm grip, an iron-like grip, steadying himself with the black walking stick. Thomas found that he could not move his head at all. He could not close his eyes either. He opened his mouth, but no words came forth.

'Greed and ambition drove you that day, Sir Thomas, and it was greed and ambition which brought you here, to this grisly end, in a back alley in Calais. Not even on your native soil, a sad way to go, but a soldier's way perhaps. Though, not in service to a king, verily, one who does not even know of your existence. Winchester never lifted a finger to aid in your cause, Thomas, I know. You had become an embarrassment to him. You were a loose end, the skeleton in the closet, an odd one out to the Herbert clan. Your name exists now only on a couple legal documents and on a couple military rolls. Even now my people are expunging even these from the official records. Soon, it will be as if you never existed at all.'

New tears formed in Thomas's eyes and fell down his cheeks only to fall from there into the dust at his knees.

'But' Tadhg continued positively, 'your death has some benefit, fear not. I will take your property and possessions, what little you had, and put them to a noble cause, and on the positive side at least you did not breed.'

Confusion formed in Thomas's wet eyes.

'Not a concern for you. You named the soldier as William le Penne. Listen closely now, can you remember any other names, faces, locations?'

'Have mercy my lord... that was...'

'Not so long ago in reality, Sir Thomas, come now. Le Penne and whom else? I am not above torture.'

Unable to whimper, unable to look away from those probing, hard, cold eyes, Sir Thomas thought harder than he ever had before. 'I... Walter... Osteler, he had bright red hair, and... Nathaniel Fodde, he was good with the horses, but a little slow in the mind. Umm, give me a moment, I beg of you sir. Philip, there was a Philip... blast what was his surname? Phelip, yes, yes, I always found it an odd name.' Sir Thomas fell silent. Tadgh took the names in.

'These men were under your command, and you can recall only three names?'

'I will remember them all sire, really I will, and I will write it down like I said.'

'It's enough to be getting on with, sir,' said a man at the entrance to the alley.

'Arthur, there was an Arthur...'

Sir Thomas heard a buzzing sound then the voice from the entrance and quieted down again. A soldier by the look of him; Sir Thomas could not make him out any clearer than that through his dried-out eyes. He noted the detail that the man was writing in a book. Then the man who held him tightened his grip, drawing Sir Thomas's attention back fully on to himself.

'Thank you, son. That will do then. Now there is one last thing for you to consider in your last moments of life Sir Thomas Herbert. When your body is found, whenever that might be, in the morning or in the days to come, perhaps when they trace the decaying stench of you, no one will know you. Nor will they care, except that you will have become a burden on the council here. Your body will be thrown into a peasant grave, covered in lime, left to rot as your body is pushed down into the earth by a layer of peasants on top of you and then a layer on top of them.'

Thomas's eyes grew wide.

'That's right; I planted that dream in your head myself.'

The penultimate image Thomas saw, one he could not look away from, held as he was, were gleaming white fangs emerging out of his capture's upper row of teeth, and his eyes becoming round black orbs. The last image he saw; that which he took with him to the grave, however, reflected orange torch-light and his own cowardly, cringing, likeness reflected in those colorless eyes.

§

Some brief time later a hand is placed on Tadhg's shoulder, and he was pulled out of his feeding frenzy. Tadhg let the emptied body slip out of his grasp. A dagger was produced and someone to his right slit the throat of the corpse. There is no blood remaining in the body, but someone poured a jug of goat's blood, to the effect that it seems to trickle out of the dead man's neck. A strong wine is then poured over the head and body of the dead man, which mingles with the blood on the cobbles of the alleyway. Tadhg was helped out of the alley to an awaiting black carriage.

He is helped into the vehicle, where three men and Talia are already waiting for him, each man wearing the livery of the Sons of Lóegaire. They are Henry Garrison, William Tanner and Richard McKeen (otherwise known of late merely as Lóegaireson). Tanner knocks on the panel and the driver (another son) eases the horses into a gentle trot, navigating the streets of Calais to the manor leased from the city for the king's convenience. There is less than a week's need for it still (if that); time to await news of the body's recovery and burial, to await any further repercussions (if any), and time needed to assess the new names and send missives back to their people at the Herbert, now the Fiallon, estate, where the new lord and lady of the manor have already settled.

'I have some thoughts on the harvest process, sir,' said Tanner.

Tadhg held up a hand. 'Give me a moment, son.'

William sat back, nodded, happy to wait.

2

"Is this the end of the Stick Man killings?"

If the Stick Man even exists, he's one of Northern England's and Southern Scotland's most prolific killers. At least 15 deaths of young men and women are attributed to the Stick Man, but most police departments say he doesn't exist at all.

Is there a serial killer stalking college-aged men and women? Scotland Yard and other policing agencies insist no one is drowning inebriated college students around the regional schools and leaving behind a painted stick figure where he dumps the bodies. The bloodless bodies! But no matter how many times officials try to squelch the theory the rumour of the Stick Man will not die. And the bodies keep cropping up. The theory originated with two North Yorkshire police detectives, Kevin Gough, and Robert Durante. They concluded that the deaths of at least 15 by drowning have too many similarities to be unrelated. Although the theory began in connection with bodies found in university towns, it spread to include murder cases from the Midlands and here in Renfrewshire, Glasgow, in North Ayrshire and in West Dunbartonshire. In at least a dozen cases, a painted stick man figure was found near a body of water where a victim's corpse was dumped.

Nine of the victims of the supposed Stick Man Killer were white college men, another five white college women and one black woman. The detectives speculate the motive may be jealousy, as all of them were good looking or athletic or academically successful. Because some of the deaths occurred the same night, but on different campuses, the detectives altered their theory slightly, believing that the murders were carried out by an organized gang of killers. They believed their theory enough to reportedly use their own personal funds to continue the investigation when official funds dried up. The Stick Man killer theory all began with the 1995 death of 21-year-old Benjamin McNeill (of Ripon) was last seen drinking with friends in a Carlisle pub. Volunteers plastered the city with thousands of "Missing" fliers, and McNeill's body was found two months later and twelve miles away near the entrance to the Solway Firth. Police found no evidence of foul play at the site, but Gough and Durante, who visited the site, were not convinced; they pledged to keep working on the case. Nearly all the subsequent deaths have also been ruled accidental drownings involving alcohol, cuts, and blood loss in the water. Scotland Yard and several police organizations have researched the deaths and concluded there is no link between them. The two officers went so far as to publish an exhaustive report, however, called "Drowning the Stick Man Theory." It lists 18 reasons that the theory doesn't hold water, including the fact that stick men are a quite common form of graffiti and that murder by drowning is extremely rare.

    This reporter, however, found a few criminologists who agree with the detectives that there are too many similarities in the deaths to put it down to pure coincidence. And there have been frequent requests to Scotland Yard, and Interpol, to pick up the investigation, including one in 2008 from a Cumbria MP. The Stick Man Killer was invoked as recently as 2016 after the drowning death of a 24-year-old in Glasgow, Michelle Lethbridge, who had last been seen drinking at a local pub with friends. Like so many of the other supposed murders, Lethbridge's body showed no signs of foul play although, like all the others, it had been drained of blood. Despite this, many Glaswegians began to panic about a phantom serial killer possibly living among them.

Despite this most recent case, however, even Gough and Durante have given up on their theory. After spending years (and seemingly a significant chunk of their money) on the Stick Man Killer theory, the pair stopped researching the case in about 2012. The victims' families and several internet sleuths, however, still hold out hope that the Stick Man Killer theory will prove to be true. It would lend some sense of meaning to the deaths of the many victims whose unexplained drownings still haunt their loved ones. Lookout for a new book on the case by the two men, to be published by Penguin in the fall.

The Scottish Daily Express
For April 3rd, 2012
by Aaron McClan

3

[It is 1522 — a small town in Hampshire called Basingstoke]

Looking back on it all, it had been a good life.

James Bedingfield lay in what he had come to assume would soon be his death bed, thinking about the things he had done, the people he had known, and the family he had sired and guided all these long years. Many men faced their last days on earth with anxiety and fear, but James was satisfied and calm at the prospect of death. He was ready to face God with a clean conscience of charitable deeds done and a life of righteous living.

There aren't many who could say that these days, he knew, but James had reached his sixth decade without too many regrets.

Indeed, he was now looking forward to a few answers.

God could finally explain to him the loss of his eldest son, also named James, just two years earlier. That would ease his curiosity at least. A deadly "accident" he could accept, but in the office of a law clerk where James had been working? The explanation just did not sit well with him. It never made sense. Sadly, he could not afford to go to Chichester and fund a full-on investigation into the matter.

Sarah, his wife of thirty years, would at least be well cared for by their remaining son. Thomas Bedingfield, and his wife Mary (a Howard by birth and a distant cousin of the great Howard clan), had already given Sarah two grandchildren to fuss over in her declining years. James' one surviving daughter, Lizzy, and her husband John Silversmith were finally expecting their own first child as well. Sarah said it would be a boy due to the way Lizzy's baps had changed shape.

James hadn't said anything about it then; he didn't care whether it was another grandson or granddaughter.

Either would keep her busy.

Sarah would have much on her mind over the next few years whatever the baby was, so the loss of her husband would not be such a sore point for too long. James had also noticed the little cough she had developed, and he thought it would not be that long before they were together again in any case.

He lay comfortably on his pillows.

Yes, looking back on it all, James was happy with his lot.

He meant to take up the small *Book of Hours* again. He had been skimming through it for the last few days, preparing his soul. It was expensively illuminated and had been produced especially for him. The names of his wife and children were written into the prayers; his own likeness (from a younger time) featured in some full-page decorations. He had never said so, but in the lavish two-page spread of the Adoration of the Magi, the four human nudes were artistic visions of his wife, his first wife, and two favored mistresses he had told no one else about except the artist (a monk of Edington Prior). He had directed the artist's hand himself when time was. Some features may have been exaggerated, and some diminished, but he had paid the artist good money to keep his mouth shut about it all, and all these years later it seems that he had done so.

What was her name again?

He had discovered a few weeks earlier that he could not remember the names of his two former paramours. One might have been named Mary or Elizabeth, but those were pretty common names nowadays.

Anne? He thought about this. *No, that was your first wife, you fool.*

Yes, Anne, so young, he answered himself with a sigh.

Despite the titillation of the pictures, he found his eyes closing repeatedly, and he was increasingly hard pressed to stop them. He was just dozing off when his wife came into the room and shook his shoulder.

James looked up into the familiar brown eyes he loved very much; he noted the wrinkles around them and the weakened brightness they had once held. Usually they were smiling; this time he noted a worried expression.

'I'm still here… Sarry.' He saw the changing expression on his wife's face from anxiety to confusion and then to the light of understanding. A small smile spread across her lips.

'Sarry? You haven't called me by that name in years, Jimmy. It's a bad sign you know.'

'A bad sign you say. Thinking about the fine times of our youth is bad?'

'Youth?' she laughed. 'You were thirty when my father contracted our marriage.' She paused. 'I was young,' she said teasingly. 'Anyway, it's nothing like that. I wasn't worried about you. There's a man here to visit you though.'

James smiled; it was good that a man has friends.

'At this time... who?'

'A Sir Lawrence Oldfield? I've seen him about the town from time to time of late, but he says you and he have friends in common? He is here on their behalf?' The change of pitch in her voice turned the claims into questions. This made James sit up a little.

Lawrence Oldfield? Oldfield?
A knight of the realm come to my death bed.
Friends in common?

He shrugged weakly.

'Well, dear, let's not keep the man waiting, show him in.'

Sarah nodded, straightened out the bed clothes some, and then left again while James readied himself to present as good a face as possible given his condition.

Click-click-tap, click-click-tap.

James heard the sound and looked to the door.

Sarah returned shortly with a fancy dressed man who was half James's age, but a man already wary of the world. His attire was rich but not gaudy (as James judged these things), fine silks, a good sword at his side — Spanish by the look of it — a walking stick in the other hand the likes of which he had never seen before. James imagined this man a royal messenger from the queen.

What would Catherine of Aragon have to do with me?

He could think of nothing.

The knight entered the chamber, which must have been small by his standards, and at once took command of the space. He looked around, taking note of every little thing (it seemed to James), as if making a mental tally, and then his eyes finally met James's own. He held them for a moment as if boring into James's mind or soul, then he just as suddenly turned back to Sarah for which James was grateful as he was growing anxious.

'Leave us, woman. We have to discuss certain private matters between us.' It was more an order than a request; politely said but brooking no denial.

It offended James slightly to see his Sarah ordered about so casually — the knight expected to be obeyed without question — and he was.

Sarah bowed, picked up the remains of James's supper, and did the best curtsey she could manage while backing out of the room. She closed the door as she left. To James the knight watched the door a little longer than was necessary, if it was at all necessary to watch the door?

What was he looking for?

Finally, satisfied, he turned again and regarded the bed-ridden man.

James noted that the man's eyes seemed larger than he'd noted earlier and strangely differing shades of violet, subtle but true. He'd never before seen the like.

'What ails you, James Bedingfield?' The man also had an odd accent, certainly not local, not a Hampshire man anyway — *Sussex?*

A Kentish man maybe?

James shook his head, but smiled at the enquiry, 'The local practitioner could not or would not say, sir. He would only say that he had seen the signs before, sore throat, swellings in the neck, trouble breathing.' James shrugged it off. 'I am cold one day and hot the next.' The knight nodded, smiled briefly. 'Not the sweat or plague in any case, but something just as deadly for me, or so it seems.'

'I'll keep my distance then.'

'As you like, sir, as you like.'

James fell silent watching the man, studying him. He certainly knew the man was unknown to him but *friends in common* Sarah had said.

They shared a social rank but clearly no more than that, and it would have been inhospitable for a commoner like James, who bought his knighthood, to ask questions of his obvious social superiors; and the man at the foot of his bed was a nobleman, James could see it in his stance, expression, and attitude.

In effect, therefore, he could only lay there and wait for the man to explain his presence if he even chose so to do at all. James could not imagine which friends of his they had in common, and he longed to ask.

As he watched, pondering that issue, the knight pulled a chair from its position near the wall and carried it to the point near the foot of the bed where he had been standing. James knew it to be a heavy oak chair, and the man had managed it effortlessly. He moved with the grace of an acrobat too. The visitor then unbuckled his sword and set this nearby on the floor.

'I will not be needing this here now will I, sir?' he smiled. James gave him a weak smile from the bed, nodding his head.

'I suspect not.'

The man smiled, not unkindly, and next removed and hung his silken jacket on the back of the chair. The jacket was a rich brown fabric and it reminded James suddenly of autumn leaves just before they turned color, and it matched the man's jerkin, under which he wore a yellow shirt, which brought to mind bright sunshine. This done, the fellow sat down, his walking stick before him. James's eyes were drawn in by the glinting lion's head grip.

If that's really gold and real silver, that stick is worth more than my house.

'It's real.' James looked up, shocked. The man shrugged, 'And I am neither of Sussex nor Kent. I am not here to discuss my place of birth... not directly. I am here to discuss you, James, and your history.'

'Oh?' James was curious now and leaned slightly forward, as much as his position and health allowed.

'You have a good reputation in this town. People tell me that you are a man of faith and a provider of good service to your fellows.' James smiled, nodded, and shrugged before pride got the better of him.

'I did what I could, sir, as should we all.'

'Humble too, I see.'

Again, James smiled and shrugged, nice as it was to be praised his confusion was growing, and more questions had come into his mind.

'This... behavior you pretense, it has not always been so... shall we say, godly, has it, James?'

'Sir?' This was a little more troubling to hear.

'Or perhaps you would prefer to be called *Lanky Jamie*?'

James was confused and started, 'Why... I haven't been called that since...' he paused for thought, 'since...' he was having trouble remembering it.

'When might that have been, Jamie?'

The knight was removing his gloves as he asked, he eyes never leaving those of the bed-ridden man. James thought about the question, but all he could focus on at the moment were what long fingers the knight had, once hidden under his gloves. He had fine rings too.

Lanky Jamie?

'It's been…'

'What, thirty-years or so Jamie? Have you forgotten all those cool autumn days and nights with Lord Herbert's fighting men in Ireland? The pillage, the rapine, the tortures done on that one day and what fun you said you had?' The knight's eyes bore into James' own and suddenly memories came flooding back in, reminiscences long buried and thankfully, long forgotten.

But no more it seemed.

He thought of names and faces long, long pushed out of his mind, and suddenly it seemed that their ghosts were in the room with him. Beside him on the bed, leaning on the tallboy, one standing beside Sir Lawrence, who did not seem to notice the apparition. James remembered things he had done then, the men, women and children massacred, and then he sank, his eyes downcast following the shame of his actions; a rising hotness in his chest; his heart beating faster than it had in years.

Oh no, not that.

These thoughts must have been revealed on his face; the knight smiled and nodded. 'You remember then?'

It was just a statement, but tears were forming in James's old, rheumy eyes.

'So, you are not quite that saint that your friends and neighbors think you are? Does this wife know? Have you told her that which drove away your first wife, Anna? Anne, was it? How the knowledge that the man she'd married was once a rapist and murderer drove her to insanity and finally death by her own hand? Have you explained these things to your remaining son and your daughter, your grandchildren? How do you tell a child that grandfather is a murderer, a torturer, and a molester, a monster? *Lanky Jamie*, your name hasn't been forgotten.'

James shook his head violently, he weakly swatted at the sound of a flying insect. 'No, they do not know, sir; I am not that man any longer.'

The knight nodded. 'Oh, you've changed your ways then have you, James? Made peace with your past? Justified what you did to your triune god as, what, the sins of your commanders?'

'No, it was only…'

'Only!'

The knight was clearly now upset and spit out the word as if it was some kind of poison. The buzzing sound of the insect increased momentarily. Sir Lawrence just as quickly composed himself in James's eye; he paused and listened to some voice or sound beyond James's old ears.

'My apologies. I am known as a man of quick passions.' Tadhg waved his hand for the bed-ridden man to continue.

'You were saying it was, only… what now?'

The man shook his head.

'Only some backwater, backward-looking Munster village of no consequence?'

Tadhg paused and regarded the bed-laden man.

'Perhaps? Or was it only a stark message sent to the mayor of Cork for his allegiance to the white rose?

True enough, it was that. 'Or perhaps was it because he had been fooled by a pretender and he must pay? But not directly.'

As he spoke James watched the knight pull a vial from a small bag hung from his belt.

'Only a bit of sport, something you remember now and then, and occasionally smile about, a misspent youth. You entertained your comrades in arms with tales and descriptions. Those remaining few, cast here and there. Your friends in arms, when time was? Lanky Jamie, and his crew?'

James shook his head in denial while the knight got up and moved to the door. Tadhg opened it, playing his role.

'Woman! Fetch a mug of beer for your man!'

The knight regarded James lying still in his bed, now visibly shaking and quite obviously uncomfortable.

Tadhg continued the interrogation. 'How long did you stay connected with them, James? Who among them do you remember from that day?'

James did not ask who the knight meant by *them* as he knew the answer. 'I didn't stay connected, sir, not for long afterwards.'

'Thank you so much.' He closed the door and returned to his seat carrying a mug. 'At least you have the awareness to look ashamed.'

'I could not. Those days… they began to haunt me.'

'I know.'

'I heard reports of some of the others dying, terrible deaths…'

'I know.'

'They all lost family, sons, daughters, never wives though.'

'I know.'

'You know? Who are you, sir?'

Tadhg smiled but ignored the question for the moment. He opened the little vial and poured its contents into the mug.

'Who am I?'

From James's point of view, the knight paused, watching the mixture, swirling the liquid, around without spilling any, smelling it, adding a little more of the vial's contents to the ale.

Tadhg then regarded James again. 'I am not a cruel being, James, not by the standards of some of my people. But you did an awful, awful thing, long and long ago.' The ghosts standing about nodded and pointed at him. 'Oh, I am sure you are sorry for it now. It troubled you for a while, gave you some sleepless nights, you tried to drink it away or found relief in the arms of other woman. Tweaks unknown to your wives, yes? Those two pictured in your little book perhaps?'

Tadhg, as Sir Lawrence, pointed at the *Book of Hours* lying on the bed.

'But you finally put it behind you and moved on. You met a good woman, two good women in fact, and you became a good man, noble even, in your own way, charitable to your fellow men. Well, that was particularly good, James. I commend you for all that. But did you never think that payment would someday come due for what you did? Did you think that, as you forgot so too would you be forgotten?'

'What, what is that you put in the beer, sir?'

'This?' The knight held up the vial for James to see. 'It is a little something one of the daughters prepared for me, extract of *the* phantom queen's helm if you must know. She is exceptionally good with herbs and plants, was trained by a druid's daughter. You might know it as hemlock. The Roman's outlawed its use here in England, long and long ago, such a powerful poison it is, but the plant still grows, and it is still used. Ah, but this version is watered down with the juices of other plants.' The knight, Tadhg, stood and brought the mug over to the side of the bed.

'Are you strong enough to drink it unaided, or shall I feed it you?'

'I'll not be drinking that, sir.'

'Yes, yes you will, James, or I summon your immediate family out there beyond the door and tell them everything you did, around your bed they will stand, with you laying there unable to deny it. How long will your saintly reputation last after that?' The ghosts all took a step closer to the bed, save the one sat at James' feet. He put his hand down; James felt it through the heavy quilt.

He consequently sat up a little, pulling his feet away from the specter who suddenly he knew to be Walter Osteler, died these past five years. He wiped the wetness from his eyes.

'What... what will it do to me?'

'The daughter who prepared it is quite skilled in the arts that used to be called alchemy. It will not impair your senses, it will, in fact, make them temporarily sharper, and it will relax your muscles, easing those pains in your chest, arms and legs. You will, if left undisturbed, ease into a peaceful death before the sun rises on the morrow.'

'This does not seem such a punishment.'

'Did I say it was a punishment?'

'No, but I assumed...'

'Do I look like some demonic being sent to torture you or perhaps an angelic being come to ease your sufferings?' James merely watched the visitor, shook his head. 'I give you this because you did not try to dispute of what I reminded you just then. You did not deny the ghosts of your past.'

James reached a shaking hand over and took the cup. 'Your word as a knight, my past dies with me?'

'You have my word as a king, no one need know.'

If James heard this last part of the oath, he did not react to it. Instead, he drained the mug of a tangier brew than he remembered it being.

'I would rather they,' he coughed out while indicating the door, 'remember me fondly.'

Tadhg nodded his head and returned to his chair, seating himself once again.

'I am sure you would, James, and for the time that remains to them, they will. I will not despoil your legacy.' James was satisfied with this, it sounded good even though he was not sure what a legacy was or what despoil meant. He was already feeling the touches of the drug at work on his body.

'I can't... I can't feel my feet, Sir Lawrence.'

'That is a good sign. As I said, peaceful, if not disturbed.' The dying man watched the knight return to the bag, stopper and deposit the bottle back inside. He was curious when the knight pulled out another vial. This one was larger than the first and held a powder rather than a liquid.

'What now is that, sir? Is it another poison for me to drink? Why, you can only kill me once, sir, surely.'

'Only once you say?'

James was very disturbed by that response.

Tadhg, the knight, nodded in agreement.

'True, in the physical sense I can only do that much as I have done. But then this one is not for you.' He placed the bottle on the frame of the bed. James regarded it with raising anxiety.

'Soothe, James, soothe. You have now paid the price of your thoughtlessness and cowardice of long and long ago. But there is more debt owed. Posterity is owed, my friend. You and your comrades killed not just people on that day, no, you killed a future. You killed what might have been. Children that now cannot be born.' The knight moved the chair back into its former position and picked up his sword, buckling it once more into place. He then replaced his gloves on his hands.

'It was war sir, men die in...' James coughed.

'Quiet now Jamie. The drug is taking effect.'

Tadhg paused, 'Was it war, though? Really? Funny, William le Penne said the same.' He pondered this thought. 'Except in their own self-defense, how many of your soldiers were killed by the people of that village? Or should we say murdered, for that is what it was. Had any of them ambushed you first, hunted you out first?' He paused to allow James to respond. 'No, I did not think so. And yes, men die in wars, of course they do. And a village can survive with the loss of a couple young men, certainly, but a village cannot survive the murder of every man, woman and child there. It becomes a cursed place. People will not come there, go there; it is avoided and best forgotten.'

Tadhg opened the vial and poured some of the powder into his gloved hands. He rubbed it into the fabric of his gloves vigorously.

'We have to be careful here, James,' he said by way of explanation. 'This is the *composition of death*. Nasty stuff is this. A contact poison, it begins working almost at once.' James listened but could no longer see the knight or speak.

'Sarah?'

James screamed in his head when he heard his wife's name called out in that friendly tone the knight used. He heard the door open.

'It seems that James has decided to rest for the night…'

No, I haven't. No, I haven't, see me wife, see me.

'…so, I will return on the morrow perhaps? Now, introduce me to your family, if you'd be so kind. I would take the news to James's other friends of so long ago. I would know his children.'

Run, Sarah, run.

'Of course, I would be delighted to do so, Sir Oldfield. It's not many of James's friends we see from the old days before we married. Tell me, how do you and my James know each other?' James heard laughter.

'It's a long and funny story, my dear, but first things first, who is this fine young man?' The door closed.

James did not have to strain to hear anything from beyond the prison that was now his body, his senses had become, as promised, sharpened. He heard muffled sounds, light sounds, like laughter, good tidings, funny stories being relayed to a humor starved audience. Maybe he had been lied to after all.

Then he heard, not long thereafter, the entrance open and close, the sounds of farewells and the complaints of the animals below, their sleep disturbed. He had almost convinced himself that he had been played for a fool when he heard the coughing start, a bad coughing. This was not Sarah's soft cough; this was fast building up and hacking of his son. Many voices, his wife's, his son's, his daughter's husband, finally everyone was coughing, some violently, others less so, none of the babes thankfully. This suddenly changed and one by one grew in volume into a confused gagging, vomiting and finally screaming. He heard things fall into other things; someone pawed at his door. Then he heard nothing else but babies crying; then he descended into madness.

§

A door opened only a few minutes later.

'Are they all dead, sire?'

'No, Bedingfield's son here is dying, but not yet dead. The young woman there is merely in a deep sleep like the others. You got the names of Thomas's children Talia?'

'Yes, sire, I know them now. I will write them down soon. What about the unborn child of the girl?' Tadhg nodded his approval; Talia was growing into her office.

'Elizabeth is not Bedington's own child. This Sarah was unfaithful, just the once. When I spoke of Bedingfield's offspring, Sarah thought only of the young man Thomas, not the girl. When I spoke of his grandchildren, she thought only of his children, not the child in the girl's womb. She lives; the unborn child will never be harmed by my hand. Elizabeth will aid Sarah's declining years along with the wife of Thomas. They are innocent. We will watch these two children though. When they are older, they too will be harvested. Speaking of which…'

Tadhg moved back to the bedroom door and re-entered the room. Sir James was still alive; barely, cried out, eyes puffy still, barely aware. His eyes would widen in terror, however, when he saw Sir Lawrence's fangs descend from his upper row of teeth and move toward his throat. The old man's last thoughts were not of his wife and children but of two prostitutes he'd once known, immortalized in the illuminated pages of a sacred book.

§

Two men awaited on horseback just beyond the edge of the town. They held a third horse between them. They were in the shadows; no one had seen them. At this time of night there were few about in any case.

Tadhg approached them on foot from the north side of the town. He was removing his gloves, carefully it seemed, and placing them in another bag. This he placed in one of the saddlebags. He flipped through the pages of a small book he had taken out of another pocket, which he then also deposited in the bag along with another, which jangled as it moved, metal on metal, coins hitting against each other.

He mounted the horse.

The man to the left of him handed him a book and a quill pen, holding an inkwell out toward him.

'Master.'

Tadhg took the book and opened it to an early page. He dipped the quill in the ink and wrote a few details in the book, writing carefully and precisely despite the shadows and the night. Details Talia may have missed. They would compare their notes later.

The other withdrew and held a flask.

When Tadhg was finished with the entry, he handed the book and pen back to the first man, then took the flask from the other and took a long draft. Some of the liquid seeped out and flowed slowly down Tadhg's chin. It was a black liquid. In daylight it would have been the color of a deep, thick, brandy-wine.

'All is well, sir?'

'A man can be killed more than twice.' Tadhg wiped away the few escaped drops.

The two sons regarded each other over Tadhg's shoulders. Neither questioned the statement having heard similar nonsensical statements before.

'When we return to our rooms, Son Harold, would you be so kind as to send Daughter Maggie a note that her mixtures worked just as she promised they would. Relay that I am pleased. Son Tobias, you will remain here. Keep watch on the house and report back to me when the Bedingfields are discovered. Children will be crying soon, women sometime thereafter. It will look to the sheriff like James killed his son and poisoned the others ineffectively in some kind of deranged state, and then died peacefully in his bed.'

'Yes, my lord, and if there are questions?'

'Bring it to me later. There shouldn't be. James was a saint you know, this will be dismissed as the devil's work, and perhaps, it is.'

'Can the wife not identify you?'

'She will try but be unable too. It will be dismissed as her mind being addled by the events of the morning.' The man nodded and rode off toward the inn of the town. Tadhg and his other man started off the other way. Talia flew to catch up.

4

[It is May 12th, 1672 — The Roundhead's Inn, London]

One of the daughters had informed Tadhg that he should come to a pub in the heart of the city as soon as he could conveniently do so as there were rumors spreading out in the lower echelons of the mortal science community with regard to blood, and this was a place he might hear them discussed.

And this one night he did hear a disturbing tale indeed.

Two medical students, or youngish physicians at any rate, began talking in an isolated booth near the fireplace, no more than a body length away from where Tadhg sat in the shadows of the great hearth. They were not worried about being overheard; it was just that this was their customary spot in the nearest pub to their work.

At first, they spoke of nothing important, trivialities to Tadhg's mind. They spoke of families, friends, incidents, to which Tadhg was on the verge of tuning out. Abruptly the topic turned and captured his full attention.

'… I read,' said the one with hair the color of obsidian, 'that this Lower chap opened the jugular vein on this dog, a good-sized dog mind, maybe a collie dog, I don't know what breed, but it doesn't matter anyway. The point is that he did this at the Royal Society, just a few years ago, before lots of witnesses. He bled the creature until it was exsanguinated, nearly, and the dog almost dead. As you can imagine, Miller, this had raised a few mumbles in the crowd.

'Ghastly stuff,' commented the one with hair of muddy brown.

'But then, Lower attached this new instrument of his own design and pumped back into the dog the blood of another dog entirely.'

'Whatever for…? These are most odd goings-on. What breed was this other creature, Jenkins?'

'Um, a bigger dog, maybe a mastiff or Saint Bernard, the article did not specify, but it would have to have been larger so there would be more blood to work with, less life-threatening.'

'Aye; that makes sense of a sort.'

'Anyway, Lower fills the smaller dog back up a bit with the blood of this other, sewed the vein up, and the dog is up and moving again in no time, no worse for the earlier doings.'

'Amazing,' said the other, Miller, sipping a fine port which Tadhg could smell from his position. 'Where did you read this, my good man?'

'In the *P.T.*, an edition of '66 or '67, I don't recall precisely, but you could find it in the stacks I'm sure if you're interested. The operation was carried out in February or March of the previous year.' Tadhg overheard this but was distracted by the fact that he did not know what the letters "P" or "T" stood for. He would later be informed it was *Philosophical Transactions*, a scientific journal first published that same year. Questioning revealed that mortal scientists call their studies *natural philosophy*, which cleared up a little confusion on his part.

'Do, Jenkins, do, it's an amazing article. In any case, a couple of years later a doctor named Denys, a Frenchie, transfers the blood of a sheep into this boy and the boy survived!'

'That's harder to believe…'

'True, true, but the story goes that it was a miniscule amount of blood, so any cross-species difficulties were made inconsequential. He repeated the procedure later on a common tenant farmer, who also survived to return to his labors. You know Doctor Bernard?'

Tadhg heard no reply to this question but presumed that the other indicated that he did know the man.

'Yeah, he witnessed this Lower chap perform at the Royal Society itself.'

'Hmm, I must send him a letter; ask for some further details.'

'He is a most accommodating fellow is Bernard. You can pay him a visit as he has a surgery here in the city. He doesn't do research any more due to the success of his inventions and procedures.' Jenkins and Miller resolved to pay the inventor a visit in the near future and their conversation moved on to other trivialities.

By that point Tadhg had heard enough. He left the pub distracted by the conversation and perplexed by the implications. He walked about the streets of London, considering the ramifications of what he had heard. It was impressive, no denying that fact, but he also feared the consequences.

He later asked the daughters to keep an eye on any new developments, leaving it in their capable hands with permission to draw resources, if necessary, and track this Bernard fellow.

A couple of years later he was told that the Royal Society, the French government, and the Vatican, had suspended the new practice on both medical and ethical grounds. The triune god had not been pleased by this work, tampering with nature.

As pleased as Tadhg was to hear of these objections, he also knew that the mortals would not stop there despite the prohibition. No, someone somewhere was even now experimenting, he reasoned, against the day when those small-minded restrictions were lifted.

It took a century and a half for that day to come… officially.

5

Who put Ken Malone in the Wych Elm tree?

    Last year (26 September) four local lads discovered a skull and other human remains inside a Wych Elm in the park near the pre-school in Turvey. A police investigation determined that the body was that of a man, possibly Ken Malone, who had missing for two years. The identification is based on the remains of his clothing. A piece of leather belt (possibly his own) was found mixed in with the bones suggesting that Malone was suffocated before being squeezed into the hollow of the tree. Rigor mortis set in thereafter. While interesting, the discovery did not capture the public imagination. That is, until last week when graffiti began to appear around the school, park, and local structures. **"Who stuffed old Ken into the Wych?"** The first such message was found at the *Three Cranes*, the next at the *Tinker* and then at the *Abbey*. The dean of St Alban's has produced no comment on the fact that the message was scrawled on All Saint's Baptismal font. As of this edition, the question is still unanswered.

The Bedfordshire Times and Bedfordshire Standard
For 8 November 1943
By Michael Osborne

6

[It is August 23rd, 1690, in the town of Dunstable]

The old soldier sat on the bench outside the Sugar Loaf tavern. He was a sad sight; a proud man, once, but people did not really see him as a man any more.

The bench had become his habitual place about fifteen years earlier; he was usually there by early evening, and his presence was as familiar to the patrons as the old sign over the entrance. Old White Head was a fixture around these parts, an old fitting. In the minds of many he and the bench were as one piece of furniture.

In any respectable gentleman's house, Old White Head and the bench would be seen as a piece that was considered much in need of repair and attention as well, but which instead got a cover thrown over it to hide its presence in a cellar or unused outbuilding (or just burnt away with the other old rubbish).

A rusted old helmet sat overturned beside him, as it always was it seems, and a few coins were already gathered there, given over from one generous patron or another. The soldier, said to be in his eighth or ninth decade, was dressed in an old, ill-fitting, and faded roundhead uniform.

It was as faded as his eyesight.

He dressed that way not only because it was his best suit (his only suit to be honest), but also to remind people of the past; of a time when he had been someone, and what some, men like him, had done for all the rest of them in the name of Cromwell and of the republic. That he had fallen on tough times was quite clear; he had been reduced to beggary (and occasionally worse) in the last decades of his life.

He had no family (that he could remember) and no one could remember his name.

It had not always been this way, of course. The bleached embellishments on his old jacket proved he had once been a sergeant, and he still carried himself as a man who once commanded others. Command requires respect, however, but he was no longer given that.

Sometimes, in his head of late, a voice would come unexpectedly. It would remind Richard Brandwhait (Old White Head) of who he was, and who he had been.

Those were the worst times though.

Remembering was like a torture for him.

§

Brandwhait was known by sight (and smell, some wag might say) by the actual residents of Dunstable and he knew them. He had watched them go by day by day, month after month for years.

He knew which ones might drop a coin in his old helmet; he knew which would ignore him altogether. He knew which might strike him if the mood took them so to do too. He also recognized which were the travelers in the crowd. Those heading south to London, when he looked, he saw hope in their eyes for whatever plan or scheme they wished to instigate (he knew they might be generous). Those heading north to, well, wherever they were going, eyes glazed over in disappointment or contentment, less generous. Some could be counted on for a little more charity than others. His old eyes had seen them come and go; they had shown puzzlement over the changing fashions; they had been disappointed at the way the youth treated the elderly, and they had watched bullies grown old enough to be poorly treated or beaten in their turn by former victims and younger bullies on the rise.

It was none of his concern, any of that though. Maybe, if his memory was still stable, as a young soldier he would have done… something.

That was another life; and certainly, no longer his own.

Personally, he had only two concerns nowadays. Keeping his belly fed and keeping enough fuel handy for the small fireplace in his small room at Mrs Logan's, a boarding house across town where he lodged.

Given that it was high summer just now the second concern was not so much at issue. It would become more urgent soon enough, however; he did not want to lose his bed for lack of a few shillings rent or his health for lack of coal and warmth. He therefore had a stockpile of small pieces of wood and coal chunks hidden away here and there about the surrounding woodland or secreted where no one else knew, about town, and he added to the collection whenever he could in the three seasons where a fire was less a dire need.

By night, abed, he dreamed of days gone by and what might have been.

Had he not been injured so long ago, had he not tripped up at an inopportune moment back then, well, he thought (against all reason) that he might just still have been able to join up with good King William's forces near Dublin a couple of months back now, and help see off the old king's mercenaries. In his mind he saw himself as maybe even an officer, a senior officer at that, gentrified by a grateful king and realm. He would then imagine being retired on a good pension, his wife and children (and grandchildren) gathered around as he told tales of his exploits, by the fire, after a fine dinner cooked by an efficient staff of servants.

Lately, these dreams filled his waking thoughts too.

What might have been occupied so much of Richard's time these days that he took it as a sign of his impending demise (which, frankly, he welcomed), and smiled and shook his head at the irony of it all.

Imagine me, a former roundhead, from a shire and city of roundheads, wanting to fight for the heir of the old king against another heir of the old king?

He would laugh aloud; the cackling sound would startle anyone nearby.

It was then that a well-dressed man, cane in hand, placed a few coins in Richard's helmet. The sound was heavy, shillings, not groats and pennies. He had been distracted from his fantasies by the clinking sound.

'Thank you, good sir.' He looked up, his eyes rheumy and his vision blurred by tears he wasn't aware he shed.

Pushing the shag ends of his ill-kempt hair away from his sunken eyes he noted a cane with a golden doghead as a grip pass by. This sparked something in the dark recesses of his muddled thoughts, but he could not recall what it was, only sound, *click-click-tap, click-click-tap,* the same sound his benefactor made now approaching the tavern.

'You're welcome, Grandfather.'

The man who spoke had an accent. By the time this registered with the old soldier, the man had already entered the tavern and was out of his sight again and out of reach for the time being.

Richard frowned. He was forbidden to go inside, so he could not follow his patron and satisfy the mental itch that was so familiar to him... somehow.

The old soldier shrugged, knowing that the man would have to, in time, come out of the tavern and pass this way again. There was no other way. Richard smiled, that's right, the man had been coming in quite often of late (of late being in the last few days) and he often remained after the working hours were over. Richard then settled back on his bench, recalling the same feeling of familiarity he had on previous nights, and wondered if it might not simply be the repetition.

Three times now; Richard had never seen him leave though, now that he thought about it.

He made most of an evening's earnings from those coming out of the tavern, despite the occasional bash about the head and shoulders from drunken churls, so he prepared to wait for the emergence of the man with the cane once again.

'This time I will, sir; this time for sure.' He swore his small oath, sat back, and pondered all the *what ifs* of his life once again.

§

Here, in this place, at this time, Tadhg had adopted the name Lord Patrick Fitzgibbon for no other reason that he liked the rhythm of it. He passed the old soldier a few coins, spoke briefly, and entered the tavern. The small gesture was enough to set up an emotional connection that he could use later that morning.

Stood in the entrance Tadhg paused and saw a pleasant enough establishment, but really, much of a muchness as far as taverns went these days. Even gentlemen's places like the Sugar Loaf were no longer unique in his eyes.

Oh yes, certainly, this one was cleaner than some but less well-appointed than others. He signaled the barman with his cane and made his way over to a free bench by one of the front windows. This position afforded him an unobstructed view of the common room, the door, and the front of the tavern outside where the old soldier sat mumbling to himself. He withdrew a small thimble from his pocket and placed this on the table before him and off to the side.

'Lord Fitzgibbon', said the barman, bringing over a bottle and a fine glass to the table nearby, now used to the eccentric thimble custom. 'The usual, sir?'

'That will do nicely, Maurice, nicely indeed.' Tadhg winked.

Fitzgibbon opened his charge purse and passed the barman a few coins, more than enough to pay for the bottle and the service. 'Keep the rest for yourself, my man, and be sure to join me for a drink before closing time. You have such interesting tales, and I would hear another if you have the time for it.'

The barman chuckled, pocketing the money and bowed. 'I will be sure to do that, sir. It is a rare pleasure for me to have a highly placed gentleman such as yourself interested in my commoner's tales.' Fitzgibbon waved this away.

'You have no idea my man how important your tales are to me. I am something of a collector of stories of the human condition you see.'

'So, you say, sir, so you say.'

It was clear that the barman was unclear on the meaning of this phrase "human condition". He looked around at the other patrons, but no one needed his service just then.

'If only my Sal were still alive to hear it said that a gentleman wanted stories from me.' According to the notes one of the daughters had been keeping on the man, Maurice, as he now called himself, had been married to an ancestor of one Humphrey Boothe, a Hampshire soldier, mercenary, murderer and thief. Tadhg had harvested the woman about eight years ago, the last member of that cursed bloodline (they had had no children, thankfully); another name, another time, another small revenge achieved. Tadhg had planted subtle thoughts in the man's head over the previous two nights; how they were acquainted one with the other; how Lord Patrick was a connoisseur of anecdotes. Tadhg had created a small legend about Lord Patrick, and his natural exuberance took care of the rest.

Maurice excused himself from the gentleman's presence and returned to serve a patron now come to the bar. As Fitzgibbon, Tadhg had already heard the story of the death of the man's wife, Sally, and a sad tale it was although embellished quite a lot in the telling since the actual event. The barman attracted more business based on the tale and even gained a sympathetic shoulder from one or other of the town's many comely matrons.

That was none of Tadhg's concern; the barman was not related by blood to any of the cursed, so live and let live. He glanced out the window at the beggar-soldier, however, whilst sipping his wine.

Tadhg watched the man for a time; he seemed friendly enough for a scrounger; there was still some of the soldier's swagger about him (hard to tell as he was sitting down), but that was also no concern of his. But time was growing short, and already Tadhg had notes from sons and daughters around the south of England eager for his attention.

Instead, all part of the act (mostly), the aristocratic Fitzgibbon pulled a little book out of his pocket; this evening's reading; the show for the masses. It was the philosopher's, John Locke's, newest publication called *An Essay Concerning Humane Understanding*. When Tadhg had found it in the bookseller's cart, he had misread the title as "Understanding Humans", only realizing the mistake later. Still, it was an interesting read, and he would very much like to meet this Locke fellow. They had much to discuss. Sadly, he did not have the time for fripperies and fancies yet.

He snickered; he even smiled.

Tadhg had already worked his way through Locke's early chapters on so-called "Blank slate versus innate understanding." This is what other human philosophers of an older generation had called *nativism*, and Tadhg remembered studying that too when it was fresh learning. He had been interested in this as a means of explaining the difference between *fae* children, who are born with some innate knowledge of themselves and their world, and human children, who gained knowledge only through, as Locke wrote, experience. Tadhg often wondered which was better and tried to engage a son or daughter of learning in that discussion. This reading had also led him to recall times when he had said something to his mother or father that a child should not have been able to discuss rationally.

What would this man Locke say about the Hidden?

Maybe he knew.

The second part of the treatise had let him down; it was, Tadhg recognized, little more than a rehash of Platonic and Aristotelian ideas mixed in with Aquinas' teleological explanation of the proof of the triune god.

As such, it was easily dismissed.

The third part (that which he was now reading) seemed much more interesting; Tadhg was looking forward to appraising the arguments. It was a mental exercise he engaged in early mornings, before the supernatural influence of the day finally forced him to withdraw into darkness and sleep.

He kept an eye on the beggar though.

The thimble was empty. Tadhg carefully poured a splash of wine.

Talia was quiet tonight for which he was thankful. Maybe he could talk this Locke into writing a study of *pixies*?

He smiled, placed the bottle down, and glanced out the window again.

Outside he could see two men, well-appointed, straight backed soldierly types, had stopped and were speaking with the beggar; they were intent on coming into the tavern; he was trying to engage them in small talk. The two men had a woman with them. She was a young and attractive brunette beauty. Perhaps the old soldier wished only to keep her in sight a moment longer. Between the three they gathered a few coins for the man, dropping these into his helmet, brushing off his effusive thanks.

Tadhg knew these three; they were sons and a daughter, and they had been watching the old man for some time on their master's behalf (unbeknownst to the old man, of course). The soldier types subtly nodded to "Lord Fitzgibbon" as they passed him by, doffing their caps, and the woman performed a nice curtsy. This impression of respectful acknowledgement would work to throw off suspicions of too much familiarity and reinforce the pretense in the minds of other patrons.

Yes, just an act to reinforce the illusion; gentry paying due deference to their betters.

Nobody had seen the four of them together; Fitzgibbon had only arrived in Dunstable half a week prior, while these three had been here a fortnight, keeping watch on Brandwhait; his comings and goings, his associations, his life (such as it was) and setting up a presence.

Fitzgibbon idly returned the acknowledgements as he turned the page in his book; the sons sat at a nearby table where they could watch the master and the door; the daughter sat with her back to him.

Brandwhait sat in his place outside and decried the unusual lack of patrons, even for a Wednesday evening no one seemed to be out and about.

§

Still, it was a warm evening, but a dull one for Brandwhait, what with the light foot traffic on the streets. After a time, his head began to tilt down toward his chest. Tadhg had been waiting patiently for just this moment. He put down the book and his glass of wine, put a finger to his lips (not that Talia was being a nuisance at all as she was well into her cups) and concentrated his will through the glass and into the unconscious mind of the old soldier…

§

'…Brandwhait!' The soldier's mind registered something and stirred toward consciousness.

'Brandwhait!' There was a light, and his head was swimming toward it, but it was a hard struggle against the opposing tide.

'Brandwhait!' yelled one of the sergeants for a third time. 'Look alive, you numbskull!'

In his dream Richard shook himself out of a stupor and rose unsteadily to his feet, following the order but still groggy. He glanced around; he was surprised that he was not on a bench outside a tavern (where he thought he should have been) but had somehow taken a position off the ground and up in a tree.

He shook his head, as if to clear away the cobwebs.

Oh yes, he now remembered, it was better here to observe the distant goings on in this small cesspit of an Irish village.

Rising to his feet, however, had been a mistake.

He tumbled out of the tree and hit the ground on his rear, just missing knocking over his superior.

He moaned out more in surprise than pain, however. The sergeant made no move to help him to his feet either.

'Get up, *lack-whait*', he bellowed, making part of the soldier's surname sound insulting.

Brandwhait did as he was bidden, however, his soldier's reflexes taking control. His legs and back were complaining (in his mind he thought he was getting too old for this), but otherwise functioning as well as could be expected. In his mind he had the passing thought that the fall should have done much more damage to him than it had. He had the image of a bashed and broken leg.

'Report, if it's not too much trouble?' Brandwhait appreciated the consideration, not catching the sarcasm in the other's voice.

'Thank you, ah, sergeant.'

The man before him next raised a hand to slap out what he took as insubordination, and then he thought better of it, shaking his head in sorrow.

'Just report, you fool.'

He shrugged. 'There is nothing to report, sir.'

Brandwhait cringed, expecting a physical assault but it did not come. 'Really, sergeant, I swear they just go about their business. It's… boring sir, really dull. Occasionally, a couple go off into the woods over that way, but from what I can see it's just a village, sir. Kind of reminds me of Dunstable.' Brandwhait paused in confusion; *what did I just say?*

'May I ask…'

'No, you may not, Brandwhait. And what's this about Dunstable? Jesu man, it looks nothing like that place. Have you ever been to that hole? Just get back into your position up there but stay alert now. We are moving toward an attack soon.' Brandwhait closed his mouth, stifled his questions, and looked back up to the stout branch he had been sitting on. He nodded and started the climb once again. The sergeant stomped off.

Brandwhait resumed his perch, wondering about Dunstable (*of all places?*) and why this tiny village was so important to anyone not already cursed to live there.

§

Tadhg, as Lord Fitzgibbon, sat back on his bench inside the Sugar Loaf and puzzled over the dreaming soldier's insertions of reality into the created mental landscape, little as it had been, pushed into the fantasy Tadhg had been building up inside his head for him.

Tadhg had long ago accommodated himself to the fact that, as an impure member of his race his power over mortal dreaming was not what it once had been, but his control had been getting better (with the death of each bloodline, or so it seemed). Still, the old soldier must have something of a good old brain in there to insist upon what was real whilst still inside a dream.

Thinking back to the time, long and long ago now, when John Brandwhait's memories of the day in question had been harshly ripped out of his mind, Tadhg tried to associate the two men across the span of years.

That had been two centuries' gone by.

Tadhg had had to consult the book to firm up the details in his own mind. Talia flipping through the pages; a daughter grabbing the book before the pixie did any damage. That soldier, John, had been ill-treated by his comrades too; recalled as something of a lack-wit. That aspect of the bloodline had stabilized apparently. Tadhg had found that soldier working in a blacksmith, practicing the armorer's trade. He had somehow found a woman to lay with him too and had a wife and child in short order. It had been child's play to arrange an "accident" in the smithy, but other related pursuits had meant that it was a good thirty years before Tadhg could return for the child, by which time he had children of his own.

And so, it went. Humans breed so fast; the world will be full of them soon.

Tadhg saw to his fulfilment of the oath, the harvest, while the sons and daughters were tracing the twists and turns of the Brandwhait progeny.

Like so many others, John Brandwhait's direct and legitimate male line had been ended decades ago, but someone born on the other side of the sheets in the meantime had re-adopted the old surname. John Brandwhait's grandsons, one of whom had somehow managed to become the owner of a small farm in Hertfordshire, had sired many children between them, legitimate and otherwise, and meanwhile, with the other families keeping the sons and daughters busy, his lineage had made it into the next century, well beyond the time of the Tudors in whose name the original atrocity had occurred. But every one of them killed did, in theory, reduce the future numbers, so Tadhg stayed the course as he must. Sometime in the 1620s an illegitimate heir was able to legally adopt the family surname again (which was a boon to the Daughter researching that family line).

Tadhg, however, for all the support the sons and daughters gave, for all the resources the *fae-courts* and he personally had at their disposal, could not burn out the old monsters' blood fast enough to keep Ireland strong and independent. Without its *Hidden* high king, the land lacked a certain vitality; already the clans had given in to English customs and culture, and even the Scottish plantations in Ulster were growing up and over the natives. He worried that a few more generations might even see off Gaelic as the land's first language. Instead of supporting the Scot on the Boyne they really should have supported the Dutchman in that dynastic struggle. Tadhg reached out with his will toward the last Brandwhait again (the last his people had found so far), and re-established control over his unconscious mind, leading him through the sudden ambush, the slaughter of the innocents, and the senseless, awful destruction of the otherwise inconsequential village. The original Brandwhait had been uncaring, but to his credit, at least this last one had been visibly upset by it.

§

At or near to closing time the barman brought over another bottle and two glasses to the aristocrat's table. He ignored the thimble or, at least, no longer asked about it. The sons and daughter had already left (waiting nearby), and Tadhg could see that Brandwhait had shaken himself awake and was stirring, soon to make for his home.

'I think you'll like this vintage, my lord,' said the barman, 'it comes from Burgundy.' Lord Fitzgibbon smiled up at the man, folded his book closed, took and examined the label.

'A Pinot Noir?'

He accepted the cork and waved it under his nose. 'I know the grape, the noirien, I believe… 1650? How did you get it, Paul, my good man? Please, sit, join me for a time.'

The barman, whose real name was Paul (after the saint), not Maurice (which was a name meant to attract a better clientele), put a finger to his nose; 'We barmen have our secrets, my lord,' he smiled, 'may I?' He moved the bottle and glasses.

'Please do, Master Shawley, and some for the *fae* if you would.'

Paul poured the wine into the two glasses and a small portion into the thimble. He picked up one of them while the aristocrat picked up the other. The two glasses were lightly clinked together.

Over the course of the next hour, wine was drunk, glasses (and thimble) refilled, and tales exchanged. Finally, Lord Fitzgibbon rose and thanked Paul the barman for his company and tales and for the fine wine. Sadly, this would be the last time they would make an evening of it; business concluded, Tadhg said that Fitzgibbon was leaving on the morrow. Perhaps one day he would come back this way.

Yes, he would mention the Sugar Loaf, long may it stand.

He passed over more coins, much more than the wine would have brought to the bar and said his final good mornings.

The tavern was shut down and locked after his parting.

It was time to finish with Dunstable and the Brandwhaits.

§

Mrs Logan's boarding house was an old, once even fashionable brick building on Winefield Street, sat opposite a small green space with a plinth but no statue. It had been under observation for days now, more attention than it had gotten in the previous century, all told. Getting a layout of the place had been no trouble, and Tadhg (who had now removed the aristocratic finery) could easily scale the exterior wall to the old soldier's digs on the second floor.

Brandwhait had a convenient tendency to leave his window slightly ajar for the night air and Tadhg effortlessly found his way inside. He had re-learned the innate *fae* ability to mask sounds, and he had employed it on the old frame with success. His use of it was still imperfect, but it worked as intended (this time).

Once inside he noted that the old soldier had the presence of mind to take the time to hide whatever money he had gathered in that evening, but not enough to remove his outerwear before he fell on to his cot. Tadhg saw this for an old campaigner's habit — hide valuables, keep in a prepared state for unexpected action.

He nodded approvingly.

It was not a large room by any measure.

Beside the bed there was a table, and a chair was set near a small fireplace, a tall boy near the bed, a coat rack near the door, and an old mid-sized chest at the end of the bed. Tadhg accepted a place sitting on the chest and regarded Richard in his sleep. He resisted the temptation to invade the man's mind again, now, as there was really no longer a need for it.

He was, however, considering how best to end Brandwhait's life when the soldier stirred and opened a wary eye as some instinct was still alive.

He rolled over then and saw the man sitting at the end of his bed.

Unsure whether this was another dream or real life, he only slowing pulled himself together, shook off the sleep and sat up. 'Are you… who are you?'

There was clearly still something of an old military discipline about the man, muscle memory, and Tadhg could not help but be impressed by it.

He bowed his head, 'I am Tadhg Roryson, and you are Richard Brandwhait, last of the indirect bloodline of James Brandwhait, who died in October 1514.' This response took the old soldier a moment to digest. He put a hand to his forehead. Tadhg whispered, 'This is not a dream, Richard.'

After a moment, 'I know that name; indirect? What does that mean?' Brandwhait came a little more into his waking senses, 'Why are you in my room anyway? You…' he blinked a couple times. 'You look familiar somehow.'

'We have… met, Richard. It was decades ago, but more recently as well.'

Tadhg pulled what looked like a baton from under his coat. Brandwhait may have taken it for a truncheon or cudgel in the bad light and shrank back slightly.

'Assassin…' his eyes grew wide but then he thought the word over and dismissed it, '… huh! Why would you come for me?' Although it was a rhetorical question, it seemed the old man was more depressed by the implications of his realization than he was the man at the end of his bed.

Tadhg ran his hand over the baton and it magically, and within a bright blue aura, expanded to take the form of a golden lion's-headed ebony walking stick. Tadhg held this up for the man to see. For his part Brandwhait was confused by the sudden appearance of the stick. He shook his head and tried to rub the sleep from his eyes again.

'Ah... the generous aristocrat...' Tadhg nodded. 'I... I know that stick.'

'Yes, I'm sure you do, Richard. You were once a sergeant in the old parliamentary forces were you not? Think back. Do you recall a battle near Worcester one balmy evening? You were leading a small platoon...'

'... against the forces of the old king? Yes, yes, I remember it well.'

'And you hurt your leg...'

'Yes, I'll never forget that it was as if a plant had reached up out of the ground and grabbed me, pulling me down.'

'In the chaos that followed you were forgotten, overrun by your own men. Afterward you crawled your way to a nearby tree, rested against the trunk, waiting for anyone to come and give you aid.'

'Yes, I sought it... I sought out a safe place to recover.'

'A walnut hit you on the head.'

'Wait, that's right. I... I looked up at the sound of laughter and saw...'

'Me?'

'You were standing on a branch, leaning against a black stick with a golden lion's-head grip, casual as you like.' Tadhg displayed the stick once again.

'The very same.'

The old man was clearly confused.

'But that man, you, whomever, he disappeared right before my eyes. They told me it was just a result of a clout to the head or something; I hit a rock in my fall...'

'No, no. That was really me. I did not disappear so much as pulled the shadows around myself. It's an old trick now. I'd meant to kill you then, you know, but my control over flora was not what it once had been, and that stubborn old walnut tree would not cooperate with an impure *sidhe*.' Tadhg shrugged, 'and in the chaos of the battle I could not risk further interactions with mortal... umm, human witnesses.'

Brandwhait was clearly struggling to take in all this information.

Tadhg smiled indulgently. 'You're wondering why I would wish to kill you.' Brandwhait shook his head to say differently.

'Nah., I have been a soldier near all my life sir, I know the way of it. I killed someone dear to you somewhere along the way and now you seek revenge or was hired so to do on some other's behalf. It's an old story… and I am ready to die besides. If I may ask though, who did I kill?' Tadhg stood up. He moved to the washing bowl on the table, poured water into it, and dipped the washing cloth, bringing that back for the old soldier.

'I've noted that you have raised no hue-and-cry, Richard,' he said, passing over the cool cloth, 'I respect that, sir, and I respect you, so I will tell you why I have come. Personally, I bear you no ill-will, but the blood you carry has to be erased from the world.' Tadhg returned to the chest, sat down, and turned to face Richard full on once more. 'You have been dreaming of a man named John, have you not, and the destruction of an Irish village of no particular consequence.' It was not a question. Brandwhait's mouth fell open and he nodded.

'The dream…'

Tadhg held up a hand stopping him going any further.

'Not a dream as such, Richard, a vague memory pulled from your own blood and enhanced by my own powers, such as they be.' Tadhg shrugged with good humored self-deprivation. 'Your ancestor, the soldier in your… dream, really did participate, willingly, I might add, in the slaughter of a small Irish village. That village, you see, was, is, dear to me. And though I was not there to see it, I have lived it now hundreds of times through the blood memory of each descendent of each man who took part that day, including John. Brandwhait, however, is not your real name though is it, Richard? Your grandfather was born on the wrong side of the sheets as the expression was and only adopted his father's name prior to having a family of his own. Your real surname is Whiteside.'

'So… if my grandfather, as you say, had not changed his name?'

Tadhg shook his head. 'It would have made no difference sir. I would still be here all the same, perhaps on another day, in another year, but all the same.'

The old man thought for a time.

'I think that I should fight against this; it seems somehow unfair, but…' he stood up then, straightened his shirt and jacket, a little unsteady on his feet. 'Sir, I am a soldier; can I not at least be allowed to defend myself?'

Tadhg considered the request a moment and nodded, 'That seems right, but I have only one weapon.' The soldier pointed at the tallboy.

'Underneath are two swords.'

Tadhg nodded, magically reduced his walking stick into its baton form and hid this back inside his jacket. He squatted down, expecting the burn that running his hands under the heavy old closet would bring with contact to the iron of the weapons. He grimaced but came away with two serviceable, well cared for, but clearly old and rusty in parts, weapons. At first site there was nothing particularly special about the swords, single edged old hangers by the looks of them, but brought into the moonlight Tadhg took note of the once bright brass pommels, fragmentary traces of silvering on the filigrees, and some punch work. The grips were still good, however, fluted wood designs, which he was glad to find. He handed one over to Richard.

'I am impressed, sir. You have kept these blades in excellent condition for their age.'

'Alas,' Richard said looking at his sword, his wits now sharper with his old weapon once again in hand, 'they have seen better days... like their master. I have no heir to pass them on to you see. Perhaps... perhaps I could beg a boon of you, sir? Find them a good home?'

Tadhg removed his jacket, put gloves on his hands, and nodded his agreement to the request. 'Agreed, that I will do.' Tadhg adopted the first position of a duel. 'First, though, present your weapon, sir.'

The old soldier did as bid.

Tadhg focused his will on the gathered dust and grime of years gone by and brought his weapon against that of his opponent. A flash of brightness momentarily overcame the soldier's senses, but when it dulled it was clear that the blades had both somehow shed their rust and the indents of service, the brass shone like new, the silvering restored, the wood grips smooth and unchipped. Brandwhait stood wide-eyed in astonishment. He held his blade closer to his eyes.

'It... it looks like the day I was given it from the munitions store.' He chuckled, 'I was young and foolish then, and thought this the most beautiful thing I had ever seen.' He turned his rheumy eyes on Tadhg.

'What manner of creature are you? Your form is human, but no man can cast such magic. Are you an angel of redemption or a demon meant to tempt me into soul destroying fantasies?' He paused, expecting an answer, but then shook his head. 'Do not answer that question, sir, do not, I beg you. I take the question back.' He regarded his old clothing. 'Can... can my attire be restored so easily?' Tadhg shook his head.

'It is all merely earthen matter, Richard. I can appeal to the elements, repair the fabric if you would like?' Brandwhait nodded eagerly.

'If I am dreaming, and these are my last moments, let me at least present a better corpse than I would have.'

Tadhg nodded agreement. 'Stand still then, sir.'

He focused his will again and appealed to the elements once more. The dust and dirt and mire of long attachment were more than happy to return to the earth outdoors once again. As he focused, something of a small whirlwind enveloped Brandwhait.

The years of grime, soaked in through sweat and weather was pulled away and funneled out the open window. Next, an aura enveloped the astonished old man, starting at his feet and moving up his body, his stockings were no more in need of repair; rends and rips in his trousers and shirt were repaired, somehow buttons were replaced, and a belt buckle made once again to shine. He stood dumbfounded, his eyes again wide in wonder, but now with tears gathering.

'Could you...'

'No, that I cannot do, sir. Each of your kind is given a span of years which can only be artificially shortened through accident or killing but never lengthened, except by a terrible curse. Superficial hurts I could conceal under the illusion of clean flesh, but I can hear the stammering of your old heart, the whispering of wheezing in your lungs. Your blood is too old and spent to support your continued existence much longer now. Already I can hear that it burns your throat to merely inhale. Your senses have served you well, sir, but they will soon abandon you one by one. It is the nature of my oath that I cannot allow you to die naturally, however. I will take no more than a week off your total span of time.' Tadhg paused and let all this sink in. 'You must have known this yourself or suspected as much?'

Brandwhait held his head down, nodding his agreement with the assessment.

'But,' Tadhg continued, 'know this, Richard Brandwhait. You have a soldier's will even if your physical condition is waning and failing. Tonight, you die a soldier's death, in combat. Not slumped over on a bench in the rain, unregarded by those who pass you by.' Tadhg crashed his sword against Brandwhait's, and at the same time concentrated his will, invading the old man's mind one last time.

The actual fight was short. In his mind's eye, however, Brandwhait fought like a lion, repelling attack after attack, a wild lunge met with a firm riposte; parry followed parry as he saw two expert swordsmen circling each other, appreciating the other's form, saluting the other's superior moves or surprising strategies, each countering the other's moves with practiced precision. Neither swordsman asking for quarter; neither offering such an insult to his respected foe. Even as he lay dying, in his mind the battle waged on fiercely. Tadhg had delivered the mortal thrust to Brandwhait's heart, but he kept the illusion going.

Tadhg put aside his blade and lifted the old soldier back on to his cot, willing away the bloodstain, absorbing it into himself. He bit into the man's neck, taking what remained of his life's blood into himself as well. He found it surprisingly vital still despite the losing battle against age. Perhaps it had been tricked into some release of arousing fluids at some point in the fight. For his part Tadhg suddenly felt a little stronger, a little more vital himself, a little more alive than he had felt in quite some time. He recognized this as an effect of the death of one of the offending bloodlines.

Richard had been the last.

The sons and daughters could move on in their searches to other bloodlines.

Tadhg had reasoned out that this vitality boost was how the gods who had appointed his task intended that he would throw off the vampyric curse and purify himself again (eventually). Some ghost or other of ancient Mallow could also now rest in peace.

After a moment's reflection sitting on the chest at the end of the dead man's bed, Tadhg gathered the two swords and placed them on the table. He then began a systematic search of the room, uncovering the hiding place of Brandwhait's fortune (the chest, no surprise there), and the few valuable possessions he had left from his life. These included an old watch, a couple medals, a diary with truly little written inside, and a silver picture frame (with no picture). This would be due as recompense to the ghosts of Mallow and would help pay for the re-building of the village.

§

'That was generous of you, sire.'

Tadhg had climbed down from the room. Back on the ground he looked up one last time. 'He had the makings of a good man, Talia, courageous to the end.' With the little pixie flying nearby, Tadhg made his way to the edge of town where a horse and three companions awaited him. One of them would explain the next harvest target and they would plan a route, stopping somewhere not far away for the day. In her own little book Talia would cross out the name Brandwhait.

7

[It is May 23rd, 1778, in Lichfield, England]

Catherine Severance has finally reached her eighteenth year today.

She has been well tutored and is the product of a very respectable upper middle class Staffordshire family. She is the very model of an upstanding modern young woman.

Catherine knew that the Severance fortune had been made in wool and leather. She was also vaguely aware that breweries were owned by her father's people and that there were shares in hotels here and elsewhere managed by employees. She knew that there was partial ownership of a coach design and building concern which was somewhere in the south.

The Severance men were members in good standing within the local Grand Lodge (whatever that was).

Her grandfather, papa, was once commander of the 38th Regiment of Foot, now, with her father, worked in government. She wasn't precisely sure where in government, in which department specifically, but she knew that they were both important gentlemen. When her brother had turned eighteen just two years earlier, he had taken on mysterious work too, between bouts of education.

Catherine, Kate to her friends, had never dreamed that she would be recruited on her own coming of age.

She knew that she had been raised to become the wife of some other important gentleman.

She knew women did not get involved in government work; that was for gentlemen.

She knew these things to be true on the morning of her birthday, May 23rd, but she would know differently by the early evening.

§

[It is May 17th, 1780, in York, England]

Eliza, Lizzy to her friends (what few she genuinely had), had never really known privilege, or security, or love in her scant twenty-three years of existence (she would not call it a life) here in York, where she had been born and trapped by circumstances. Her mother had told her long ago that her father had been a "no good beard splitter".

She never mentioned the fact that she had herself been nothing better than a hedge whore at the time.

Eliza imagined that must have been where she'd been conceived, somewhere under a hedge, as mother sold off another piece of her virtue for the price of a loaf of bread (if that much). By the time Eliza knew that it was shameful, her mother had become little more than an old, used *blowse* who could no longer sell herself.

She instead now oversaw younger whores.

Eliza was determined to avoid that life, but with no education of any kind and no opportunities she had turned to the one thing she had aptitude for, shoplifting. She had made that her stock and trade. Sure, it was more dangerous than whoring, but she was good at it and got better as she grew into womanhood.

Somehow Eliza had also been gifted with a pretty face, full and curly auburn hair, attractive chestnut brown eyes (on the larger side) with thick dark lashes. She had been taught from an early age, by an "aunt", that careful application of make-up "accentuated" her good features and could even change her "aspect" when needed. It was even possible to change her hair color (but wigs were cheaper!) Mother owed auntie money; or something like that, from some time ago, so Eliza was primed for working off the debt as well as work as one of auntie's "girls".

Not the *bob-tail* trade for her though!

Eliza pulled in all the un-licked cubs from around York society and used them to gain valuable gifts in exchange for promises of future favors (rarely ever actually gifted).

Eliza was not a virgin; that commodity had been sold off a decade earlier to a gentleman member of parliament. Eliza wasn't appalled by the trade in sexual favors as such. Realist that she had become, she just preferred not to end up like her mother, so she had concentrated on fast hands and misdirection.

§

[It is May 23rd, 1778, in Lichfield, England]

What a splendid day Catherine was having. There were gifts, and her favorite little cakes, and there was a promise of so much merriment to come.

She would be formally introduced to the cream of Staffordshire society at the official celebration later that evening. All of her friends, their families, and all the eligible bachelors of the region would be in attendance.

She planned to dance all evening.

She planned on being abundantly gay and charming.

She planned on lording it over her friends who were still *children*.

There might be one or two "unplanned" trysts.

While she would still be her parents' babe (as the youngest child), and her brother would still call her *"squib"* for reasons of his own, she would no longer be considered a girl after today. She was an adult now, but she was given this one last chance to play before she had to give up the things of childhood.

The best thing about the day, though, was the presence of papa, her father's father. He was a widower from a youthful age (Catherine was named after his dearly departed wife), and she had a special place in his heart. Many was the time she would sit on his lap by the evening fire as he told her and Daniel (her brother) stories about his life in the army and in government and business, their grandmother, and the stories that his own papa had told him about life in Ireland.

Silly stories though they were.

Catherine had come to think the stories about all kinds of mythological creatures and strange events must be allegories for something. Papa had over the years given her a library full of books on the subject, from picture books for the young to scholarly accounts of legends and folklore. She had read them all because papa also had a tendency to ask a great many questions when he came to call upon his son's household. Father had not minded this impracticable education encouraged by his father (whom he obeyed as a good son should). Father made sure Catherine had learned other more important skills, like languages and writing. Daniel, on the other hand, did not get so much of this as he did preparation for the business and legal worlds. He had a self-defense tutor as well (but he secretly passed on the lessons to Catherine in his turn). Their mother oversaw all the "womanly" arts Catherine would need to know later in life for when she had her own children and a household to manage.

It was late afternoon when Catherine was summoned into her father's office.

§

[It is May 17th, 1780, in York, England]

That afternoon Eliza was wearing her favorite canary yellow, silk, sack-back dress, this time with a cane petticoat. Her hair had been combed up and over the padded roll in the way auntie had taught her to. She had taken on the role of the very model of a modern society woman. She walked the length of the Great Flesh Shambles but there was nothing for her there today. She headed instead toward Christ Church and the better shops, those on the streets which led toward the great Minster.

She had rarely ventured inside the cathedral as she did not want to draw God's attention to her situation as this would draw His attention to the sins of her mother too.

She walked on by, suddenly in the mood for a *pomatum* treatment.

She sang, quietly, "*orange or lemon, orange or lemon?*" Eliza hummed the question like a chant as she walked along and very much alone. Mother had asked her to buy bread too, and auntie had given her a list of required items.

No money to buy them though.

Money would not be needed as Eliza knew her business.

Auntie's lists were never long or overly complicated, and Eliza knew that she was not the only girl sent out to fetch listed items. Other girls, whom she did not know and would not recognize, worked other parts of the city. Men too, but Eliza worked the middle class and upper-class salons and shops because she could be made to fit into that world either as a servant or a lady.

§

[It is May 23rd, 1778, in Lichfield, England]

Catherine was confronted by a sobering sight upon opening the door.

Papa sat at father's desk, his hands folded and resting on the thick leather-bound blotter while father stood behind and to his right, with Daniel standing to papa's left. An unknown man sat in a chair off to the side of the desk near the bookcases. His chair was situated in such a manner that he could comfortably view all three men and an empty chair sat before the desk.

Each man wore the same serious expression.

Her first thought after closing the door was *my future husband is wealthy but not good looking*. She glanced at the unknown man. *Well, not ugly at least... ears a little long.*

'Sit down, Catherine.'

Father used her formal name rather than the casual "Katie".

Catherine decided that she would accept whatever decision had been made about her future stoically and with a smile. She would make the best of it. She would make papa and father happy if she could. She moved forward and sat in the chair, folded her hands in her lap, and smiled at the three men in turn signaling that she was prepared for the news.

'First,' said papa, 'happy birthday my dear. Eighteen?' he shook his head. 'A grown woman now and so pretty and smart. I remember when your father presented you to me. I was afraid to hold you; afraid I would break you; you were so small in my hands.' Father put a hand on papa's shoulder, patting it, as a reminder that there was a purpose here beyond fond memories. He looked up and nodded at his son as if to say *of course*.

'Let me introduce Baron Cain,' he raised a hand and indicated the sitting man, who nodded but otherwise remained oblivious to the proceedings. Catherine was certainly taken by surprise by the revelation of the man's title (a shame that his name was unfortunate, given its biblical origin). She put her hands on the arms of the chair as a prelude to rising and curtsying, but the man raised his hand first and stopped her.

'No need for that, Miss Severance. I am pleased to make your acquaintance.'

'And I you, sir.' She gave him a small, shy smile, her future husband, and turned to face papa again. *Not really ugly at all… and a nobleman!*

'Second,' papa said as if listing items on an agenda. 'Baron Cain is here because we need to discuss your future, my dear, and he will be a big part of it if you agree.'

I should think so, thought Catherine, *being my husband and all. My but he does have fine black hair.* The Baron smiled for reasons unknown. *Is he pleased with me too?*

'But before we discuss details there are a few questions I need to ask you, my dear.'

'Questions? What kind of questions, papa?' Catherine did not think that she was speaking out of turn with her query. *Mother had made no mention of questions… his eyes are violet!*

Papa smiled, 'Questions, the answers to which I have been training you to know all your life.' Catherine wasn't sure how to take this response, nodding, nonetheless. *Not fat either.*

'Tell me of the *phookas*, my dear.'

Catherine sat a moment, confused, thinking she had misheard the question. She glanced at her father, who nodded, and then her brother, who smiled encouragement and winked at her. The Baron looked at her with intense eyes, his thick eyebrows drawn in, and sitting slightly more forward than he had been.

'Sorry, papa, did you say *phookas*?'

'Yes. What do you know of them?' Catherine thought for a moment, her mind scrambling for purchase.

'*Phookas*,' she repeated. 'Well Papa, Gentlemen, in the original Gaelic the word means ghost, but it is considered now to be just one of many descriptors in the category of *fae*. *Phooka* are traditionally known as shape-changers, usually into domesticated animals all the better to prank human victims, although, this is without the malicious intent of their Welsh cousins the *Bookas*.'

The Baron made a noise like a huff.

This momentarily distracted Catherine, but she easily picked up the thread of her discourse again. 'It is said that *phooka* will destroy any unharvested crop or, at least, claim ownership of any such crop left unharvested after Samhain. If I remember correctly, I've read that they sleep between Beltane and Samhain, but there is much debate in the scholarly works over the truth of this claim.'

'Very good, my dear, very well remembered. Now, again, tell me of the *bogies*.'

'Yes papa. *Bogies*... are classified as *bug-bear*-types, categorized alongside *bogles* and *boggarts*, said to have descended from bog spirits. They inhabit gloomier regions, hoarding collections of discarded items which they gather from disused attics and cupboards, lost if one is not careful in their household cleaning regimes.'

'And their forms?'

'Their forms... yes.' Catherine paused for thought, her brows slightly furrowed. *This was clearly a memory test.* 'They are the amorphous ones, vague in form, almost wraithlike in aspect which may account for the variety of reported descriptions in the literature. This is particularly true of the so-called *bogeymen* who tend to hector children... naughty children... and usually at night. There is no accepted explanation behind this behavior except for its convenience to badgered parents.'

'They hope only to turn the children from their misbehaviors. That is their only true duty.' Catherine regarded the Baron.

'Is that true... while... is that the accepted understanding?'

'It is,' he spoke again. 'A *boggart* or *bogie*, by whatever species, inherits a mort... human household over which it holds domain from that point to the end of the human line. Dark in nature they may be, but they are not bloodthirsty by any means. Indeed, they actually protect their humans from the truly bloodthirsty ones.'

'Which,' said papa, raising a hand, 'brings us nicely to the next question. What is the relationship between *boggart* and *hobgoblin*?' Catherine was still looking at the Baron as papa spoke, and she almost missed the query.

'Well, my understanding of the matter,' she turned and faced papa again, 'is that *hobgoblins* are rather good-natured fellows but sensitive about their hirsute seeming. They will turn into nastier sorts if they are slighted once too often about it. The same can be said of *brownies* too, named for their earth tone hoods and mantles.'

'How do you rid a household of a *brownie*?'

Catherine turned her attention from her grandfather to her brother. 'One offers them clothing, Daniel. The little creatures tend to work their odd jobs unclothed, but they are helpful little fellows nonetheless and I'm sure one could learn to disregard their personal habits in time.'

'Have you ever seen one, Miss Severance?'

'No, sir, I have not.'

'Short, stocky, hairy, as you said, quick to anger, but they are equally quick to forgiveness if apologized to promptly and sincerely. Despite their reputation it is the case that no species of the *Hidden* actually wishes permanent harm on humans, but like anyone they can only be pushed so far.'

'Unless the human is himself evil,' Catherine replied, 'liars and murderers can expect no mercy.' The baron conceded the point with a quick affirmation.

For quite some time it seemed to her, papa, sometimes father, and sometimes her brother asked Catherine questions about these and similar mythological beings. *Bogles* and *Buggars*; the stupid *Dobies* and the helpful *Brownies*; *Ghouls* living underground in churchyards and among the roots of ancient trees, the primordial tempters of humanity; questions of how or why every manor house was gifted with a *ùruisg*; of the malevolent, and of the beneficial sorts of creatures. Catherine was hard pressed to recall knowledge but came through well in the end or so it seemed.

Papa smiled and sat back in the desk chair. He nodded and the Baron assumed the discussion from that point.

The Baron stood and sat on the edge of the desk, closer to Catherine but/and blocking her view of her brother. She found she had no desire to turn away from the Baron now anyway but wondered if his choice of position was purposeful.

'Miss Severance... may I call you Catherine?' She glanced at her father, who nodded.

'You may, sir.'

'Then you may call me Cain, I insist.'

'I shall if that is your wish.' *What else would I call my future husband?*

Cain had taken on a tight-lipped smile, but a smile, nonetheless. It did not, sadly, reach up to his eyes.

'Do you think, Catherine, that these *bogies* and *boggarts*, *dobies* and *goblins* are real beings or merely the stuff of children's stories and useful illustrations of moral behaviors and life lessons? You are under no obligation so to think either way, of course, but I am interested in your opinion.'

Catherine smiled at this, a nobleman asking her opinion, and gave the question serious thought. This was something she had never done until this very moment.

Could they be real?

She started to answer the question a couple times before she finally had to admit that she did not know one way or the other.

'I've never seen one, Cain, you see. I would like to, of course.'

'All right, but for the sake of argument, Catherine, let us say that the various species of *fae* are real creatures. When wronged do you believe that they are in the right to seek justice, even vengeance, if it comes to that?'

'All God's creatures have the right to justice, Cain, perhaps vengeance as well, but that is a deep-seated moral question perhaps better left to philosophers and clerics.'

'But humor me, child. If there was such a crime perpetrated against the *fae* that even the death of the perpetrators itself was not enough to cleanse the stain, would you, if asked so to do, give aid to the *fae*? Even should it be the case that you, personally, would not live to see the final reckoning in your lifetime?'

Child?

'Oh my... well, if...' Catherine said, perhaps a little flustered by the question and the implications of it and the Baron's powerful presence, 'if there was something I could do I would do so, Cain. I would see justice done. But this all seems... odd qualities to look for in a wife.'

The Baron's eyes widened at this statement. He stood and turned to regard the three men behind the desk.

Daniel was smirking now, on the verge of laughter, no doubt the word "*squib*" on his lips; papa too was smiling. Father had, however, taken on a sterner expression and was red in the cheeks.

'Catherine!' he said perhaps a little loudly. 'This meeting has nothing to do with marriage. Baron Cain is not a suitor come to call or seek your hand. He is here only to assess your knowledge and suitability for membership in the Daughters of Feidlimid.'

Catherine's mouth hung open a moment and her lovely, cared for skin reddened significantly. 'Oh my... you aren't... we're not...' the Baron shook his head that no, they weren't, but he was now smiling a smile which finally reached his eyes.

'I am flattered of course, Catherine,' he said softly. 'But my people do not believe in marriages in quite the same way that yours do.' Catherine did not know what to make of such a statement, so said nothing, turning back to papa for guidance.

§

[It is May 17th, 1780, in York, England]

Eliza showed no outward annoyance at having to wait patiently before the shop, no woman of the middle classes or higher would ever think to show impatience.

She wanted to be invited in to view and assess the newest fabrics.

Here they sold only the best silken threads, ribbons, and bows from the orient, as well as the finest lace craftworks from Nottingham. Auntie needed specific colors, specific textures and materials, but one must not appear too anxious, that would draw suspicion. Eliza carefully slid a hand into a hidden pocket in her gown. The hoops of her skirt were perfect; bags had been sown in and attached to reinforced leather straps on either side of her body. The bags hung down under her hips and against her legs... undetectable. There were no obstructions at all left or right. The pocket holes were concealed by the folds of the gown.

A customer was finally let out of the shop.

She looked like a mender, perhaps she was a maid out on errands. Her dress was plain, nothing compared to Eliza's own, and Eliza gave the woman a patronizing *hmphed* meant to show that she did not appreciate being made to wait by the likes of *you*.

This was no less than expected of one of her position. Likewise, the maid ignored the rebuff. A man with a clean white wig and stylish attire waited on the other side of the closed door looking off to someone Eliza knew was there but could not see, the owner of the shop. Probably counting and hiding coins or notes of promise. The gentleman awaited a signal to allow the next patron inside.

The door was finally opened.

'Welcome to Halson's Fabrics, Miss, how can we be of service today?' Eliza stepped over the threshold and the door was shut and locked behind her.

'Mr Benson, how lovely to see you again, and Mrs Ramsdale, how is your husband's gout?' Mrs Ramsdale, the owner, was a larger woman; she wore far too much powder; her lips were a tad too red. She looked to Eliza like a fat harlequin.

Eliza softly giggled at the imagery.

Mrs Ramsdale took this as girlish enthusiasm.

'He is in constant discomfort, Miss Granger; it grieves me so to see it and you are so kind to enquire. The surgeons do nothing, nothing!' The fat woman threw her hands into the air, appealing to God for relief. 'But we are all sent trials, my dear, all sent trials. Speaking of which…' the woman now toddled (there was no other word for it) over and took Eliza's hand in her own. She lowered her voice, 'Did you hear about Mr Carlisle?' Eliza moved her other hand to cover her shocked expression at Mrs Ramsdale's unspoken insinuation.

'Did he…' she asked, as if she meant to finish the thought, knowing she did not need to.

'Yes, he did, he did, and…' so it went, on and on for a good quarter of an hour.

All the while Mr Benson, the doorman, who may have been Mrs Ramsdale's son or nephew (Eliza was unsure), ignored the gossip and restocked shelves and rearranged hats on wooden busts and performed other busy works. Eliza was treated to all the tittle-tattle and blather from Mrs Granger's circle of friends (none of whom Eliza knew, but all of whom she could picture in her head).

Eliza was skilled at pretending to know people; repeating gossip she had heard elsewhere was a good cover for ignorance; pretending to be shocked, or intrigued, or outraged, as the case may be, was a valuable talent and her acting matched expectations again. She listened, reacted, and meanwhile subtly eyed up the samples behind the main desk, spotting one of today's target acquisitions. There, within her reach, were the valuable and thick silk threads and ribbons auntie needed for… something.

'But you didn't come today to listen to me chatter on and on did you, dear? No of course not!' The shop owner patted Eliza's hands and turned to move behind the counter once more; Eliza gave the shelf stocker a subtle wink, so subtle in fact that he wasn't sure he had seen it at all.

It was meant as another distraction.

His cheeks took on a slight reddish coloring. He was a weak, piteous sort of man, and he would not look in her direction again for the rest of the time she was in the shop just in case she had meant something by the gesture.

'Now, what can we do for you today, dear?'

Eliza shifted her eyes away for the hat displays and back to the silks on the shelves clear on the other side of Mrs Ramsdale's considerable bulk. She made a show of extracting a small piece of paper from her tiny purse (making sure to jiggle the coinage within).

'My auntie,' she said, softening the *au* sound in the way the upper classes do, 'has sent me out with a list. She said this could not be entrusted to the maid.'

She passed the list over the counter.

Mrs Ramsdale extracted a pair of spectacles from a pouch at her side and looked over the list with a critical eye. She nodded and turned around, shifting and moving spools, bobbins and reels between the shelves and to the countertop. Glancing again at the man, Eliza noted the clear opportunity to pocket a couple bright colored coils of silk ribbon. For the next half hour, she closely examined many samples while distracting the older woman with questions and observations and requests for this or that hue.

Finally, having made legitimate selections, a tenth of what she left the shop with, Eliza noted that the man was now waiting patiently by the door, another customer without. Mrs Ramsdale would be busy with the next woman; Eliza would be long gone even if she did finally wonder where the rest of the stock went.

Such an act would be much of her day.

Little needful things were found; ribbons, bows, and threads, a bottle of perfume, a silver snuff box, a Dublin gold spoon set, two oriental fans, an ivory love-letter case (that had been a trying time and Eliza was almost caught out). The most difficult item on the list, by far, was a pearl choker. Eliza had worn a well-made fake into the shop (it was a Mr Halenbury creation, especially build to auntie's requirements for just this occasion), and she walked out with the authentic one around her throat. By that time, however, it was approaching an hour when good mannered girls were heading back home.

Eliza was just walking past the fabrics shop from earlier in the day again when she was lightly bumped by another woman. She turned, was about to swear, when a fine-looking young man came along in the opposite direction. Neither woman had seen the other's approach, but Eliza liked what she saw. The man doffed his hat graciously, and the woman apologized sweetly at the same time. Eliza noted a family resemblance between the two but said nothing, accepting the apology, and offering one of her own, no harm done either way.

'Is this your napery, Miss?'

The gentleman, mid-third decade of life, held a lovely silk napkin in his outstretched hand. It had a pearl-like sheen and was gaily decorated around the edges with little white pearls and white-green opals.

Eliza's eyes grew wide; her pupils dilated at the sight of the object; she knew a luxury item when she saw it. It took her a moment to realize she had not answered.

'Yes, yes, thank you, sir. It's most gracious of you, both of you, to retrieve it for me. I'm so clumsy.' She put a hand to her forehead. 'Mother says I will never find a husband until I can correct this *glaring* defect in my character.'

The others laughed politely as did Eliza, self-deprecating and pretty. The man's chuckle was deep, kind-hearted, and attractive; the woman giggled and put a hand to her mouth, saying "No" quietly, surprised.

'The least I could do, Madam, the very least for causing inconvenience in distracting my sister's attention. And worry not for your mother for you are… it is a charming characteristic in a woman, I think it so.' Eliza liked the looks of him; she studied his face as well as that of his younger sister. She took the implied compliment well, felt a little heat in her face in fact, and determined to keep an eye out for one or the other in future. After an awkward silence they parted ways.

'Well, good day, Miss…?' The man doffed his hat once again.

Eliza took the hint, 'Eliza.'

'Miss Eliza then,' he proffered a kid-leather gloved hand.

'Anthony Stabler at your service, and may I present may own dear sister, Miss Grace Stabler.' The two women eyed each other up and nodded politely one to the other.

Afterwards, Eliza continued in the opposite direction to the couple, after a final subtle glance at Anthony. In the back of her mind, she wondered if the Stablers were any relation to the current Lord Mayor.

Once the target was out of earshot, Catherine leaned into her brother, 'You made quite an impression with that one, Daniel.'

'And you, *squib*; you didn't give the game away at all, well done! Was she carrying?' Catherine smiled. It had been her very first assignment for the daughters.

'Left pocket seemingly filled to bursting. Look at this fan… oriental surely, and silk webs.' Catherine opened and closed the find before putting it away in pockets of her own 'Right pocket, smaller items, and this little snuff box,' Catherine showed Daniel and stuffed it also into a hidden pocket. 'Can we not just follow her though?'

Daniel shook his head.

'I don't think so, *squib*. She has the napkin now; that was our goal today. Our friends will take it from here until it is time to meet Miss Eliza again of course.'

'What will happen to her then do you think?'

Daniel sighed. 'I don't know, Katie. Other sons have spoken of… dreams, nightmares, visions… but I prefer not to think upon that part of the work too often.'

§

[It is May 23rd, 1778, in Lichfield, England]

'Who is this Feidlimid?'

The Baron named Cain spoke in answer to the question. 'Feidlimid "the Celebrant" was in the company of the king when he sought out the gods' will at *An Seisear*.' Catherine looked a little confused.

'George III? Is this about the colonies?'

'No,' said papa, 'it has nothing to do with that.'

'Not the king of the English, Catherine, the *Hidden* high king of Ireland.'

'Is King George not also the King of Ireland Baron Cain?'

'No, the *Hidden* king, I said.'

'A Jacobite?' The Baron smiled.

'No. The current *Hidden* king was born in what you know to be 1425, and he is currently in Chichester.' Now Catherine really was confused.

Chichester?

The Baron spun a wild and meandering tale over the next thirty minutes, one which Catherine could only just follow, silently interrupted by so many questions springing into her mind from the start. So many emotions made their way into her heart and across her brow as the Baron spoke. It was such a catastrophic, heart-breaking story. Such loss, and such a senseless, wretched crime committed, but somehow, it seemed that fate or God or the gods had brought other elements together in such a way so as to begin to repair the unintended collateral damage.

'…and when the supplicants returned to Mallow, Catherine,' he drew the tale to its conclusion, 'it was decided that persons, male and female, from the stoutest families of the old ways, would be recruited to the cause, trained, funded, educated, whatever was needed. Their special talents, if any were to be found, were discovered and worked into fine, fine, mastership of whatever art or artifice was clear within them. Where skills considered necessary were not to be found, they were bought… rented, that might be a better word. Skills present were honed to perfection wherever possible. The Sons and Daughters are also… have become something of an experiment Catherine. We… that is, my people, can sometimes strongly influence yours, and so we try and find the best matches for the sons and daughters, the most suitable mates from the finest families.'

'Oh my, but Cain, you make it sound like a breeding program for dogs.'

The Baron smiled and shrugged.

'At heart… yes perhaps that is true. But so crudely put Catherine; let us say instead for thoroughbred horses rather than dogs, shall we? That is a much more favorable example, I think. Going with this theme, however, one breeds horses for either speed or endurance, yes.' Catherine nodded. 'You could breed them for speed and endurance and for intelligence too could you not?' Catherine paused only briefly and nodded again. 'No offence, Catherine, but humans can be specially bred in the same way; any creatures could, yours, mine, whatever… but imagine if you will what might one day become of humanity if led by perfected specimens created after generations of experimentation?'

'Oh my!'

The Baron smiled softly, waving it away. 'It's an interesting thought experiment, Catherine, but it is only that for the moment. The need for the stain to be removed is dire, and our first and only cause at this time is just that; the curse overcome; the bad blood taken away; the king restored, and the world set aright. Then, who knows what dreams might come of it eh?'

The only two words she had spoken for the previous quarter hour were again on her lips, but she refrained from saying them. 'I am still unclear on my proposed role here?'

'Like all the sons and daughters, Catherine, one role will be to parent the next generation. Even now candidates are being considered for you, men both physically appealing but also intellectually and spiritually compatible with your own unique characteristics. Once you have taken the trial this process can be finer tuned.'

'Trial?' Catherine was obviously unsure about the sound of that.

'Trial, yes. Not a trial before a court mind, more like various examinations, as you might have in a school for instance. Tests of your mental capabilities, your suitability for disciplines that you may now be unaware even exist, and tests of your physical capabilities too of course. Your father tells me that you are proficient with a sword…' Catherine glanced at him and then at Daniel, they had fooled no one, '… and gymnastic specialties, and that you have been tutored in many fields that women of your class are not usually mentored.' Catherine smiled and affirmed this was the case. 'Good, working with the results, we are better able to find you a superior mate. But if you decide you do not find any of the potentials suitable, or if you have proclivities otherwise for…' he waved his hand as if searching for the right words.

'Proclivities?'

'Never mind that, Catherine,' said father.

Cain looked from father to daughter, shrugged as if this was unimportant, and continued. 'And you will participate in the furtherance of the mission in a capacity suited to your talents.' Catherine raised an eyebrow at this. 'You will be expected not to speak of these things with anyone outside the orders and the king's chosen few, or those like myself, tasked with handling specific circumstances.'

'You know this king?'

'Your people would term our relationship as familial... as cousins once removed, I believe is the correct connection.'

'You keep referring to my people and to your people, Cain. What do you mean by this? Are you Welsh?' Cain smiled; Daniel laughed aloud.

Both father and papa turned sharply in his direction and looked at him sternly until he quieted down again. Catherine, for her part, had never considered the Welsh as a particularly humorous people, nor as particularly sober for that matter, and could not reason out what she had said that caused Daniel to disrupt the seriousness of the discussion so.

'No not Welsh, Catherine. I am a *sidhe* of the Hidden.' Catherine smiled now; understanding what jolly japes were being played out at her expense. Daniel had given the game away.

'Baron, if you are that, you have erred there and let slip the ruse. I know what a *sidhe* is; it is nothing more than an earthen mound. You and my family here wove a fascinating tale, certainly, and you had me captured for a time, quite entangled in it admittedly, but...' Catherine's words dried up on her tongue as the Baron began to glow.

It was subtle at first and she thought stray beams of sunlight were coming in through the blinds, but this proved not to be the case. Standing before her Catherine would have estimated his height at a respectable 5'9", but he began to get taller, 10", 11", six foot tall, and still he grew. His body grew thinner, however, and his face longer, his ears become pointed and too large by half for his face, his hair changed color from black, to white, to a salt and pepper mixed pattern. His clothing, respectable, changed too; from black to green and brown, from solid to a leaf pattern with gold and silver thread work on his robes and cape, a silver crown seemed to sit upon his head. Within a short span of few heartbeats Baron Cain had become an entirely different... *being*.

"Not human" were the only words Catherine could think of to explain what he had become.

'People... humans,' the Baron's voice was more melodic now and it sounded as if there was a chorus of voices behind his own, 'came to associate my people with these earthen mounds of which you speak only because some of these held gateways between the *Hidden* lands and the human lands. We live among you, Catherine; hidden in our way, but our influence is the stuff of myth and legend. Legends, I say, which you should have been tutored into a detailed understanding.'

Catherine closed her eyes, *of course, all those books and stories*. 'Crom Cruaich?' she whispered.

'The "Crooked one of the Hill", yes? You would think of him now as a mythical sun or fertility god, but in fact he is the ruler of our celestial host and quite a real being after all. All the gods are genuine.'

'But is God not authentic then?'

'Your triune god you mean?' Catherine paused at the description then nodded in understanding. 'Certainly, I believe so,' said the Baron, 'and a powerful god to be sure. Look at all that's been accomplished in his name, witness the work of Saint Patrick alone.'

'How can that be?'

Cain took in a deep breath and his continence changed back to what it had been when Catherine had first entered the room. 'Our king has said that, and he has experience of this from long and long, that the gods were always there, altered in aspect by the people of differing regions to meet what he called "cultural norms". I am not a scholar myself, but this explanation would appear to explain why there is so much commonality between the regional so-called "myth cycles" and the sacred history of modern humanity, whether Christian Europe or Hindi sub-Asia. But beyond that over-simplification of the matter I have no particular expertise or interest in the question.'

'So, I would not be expected to forsake my Lord God?'

'Of course not! You would be expected merely to understand that your triune god is not the only such creature, although, granted, he is perhaps currently the most powerful.'

Catherine took in a deep breath and let it out slowly.

The idea that she was at all religious or spiritual had never occurred to her before this moment, but there it was, it seemed important just then and the answer reassured her.

'The question you truly need to consider, however, here and now, is whether or not you are interested in committing to the cause?'

'And if not?'

'Then this conversation never happened. You will not remember any of it. Life will return for you as it was. You will put down to fate whatever influence we have to assert over you from now on, luck will always be on your side, as you humans say, but whatever you do from this point will be of your own making within certain parameters. Someday, your father may call into a closed meeting your child and one of my kind to have a similar discussion as we have had, like your own mother once had but does not remember. You will most certainly be similarly unaware of our influence and that of the sons and daughters.'

Catherine glanced at her father, 'Mother does not know of this?'

'No, Catherine, she declined to be involved and so... her memory was cleared of it is the best way I understand the process. Her mother knows of this, however, but her husband, your maternal grandfather, does not know.'

'Is that because he too declined or that he is not Irish?'

'Well,' Cain assumed the discussion from there, 'being Irish really only makes one more willing to accept the truth of these revelations. They are a race given to mythic tales and allegorical meanings, similarly the Greeks. Songs and poetry are in their blood, you see. It may be that he too declined the invitation, long and long ago, or no. If so, there would be a record of it in Talia's archive, I'm sure.'

'Talia?' The Baron smiled again.

'She is a pixie as well as the king's amanuensis.' Catherine considered this.

'Do you have geese so small?' The Baron laughed merrily.

'She is a "remembrancer" rather than an archivist or secretary as such,' he explained, and Catherine accepted the explanation in light of the fact she had no knowledge or evidence that she was being fooled or being made sport of otherwise. 'But her stories of the king's actions have been transcribed by genuine archivists, scholars, scribes and historians and examined for accuracy. Talia has something of an imagination, and a let us say... heightened regard for the king. A part of the *geas* laid upon the king by the gods was the requirement of a complete and correct record of the cursed families and the steps taken to rectify the matter. You will have access to that archive, of course, and it is written in Latin, English and Gaelic.'

'Latin?'

'By the king's own command. He is fluent in that tongue of human scholars, diplomats and monks and is also something of a traditionalist... despite his wintery aspect.'

'I do not understand that phrase, Baron... umm Cain.' Cain looked toward papa and father.

Papa spread his hands, 'It rarely comes up in the literature, Baron.'

'We should rectify that.'

He turned back to the young woman recruit.

'It is the changing of the seasons, Catherine, although it has nothing to do with what you know to be winter or summer. For us, a court is either wintery or summery, never at the same time, but one inevitably leads to the other over the course of time. A summery court, you should have met the term *seelie*, is more a traditionalist establishment, holding forth such ideals as chivalry and the life of the positive emotions which are strongly shown by the courtiers themselves. The wintery aspect respects tradition less so, reveling instead in individualism, freedom of action, passion, and changes. It is the... tearing apart of the old as a means of ushering in the new. Often these are termed as *unseelie* qualities. It's not a question of good or evil, as your human poets and bards have written; but more the personal nature of the crown-bearer holding sway. That and necessity.' Catherine's raised eyebrow and slight head tilt told the Baron that she was not entirely following the reasoning.

'Think of it this way my dear. It is said that the actions of strong men lead to stability and good times, yes. But stability and good times produce weaker men. Weak men create instability and bad times which, in turn, necessitate the rise of strong men again. You see, the seasons pass in just such a way and so on *ad infinitum*.' Catherine was happier with this understanding. 'Our king was born to a summer king and queen, but circumstances changed him...'

'This history of Mallow?' The Baron nodded at her.

'Partially that, yes, but there is more to the story, and I do not know at how much liberty I am to disclose those other pieces, even to members in good standing.'

'Oh my!'

The Baron returned to his chair. 'The next step, Catherine, if you agree to the terms, I've laid out, is relocation. We have facilities in Winchester and Cork, and of course, all the amenities are supplied for you while there, including a stipend. Your capabilities and talents will be further assessed, and a personalized training program laid out for you.'

Catherine looked at Daniel, 'I thought you were at Winchester School training for Oxbridge or the Inns?'

'I was, am, yes that as well, Catherine. I was invited to Hertford College at Oxford for this coming fall semester to start common law studies, or I could attend Doctors Commons or Lincoln's Inn in London to read civil law. I am unsure which offer to accept.'

'Oh my. I would like to go to college too.'

'We are working on that,' said the Baron, 'that is, the sons and daughters are trying to influence government to institute higher education for women. Our seers think this will be long in coming though. However, if you have the temperament, we can make special accommodations and tutoring.'

'That all sounds marvelous, Cain, so many advantages, but what would I be giving up?'

'Once you join the daughters, swear the oath, you will always be a daughter, so you give up some liberty and free action. You give up innocence; the world is not as you thought of it before this meeting. There is risk; but there is risk in any worthwhile act. The harvesting of the blood is not a pretty or pleasant thing. There are some who find the rumors repulsive; death always is, but you would be, if not personally responsible... you might say, indirectly accountable, should it come to a court of law. Although, I can't foresee how that might happen. But this weighs on the souls of some. If you have the,' the Baron paused, 'aptitude for public work you would be made an envoy.'

'Sometimes the work is hard, Catherine,' said papa in his stern voice, 'and you will sometimes feel yourself blamable, but it needs to be done, and it is for the betterment of our species as a whole, and theirs as well,' he said, nodding toward the Baron.

'Harvesting, you said harvesting, Cain, what does that mean?'

'I cannot speak of it, Catherine, and I hope you never find out. I will say the gods are fair if not always kind.'

§

[It is May 20th, 1780, in York, England]

Auntie's work went ahead as usual but now, Eliza had a self-assumed mission of her own. She lay on her bed, turning the fanciful napkin over and over, counting the little pearls and opals, tracing her fingers along the gold and silver threading.

Auntie did not know about this piece of work and Eliza opted not to tell her, after having been slapped for inexplicably losing a couple items on the list.

Mr Anthony Stabler, and his sister, lived near Saint Anthony's Hospital, on St John's Green, within sight of the river and the farmlands beyond the walls of the city. Even on her best behavior and in her best costumes Eliza would have to be careful even walking along the streets nearby it. The upper gentry knew each other by face; hers was unknown there.

Perhaps Mr Stabler could be persuaded to change that?

Eliza's spy had uncovered the fact that Grace Stabler frequented a café on Coney Street.

Her new plan of action, the third such scheme thought up already today, centered on the sister. Auntie would be told that this was an insinuation, and nothing personal. If Anthony was not interested, he did not strike Eliza as a sodomite on first impression… well, Eliza had played the role of fallen angel and lesbian in the past, perhaps through Grace… *maybe it ran in the Stabler family?*

But wouldn't there then be far less Stablers?

Fewer, I mean fewer Stablers that way?

Eliza giggled to herself. She was being a little bit silly, and she knew it. But she let herself be a little silly for the moment, having had a hellish nightmare the previous evening.

Eliza had dreams, many of them in the space of a night. Usually these were fantasies of a better existence. Last night's had been a terrible dream of death, and war, and of a slaughter in which she reveled. She had been herself in the dream, but she had a man's body and countenance. She was a soldier, with other soldiers, engaging in butchery but she knew not why. Eliza could still smell the blood and shite long after she had awoken in a sweat; she was still shaking at breakfast but kept her answers vague when questioned about it.

'Just a bad dream, Mother… just a bad dream.'

She could not reason out the cause of the nightmare though, nor her role therein, except to commit carnage and death over and over. Stealing from the rich merchants about the city was one thing, but only a sick mind would enjoy such massacre writ large, as she had seen in her dream.

She shuddered again.

Forget it girl, you have work to do.

Today she would be the maid of some presumed middle-class household. Brown hair, mousy, she would be timid in dress and attitude; just one of the many such girls on the streets and in the markets this morning. She would be near enough invisible to all.

§

Catherine sat in the garden area of the café Trinidad, having arrived promptly at eleven fifteen a.m. She sipped her coffee and waited, as instructed, for the Baron to show. She daintily nibbled on a tasty ginger biscuit.

It was here that she and her brother received new instructions from their "handler". They, or one of them, as today, would come at an agreed upon hour. Cain rarely showed up though, in which case they were to continue as per the last set of instructions.

At least the coffee was bracing, hot, and healthy, and she liked it unflavored by syrups or spices (unlike how Daniel took his). Both she and her brother had made their movements fairly open about the city, but the target had not made contact again. Catherine had been assured Eliza was under observation and that the "treatment" (whatever that was) had already begun. She sometimes wondered, especially at times when Cain did not show up, what his people needed her and her brother for, exactly.

Speak of the devil.

'May I join you, my dear Catherine?' And just like that, he was there, as if thinking of him summoned him somehow.

Perhaps it did.

'No, it doesn't,' he said, as if reading her mind.

He sat down placing a cup of strong tea before him. His violet, elongated eyes, almond shaped but stretched out took her in. Today he wore darkened spectacles to hide the *fae*-ness of his eyes. He cocked his head to the side as if reading her. 'You have something on your mind, Catherine?'

'As a matter of fact, yes, I do. Tell me, Cain,' she glanced around at the other patrons but no one seemed to be within earshot, 'why do you really need Daniel and me here?' The Baron's face took on a confused expression and his head tilted to the side as he regarded her.

'I beg your pardon?'

'You went to a great deal of trouble, I think, to procure a suite of rooms, finances, materials, and time, all so Daniel and I could finagle a fancy napkin into the possession of one otherwise anonymous girl? Why could you not do all that yourself?' Cain put down his tea and steepled his fingers before him, elbows resting on the edge of the table.

'What do you know of magic, Catherine?'

Catherine sat up a little straighter in her chair and her tongue ran lightly over her lips. To other humans she might have appeared calm, but to the *fae* it was clear she was suddenly quite excited. She was practically bouncing in her seat with anticipation at this turn of the conversation.

'Why nothing, Cain, at least, no more than what is written.'

'Look about you then, what do you see?'

Catherine did as bid to find not a few of the patrons were looking in her direction, but more at Cain than herself although there was still some interest in her as well.

'Humans are sensitive to the supernatural in a way few of you understand. Perhaps the *enlightened* fathom it… I do not know. Those surrounding us; however, they peek over and quickly look away, and then look again, repeatedly. Something in your nature understands the presence of the *other*. Were I, for instance, to sit here more than an hour those surrounding us would inch closer and closer, unbeknownst even to themselves, until they were upon me. And I am no great magician; it is simply the elemental nature of my being which invites this interest. You would also be a target of curiosity. Even now the other patrons look at you, wonder over you, and ask themselves where they have seen you before? You are the subject of my interest, so you become the confidential subject of theirs also. Now, the napkin was carefully assembled according to certain ancient principles that I do not pretend to understand. It was in the hands of only humans; no one of the *Hidden* ever managed it at all. It had to be delivered to a particular woman, Eliza, by a memorable man, your brother, so that it would be accepted and kept close for the effects to work. Were I, or another like me, to have handed it on Eliza would have rejected it, perhaps even discarded it in the nearest refuse receptacle.'

'So, you needed Daniel to hand it over.'

'Yes.'

'Why did you need me?'

'In order to establish conflict.' Catherine pulled back in shock.

'I beg your pardon… conflict?'

'Yes.'

'I do not understand.'

'You have not studied human behavior as long as we have.'

'Please, Cain, I wish to know.' Cain eyed Catherine's face until he was satisfied that he found what he needed to find.

He leaned forward.

'All right. As I understand it, the napkin amplifies emotions. Eliza took an interest in Daniel, a handsome man by modern standards and a well-mannered man, an obviously wealthy man, potentially a good provider. She recognized the name supplied as well. That was three days ago. She has been trying to find Daniel, or you, since. She has spies who think they are well versed in the practices of subterfuge and obfuscation.'

'We have not hidden ourselves away, sir, as you directed us to do.'

'No, I understand that. But she has been kept out of step with you by other sons or daughters or hired actors. Remember that my people are great pranksters, Catherine; we know a thing or two about creating deceptions, muddying the waters, putting up smokescreens. Little incidents, tiny inconveniences… we have interrupted her efforts to find you at every step. When she made to turn right, we turned her left. For some of us that sort of thing is great fun. In any case, her heart grows fonder in the delay of gratification.'

'And this *conflict* you mentioned?'

'In her mind elaborate schemes are… have, taken shape. Daniel, she imagines, dutiful to his kin of course, cannot pursue her, which she assumes he would do given how obviously ideal they are for each other in her mind.

You, his sister, representative of his family, tradition, custom, holds him back from pursuing his own heart's desire.'

'It sounds so scientific when you spell it out like that.'

'Finish your coffee, Catherine. If you notice, we are now drawing more attention to ourselves.' Catherine glanced around them and noted how others turned away, embarrassed, as their eyes met hers. Caught in the act of social impropriety, some even flushed. Now that it had been pointed out to her Catherine could not recall Cain sitting at their table as long as he had this day already.

The pair left the Trinidad café's tea garden shortly thereafter through the common gate (Catherine had dropped two ginger biscuits into her purse) and strode along the road toward York Minster. Catherine knew that Cain admired the cathedral.

'But…' Catherine hesitated, unsure of the correct wording needed to pick up the conversation again 'Eliza is some kind of threat… is Daniel in any danger?'

'There is always danger; life is risk, my dear. A carriage may pass near to us at any time and a horse, distracted, run us down. There is no intended danger to him, I can assure you of that much.'

Catherine was now on the lookout for horses and carriages while the Baron collected his thoughts. 'For whatever reason, the king requires that Eliza be in a strong emotional state when he finally confronts her. She must be made to understand the loss which her blood inflicted on the victims of Marrow. I do not pretend to know why this must be, to understand it, but it must be done. As I said, I am no great magician or seer.'

Catherine walked in silence beside the Baron, thinking over what he had said. Cain led her along the streets, turning left to walk parallel to the cathedral, and then right again in the direction of the better shops. 'Pause a moment now, Catherine,' he said, 'as if you are interested in these fancies and baubles.'

Catherine noticed that they were standing before a jewelry seller. He pointed at something on display. 'Not the necklace, Catherine, look at the reflection in the glass. Do you see yon housekeeper across the street?'

Catherine looked, 'Yes, what of her?'

'That is our Eliza in disguise. See how intently she watches you?'

'Oh my, that is her isn't it, but…'

'She is a gifted actor and disguise artist. She owes her life to a woman of ill-intent, although Eliza does not realize this fact of malevolence. Our friend there is a thief, a pickpocket, I believe is the correct terminology, committing small frauds about the city in exchange for a future freedom that will never materialize. She was in the disguise of a lady when you met her on that occasion days ago, and now she purports to be the servant of a middle-class family of means. She moves between these societies but is part of none save the criminal class. She does not realize in her waking mind that she is trapped in that life, but in her sleeping mind, for lack of a better description, she is aware and searching for escape. Again, your brother fits that bill nicely, in her mind. Seeing you, with another man, gives her hope. A false hope certainly but hope nonetheless that her path to Daniel and the life he represents is now more available than previous.'

'I pity her, Cain.'

'Understandable.'

'It seems a cruel jest.'

'Agreed.' He paused and watched a bird fly away as they started walking again. 'I am sure that if there were another way to accomplish the cleansing of the blood the gods would have ordered that way instead.' Catherine shrugged, joining the Baron a couple steps ahead.

'That is a convenient answer,' she chided. The Baron said nothing. 'Did you know she would be here at this time?'

'I was made aware of the possibilities as we walked.'

'So, you took a route to intercept her?'

'Indeed. But we could not stand there long...'

'Due to the effect of magic... on my kind, on humans I mean?'

'Yes, that but also because now that she has found you, it will be her intention to follow you back to your rooms, even though she knows already where you reside. There, she will wait for Daniel to appear; today, tomorrow, the following day, as fate would have it happen. So, let me walk you back now. Take my arm, Catherine, we are a happy couple.'

Catherine did as she was bid to do but was at loggerheads within herself.

In her mind she understood the Baron's explanation or thought she did (but not really on reflection). This subterfuge was necessary; the reasons ancient (in her reckoning), but well beyond her wits. In her heart, however, she was telling the truth of pitying the other woman. To be so desperate for escape and for a different life, and yet destined for... what? Degradation? Death? After only a lonely existence?

'Will it be painful, Baron, this... harvesting?'

The Baron sighed.

'The king is not a cruel *fae* though he has such capacity for brutal actions you would swoon to hear it.'

'This wintery aspect you spoke of some time ago?'

'That, and something even more... *evil* is not the correct word for it. Let us say...' he waved his hand, 'unpleasant. Only a chosen few have seen the actual process of the harvesting, and I have not been among them. To be honest, from what I have heard, neither do I wish to be so honored. Those sons and daughters who have been privy to the event lose something of themselves... hmm, their innocence... something else I cannot name. I know that it puts off the silver prince, but the king's *red cap* advisor revels in it all.'

'The "silver prince", Cain? You have not spoken of such a man prior to this.'

'No man he, but a noble sidhe of the court of Armagh is the Silver Prince, and the king's regent in his absence from the court of Cork. He is a closer cousin to the king than I.'

'Is he made of silver?'

Cain laughed.

'No. His ancient familial plate is of the best silver ever mined, or so the *goblins* say and they would know. He is the king's closest companion, save for Talia, and his truest friend. His rescuer, so they say.'

'Does your king not have a queen?' Cain stopped suddenly to allow a carriage to drive by pulling Catherine back abruptly.

'Forgive me for the rough handling, Catherine, but the horses were distracted by my presence. I should have been more careful, but my mind was elsewhere.' They paused a moment while Catherine recovered her equipoise. 'You have another question?'

'Yes,' she said once they were walking again. Eliza was still following. 'Does the king have a queen?' The Baron shook his head.

'I have been told that there was once, long and long ago, a female fancied by the king, not a human woman as such, although there is some confusion about that aspect of the tale. He loved this female and she him, but she died, or killed herself, or was killed in some tragic *accident*. It was an unnatural death, or so I understand. To my knowledge he has taken no other to mate.'

'To "mate" makes it sound so primitive Baron. These are enlightened times you know.' Catherine smiled and the baron was taken in by her cheer.

'A culturally different understanding of the process my dear Catherine, that's all. Your kind has divorced itself from nature while mine has never left it. Perhaps someday you will romp naked in the woods with me and partake of the freedoms nature provides.'

'Baron!' Catherine flushed hotly (her fan working and hiding a slight smile), while the Baron chuckled.

§

[It is May 22nd, 1780, in York, England]

'There she is again, brother.'

Catherine pulled back the curtain ever so slightly away from the opened window. Eliza, in an attractive bright canary-yellow day dress and matching dainty parasol strolled along the green avenue before the townhouse. Catherine, and sometimes Daniel, noted her passage, on the half-hour between two and four in the afternoon. The Baron had organized a plant in the gossip networks of the women of York which had been able to get a message to Eliza that Anthony Stabler, lawyer, often returned home and left again between these two hours. He had been instructed to do so until Eliza had evidence that this was indeed the case.

She had been coming like clockwork over the last two days.

Daniel had been instructed to leave the house at 3.50 p.m. today and "interact" with Eliza, walking with her to the law office in which he was a young barrister.

It was a genuine law firm; Daniel had a genuine position there, having kept the terms and passed the bar exam years earlier. The senior partner was a Son of Lóegaire and had taken a special interest in Daniel's advancement.

This was not all mere dalliance in point of fact; Daniel would eventually come to concentrate his efforts in the name of the various

Severance concerns, but for the moment his work and growing experiences served both the family and the Sons and Daughters.

Daniel consulted his pocket watch. It was 3.43 p.m. He went to the hall and donned his jacket. 'Wish me luck?'

'Luck?' asked Catherine while still at the window. 'She loves you, dear brother, try not to lead her on too much, and don't take advantage of her either.' Daniel smiled.

'Thank you… Mother.'

'I'm serious, Danny.'

'I know, *squib*, I know. I promise.'

'Okay, go now. She will be coming back around any second.'

Daniel shut the outer door loud enough that Catherine could hear it. He walked down the pathway toward the street gate, opening it and stepping out just as Eliza, face flushed from walking a little faster, breathing a little heavy, approached him. Catherine closed the curtain shortly thereafter and sat down to her afternoon reading, at least until Daniel returned for tea. She had been on something of a diet, unconsciously, ever since the Baron had spoken of "naked romps" in the woods, and pondered, often, what she might say should he mention it a second time.

§

As if it were planned Daniel closed the gate and turned to his left just as Eliza ran head-long into him. He caught her (deftly, he later thought) and set her upright once again, stooping to retrieve her parasol.

'Please excuse me…' he pretended to look at her with a confused expression. 'Do we not know each other?' He paused, then snapped his fingers, smiling, 'Miss Eliza, isn't it? I found your lost napkin that one time.'

'Of course,' she pretended to recall. She had the napkin. She fluttered it and used it to wipe a small bit of nothing off her forehead. She was wearing the same yellow dress, Daniel noted, but daring to go out without the under-structure hoops this time.

It was very risqué and Daniel found himself both amused and interested.

'Why yes,' she said retrieving her parasol, 'Master Stabler, I believe, young gentleman lawyer about town.' She looked at the house, 'Do you live here, sir?' He looked at the house and saw Catherine just closing the curtains.

'Why, yes I do. This old pile has been in the family for ages. But what a pleasant coincidence this is. Do you live in this neighborhood?' Eliza's eyes widened; Daniel noted that her eyes were cornflower blue (although with a slightly more greenish hint). 'No, I was just… walking… through on my way to… auntie's house.'

'Perhaps you would let me walk you then?'

'No, no need for that, sir.'

'Call me Anthony, please.'

Eliza's pupils dilated, clearly signaling her interest in the suggestion but her eyes dipped too late to hide the fact. She smiled coyly and looked up again seconds later.

'If you will call me Eliza, I will.' Daniel smiled, not sure if hers was an act or no, but he was having a delightful time despite himself. 'Where were you off to in such a hurry, umm, Anthony?'

'The office; I am taking the lead in a case for the court tomorrow,' which was true.

'How exciting!' By Daniel's expression, Eliza might have deduced that this was not as exciting as her proclamation suggested.

'Would you like to see the offices?' Eliza produced a fan from nowhere and tapped Daniel on the shoulder, a carefully contrived flirtation.

'Do you keep your etchings there?' They both laughed at the implied joke.

'Oh no,' Daniel replied, 'such things would absolutely confound and scandalize the senior partners. I keep only the tamest examples on site,' he winked, playing the rogue. Unbeknownst to him, this statement was only partially true. Daniel had not been in all the senior partner's private chambers, where certain illegal books were stored and where he had a fine collection of erotic Japanese prints. Eliza put her arm through Daniel's own.

'I should very much love to see where you work Master Stabler… Anthony.'

'What about your auntie?'

'Bother auntie, she is going nowhere anytime soon.'

Daniel, eyebrows raised, and Eliza had a fine stroll into the city and finally to the law offices of *Severance, Patton & Stabler* (est.1743).

§

[It is May 26th, 1780, in York, England]

Daniel was despondent.

Catherine had tried to console him but even her best efforts were wasted. Baron Cain sat quietly in the chair opposite; his thoughts very much kept to himself.

'It's for the best that you were not there, Master Severance,' he did offer.

'I would have liked one more day with her,' Daniel replied.

'We could not take the risk.' Daniel looked up and Catherine looked over at the Baron, confused by this.

'What risk, Cain?'

'Well, had Eliza become with child…'

Catherine made a silent "oh" and turned away; Daniel looked angry.

'What kind of gentlemen do you take me for, sir?'

The Baron smiled sadly. 'a human one sir, a human one.' Daniel paused, and finally nodded.

'What happened, Cain? Do you know?'

The Baron shook his head. 'I was not privy to the event,' he explained. 'The king came with two Sons and a Daughter; one of whom alerted the constabulary to Eliza's… house. The body was found early this morning. There is unlikely to be an investigation given her… social status and profession. It is doubtful that a connection between that woman there, and the woman who was seen on your arm about town, Daniel, will ever be made, but you will remain in York another month. A daughter of similar bearing is available to reinforce your innocence in the unlikely event a connection is made. I believe, moreover, that you have another court date in any case. As for you, Catherine.' The Baron reached into his jacket and passed over a heavy envelope. Inside was a first-class carriage ticket to St Albans, leaving the same afternoon from York city center, a five-pound note, and that much again in loose coins. 'Once in St Albans you will be met by another daughter and given another assignment in that locality.'

While the Baron explained this, Daniel had moved to stand before the opened curtain to the window looking out into the street. It was shaping up to be a sunny day, a good day for travel. Cain joined him there and the two stood in silence.

The noble *fae* reached into his jacket's inner pocket.

'The daughter collaborating with the king retrieved this for you, Daniel.' It was the very napkin which started the whole adventure here in York for the Severance siblings.

Daniel took it. 'Something to remember in times to come,' said Cain. 'Its magic spent, it is no more than an expensive piece of cloth to anyone else, but it was thought you would appreciate it for more than its material worth. Keep it, sell it, treasure or discard it, whatever you prefer.'

§

[It is March 7th, 1800, in Northampton, England]

Matthew knocked on the door to his father's study. A familiar voice from within bid him enter. Matthew smiled, *papa!* He composed himself, straightened his tie, and went inside, closing the door behind him.

Turning, he was confronted by the sight of his maternal grandfather, *Papa* Severance, seated at his father's desk. His mother stood to one side, smiling proudly, and his Uncle Daniel stood to the other side behind the big chair; he gave his nephew an encouraging wink. A stranger sat in a chair near the desk, facing the three as well as the empty chair before the desk, into which Matthew was directed.

'Sit down, Matthew,' said papa. It was serious; papa usually called him Matt or *sport*.

'First,' said papa, 'let me say happy birthday. Eighteen?' he shook his head. 'A grown man now, handsome, smart, a gifted athlete too! I remember when your father presented you to me. A small boy, a shock of black hair…' Daniel's mother put a hand on papa's shoulder, patting it, perhaps as a reminder that there was a purpose here beyond fond memories. He looked up and nodded at his daughter.

'Let me introduce Baron Cain,' he raised a hand and indicated the sitting man, who nodded but otherwise remained oblivious to the proceedings. 'The Baron is here because we, the four of us, need to discuss your future, and he will be a big part of it if you agree to the terms laid out. But before we discuss details there are a few questions I need to ask you, Matthew.'

'Questions, Grandfather?' Matthew was an adult now and decided that he would not refer to *papa* in the way he had his previous eighteen years. Let Katie and Matilda do so. 'What kind of questions, sir?'

Papa smiled, 'Questions, the answers to which I have been training you to know, son.' He sat back in the big chair and steepled his fingers before him, elbows rested on the desk.

'Tell me of the *phookas*, Matthew.'

'Sorry Grandfather, did you say *phookas*?'

§

[It is September 29th, 1843, in Rochester, England]

Kenneth and Kathleen stood by, nervous, before Kenneth took initiative and knocked on the door to their father's study. A familiar voice from within bid them enter. The sibling's, fraternal twins, smiled, it was Grampa Dan! The twins composed themselves; Kath straightened Ken's tie for him. He opened the door and ushered his sister through, coming in behind and closing the door.

Turning, he was confronted by the sight of his paternal grandfather, Daniel Severance, seated at his father's desk. His father stood to one side, smiling proudly, and his cousin Matthew McGrath stood at the other side of the man in the big chair behind the desk.

The men looked sober indeed. But as was his habit, Grampa had his favorite handkerchief (a woman's pearls and opals creation) in his breast pocket. A family heirloom but once again, it did not match his tie (it never did).

A stranger sat in a chair near the desk, facing the three men as well as the empty chairs set before the desk, into which the siblings were directed.

'Sit down, Kenneth, Kathleen, there is much to discuss here today.' It must have been serious; indeed, Grampa usually called them Kenny and Kathy.

'First,' he said, 'let me say happy birthday to you both, obviously. Eighteen?' he shook his head. 'A grown man now, Kenneth, a handsome youth, and a grown woman now, Kathleen, smart as a whip. I remember when your mother presented the two of you to me. What a shock, twins do not run in our family, still...' Father put a hand on papa's shoulder, patting it, perhaps as a reminder that there was a purpose here beyond fond memories. He looked up and nodded at his son. Then he paused looking at the hand on his shoulder, reminded of something.

'That's my influence, Daniel; tradition matters to me.'

'Yes, of course.' He glanced from the stranger to the twins. 'Here, let me introduce Baron Cain,' he raised a hand and indicated the sitting man, who nodded but otherwise remained somewhat oblivious to the proceedings. 'The Baron is here because we, the five of us, need to discuss your futures, and he will be a big part of it if you agree to the terms. But before we discuss details, there are a few questions I need to ask you both.'

'Questions, Grandfather?' said Kathleen.

'What kind of questions?' asked Kenneth at the same time. The twins had a tendency to talk over each other and finish each other's sentences and thoughts.

Grampa Dan smiled, 'Questions, the answers to which I have been training you to know.' He sat back in the big chair and steepled his fingers before him, elbows rested on the desk. 'Tell me of the *phookas*, Kathleen.'

'Sorry Grandfather, did you say *phookas*?' She glanced at her brother.

Cain smiled.

§

[It is June 18th, 1846, in Northampton, England]

'She's asleep now, my lords, or was, the last time I looked in on her.'

'She would be angry if she discovered we were here and you denied us entry, Mary.'

It was a mere statement of fact. There was no threat or malice behind the words. The maid knew it was true as well, so she simply curtsied and opened the door.

Mary looked in to make sure that there was nothing untoward and then pushed open the door for the three men. She knew her mistress's son, of course, Sir Charles Franklin, and she recognized the baron, an occasional visitor to the manor, but the last person she had never met before and she would have remembered him His walking stick alone was the most fantastical object she had seen in her life. He must be something especially important; the other two deferred to him. It was slightly embarrassing that a fly or bee had also got into the house. Mary could hear the buzzing but as yet could not see the creature.

The men filed in. The door was closed between the bedchamber and the hall.

Mary could no longer hear the buzzing. Maybe she had been mistaken. She walked away, her duties awaiting her.

Sir Charles approached his mother's sleeping form; he would prefer not to awaken her, but the same thing he told Mary applied equally to himself.

'What do your doctors say, Charles?' The baron had moved to the other side of the bed and looked down upon the woman. He had a gentle expression as he looked upon her.

'Today, perhaps tomorrow,' he shrugged, 'no more than a few days now in any case, Baron. Nothing more can be done but to make her comfortable as possible.'

'She dreams,' said the third man from the foot of the bed. 'She dreams a dream of forested landscapes and streams of clean, fresh cool waters. Ah, you appear in her dreams, Cousin.' The Baron put a hand on the sleeping woman's shoulder; it did not disturb her.

'It is a dream of long-ago, sire. She was... much younger then. Sadly, it never happened.'

'Shall I awaken her, Baron?'

The Baron turned to the other. He paused, studied the woman, finally nodding.

'Do so.' Sir Charles bent toward his mother.

'Mother?' he gave her shoulder a gentle squeeze and leaned closer. 'Visitors, Mother, the baron has brought a guest who wishes to speak with you.'

'Cain?' the woman said. She opened an eye, tentatively looked from right to left. A tear formed. 'You... you came at last.'

'Of course, Catherine, of course, a promise was made. I have brought another.'

'Another? Danny?'

'No, Catherine, not your brother. He passed away, remember, three years now.'

The baron pulled a chair over to the side of the bed and stepped back. A stranger to Catherine, the third man sat down, laying a great walking stick across his lap.

'Miss Severance,' he nodded, tipping a fancy but odd hat.

'Mrs MacKinley if you will, sir. I worked hard to achieve that status.'

'Of course, Mrs MacKinley then.'

'What can I do for you? Sir, please excuse my condition, but they will not let me leave my bed... bother doctors.'

'I quite understand.' Catherine opened her eyes a little further. There was a darkness now about the edges of her vision; inoperable, or so she was reliably informed.

'You have a kindly aspect, sir. Do I know you? My memory is not what it once was... I apologize if I should know you.'

The man shook his head slowly, 'No, we have never been formally introduced, but you have been in my employ these many years now.'

'You look something like my baron. He was just here, I think.'

'I am still here, Catherine.' Cain stepped closer to the bedside.

'Cain! You came, I knew you would.'

'Her mind comes and goes like that, sir; the doctors cannot fix it.' Sir Charles explained from the other side of the bed.

'Bother doctors,' said Catherine with passion. 'My mind is perfectly fine, Danny!'

'It's Charles, Mother, not Uncle Daniel.'

'You've aged, Charles, when did that happen?'

Her son laid a hand on her arm, giving it a squeeze of reassurance. He held it and sat down on the side of the bed. His mother had grown small, it seemed to him. Small and frail; no longer the vital woman she had once been not so long ago. Such adventures she'd told him of, and mostly if not all true, apparently. Sir Charles was a Son of Lóegaire, not a field agent but a gifted financier. He had met Cain on several occasions but did not know the other man. *Mother had worked for him.*

Realization dawned and he stood back up, standing at attention, remembering his military training of years' earlier. Cain nodded in his direction, affirming the assumption, and turned once again to Catherine.

'Catherine, do you remember those tales I told you, tales of my king?'

'Of course, I do!' Cain smiled and directed her attention to the seated person.

'May I present King Dubhgall of the Court of Munster, *Hidden* High King of Ireland.' Catherine turned from one to the other. She began to sob.

'You came, oh you brought him, Cain, you promised and you brought him!' She tried to sit up straighter.

'Please, Miss... Mrs MacKinley, relax yourself, I expect no ceremony. I understand that you desired to meet me, however?' She nodded, happy.

'I did, Your Majesty. I longed to; I've heard so many stories of you. You look so young to be so old.'

Tadhg smiled at this. 'And you are far more charming than Cain has led me to believe, Mrs MacKinley.'

'Oh bother... call me Catherine.'

'Catherine then.' Tadhg briefly glanced at the door, shook his head and turned his face back toward Catherine. 'I am remiss, Catherine, in that I did not introduce myself sooner, but there are... reasons I tend to remain in the background...'

'Your *fae* magic, and its effects on humans your majesty?'

'Ah yes, the baron explained this. Even now, your staff assembles outside the door, none brave enough to open it though.' Sir Charles made an angry sound at this, stood and exited, scattering the servants. The door remained closed, however.

'I am glad you understand, Catherine. I cannot stay long, sadly, we do not wish to tax what energy remains to you. My cousin, Cain, tells me that you have longed to ask a boon of me. If it is within my power, I will grant it you. You have more than earned my gratitude after all.'

Catherine closed her eyes.

For a moment she appeared to be sleeping again, but then she opened them once more. 'I... it is a delicate matter, Your Majesty.' She looked at Cain.

'Do you wish privacy, Catherine? To be alone... to speak alone with the king?'

'If I may, baron.'

'I am never alone, Catherine.'

'I don't understand.' Tadhg said something Catherine did not understand and suddenly there was a tiny, winged woman sat on his shoulder. Catherine laughed.

'Talia, the king's amanuensis?'

'In person!' the pixie giggled and bowed, her hands covering her mouth and her legs swinging back and forth like a child on a swing set. Tadhg smiled too, and nodded to Cain, who reached down and gave Catherine's hand a squeeze.

'I will be right outside the door, my dear, with Charles, fending off the servants.'

He left.

Tadhg looked from the door to the woman lying on her death bed.

'Now, you have a question?'

Catherine licked her lips. 'I have heard so much about you, Your Majesty, from Cain, from others of your kind, my kind, sons and daughters. There is one thing I have never uncovered.' She hesitated. Tadhg saw it in her eyes, a curiosity he had witnessed many times. A curiosity, yes, but a deep, fellow-feeling sorrow as well.

'You would know of *her*. That is your wish, Catherine, to know of my love of long and long ago?'

'Oh yes, so sad and so romantic a tale, please, Your Majesty.'

Talia jumped off the king's shoulder and flew down to sit on the pillow near Catherine's head. Tadhg got up out of the chair, removed his jacket.

'Usually, I am asked to reveal my true form. You are the first person to ask after a love story.' He hung the jacket and made himself comfortable again. He reached down and took the woman's hand in his own. Her hand was almost as cold as his own.

'It was long and long ago when I first laid eyes on Mikaela. This was in a Greek *taverna* in a country that no longer exists…' Catherine laid back and sighed.

§

An hour or so after the baron had left the room Tadhg appeared as well. He gently closed the door behind him. 'Your mother has fallen asleep once again, Sir Charles. I think she will rest easy now.'

'What did she ask of Your Majesty?'

Tadhg smiled but said nothing.

Cain nodded in understanding, however, and turned to the human. 'The king and I must leave now, Charles. I think it best if we do not speak of this visit. This was a rare privilege granted your mother for her years of faithful service. I will ensure that the servants do not remember it.'

'Keep watch over your mother, sir,' said Tadhg. The man said nothing, bowed formally, however, and re-entered the bedchamber. Tadhg waited a moment then turned to face Cain.

'Naked romps in the forest, Cousin?'

The two *fae* left the building, laughter echoing throughout.

8

"The Unsolved Killing of Georgette Bauer — a retrospective"

Although her screaming has long been silenced, and her murder a mystery still, nevertheless her spirit cries out for justice!

Georgette Bauer was a pretty, young woman, brown hair styled in the latest fashion of the 1990s, a girl on the verge of adulthood with a bright future, but with a tragic past. The darkness lurking at the edges of her yearbook picture tells the tale of a murdered mother (case unsolved) and a father taken to drink. Hers' was a good family, once, perhaps celebrated even. That is, before the strange death of young Georgette's uncle and cousin (her mother's brother and nephew). As for the girl herself, oh yes, a socialite in the making (as they used to say). It all ended for her on October 15th, 1994 (exactly fifteen years ago).

The story is almost worthy of a Hollywood movie.

Born to a Cincinnati publisher, Georgette lived a life of privilege. She attended an exclusive private school in Chicago; she had ambitions to be a writer herself, and had some poetry published in local arts magazines. Well regarded. Her father said that Georgette did it all herself; she did not want his connections. Bauer sits in his office for this interview; he picks up the frame picture of his daughter; he is off the drink (three years sober).

"My daughter graduated Vassar College in '92 and she moved to New York to pursue a career in publishing. As she wanted to make it on her own it was hard for her. She found work with the *New York Post* while she was working on a novel. She moved with the literati, or so she told me. She enjoyed the attention of many suitors. That's an old word, suitors, I mean." Bauer picks up his drink, a soda, and takes a sip of it. "Maybe too many nights on the town when she should have been working, maybe she fell in with some troubled elements. She never said; I never asked. She had a good head on her shoulders."

Exactly what happened on that Saturday night fifteen years ago is still a mystery. She was out with her crowd; she was seen in a nightclub here and a café there about Long Island. She was last seen getting into her own vehicle, left in the *Post's* parking bays, apparently driving home. The bay supervisor is sure that she was sober that morning. "Probably just driving home, you know, to sleep off the rest of the morning before another night on the town."

At 11:00AM that morning, Georgette's friend and roommate, Alice Carlisle, arrived back from a night with her parents. She found the front door shut but unlocked. She found Georgette's lifeless body face down in her bathtub, the water was still running, the body was bloodless, chalk white, but a smile was still on her lips. Carlisle turned the water off, possibly obscuring any chance of finding fingerprints there. Georgette was wearing only the top part of a smart pantsuit, silk, blue with white diamond patterns. Her brown hair, which reminded people of the color of roasted chestnuts, was floating in the water. When the police surveyed the scene, they found no evidence of a struggle. The coroner did later confirm that there were some light bruises on her body, but whether this was evidence of a fight before her death, or the attentions of a lover could not be conclusively determined. The blood loss was puzzling of course. A broken lightbulb in the bedroom suggested to investigators that someone could have been waiting, hidden in the darkness. Perhaps her attacker had somehow entered the apartment before Georgette got home, lay in wait, and attacked as she was changing in the dark.

Lieutenant Peter Filbert, leading the investigation at the time, released a rough note of Georgette's last moments. Investigators believe that she came home, early that morning, made herself a snack in her kitchen, prepared to take a bath and undressed in the dark of her room. There she was killed, possibly, by someone who may or may not have been a stranger to her. No viable fingerprints other than of persons eliminated as suspects were ever found, but a neighbor

(John Dexter, 35) said he'd heard "very loud moaning" at about 3:00AM, along with shouts of "Oh God, you're killing me," but the neighbor assumed it was nothing more than Georgette's *"exuberance"* and closed his window to the noise. Another neighbor, coming off a nightshift, said he heard the sounds of shoes and something else on the wood flooring of the building. "Click-click-tap", he said, 'not loud, but someone not hiding their movements. *Click-click-tap*? He could not confirm that the sounds had come from Georgette's apartment precisely though. Whatever occurred there, Georgette's last moments were, or could have been, a desperate attempt to save her own life.

In November 2001 police received a note from a Detective Charles Madlin of the Columbia fraud unit here in Ohio. The note alleged that a woman matching

Georgette's description had given the author of the note a lift through the streets of Long Island on the morning in question. In the note he wrote that the woman, presumably Georgette, was quite nervous about something, watched the mirrors repeatedly, and had giving him a lift for the company and safety. He explained they knew each other but were not involved and did not leave his name. Police have been waiting for the man to contact them again after several appeals in the local papers. In any case, Carlisle said that nothing had been taken. The killer, meanwhile, had vanished into the morning driving off in Georgette's car, which was found sometime later, miles away, abandoned and out of gas. Sadly, no unknown prints were found in the car either. The killer may have been heading to Buffalo, the last trace of the killer's movements.

Georgette's body was shipped back to Columbus, where it was interred in the Bauer plot in the Ascension Lutheran Church's cemetery. While much was written and guessed about the death of Georgette Bauer, little is firmly known. John Dexter has not been able to supply any more clarity to his statement and the rider-friend on the fateful night has never been named. Who was the *click-click-tap* man (woman?) is not known? The murder stays a mystery to this day. Fifteen years to the day, there's little chance now that Georgette Bauer's death will ever be solved.

Columbia City Paper
for October 15th, 2009
by Roberta Callum

9

[It is October 10th, 1820, in the city of brotherly love]

Tadhg was in Philadelphia harvesting the last of the Ralph Holsey bloodline.

As they worked to clear away the evidence, one of the sons handed him a letter from another, a London-based daughter.

He paused to read the letter and was disheartened by it. He had known this day would come, of course, but it had taken no supernatural talent to predict it.

A doctor, a man named Blundell, had performed a successful transfusion of human blood having, or so it was claimed, been experimenting on animals for some years beforehand. The story in the report was that a brief time earlier a man had volunteered to allow his blood to be taken for his wife, who had suffered a postpartum hemorrhage. This was explained in marginalia as a post-delivery condition many women suffer. Tadhg later uncovered that this was overt blood loss due to birth, and remembering events from his youth, was pleased this would no longer be a problem, medically speaking. The report mentioned that four ounces had been transfused from man to wife; a success, predicted to be the first of many, all going well.

Tadhg sat down on the nearby bed.

The sons left him alone.

He made a crucial decision.

The medical procedure was obviously too important to try and stop. Religious and moral arguments would be raised against the work again, of course they would, or one government or another might be persuaded or bullied into outlawing the research, for reasons vague and self-serving, or over-regulating of the techniques would over-police it out of practical usefulness, but these too would not last long... a decade, a few years more. The relentless pursuit of knowledge was a human trait that Tadhg approved and envied in the species. He could not and would not, however, ask the sons and daughters to support the forces of retrogression. No, the resources at his command would be used to further the research.

From that day forward the sons and daughters would, together, or separately, spare no expense to support this Blundell and any further research and development of the transfusion methods. And in so doing, he told them, they would be privy to every new advancement and procedure made. The *Hidden* were also informed, and envoys were sent to cities with renowned medical science institutions to lend aid in the affair, if they would. Any resulting profits would be funneled into causes of their choice in exchange.

The only stipulation was that the twin charities would always have access to the files on new patients.

This was readily agreed.

10

"The Herne Bay Murder: Who Killed Jennifer Lord?"

In 1902, Charles Lord (52) found his wife Jennifer (*nee*: Jonson, 47) shot dead at a neighbour's country house. Jennifer and Major Charles Lord were considered upstanding members of their community in Canterbury. Then, tragedy struck, robbing them of the life they had been building and enjoying together those many years.

In the first place Jennifer was found murdered at a neighbor's country home in Herne Bay. Sadly, just scant weeks later, in the second place the major took his own life. Though there has been a great deal of speculation over these events the case, widely known as the Herne Bay murder, was never conclusively resolved.

Charles Lord was a former military man, a keen golfer, and sometime local politician who had founded the Patriotic Party with his friend and fellow golf enthusiast Major-General Charles Luard. Jennifer was a well-liked friend to many, a helpful neighbor to some, and a frequent volunteer for local charitable causes. The parents of two grown sons, one of who had died under mysterious circumstances himself five years earlier, the couple was putting the death behind them and trying to settle into the golden years of their life. Their social standing, as upper-class members of the late Victorian society, made their untimely deaths especially shocking and noteworthy.

The series of events which led to the deaths began, or so witnesses tell, on or about 23 August 1902, a typical summer's day on the coast for the couple in their vacation home. They left their home together, on foot, at about 2:00 PM. Charles was heading to the golf club to retrieve his irons, while Jennifer was planning to enjoy some exercise before returning to the house for an afternoon tea with a friend. At 2:30PM, the Lords parted ways at a particular gateway. Jennifer headed through the gate and down a path that would take her through the woods, past their neighbor's mostly unused summerhouse, and back to their own summerhouse. Charles, meanwhile, travelled onward to the golf club, where he had a brief unplanned meeting with Luard.

Little did the couple know that the parting at the gate would be the last time they ever bid each other farewell.

Several townspeople saw the major over the next thirty-five minutes as he made his way to the club, and of course, at the club itself. At or about 4:10PM, after leaving the club, the local vicar, Father Rowlin Capstone, driving in the opposite direction, promised him a ride home after completing an errand. The vicar made good on his word, driving by again and picking Charles up at or about 4:20PM, and dropping him off at his home at or about 4:30PM.

Thus, arriving home, Charles was surprised by the presence of Mrs Eleanor Steward, the friend Jennifer had promised to host for tea, waiting patiently for his wife's return. After a brief discussion, the major presumed that Jennifer may have fallen victim to an accident in the woods, and with Eleanor, set off in search of her at 4:45PM.

Forty-fine minutes later, their search came to a tragic end with the discovery of Jennifer's lifeless body on the veranda of their neighbor's summerhouse.

The major and Mrs Steward discovered that Jennifer had been shot in the back of the head, at least twice, and that her purse and jewelry were missing (presumed stolen). No cartridges could be found on the scene, no blood; in fact, there was no evidence of the killer at all, save for a few footprints in the soil beside the footpath. The fact of no blood on the scene surely suggests that Jennifer was killed elsewhere and moved?

In the aftermath of the discovery of the body, many strangers and self-proclaimed experts

acccunts from another neighbor and a gardener, both of whom heard three shots fired in the general direction of the empty summerhouse.

Major Lord, an expert with firearms, offered up all three of his own revolvers to the authorities for examination, and none of them matched the bullet holes found in Jennifer's skull. Still, rumors proclaiming Charles's guilt spread nonetheless, and despite a quick official exoneration. Some believed that Jennifer's missing jewels had been removed by Charles. This, despite the presence and witness of Mrs Steward, was done to throw police from his trail. It was guessed that the major and the friend engaged in an affair (never proven) and the events described were a bid to rid them of the wife. Soon, Charles was receiving hate mail and threats from people vehemently accusing him of his wife's murder.

As the days progressed to weeks with no new evidence leading to any likely suspects, Charles' hope of finding Jennifer's killer dwindled to nothing. Devastated personally, and now a pariah in his summer community, ousted from the party and the golf club both, the major put his summer home up for sale intending to move back to Canterbury earlier than usual.

A member of Parliament, Colonel Jonathon Ward, offered the major a place to stay in the meantime. On 16 September, as soon as the official inquest had ended, Colonel Ward collected the major and took him home. Additionally, the Lord's surviving son, stationed in Rhodesia, had finally gotten news of the tragedy. He was rerouted back to England to be with his father the following day. On the morning of 23 September, the day his son was due to arrive, Charles Lord woke up, bathed, and walked to the local train station. There, he hid in the bushes beside the track, then committed suicide by jumping in front of a passing train. The major met his tragic end exactly a month after his wife had met her own.

Of course, Lord's suicide fanned the flames of the Herne Bay murder mystery. Over the nearly ten years since these events, investigators have come to believe that the crime was committed by someone the major knew, rather than by a random passer-by. They still believe that her jewelry had been taken to mislead the authorities as to the true motive of the murder, whatever that may have been.

The upcoming ten-year anniversary of the case sees the release of a book by Sir James Morney Rowan-Spearman (soon to retire Chief Justice of Jamaica) covering the unsolved murder case exploring his own theory of the events. Sir James has put forth the notion that Jennifer's killer was a man named John Diceman. Diceman was sentenced to death in 1910 for murdering a man on a train. Sir

James asserts in his book, *The Herne Bay Murder: Who Killed Jennifer Lord?* That Diceman was connected to Jennifer Lord through an advertisement the former placed in *The Times* of London.

Sir James' guesses that Jennifer responded to John Diceman's advertisement asking for financial help, by sending him a check, which Diceman then forged, possibly by changing the amount. Upon discovering the forgery, Jennifer contacted the man and arranged to meet with him, without telling her husband, for reasons unknown. So, the new theory goes that Diceman then murdered Jennifer at this meeting in the woods, presumably off the well-worn path, to cover his tracks for the financial crime (which subsequently proved to have been quite a profitable fraud). How Diceman managed to move the dead woman to the unoccupied neighboring summer home without being detected is still unexplained. This is just a theory, however, and neither Sir James' nor any other theory has been conclusively proven, although Sir James' offers interesting speculations. To this day, the Herne Bay Murder case is still unsolved.

The Kentish Gazette
for 10 July 1912
by Maurice Taltson

11

[It is February 18th, 1892, in the city of Edinburgh]

It has been over seventy years since the last major development.

Over the years between then and now, a son or daughter would send new information of successful operations to the others and to Tadhg himself, whatever new information was uncovered, and the charitable institutions they controlled would respond appropriately.

So, blood types appeared, plasma was isolated from whole blood, different cell types were discovered, and suddenly, hemophilia was treatable. The sons and daughters had kept pace with, and funded much, of the research beside other dedicated charities and government medical offices.

Tadhg, ironic given his condition, was not particularly interested in the science of blood. He was aware, of course, in the close relationship between the industry of blood and medical sciences and the societies over which he was officially but secretly the head. As a result of decades of attentiveness to these new areas of knowledge a few of the sons and daughters became more actively involved in the science and experimentation itself. Tadhg heard terms such as *blood products* and *whole blood*, *red cells* and *white cells, platelets, hemoglobin* and *clotting factors*, but these of little real interest to him despite his rediscovered *joie de vivre*.

In a way, however, it was a boon to his purposes that the medical establishment did not fully endorse the procedure yet in the nineteenth century and probably would not do so in the early twentieth either, finding it of "dubious utility"; so many patients died as a result of the developing techniques.

"Too, too risky," the authorities had determined.

Tadhg knew it would not stop, of course.

For all the same reasons he thought of in earlier times he kept his people on it, funding it, administrating, keeping involved as benefactors, or as investigators, technicians, scientists, and occasionally, as anti-procedural agitators and moral busy bodies. He tended to keep his own thoughts about it to himself. It was genuinely great for human science and for the inflicted, of course, those who could be helped, but left unchecked it would be bad for him and the ghosts of Mallow.

The gods had been clear; *all* the cursed blood had to be collected.

The question was, which part of the blood carried the curse?

§

There was no turning back the matter now, but the sons and daughters were well on top of it, for which Tadhg was grateful. The Edinburgh Royal Infirmary had perfected the procedures of blood donation, classification, and transfusion, according to the new report.

Tadhg folded up the letter informing him of this fact and the description of events.

It made him wonder if his explanation of why *vampyres* (of whatever species) went insane was not in fact the mental fragility of humans that he had always assumed it to be. Could it be instead the mixing in one body of incompatible blood types? The more information he was sent the more this new idea appealed to him.

But it raised a moral issue.

Was he bound to share this consideration with anyone, a human scientist perhaps? The *enlightened* may already be on it, he concluded, absolving himself of further worry. Perhaps someday he would ask an *enlightened* if he ever met one.

In the meantime, while his people could do a great deal, they could not be everywhere all the time. Even the other *Hidden* courts could do only so much from the shadows. There was only one thing for it. To make sure that he did not miss anyone, well, any cursed blood he needed the services of a *vates* or an *ovate* (as his own gift of prophecy was limited to random impressions at best).

This raised another problem.

Sadly, all the true druids had been long killed off by the forces of the Christian triune god. There were still druids, if *in name only*.

True bards were sparse on the ground, as they say, as well, not entirely died out but certainly rare in these modern times. Human prophets and seers were numerous (in the carnivals and seaside boardwalk attractions on the east coast of America), but few if any had real talent. Romani mystics were withdrawn from regular society and shunned as vagrants and social pests. Any information gleaned about them was also subject to bias and bigotry.

Tadhg decided that he would send a missive to the daughters later, in the morning perhaps. Tonight, the fate of the last of the bloodline of soldier Lawrence Backnell was to be decided.

Vigilance was needed, he would write later; *chances were slim but not zero. Better safe than sorry.*